—*DRAGON? WHERE ARE WE?*
—*I have no idea. But . . . look!*

Abandoning the language of words that he'd only recently learned, the dragon poured into her head a quick reminder, images culled from the dark and noisome dreams they'd shared of late. Erde had to agree this could be the very place, the landscape of their recurrent nightmares, a place of horror. There was the same burnt yellow sky striated with gray, the same acid smells, the constant roll of thunder. Despite the heat, Erde shivered. It had been night when they'd left Deep Moor, mere seconds before. Here, everything was suddenly too bright. Her eyes burned. She squeezed them shut. She didn't want to see this place anyway.

—*Look!*
—*I don't want to look! It's ugly! Why have you brought us here?*

She hoped her voice in his head did not sound as querulous as it did in her own. Yet maybe he would reconsider, and spirit her back to the meadows of Deep Moor where she could breathe again.

—*Here I am Called. Here the Quest will truly begin. . . .*

Be sure to read the first novel
in MARJORIE B. KELLOGG's
powerful DAW fantasy series—
The Dragon Quartet:
THE BOOK OF EARTH (Volume One)
THE BOOK OF WATER (Volume Two)

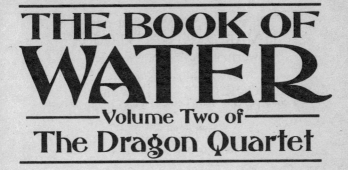

THE BOOK OF
WATER
Volume Two of
The Dragon Quartet

MARJORIE B. KELLOGG

DAW BOOKS, INC.

DONALD A. WOLLHEIM, FOUNDER

375 Hudson Street, New York, NY 10014

ELIZABETH R. WOLLHEIM
SHEILA E. GILBERT
PUBLISHERS

First Printing, September 1997
1 2 3 4 5 6 7 8 9

DAW TRADEMARK REGISTERED
U.S. PAT. OFF. AND FOREIGN COUNTRIES
—MARCA REGISTRADA
HECHO EN U.S.A.

PRINTED IN THE U.S.A.

FOR SHEILA

editor, friend, soul of patience
. . . and the one who got me into all this in
the first place.

And many thanks to the usual suspects and a
few new ones, all of them more generous with
their time, advice, and encouragement than
any author has the right to hope for:

Lynne Kemen and Bill Rossow
Barbara Newman and Stephen Morris
Antonia Bryan
Martin Beadle
Kenny Leon
Charlotte Zoe Walker
and the dedicated organizers and supporters
of **Oneonta Outloud,** where portions of this
book were first read.

PROLOGUE

The Creation

IN THE BEGINNING,
and a little after . . .

In the Beginning, four mighty dragons raised of elemental energies were put to work creating the World. They were called Earth, Water, Fire, and Air. No one of them had power greater than another, and no one of them was mighty alone.

When the work was completed and the World set in motion, the four went to ground, expecting to sleep out this World's particular history and not rise again until World's End.

The first to awaken was Earth.

He woke in darkness, as innocent as a babe, with only the fleeting shadows of dreams to hint at his former magnificence. But one bright flame of knowledge drove him forth: He was Called to Work again, if only he could remember what the Work was.

He found the World grown damp and chill, overrun by the puniest of creatures, Creation's afterthought, the ones called Men. Earth soon learned that Men, too, had forgotten their Origin. They had abandoned their own intended Work in the World and thrived instead on superstition, violence, and self-righteous oppression of their fellows. They had forgotten as well their primordial relationship with dragons—all, that is, but a few.

One in particular awaited Earth's coming, though she had no awareness of the secret duty carried down through the countless generations of her blood. But this young girl knew her destiny, when she faced a living dragon and was not afraid.

Thereafter, Earth's Quest became her own, and together they searched her World for answers to his questions. Some they found and slowly, with his memory, Earth's powers reawakened. But the girl's World was dark and dangerous and ignorant, and the mysterious Caller who summed Earth could not be found within it. One day, blindly following the Call, Earth took them Somewhere Else.

That Somewhere Else would prove stranger than either of them could have imagined . . . except in their dreams.

PART ONE

The Summoning of the Hero

Chapter One

He thinks he's safely away, then he hears the rubble shift behind him, and again, to the right. He shrinks into the hot shadow of the shuttered doorway, thinking fast. His hands are wet, his breath too loud for comfort. He has not expected pursuit.

N'Doch quiets his breathing and awaits their next move. He considers his alternatives. Deeper into town would provide the most cover, but no strategic advantage. His pursuers—her brothers, no doubt—know the maze of alleys and junk lots as well as he does, maybe better, and though he thinks he has the advantage of speed, they're sure to have the advantage of numbers. He tries to recall how many brothers the silly girl has still living. He stops counting at four and wonders instead how likely it is that all of them are out of work at the same time and therefore at home, too bored and idle to sleep soundly through the midday heat like everyone else in town. He can't remember if she'd said. He was too busy being charming.

Now he also wonders if it was a setup. Too easy, maybe, those five plump globes glowing in the sun on the girl's unguarded windowsill, their green-orange ripening toward red, their warm tart juice almost a sure thing in his parched mouth. N'Doch cannot remember the last time he's eaten a ripe tomato. Especially a safe one. He feels them now, inside his T-shirt, bunched up against the waistband of his shorts, as smooth against his skin as the girl's firm brown breasts. N'Doch grins, feeling her again in his hands. Silly, but pretty. She'd almost distracted him from his purpose. Maybe he should have taken her first and *then* the tomatoes. Maybe she wouldn't have set her brothers after him so fast.

Around him, the quiet is unnatural. Even the flies and crawlies are waiting to see who'll break the stalemate first. N'Doch squints into the hazed white glare at the end of the street. The market square wavers and dips, intoxicated with the heat, reminding him of his mama's old video in a brownout. He decides that if he actually escapes with the tomatoes, he'll bring her one. Maybe the promise will bring him luck. For now, he'll head for the market and hope for the best. Lately, the stalls are shutting down during the day, to open again in the faint cool of dusk. Still, some shelter might be found among the thicket of carts and canopies, enough at least for him to double back and lose his tail.

Across the hot street, a skintight alley cuts between two crumbling stucco facades. The windows are high and barred, boarded with corrugated plastic, pairs of faded green squares in a bleached flamingo wall that's shedding old campaign posters like dying skin. No entry there, but the alley is shaded and promising. A few sharp bars of sunlight drop through the dust to spotlight piles of litter scattered along the left-hand wall. Briefly, N'Doch is speared with envy. It should be him in that hard bright spot, singing his songs for the eager multitude. He catches himself surrendering to the familiar reverie and hauls his attention back to the alley. Halfway down its length, some squared-off bulk makes the narrow darkness darker. But N'Doch counts no obstacle as impassable. He is younger than most of Malimba's brothers—taller, but thinner and lighter. He's got no one at home raising safe food to fatten him up, no walled and locked courtyard in which to grow it. For once, he'll consider that an advantage. He'll go around that darkness, or over it.

He shifts his weight soundlessly. Wedged into the shallow doorway, he has no view of the street behind him. He leans forward, his head cocked sideways like a wary bird. His bare arm scrapes the peeling shutters, and chips of dry blue paint tickle his toes. He's sure it's a rat, probably a sick one if it's out in broad daylight. He doesn't flinch, but his reflex gasp sounds to him like a vast sigh across the white-hot silence. Up the street, the rubble stirs again. N'Doch readies himself. He'd gladly wait forever in the safety of this doorway, eating his tomatoes in peace like he'd planned. But he can't risk a rat bite. Besides, his pursuers won't wait out there in the rubble forever. He must gain that crucial survivor's one step ahead.

He coils his muscles, then springs across the street into the alley. The sun is a breath of flame across his back as he sprints sideways into the shadow. The brothers erupt from hiding, but they lose a step or two, blocking each other's way, so eager to be after him down the narrow passage.

N'Doch risks a lightning backward glance. Four of them, no, five—yes, indeed there are, one for each tomato. They are thick and muscled. They wear only the light briefs they sprang out of bed in when roused by their sister's outraged squeals. The dark obstacle midway down the alley is a pile of discarded plastic crates. N'Doch leaps, grabs, and climbs like a cat. The crates sway, threatening to buckle, and a voice squawks vague curses at him from inside. He slaps the tops and sides as he scrambles over. Maybe he can roust out the denizen of the boxes to slow down his pursuers. With luck, there's a whole family in there. He doesn't wait to find out. He leaps to the ground on the other side and pounds away down the alley. No point in stealth now. Almost more than fear, hunger propels him. He bursts into the glare of the market square, scattering a flock of scrawny hens that rise up around him in a flurry of grit and feathers. Heat and sun engulf him. He cuts sideways down an aisle of bread stalls into the gauzy shade of the canopies. The smells make his mouth water, but every stall has its razor-edged grillwork locked down tight. Halfway to the end, he swerves left, hoping his pursuers won't see him turn. Next, it's a hard right past the software carts. The vendors doze behind tinted plexiglass shields, only their bright arrays of solar collectors left open to the air. Normally, N'Doch would linger here, longingly, trying to bargain for what he cannot afford. But not today. He makes a few more sharp zigs and zags, and then he's across the square, free of the stalls and racing down the wide main boulevard toward the town gates. The black tar is soft and steaming. The heat is like a weight. It doesn't occur to him until he's well out into the open to wonder if the brothers took the time to grab their guns. He's seen no flash of sun on metal in his quick looks backward, but a big enough hand can conceal all the firepower necessary to blow a grown man away. The thought makes him shiver. The drab blighted trees that line the boulevard are his only possible cover.

But no spray of bullets comes after him, only the steady rhythm of multiple bare feet slapping against pavement, still a ways behind him but gaining. N'Doch speeds past the tall steel mesh gates. He wishes they still worked, so he could slam them in the brothers' faces. But no one bothers to fix anything anymore, especially something in public use. Now the scorched peanut fields spread white and brown to either side of him. Ahead, the red laterite road snakes through the palm grove toward the port. Tall trunks are down everywhere, uprooted or snapped off by the last big storm. There've been a lot of those coming through lately. The TV guys blame it on global warming and try to tell you what to do about it, but N'Doch zaps the channel when the weather comes on. He doesn't see how you could fix anything that big, and he's got more important things to worry about, like right now, saving his skin. He stretches his rangy legs like a thoroughbred and runs for all he's worth. But he notices the pressure inside his ribs, the merest hint of a cramp in his side. He begins to think maybe he won't get to eat any of these tomatoes after all. But that can't be, all this risk and effort for nothing. Still, if he drops them now, the brothers might let him go. He wonders if they've counted them, decides to take the chance. He yanks his shirt out of his shorts, lets the round red fruit roll free but catches the reddest, the ripest one as they fall. The soft thud of tomatoes hitting the dust behind him is the saddest sound he's ever heard.

The road through the grove is as dry and slick as flour, and danger hides in the ankle-deep red silt—shards of metal, rigid scraps of plastic waiting to slice up the unwary foot. N'Doch follows the track of a dune buggy, wishing such a vehicle would come along right this moment and spirit him off to safety. But he's managed to pick the only time of day or night when the road is empty, another in what seems to be a series of miscalculations. The *bidonville* under the palms is mute and motionless, everyone napping out the worst of the heat except a mangy young dog who bounds from the shade of an oil drum, sure that N'Doch has come to play with her. She springs up noisily, tangling in his legs. N'Doch does not kick her away. He had a puppy he loved, back when he was a kid in the City, and he knows it won't be long before this one, too, is somebody's dinner.

But her leaping and yapping gets in his way, so he snatches up a twig from the road and tosses it behind him. With luck, she'll chase after it and tangle in the brothers' legs instead of his own. Through the scythe-curves of the palm trunks, he sees the smoky glare of the water, drawn up against the yellow sky in a fuzzed line of haze. He thinks if he can make it to the beach, he's safe. Malimba's brothers don't hang out at the beach. They won't know their way around the wrecks like he does. He can lose them there.

But he is slowing, and the cramp in his side is harder to ignore. He risks another backward glance. The brothers are slowing, too. One has dropped back to rescue the lost tomatoes from the dust. The other four pound after N'Doch, fists clenched, blinking sweat and grit from their eyes, and snarling. The brother in the lead trips over the panting eager dog as she scrambles to retrieve the stick. He lashes out, kicks her sideways. She tumbles, yelping, into the red gravel along the verge and lies there, stunned.

N'Doch feels his soul rebel, the way his stomach would against rotten food. He'd pull up short to help the pup, could he do so and live. He's had nothing against Malimba's brothers so far, except their understandable urge to chase down the thief who stole their supper. But the pup's only crime is being innocent enough to think that humans are her friends. N'Doch's nostrils flare. He surrenders up his luscious vision of eating the remaining tomato slowly and with great ceremony once he's gone to ground. Instead, he'll eat it *now,* while the brothers watch, while the sweat pours salt into their angry eyes, and their bodies strain to match his stride. And then, his final act of revenge, when he's safe and alone again: he'll make up a funny song about it and sing it all around the neighborhood, about the pup and the tomatoes and the stupid mindless viciousness of Malimba's brothers.

Anticipation makes him grin, and the notes are already stringing themselves together in his head. Sure, his friends will think he's weird, singing about dogs and tomatoes, but hell, they already do. N'Doch wipes the tomato on his shirt as he runs, then takes a bite. The skin is taut and hot but the juice is cooler than his tongue and so tart-sweet that he groans with pleasure and forgets to savor it. Between gasps for breath, he devours it in great gnashing gulps. His mouth and throat vibrate with sensation, and then the precious fruit is gone and all he can do is taste the sour regret that he dropped the other four along the road.

He's past the last shanties and lean-tos of the *bidonville*. The palm grove is thinning. Ahead, he sees the gray stretch of water and the long bright arc of sand, littered with the black hulks of the wrecks. N'Doch is glad he's eaten the tomato, though it sits like a cold acidic lump in his empty belly. He can afford no distractions now, for the beach is even more treacherous than the road. Shoals, entire reefs of debris lie submerged in its deeper sands, ready to cut off a toe or slice through a tendon, leaving you hamstrung. N'Doch thinks the beach is like life, full of hazard. He negotiates it very carefully. He's written a bunch of songs about it, like the fact that there's less of it each time he comes here, as the sea level rises. As he breaks out onto open sand, he hears one of the brothers curse and fall behind, hopping on one foot, stopping short. N'Doch crows silently. Score one for the mangy pup. He dodges right and left, his eyes fixed on the pocked ground. The first wreck southward is a burned-out sea tug. N'Doch knows the family living in the aft section above the high water mark. He's sung at their hearth on more than one occasion. It's low tide now, so he chooses the farthest-away path through the pieces of the wreck, right along the water's edge. The old man is just up from his siesta, taking a piss from the rusted rail of the mess deck. He waves.

"Yo! Waterboy!"

N'Doch grins breathlessly and returns the wave as he passes. He doesn't mind the nickname. Water seems to him a fine and precious thing to be named after. Had he been named "safe water" or "pure water" or even "cold water" instead of merely "water," he'd have liked it even better. But his mama preferred names that could be yelled quickly and easily, so "N'Doch" it is, or "Waterboy" to the old geezer who lives in the tug wreck.

Now, Malimba's brothers haven't heard this nickname before, and when they pick up on it, it doesn't sound so fond or playful. It's mockery pure and simple.

"Water boy!" they screech in coarse falsetto. "Waaater boyh! Come heah, boyuh! Yah, boy, yah, yah, yah!"

N'Doch knows what they're up to, trying to rile him, slow him down with a little extra burden of rage, maybe even goad him into turning and standing for a fight. But N'Doch has learned to be slow to anger. He's never been much of a fighter. His speed is his strength. As for Malimba's brothers, let them ask their silly sister if he's a *boy* or not.

Already he thinks of the girl with the same regret as the lost tomatoes. Silly, perhaps, but pretty enough, clean and healthy and a virgin, he's sure of it. Not so many of those around, though at almost twenty, N'Doch has had his share. It would have been nicer to lie down with her a while instead of just snatching the fruit and bolting. Then she might have *given* him one, if he'd pleased her well enough, and there'd be no need for all this sweating and racing about. N'Doch knows he has a gift for pleasing women, even those he doesn't take to bed. It's one reason he hasn't had to fight so much. Whatever trouble he gets into, he can always find a woman or two to take his side. In groups, he has found, women can be very powerful allies. This is maybe his worst miscalculation this time—to attempt such a serious snatch when the aunties and grandmothers and the satisfied widows who might have hidden and protected him are all shut up in the shade of their houses, fast asleep.

He clears the last chunk of the sea tug and cuts shoreward to skirt the sand-filled hulks of two landing craft left unclaimed after the most recent failed coup. Together, they form a solid wall of rust and bullet holes and peeling camo paint, half in, half out of the water at low tide. N'Doch considers whipping around the hind end and climbing the far side to drop down onto the wash of wet sand inside. But the brothers are too close behind to fall for this ruse. They're sure to see him fling himself over the top, and then he'll be trapped and done for. But he can use the great bulk of the landing craft to cover his sprint to the next wreck down, one of the really big ones, a storm-grounded supertanker whose half-submerged stern juts into the water for the length of several soccer fields. N'Doch has a long run over open sand, but if he can reach the tanker before the brothers pass the landing craft, he'll be home free. He can hide himself forever in the dark and complex bowels of that derelict giant.

But as he rounds the end of the landing craft, his next disastrous miscalculation is revealed. This time, N'Doch curses himself out loud. The fishing fleet is in, as he'd have known it would be, if he'd given it a moment's clear thought. Hauled up on the sand between him and his refuge are thirty high-sided, high-prowed, brightly painted boats shaped like hollowed-out melon slices, heavy old wooden boats with galley-sized oars pulled by four men each. They're as tightly packed as a school of tuna. N'Doch can see no alley through them. A path around will take too long. Over the top, then, it has to be, though even at midships, they're half again his height. He races at the nearest, leaping to grab for the gunwales. He misses, catches a strand of fishnet instead, then flails and falls back, pulling the load of netting and floaters over on top of himself. By the time he's struggled free of the web of slimy, stinking rope, the brothers have made it around the landing craft. They slow and walk toward him, with nasty grins on their faces.

"Hey, water boy . . ."

"D'ja eat good, water boy?"

"Time to pay up now . . ."

They fan out in a semicircle as they approach, cutting off his chance of a last minute end run. The shortest and lightest-skinned of them has picked up a ragged scrap of metal. He swings it casually, like a baseball bat, but there is nothing casual in his eyes. N'Doch shakes off the last of the netting and backs toward the water. Maybe he can outswim them. He knows this is folly. He has hardly a full breath left in his body. His chest is heaving like a bellows, but then, so are theirs.

The surf pounds. A long wave foams up around his ankles. He hopes there's nothing too lethal hiding in the sand behind him, or in the water. The beach slants sharply. It drops off fast here, so the waves crest and break close to shore. The undertow is already pulling at his calves, sucking the gravel from beneath his heels, tipping his balance. He feels not so much driven backward into the water by the brothers' approach, as drawn inexorably into its depths, like he's being inhaled by the ocean, as if the water itself was alive. It's a peculiar sensation. It makes him light-headed, and now he's thinking he hears music in the crashing roar of the surf. He thinks maybe this is how you feel when you know you're about to die. He doesn't understand why he isn't terrified.

A particularly big wave breaks loudly behind him. The spray flings needles at his back. He braces himself against the hard swirl of water, the boil of foam around his knees. Another big wave coils and crashes, then throws itself at his thighs. And another. N'Doch backs deeper into the water, wondering if there's a new storm offshore that he hasn't heard about. Two of the brothers are wading in after him now. The short one is in the lead, brandishing his metal club. He lashes out suddenly. N'Doch ducks. It's a near miss. The short guy has very long arms. Another monster wave breaks. N'Doch knows he'll have to swim for it soon. He can't back out much farther in this high rough surf and keep his footing. The very next wave knocks him off-balance, and the club-wielder lunges after him with such a splashing and buffeting of metal and limbs and water that it isn't until the swell is pulling back and N'Doch has his feet under him again that he feels the sear along his upper arm. A thin trail of blood slips out with the wave like a coil of brown kelp. He claps his hand to his bicep. The bastard's cut him!

Finally N'Doch begins to feel afraid. An open wound in *this* water? Any number of nasty things he could pick up. And then there are the sharks that cruise the beaches, for lack of prey farther out. The merest whiff of blood will bring them in, and a starving shark is more fearsome than any number of Malimba's brothers.

The biggest wave so far thunders into its curl behind him. N'Doch waits to be engulfed. No, he'll dunk fast just before it hits and let it pummel *them* into the gravel. He scans the brothers' faces for a measure of the wave's size and sees instead a stark and uncomprehending terror. The short one has dropped his club. Suddenly, all three of them are backstepping through the surging water as fast as they can, heading for shore. N'Doch is sure the sharks have come in with the wave, but he cannot bear to look. He throws himself after the brothers, paddling frantically with his hands. Briefly he worries that it might be a ruse to draw him within range, but he doesn't believe they're *that* gifted as actors. Their terror is pretty convincing. The minute they're out of the water, they're pounding away up the beach. They seem to have forgotten him entirely.

N'Doch struggles against the pull of the undertow. He expects jaws lined with razors to clamp onto his thigh and haul him back again. As he stumbles into ankle-deep water and regains his balance, two of the brothers halt, high up on the beach. The short one is yanking on the taller one's arm. The tall one shrugs him off. He's yelling, and pointing toward the water. With his feet safely under him, N'Doch can resist no longer. He turns, and he sees a thing beyond his wildest imaginings.

It's not a shark. At first he thinks, *Damn, that's a really big porpoise.* Then he thinks, *No, it has legs. It's a giant crocodile.* No, the head's too small, neck's too long, it's . . like something he's seen in the movies. The only word he can come up with is *dinosaur.* Right. Okay. A dinosaur. It can't be, but there is it. And now he's sure he's hearing music. Very strange music, like, inside his head. Maybe that tomato wasn't so safe after all. *It's poisoned me,* he thinks. *I'm hallucinating.*

And then, for a moment, he stops thinking anything at all.

With a flash of wet blue-gray and silver, the creature rises out of the waves in front of him. It has four mammalian legs and a sleek, close-eared head set on a sinuous muscular neck. It stands motionless in waist-deep water but he can *feel* its liquid grace. He thinks of a big cat inside the skin of a seal. He's never seen anything so beautiful. Though it seems to tower over him, it's actually no bigger than a large horse. Its eyes are dark and round, almost level with his own, and they are staring straight at him.

N'Doch takes the obvious step backward but that odd absence of fear has taken hold of him again. He feels no need to run. The music fills his inner ears and mostly he's thinking how absolutely fucking weird this whole thing is, and could the brothers have poisoned the tomato on purpose? Were they only chasing him to be there watching and laughing when he freaked out? Well, he isn't going to give them the satisfaction. Besides, they're the ones who're freaking out. Which means either they're pretending to see something terrifying, or they really *are* seeing something terrifying, which means . . .

N'Doch notices his legs have given up supporting him. He sits down hard on the sand and stares dumbfounded into a pair of round, dark eyes that are beginning to show signs of impatience.

Behind him, he hears someone coughing.

Chapter Two

At first she was sure he'd landed them in the middle of a fire. The hot light was so hazed and the air so thick with soot and fetid odor. She shrank against him, pressing her shoulder to the dragon's side to take comfort from his girth and solidity, from the hard geometry of his leathery hide, retreating into his shadow from the glare of this sun, this searing angry red-faced sun so unlike the sun she knew. Even in the dragon's shade, she felt heat radiating upward from the scorched sand. Her nose tickled and her lungs hurt. She coughed, tried not breathing, then realized why that couldn't work, so drew a breath and coughed again.

—*Dragon? Where are we?*

—*I have no idea. But . . . look!*

Abandoning the language of words that he'd only recently learned, he poured into her head a quick reminder, images culled from the dark and noisome dreams they'd shared of late. Erde had to agree this could be the very place, the landscape of their recurrent nightmares, a place of horror. There was the same burnt yellow sky striated with gray, the same acid smells, the constant roll of thunder. Despite the heat, Erde shivered. It had been night when they'd left Deep Moor, mere seconds before. Here, everything was suddenly too bright. Her eyes burned. She squeezed them shut. She didn't want to see this place anyway.

—*Look!*

—*I don't want to look! It's ugly! Why have you brought us here?*

She hoped her voice in his head did not sound as querulous as it did in her own. Yet maybe he would reconsider, and spirit her back to the meadows of Deep Moor where she could breathe again.

—*Here am I Called. Here the Quest will truly begin.*

He sounded very sure, but Erde could detect in his formality just the faintest hint of false bravado. This place they'd come to wasn't exactly what the dragon had hoped for either.

Which meant he would need her to be strong. No time for girlish hearts or a lady's refined sensibilities. Not that she was ever very refined. Erde thought of Hal, who had yearned so to be a part of the dragon's Quest. He hadn't even minded that the dragon could not identify the object of that Quest. She wished the elder knight was with them now, to apply his skills and discipline to this unfamiliar situation, and all the equally unforeseen ones likely to come out of it. But he was back at Deep Moor with Rose and the others, up to his elbows once more in the game of king-making. Of course, he didn't consider it a game, and Erde knew she shouldn't either. No more a game than the dragon's Quest, which she'd taken seriously from the moment she'd been faced with it. Therefore, she must follow Sir Hal's example. If he was not there to tell her what to do, she must imagine his advice and be guided by it. The child in her complained that she was too young to shoulder such a burden, too exhausted from the upheaval of the past two months of fear and constant flight to face an even greater uncertainty. The adult, so recently come to consciousness, reminded her she had no choice.

—*So, Dragon. What shall we do?*

—*Wait. Watch.*

The dragon eased himself down on his great haunches, claws and head forward like an alert guard dog, and evidently just as willing to sit still forever until what he waited for came to him.

Watch. Erde remembered Hal's habit of observation. Wherever they'd camped on their long journey from Tor Alte, his first task before any was to take careful stock of the area, not only to search out ambush or pursuit, but to learn which local resources were available and which were not. Water, firewood, food perhaps. Shelter from the weather, cover from their enemies. There were always enemies.

At least, Erde thought, *we've escaped from them this time.* To this dry landscape, alien yet familiar, not just from the dragon's dreams but her own as well, she realized. The dreams where her father and Rainer fought, and their swords clashed and sparked in a harsh and smoky place was more like this place than the one she'd left behind.

Rainer. Ah, Rainer. But it did not do to think of Rainer, not in any way except as lost, as she'd thought he was until mere hours ago, hours that now seemed like years. He was lost again anyhow, even before she'd left Deep Moor. Erde raised her head from her crouch at the dragon's side and turned her mind to her surroundings.

She'd felt the hot sand underfoot but had not realized there was so much of it, more than she'd ever seen in one place. It stretched behind her like a dry riverbed toward a long line of trees, impossible trees with tall, curving trunks as slim as needles and a pincushion of leafy branches sticking out on top. There was lots of stuff in the sand, broken stuff. Some of it was wood, sun-bleached and weatherworn, but most of it was shiny or glittery, materials she couldn't identify. Erde pushed off the dragon's shoulder for a better look, teetering along his forearm and grasping one long ivory horn for support. Balanced on his right paw, her eyes were level with his own golden orbs, each one as big as her head. She peered over his stubby snout.

First she saw a mass of huge bright boats crowding the sand off to the left. They were nothing like the flat-bottomed scows that plied the rivers of the lowlands back home but they were surely boats, none the less. She'd seen such boats sewn into the tapestries that softened the stone walls of Tor Alte. But she could put no label to the square dark hulks looming to the right like a range of hills. They could be buildings, she supposed, but she saw no doors or windows, only seams and slits in the rusted metal. Fortifications of some sort, she decided. And then, between that grim and faceless wall and the rainbowed hulls of the boats, there was the water. So much water! Now Erde understood the source of the continuous rolling sound of thunder. She knew without being told that she was looking at the sea.

The sight of it lifted her spirits. She had always dreamed of visiting the sea. But the dragon regarded the roaring, tumbling water with evident trepidation. Erde patted his bony nose reassuringly. Moving water was not his favorite thing. She thought this odd, since in the bard tales, it was the uncharted seas from which the dragons of legend arose to swallow unfortunate sailing ships and their crews. But Erde had learned to think differently about dragons since meeting this one. Her dragon was definitely earthbound, and unlikely to swallow up anything without first asking its permission.

Then, over the din of the waves, she heard shouting. Male voices, several of them. She couldn't make out the words, but there was no mistaking the high-pitched tone of derision. Around the end of the dark unknown hulk, a man came running. At least, she thought it was a man. It was shaped like one, though he ran with the rangy sure grace of a young colt. But there was something wrong with his skin. It was unnaturally dark, darker than a farmer's after a summer in the fields, darker even than the gypsies who sometimes pulled their wagons up to Tor Alte's gates to barter for food and shelter with their exotic trinkets.

The dark man pulled up short when he spotted the bright fleet hauled up in front of him on the sand. Even from a distance, his dismay was obvious. Beside Erde, the dragon tensed. She could feel him stilling, preparing to make himself invisible. He sent her an image of hiding behind the nearest boat. But it wasn't the running man who was shouting. It was the three others behind him, as dark as he but shorter and thicker. When they spotted the first man, one stooped to snatch up a club. Erde thought they looked terrifying.

—*Now, Dragon! Before they see us!*

Erde prepared to dash for cover among the boats. But the dragon was no longer watching the events unfolding on the beach. He sat up very tall, intent on the churning water. A sort of thrumming sang through his body, like the vibrations of lute strings after the music has ended.

—*Dragon, what is it?*

—***There! She comes!***

—Who?

—The one who Calls me!

Erde squinted at the line of dirty froth. Was there someone else approaching along this crowded shore? Then she saw it, the snakelike neck and narrow head, lifting above the cresting waves. The body was slim and streamlined and surprisingly small, but Erde had grown up with legends. She had no trouble recognizing one when she saw it.

Another dragon was rising out of the waves.

Chapter Three

N'Doch decides he can't be hallucinating. Instead of the usual speed buzz, there's music in his head. And it's pretty interesting music, too. He's tempted just to give in and listen, when suddenly, he figures it out. He laughs with relief, and right away starts looking around for the hidden lights and camera crews.

A dinosaur on the beach. Yeah, sure.

He knows what's going on. This is no poisoned-tomato vision, it's a special effect, got to be.

Of course the vid people won't know they've stumbled on a veteran. Usually they want amateurs for these "true-life" guerrilla shoots, so N'Doch won't tell them about playing background last year in *War Zone*. He'll let them see him do his stuff first.

Meanwhile, the special effect continues to stare at him like it wants something important. He's impressed. It's very realistic. Not your ordinary robot, then, but some new kind of cybercritter, maybe, or even . . . a cleverly engineered mutant! That means the vid company must have money, lots of it. N'Doch sees this might be his big break. If they're rolling tape now and he plays his part well, they'll keep it in and he could be famous. He'll have to guess what he's supposed to do. They never tell you in advance, or it wouldn't be a "true-life" pic. And if he can figure out a way to work in a song, he'll really have made it.

He springs to his feet, but his legs are still shaky. They don't really want to carry him the several steps it would take to come within arm's length of the critter. It, no, *she*—somehow he knows this—shifts her feet restlessly but does not approach. N'Doch wonders idly, if she isn't a robot, how the wranglers give the creature her cues.

A deep wave recedes across a stretch of wet sand, revealing the critter's long flat tail: a blade of muscular flesh, which she coils neatly around her webbed feet as she eases onto her haunches in front of him. N'Doch looks her over, calmer now that he's settled on a logical explanation for her presence. His legs decided to hold him up, and once again, he is taken by the creature's beauty.

What seemed from a distance to be shiny fish scales is actually a fine silvery fur as silky as the richest velvet. N'Doch has never touched real velvet, but he's seen it on TV. Immediately, he longs to touch it. What he covets most are its strange electric-blue highlights. He wonders if it grew this way, or if they've somehow wired her for it. And probably she's bred small so they can fit her into the frame with human actors. Otherwise, they'd need a long shot to see all of her.

Her head, which he'd taken for naked but for her large dark eyes and little seallike ears, is set with a ruff and crest of gauzy iridescent flesh. It lifts lightly as it dries in the sun, softening her sleek profile with curls and complications. The crest trails down her slim neck and along her spine. N'Doch thinks of the gossamer-finned carp he saw once in a rich woman's backyard pool—the first (and last) time he's ever been confronted with food just too beautiful to eat.

He can't settle on any one of the current vid series to connect with this particular situation. It's been a few days since he's caught up on his TV-watching. It could be a new story line in an old show, or a pilot for a whole new program. Maybe they don't even know the story yet, and they're waiting for it to develop naturally out of the Precipitating Event—how 'bout it?—**a man meets a dinosaur on the beach.** N'Doch wishes he'd been at *that* story conference. But this must be why the creature looks so impatient. She's waiting for him to get on with the action.

Since the ball's apparently in his court, he tries imagining the song he'd write about such a meeting. He decides the first thing he should do is *touch* the creature. They're sure to love that, him looking like he's totally amazed and trying to prove what he's seeing is real. No problem playing it, either, since it's exactly where he's at. But it's a hard thing, he discovers, to make himself cross the narrow but infinite space of sand between him and the critter, and lay a palm to that blue-lit silver velvet.

Still, his career's at stake. He manages it. The first impossible step is all it takes to draw him swiftly the next three or four. He reaches out, trying not to look too tentative. The critter's fur is the softest thing he has ever felt. As he smooths his hand from shoulder to ribcage, he feels a rush of heat and embarrassment because the touch is so oddly intimate. Bemused, N'Doch retreats a step. Again he hears coughing behind him, but now he cannot look away. The creature fixes him once more with her liquid gaze, then opens her wide mouth and sings to him.

It is the music N'Doch has waited for all his life. He doesn't realize he's been waiting until he hears it, but there it is, and his first response is tragic: the only *right* music has already been written, and by someone else. His next is relief that it has no lyric. At least it has waited for him to put words to it. He begins to hum along. The melody comes into his head just as it is leaving her throat. He knows already the words he will write, words of awakening and discovery and of a great task to be accomplished, notions he's never concerned himself with in his music so far, but N'Doch knows better than to argue with inspiration. He slips into harmony. They are a perfect duet. They build a crescendo together, append a short coda and finish on the same drawn-out high note. They stare at each other in silence. Even the surf has quieted to a rolling caress.

N'Doch thinks: *Wow. This is even better than sex.*

Then the creature lifts her gaze above his head and sings again. The bulged reply is so harsh and unmusical that N'Doch whips around, offended.

What he sees first is a white girl standing beside a big rock. He's perplexed by the white girl, who is very strangely dressed, but mostly by the rock, which is the size of a semi. He can't remember a rock that big on this part of the beach and it's not exactly the sort of thing you'd miss. Just as he's deciding the white girl is part of the production crew and the rock is a piece of scenery, the rock moves. In that instant, it is no longer a rock, but a bronze-and-green beast, also the size of a semi, and looking even more like a dinosaur than the one that came out of the water. This one even has horns, and claws each the length of a scimitar.

Two of them. Wow. N'Doch grins. Now he's *sure* the producers have money. He smiles at the white girl, in case she's one of them, even though she does seem kind of young. But he knows the media are run by young people. He's been worried about being over the hill at twenty.

When she doesn't smile back, only stares at him wide-eyed, he sees she must be an actress—she's thin enough, maybe a little too tall—and the director has told her to be afraid of him. N'Doch thinks she's doing a pretty good job. He gives her a brief nod which he hopes looks professional. He's a bit jealous that she seems to know the script and he doesn't. Her costume is weird, like something out of a gladiator epic. Well, maybe not gladiators, but something with swords, from a much colder part of the world than this one. He tries to figure what country she's meant to be from. No place is *that* cold anymore, except maybe Antarctica in the winter. The dumb girl's wearing leather and long sleeves and heavy woven trouser-things and boots, more clothes on her back than N'Doch's ever owned in his life, and she looks like she hasn't washed in months. Plus, her hair's all choppy. N'Doch admits he doesn't know much about white girl's hair but he does know a bad 'do when he sees one. He likes the neatly sheathed dagger at her belt, but can't help thinking how she must be dying of the heat under all that stuff. Right now she's not doing much but staring at him, but he can see she's beginning to sweat.

The two cybercritters are staring, too—at each other. N'Doch wonders if they're supposed to fight. That would account for the strange tension he senses in the air between them. Some kind of communicating going on, he decides, so they *must* be machines, remote controlled by the technicians.

The big brownish one rises from his couch. He takes a few big steps down the beach. The smaller silvery one goes to meet him. She's quicker, more lithe. Her greater grace makes N'Doch feel proud, though he can't imagine why, particularly since she moves right past him like she's never seen him before in her life. And after all that music and touching. He stands aside, miffed. He's really hoped this part would be more than a walk-on. Then he notices the white girl is sticking right by her beast as he moves. N'Doch thinks, *Hey, you can just accept what you're given or you can try to make the most of it.* He turns and follows the silver one up the beach.

The two creatures meet halfway. N'Doch waits, or rather, hopes for sparks to fly. Instead, they halt a few paces apart and bend their long necks in simultaneous bows. The brown one towers over the silver one. His curving ivory horns pass like scythe blades to either side of her blunt, sleek head. The formality of it raises the hair on the back of N'Doch's neck. It seems so proper somehow, so . . . *ancient,* even if it is all for the camera.

The big brown one twists his golden gaze back at the white girl. She comes immediately to his side, her hand sliding familiarly up his rough cheek. She smiles shyly at the silver beast, then dips and rises in a gesture of greeting that looks awkward in leather and pants. N'Doch guesses it would look all right if she were wearing some kind of ball gown. He tries picturing her in fancy dress, lots of makeup and jewels, a little less hair or a whole lot more. The effect is not unpleasing. Maybe they're planning something like that for the finale.

But next, all three of them are staring in his direction. To N'Doch, it feels like an assault. He just knows someone is expecting something of him. At a loss, he spreads his arms and grins, and again his head is full of music, sounds he's sure he's been on the point of imagining. It crowds his thoughts, drowns all awareness, of the beach around him, of the thick heat and the subdued crashing of the surf, all this fades before a rush of tone and rhythm and harmony. N'Doch struggles to keep his cool. He's had his moments of mad musical inspiration, but it's never come to him like this, fully orchestrated, damping his other senses as it demands his immediate and total attention. His body is actually vibrating like a drumhead. He thinks maybe they're beaming the sound track directly into his brain. Last he'd checked, this wasn't possible, but there it is inside him, this sound, this music that's like someone else's voice singing in his head. He is helpless to do anything but surrender and listen to it.

Then it becomes clear to him—he doesn't know how—that the source of the music is the silver beast herself. It's like the music she was singing aloud a moment ago, a further development of the same theme, only this time less of a declaration . . . more of a demand. N'Doch gazes at her in wonder.

"How are you doing that?" He's just gotta ask. She's probably not programmed to answer questions, but if she can sing, maybe she can also speak. He does not ask, "What do you want with me?" That would be like asking, "Um, what's the next line?" It sounds wimpy, and it'd spoil the take.

So he moves in closer to join the group, trying to look like he knows what he's doing. The girl retreats from him a bit, into the shadow of her beast like a child into its mother's skirts. She's definitely on the tall side, he sees now, and her eyes, studying him so carefully, are very dark for a white girl's, almost black. Her skin is a fine pale olive roughened by sun or wind or maybe, though N'Doch cannot truly imagine it, by actual cold. And it looks real, now that he sees her close, like she's not even wearing makeup. He guesses her to be about fourteen.

The brown beast shrugs gently, a slow earthquake that jostles the girl sideways off her perch on his forearm. She regains her balance easily on the sand. N'Doch can see she's no stranger to exercise. She tosses the beast what N'Doch reads as a dirty look, the first sign of spirit he's seen in her. Then she squares her shoulders as if preparing for some onerous task, and turns to face him.

"*Mein Name ist Erde,*" she announces. "*Erde Katerina Meriah von Alte.*"

"Ummm," says N'Doch. He recognizes the harsh gutturals of one of those white northern European languages, but does not understand a word. He can't recall the last time he saw a vid in anything but French. Even the American ones are mostly dubbed. Are they trying to trip him up? Okay, it's gonna be a scene about communication. He smiles. "*Comment ça va?*"

Her dark eyes narrow. She doesn't understand him either. N'Doch is surprised. Most Europeans speak French. Will the viewers buy that she can't? Maybe she's supposed to be from some boondock isolationist principality. He's heard of such things. He's sure now she won't speak Wolof, so he switches to English, which he's learned only from vids. "Hey there, how ya doin', kid?"

She still doesn't get it. N'Doch gets ready to try sign language. So far, he doesn't think much of this script. He thumps his bare chest, like some guy in a bad jungle movie. "N'Doch," he says, "N'Doch."

The girl gives the big brown guy a quick sidelong glance, as if he's said something she didn't quite hear. But next she looks back at N'Doch with a gleam of understanding. She points at him and forms the sounds carefully.

"En-doche."

He nods encouragingly. "N'Doch," he repeats, correcting her pronunciation. He points back at her and cocks his head.

She taps her own leather-clad chest. *"Erde. Mien Name ist Erde."*

N'Doch tries it out. "Airda?"

"Erde."

"Right. Airda." They both nod, but N'Doch is thinking, *God, this is stupid.* He's never met anyone he didn't share at least one language with before.

Then he notices how the two beasts are regarding them with patient indulgence, like parents whose toddlers are meeting for the first time. He relaxes a little. *Well then,* he thinks, *I guess it's okay. Must be I've kept to the script so far.*

Chapter Four

In her eagerness to follow the dragon's Quest, Erde had expected to travel a goodly distance, but she hadn't counted on finding herself in a country that was so hot and where people didn't speak German. Never mind that she'd only recently gotten her own voice back: Just what did you do if somebody couldn't speak your language? But she was fairly sure language would be the least of her problems—the dragons would figure it out between them. Certainly the two of them were having no problem understanding one another. She felt Earth's relief and excitement humming through his body like a murmur of gratitude. Not since he'd woken up in that deep cold cave above Tor Alte had he been able to communicate with another being so fast and so fully, too fast for Erde to keep up. But she had snagged one astonishing revelation as it flashed by her: This new dragon from the sea was apparently Earth's relative. She'd actually heard him call her his sister.

Erde recalled how she'd felt when Rose of Deep Moor had proved able to sense and decipher Earth's image signals in her head. Not as clearly or as easily as Erde, certainly—the dragon had to be gentle with his sending to avoid burning Rose out. But she'd been the first since Erde and Earth had found each other and learned that they could speak in a way that did not (at first) include language. It helped that Rose was Sir Hal's longtime beloved, and a truly remarkably power in her own right. But mostly, instead of feeling the expected jealousy, Erde was glad to have someone to share the burden of communicating with the dragon's ferociously curious and demanding intellect.

And, even better, another dragon to help answer Earth's difficult questions. It wasn't that Earth considered her ignorant or inadequate. His generous nature was not given to that sort of harsh judgment. She was still his boon companion, his Dragon Guide, and forever would be. But Erde sensed she had come to the end of her useful knowledge, at least as far as helping Earth discover the reasons for his recent reawakening. And just when she'd needed help, help had arrived. It occurred to Erde that she and the dragon had been lucky that way. Sir Hal, too, had appeared out of nowhere to aid their escape just as she was about to fall into the clutches of Fra Guill's army of monks. It must mean that, like it or not, this hot, ugly, scary beach was exactly where they were meant to be to continue the dragon's Quest.

Which also meant that this dark young man—he seemed younger now than he had from a distance—this "Endoch" was meant to be also. If he was here with this sea dragon, he must be her dragon guide. But what Earth seemed to take for granted, Erde had a harder time accepting. He just didn't look like a dragon guide, running abut half-naked and grinning, so full of himself, yet at the same time a bit too eager to please, as if there was something he thought she might give him if only he was charming enough.

Well, thought Erde, *I have nothing, and I wouldn't give him anything even if I had. Besides, he must have done something wrong, to have people chasing him so furiously.*

At the back of her mind, she felt the pressure of the dragon's censure. He was not too involved with his new-found relative to remind her that people had been chasing her very recently. And what, after all, does a dragon guide look like? The image he showed her was like a mirror held up in her mind. Did a scrawny, wide-eyed, wind-roughened fourteen-year-old girl inspire any greater confidence?

Chastened, Erde reconsidered her inner tirade. The dragon was right. It wasn't proper to take on so against an innocent stranger. It was just that, well, he was so strange. But judging from the men who'd been pursuing him, dark skin and no clothing was the way things went in this smelly, steamy country. Erde had a sudden sense of reversal, like being tossed head over heels in a torrent. The sense of it was so physical, she grabbed Earth's neck crest for support. In this place, it could be her own pale skin and heavy clothing that seemed unnatural. As the thick heat wore on her, she was already prepared to shed a few inappropriate layers.

So she'd better give this young man a second chance. If the sea dragon was Earth's sister, it then followed that this Endoch should be, in a way, her brother. Erde found she could warm to that idea. She'd always wanted a brother or a sister. Someone nearer her own age to talk to. Her life in her father's castle had been filled with adults twice her age or older. Except for Rainer. Well, Rainer had been sort of her brother, until he grew up so tall and handsome and she was dumb enough to fall in love with him. She wasn't going to do that again. Tentatively, she smiled at Endoch and he grinned back, revealing the whitest, evenest teeth she'd ever seen, set in a round mobile face as smooth and fine as polished walnut. His grin asked, Well, what's next? Erde hoped Earth would have an answer.

She tapped at him mentally to get his attention.

—Has she said, Dragon, why she's Called you?

A flood of images burst into her head, tumbling, crowding, flashing past too fast to be made sense of. Erde slammed up a barrier of protest and sent back an image of herself drowning. Earth relayed apologies and braked reluctantly to the snail-pace of language.

—Oh, wonder! Oh, devastation!

—What? Dragon, what is it?

—Wonder that I have found my sister again!

Again? Erde puzzled at that but there was first a more pressing concern.

—What could be bad about that?

—Devastation that it is not she who Called!

—Not? How do you know?

—She, too, has heard the Call, from the depths of the sea, and has waked to answer it.

Erde conjured images of comfort and reassurance.

—It is another who Calls. She thinks she knows who.

—Can she tell you your Purpose?

*—She's hardly sure of her own. But she remembers
more than I.*

—What is her name?

Erde hoped she did not offend by asking. She knew
how sensitive dragons could be about their naming. But
Earth seemed to find great joy in the announcement.

—Her name is Water.

Water. Earth and Water. A notion began in Erde's
brain that slid away forgotten as Endoch stilled suddenly, losing his grin. He turned to stare at the narrow
space of sand between the dark rusting wall and the
impossible pincushion trees. Erde listened as he was listening, hard with bated breath.

"Uh-oh," he said, and she had no trouble understanding his meaning.

Chapter Five

N'Doch hears it now, an approaching throng. He'd have heard it a lot sooner if he'd been paying less attention to his chances for stardom and more to his personal safety. He can even hear the clang of the weapons—hoes, rakes, tire irons. They've brought whatever was to hand, and probably a raggedly lethal assortment of firearms. This'll really give the cameras something to focus on. He's surprised the brothers didn't recognize a vid-shoot when they saw it, but he knows they could never have roused the *bidonville* with a complaint about stolen tomatoes. The bunch of them must have charged in hollering about mutant monsters attacking the beach. It's mostly fishermen who live in the shantytown, a hard life and getting harder. They'll be worried about their boats, and these days, they'll believe anything bad about the water.

N'Doch has to laugh at that. If they think his own little silver-blue critter could do damage to one of those old hard-built boats, wait till they see this big brown guy. Then he wonders if the fishermen are in on it, too. Maybe the whole town knew about the shoot except him.

Doesn't matter. He's deep into it now. For at least the fifth time that day, he ponders his routes of escape. He can see the white girl has the same idea. She's casing the nearest fishing boat with obvious intent to board.

"Can't hide there," he cautions. "First place they'll look."

She gazes at him uncomprehendingly.

"Damn. Forgot." He'd felt like they were communicating pretty well until he'd had to fall back on words. Then he gets excited all over again. This has got to be it, his big moment, where he gets to rescue the girl from the ravening horde and be the hero. He wishes he'd found more to eat today. One tomato is hardly an energy-builder. He's not sure yet how the cybercritters fit in. The brown one, at least, is much too big for the hidey-hole N'Doch is contemplating. He thinks the blue one will just make it, but probably they're meant to face down the crowd first as a diversion while he makes a run for it with the girl. He finds he's not very happy about that. It means one or both of the critters will likely be torn apart by the mob, to rouse the viewer's blood lust a little and create more sympathy for the hapless escapees. He hopes it's not the little blue one, though her size and beauty make her the prime candidate. But he reminds himself she's only a prop. He shouldn't be thinking of her as *his*.

Anyhow, he knows what he should do. The only question is, whether he should wait until the crowd comes into view around the landing craft, to help build suspense and give the cameras a dramatic long shot. By now, the critters have their heads high and searching. The girl is looking this way and that, especially at him. Her eyes are very clearly demanding help. He remembers she knows at least some version of the story line—probably she's trying to cue him that it's time to make his move. Besides, he's hearing that weird music in his head again.

"Okay, let's go!" N'Doch beckons hugely, then recalls how, when he did his walk-on, the director singled him out of the whole crowd of extras and told him to stop acting so hard.

"*Act*ing!" she'd said, as if it was some kind of dirty word.

So N'Doch backs off his mugging and gesturing and trots up the beach to cut around the end of the fishing fleet. He expects the girl to follow, but beside the last boat he looks back and she hasn't, though the silver-blue critter is close behind, tailing him like a big long-necked dog. Her manner isn't doglike, however. She seems to be urging him to hurry. The mob is so close, he can distinguish individual voices and words. Any moment, they'll be in sight. N'Doch sprints back down the beach and grabs the girl's hand to haul her into action. She resists only briefly. Now the brown guy is moving, too. They both get the idea and hurry after N'Doch. He gestures at them to watch where they step.

On the other side of the fishing fleet, the super-tanker awaits them, as long and high as a city block, its bow broken and sunk so deep into the sand that it looks like it grew there. Gaping holes smile darkly, scars of the harbor mines that took it out when it blundered into them during the storm. The girl stares at it horrified, as if she has no idea what she's looking at. Even the critters seem to hesitate. N'Doch takes the girl's hand again and races for the largest gap, but when they get there and he's pulled her into its shadow, it's plain the big guy will never fit.

The one from the water, *his* one, checks out the ragged opening. It's close. She's wider than he's guessed and the metal edges are nasty. But she heads right in. N'Doch winces, worried for her fine silky fur or her delicate fleshy crest, then blinks as she seems to thin and elongate, and slip through easily. N'Doch is sure his eyes have given out for a moment, as if his vision blurred, just for an instant, then the moment passes and the sea critter is there inside the hold with him and the girl, looking very self-satisfied. He shakes his head, wondering, but he can't spend time on it now. The big guy is still outside in the hot sun, nosing around the sharp edges of the gap. His curving horns clank against the rusted metal, then he withdraws. N'Doch goes to help him, in case he's been wrong about this one's size as well.

When he steps out into the sun, he can hear the mob just about to spill, foaming at the mouth, from behind the fishing fleet. He glances swiftly about. No sign of the big cybercritter. The wide stretch of sand is empty, but for scattered rubble and a big rock halfway toward the water. A big brown rock that wasn't there before.

N'Doch squints at it, frowning. For the barest instant, he can see it as the cybercritter, settling in to wait out the battle. Then it's a rock again, and he knows the mob will also see a rock, and ignore it.

Man, he marvels *that is one amazing piece of equipment.*

Then the girl is behind him, pulling him out of the sunlight.

"*Gehen wir,*" she whispers urgently.

N'Doch holds back, pointing to the new brown boulder, but she only nods and yanks on him some more.

"*Ja, ha, gehen wir! Schnell!*"

Finally he gets it. This miracle is nothing new to her at all. Probably she does lots of these high-tech vids. Feeling obscurely put down, N'Doch shrugs and brushes past her with a sharp gesture. "This way."

The blue beast is waiting in the shadows. She chirps at him briskly as he nears. It sounds as much like an order as like encouragement, but for her sake, N'Doch chooses the widest passage into the bowels of the downed ship-giant. He leads them toward the stern, the seaward end, where the lowest holds are filled with water and hung with seaweed and barnacles and mutant starfish with too many arms. The fishermen don't like the tanker. Not even the most destitute will live in it, though the upper decks are mostly intact and dry, above the high water mark. They claim that the rotting bodies of dead sailors wash about in the holds to rise at night and walk the shredded decks. N'Doch has found a bone or two, nothing more. After all, the fish visit the wrecks at high tide, and with food as scarce as it is, they're not likely to leave much behind. As for any lurking ghosts, he's grateful to them if they keep unwanted visitors from penetrating as deeply into the tanker's wet gloom as he dares to go.

This girl, he guesses, would side with the fishermen. She looks near to panic in the close dim passages. At the raised sill of a door hatch, N'Doch puts on the charm to urge her forward. She returns him a look of offended bravado but takes his offered hand anyway, sticking close behind him as he negotiates a section of collapsed decking. The hole is filled with surging black water. N'Doch isn't worried about his footing. He knows every nook and cranny. What's bothering him is the cameras, now he's disappeared inside the ship. Then he figures the girl must carry a camera with her, maybe one of those microimplants that uses her eyes as the lens. He's seen an infoshow about the r & d on that but he's surprised to see it's already in commercial use. Of course, the Media get all the good tech before anyone. They're the ones with the real money in this world, after all.

Past another hatch, he reaches a dry level spot where

light drops through a blown-out exhaust stack. The girl looks up, as if light alone could save her life. She hugs the dank wall, breathing hard and shallow, but ready to continue. N'Doch checks back for the blue cybercritter. She's just stepping daintily through the hatchway behind them, and again he finds himself blinking at her and staring, because she seems so much shorter and longer than she did outside, almost an entirely different shape. And if she was human, he'd say she's preening a bit, to be sure he's noticed. He thinks of the big guy's gift for looking like a rock and begins to suspect this one of harboring other equally mysterious skills.

Then he hears banging and raucous shouts echoing from the gap amidships. The mob'll be in after them soon, worked up enough to dare coming inside a ways. He's got to get moving again, now the girl has caught her breath. The hardest part's still ahead of them.

He signals the girl and moves on down the slanted passage. He wishes he could tell her how he thinks of this huge vessel as a man lying dead in the water. They'd been threading through his stove-in rib cage, and now they've reached his broken, sunken spine. N'Doch eases around a mass of wreckage, some vast engine or turbine hurled upward by the blast, only to fall back, crushing everything in its path. When he's in here, N'Doch can't help picturing the ship's gallant last moments. He's written songs about it, but none yet that's satisfied him. The mammoth scale of the event as he imagines it is beyond the range of his ancient keyboard and amps. One of the reasons he wants so badly to be famous is so he can afford better equipment.

He slows a bit, knowing what's just ahead. They creep around a particularly dark corner—even N'Doch has his hand to the wall, feeling his way. Then, in front of them, the dark gets darker and the floor falls away. There were stairs here once. Now water laps along the base of the walls where they end in blackness. This hold was breached only below the waterline. It is lightless and vast, and the moist air is close with rank sea smells. The ebb and flow of water makes the stressed and rusting metal creak and groan. It's this part of the ship that gives rise to tales of the walking dead.

"And here's the bad news," murmurs N'Doch from

the edge. "We gotta swim across." He doesn't mention
that the local shark herd likes to hang out in this cooler,
darker water. As his eyes adjust, he sees the whites of
the girl's eyes shift. She's staring at him as if she suspects
his meaning. He nods, making broad swimming motions
he hopes she and her camera can pick up in the faint
light.

"*Ich kann nicht.*" She backs up sharply, shaking her
head.

N'Doch doesn't blame her really. This part couldn't
have been in the script she read 'cause he's just written
it in. But she's getting good pay for this, so he shrugs
and jabs a thumb behind them, where the shouts and
banging make it sound like the ship is being torn apart
for salvage. He tries to sound tough and heroic.

"No choice, babe. Sorry."

The girl eyes him owlishly. N'Doch likes her little
glower. It makes her look brave, even if she isn't. Except
really, she is, to have come this far past the scripted action. He wonders if the story includes a big love scene
where she gives herself to him in gratitude for being so
manfully rescued. Usually, he'd be up for that, as it were,
even on camera, though he's never tried *that* before. But
somehow, this is different. *She* is different. First, she's so
young. He knows all the hot sexpot vid stars are around
her age, but somehow, she seems even younger. He can't
bring himself to undress her in his mind. He's embarrassed to think that "innocent" might be the word he's
looking for, but there it is. He doesn't have a sister, but
this is probably what it's like. He feels more like protecting her than making love to her.

And it's weird, feeling so responsible. N'Doch figures
he's really getting into the role now. In which case, he'd
better set a strong example. He crouches at the edge, then
shoves off lightly into the water with hardly a splash. No
use announcing your presence to the damn sharks. If
they're here, they'll find you soon enough. Reciting private incantations against all sea vermin, he beckons encouragingly and treads water to give the girl a moment
to work up her nerve.

But she's still shaking her head and making big warding gestures with both her arms.

"*Nein! Nein! Ich kann nicht schwimmen!*"

She seems to be trying to explain her reluctance. N'Doch is glad she's smart enough to keep her voice down despite her panic. He's not too hot on strange dark places either, but all he wants right now is to see her in the water. The sooner she's in, the sooner they're both out. He'd like to tell her to stop acting so hard, like the director did to him. Instead, he frowns at her fiercely. She just glares right back at him.

Suddenly there is motion in the darkness. N'Doch makes for the edge, sure it's the sharks. But it's the blue cybercritter, barely visible, sliding silently into the water. She glides over, nudging him insistently. She doesn't give up until he wraps an arm around her neck to keep from being swamped. He feels like he's just been boarded by the Harbor Patrol. Dragging him with her, the critter eases sideways against the edge of the drop-off, warbling calming music to the girl.

"*Gott sei Dank!*" the girl murmurs. To N'Doch's amazement, she starts stripping off her tall leather boots and vest. She bundles them up and, clutching them to her thin chest with one arm, she lowers herself into the water to hang on to the edge for dear life while the cybercritter coasts along beside her. With a desperate lurch and grab, the girl flings herself astride the critter's back and holds tight with her free arm. In the dim reflected murmur of light sifting through random cracks and punctures, N'Doch sees both terror and determination sculpting her face into something as steady as stone. She doesn't seem to care that she's gotten wet, just that there's something solid underneath her.

Now N'Doch gets it at last. He's thought it was the sharks she's afraid of, not the *water*. He's a little embarrassed, hopes he hasn't messed up the script. But hey, how was he to know a grown-up girl like her wouldn't know how to swim?

But now the cybercritter is singing an impatient demand for directions. He can tell she's not too interested in hanging out in a shark tank either. N'Doch pulls himself together and points, and the blue beast bears them secretly into darkness.

Chapter Six

*D*ragons are certainly the world's cleverest creatures, thought Erde gratefully as she clung to Water's long silky neck and struggled to keep her boot bundle dry. She understood that Endoch wasn't being cruel or stupid, trying to force her into the water. He didn't know she was a baron's daughter and lucky to have been taught how to read, never mind a skill so unladylike as swimming. Indeed, she envied his ease with it—to be able to glide over this fathomless black without fear of sinking would put an entire category of nightmares to rest. Hal had promised to teach her, but they'd never found the time. Besides, it had been so cold up there— she thought of home now as "up" because she knew it got warmer as you traveled farther south and surely the Germanies must be very far north of any place as hot as this. But the cold hadn't been normal. Right in the middle of August, it had snowed. The smaller ponds had even iced over. And terrible storms and hail and too much rain. Just thinking of it made her shiver. That weird, unseasonable weather had roused the villagers to go out hunting the witch responsible for the curse. She would have been their victim, had Fra Guill had his way.

Meanwhile, here she was, running from another howling mob, hiding in another cave. Erde recalled the peace and pleasure of Deep Moor and nearly wept. She'd had such a short time in that magical valley, with Rose and the other women who guarded and nurtured its secrets, yet somehow she had come to think of it as home. She had no other, certainly not Tor Alte, not as long as her father remained under the priest's evil sway. And now she didn't even have Deep Moor—she had a dark and noisy pit filled with salty, smelly water.

She caught herself whining, and didn't at all like the sound of it. At least the water was cooler than the fetid air. And how dare she whine when they'd found another dragon, one who could understand her, even if its dragon guide could not? Erde did not feel Water in her head like she did her own dragon. Water responded via a fast relay to Earth and back again. This dragon-to-dragon communication seemed virtually instantaneous, as real magic should be. It was as good as having an interpreter standing right at your ear.

What did not seem to be so clear or instantaneous was Water's communication with Endoch. But Erde remembered that it had taken her a while, several days in fact, to learn how to "talk" properly with Earth. Endoch was probably "hearing" more than he realized. It had been that way for her, and then understanding had arrived rather suddenly, like a morning fog lifting off the mountains. From then on, it had been as natural as breathing.

For now, Endoch had fallen into nodding and pointing a lot, rather like she'd had to do when she'd lost her voice. But she guessed he had met a lot of people who didn't speak his language, since he acted as if it was nothing odd, merely inconvenient.

And so, with broad gestures and murmured incoherencies, he led them far across the dark lagoon to an equally dark shore. Finally, Erde heard rather than saw him let go of Water's neck and swim several long strokes to clamber up on a bank that rang softly under the weight of his step. Water slid alongside this shore while Erde felt for stone or sand, anything solid to stand on. Instead, she found Endoch's hand, hauling her out of the water. He drew her quickly away from the groaning edge, which was hard as stone but smelled like a smithy's rubbish pile.

"Come on," he said quietly. "This way."

Erde's alert ear detected familiar syllables. "*Kommen?*" She felt him stop short and turn in the darkness.

"Yeah," he said with slow surprise. "That's right, come on."

"*Ja,*" said Erde. "*Ich komme.*"

"Yeah?" He gave a little laugh of disbelief.

"*Ja.*"

"*Ja,*" he repeated experimentally, mimicking her with an actor's precision. Then he slapped his forehead. "Of course! It's German. You're speaking German. It sounds a little different, y'know? I didn't recognize it at first."

Erde was sorry to disappoint him, but her silence told all.

"No, huh? Okay, lemesee . . . German . . . I know that one. It's all over those big trucks we scavenge. It's, um . . . Deutschland!"

"*Jawohl. Deutsch.*" Erde almost giggled. He was close, but how funny that he had turned a mere language into an entire kingdom. Deutsch*land?* Didn't he know that a whole lot of kingdoms and duchies spoke German?

"*Deutsch,*" he repeated. "That's right, Deutsch."

Water announced herself with a wet nudge at Erde's shoulder. There were lanterns or torchlight flickering along the walls of the opposite shore.

"*Sei ist hier,*" Erde whispered anxiously. "*Gehen wir, ja?*" But Endoch had spotted the approaching light and was already drawing them away from the water. Erde sensed the tunnel closing in around them again. She put out a hand and immediately jerked it back, suppressing a squeal. The wall was slimy. Cold strings of stuff gave damply under her fingers. Probably the same stuff so soft and slippery beneath her feet. A childish horror rose up in her gullet. Surely, like Jonah in the Bible, she was being swallowed alive!

But Water was there at her back to nudge her along when she froze. The dragon's breath was like a warm breeze beside her ear. Erde thought of her beloved horse Micha. Her terror eased, and she was able to move on. Only for the dragons' sake would she set foot in such a terrible place.

Soon she realized she could see again, mostly faint shapes of gray and grayer, but at least now she could make out Endoch's tall, slim form moving along the passage ahead of her. The ground slanted upward, which Erde took as a fair and welcome sign that she might soon see the light of day again.

At the bottom of a flight of steps, Endoch paused and glanced back. "Everyone okay so far?"

Erde understood only his tone of concern. She nodded and picked up her pace a bit.

"Almost there."

She heard anticipation in his voice now, and a hint of pride. She climbed the steps behind him thoughtfully. This place he was taking them must be something special, maybe his family stronghold, and this was the hidden entrance. Erde was surprised by his generosity. She wasn't sure she'd reveal such a secret to someone she'd just met. But after all, it was his own skin he was saving, as well as hers.

A thin shaft of light from above lit the top of the steps. A glow down the passage promised a lot more beyond. Erde gazed about as details rose into visibility, like riders appearing out of a mist. She saw a long narrow corridor with a flat floor and a low, absolutely flat ceiling. She'd never encountered a place so rigorously rectangular or even imagined such a thing was possible. Yet, for all the apparent right angles, there was not a sharp edge anywhere. The walls were very light-colored and entirely smooth, without a crack or mortar line, only a seam every so often, flanked by rows of close-set little knobs, either decorative or some kind of fastener. Cautiously, she put a fingertip, then her entire palm to the surface. It was dry and faintly cool to the touch. Clearly, they had left the cave without her noticing, and climbed up into a strange sort of building. Endoch's family must be very powerful if this was the castle they lived in.

She was so busy studying the odd walls as she moved along them that she was unprepared for the space beyond. Passing through a doorway, she stopped short, letting her boot bundle slide unnoticed to the floor.

A great-hall, she thought, *or even a cathedral.*

But there was no altar or throne to be seen, no choir stalls or banqueting table. She stood in a tall, square room with rows of huge, many-paned windows set high up on three of the four pale walls. The ceiling above was lost behind the bright glare through the glass. Many of the panes were cracked or missing, letting currents of air into the room to swirl dust and insects about in the long thick pillars of light falling past shadowed corners toward the floor.

The floor made her nervous. It seemed to be floating.

Erde bent and laid a hand to it. It felt and looked like wood but was as seamless and smooth as pond water at dawn.

Endoch appeared out of the shadows, grinning boyishly. "Isn't it great? Isn't it just mega?"

Erde hated to dampen such luminous pride, but how long should she go on pretending she understood what he was saying? Water slipped in behind her and padded into the sunlight and smoky air. Erde watched her slim and lengthen toward the high bank of windows, and knew her for a shape-shifter. Quite astonishing to observe for the first time, really, but nothing surprising. Shape-shifting was an attribute of dragons often mentioned in the lore, one that Earth, being tied to soil and stone, did not possess. Erde hoped he would not be jealous.

She glanced at Endoch, and found him watching the she-dragon with a narrowed eye. He, too, had noticed the shape change, but he seemed puzzled by it, as if unsure that he'd actually seen it. She wondered if his study of the dragon lore had been as complete as her own. She knew that much of a young man's time must be spent in the armorer's practice yard or out with the Hunt, but surely he could have picked up the basic essentials just by paying good attention to the bard tales or the old songs sung at the village festivals. If he didn't know the lore, he'd have no idea what his duty was as Water's dragon guide. She could certainly tell him, but Erde wondered if he'd even listen to advice from someone so much younger, and a girl.

Whatever conclusion he'd reached, Endoch finally pulled out of his stare with a quick doglike shake of his head and went back to the entrance to yank on a piece of the wall beside it. When it began to swing forward, Erde realized it was a door, huge and rounded at the corners. Endoch pivoted it carefully into place so it settled against the opening with a heavy muffled clang. He twisted some kind of latch that squealed as he turned it, then came away, dusting his palms together with a satisfied air.

"That'll keep 'em guessing. No one's ever got past the shark tank so far, but you never know. . . ."

Erde nodded helpfully, which she thought was more polite than shrugging and pointing. The newly relaxed tilt of his shoulders did suggest that he felt they'd finally escaped their pursuers. Taking her first easy breath in a while, Erde rolled up her dripping legging and began to worry about Earth.

She had no sense of how far they were from where they'd left him on the sand beside the ocean. Since finding each other two months before, she and the dragon had hardly been separated. The void his absence left inside her was an almost physical pain. When he used his gift of stillness to become rocklike, or to still even further to virtual invisibility, it took all of his energy and concentration, or at least that was his explanation for why they could not communicate while he was being invisible. Erde had been sending him a stream of images just in case, ever since following Endoch into the cave. Now that they were in a more dragon-sized room, Earth could join them if only she could send him a good image of it, for he was able to transport himself to any place he could picture clearly in his mind.

Just as she was pondering what to do next, there he was, winking into existence beside Water in the middle of the room. Erde ran to him joyfully.

—*Dragon! How did you get here?*

—**My sister! She showed me and I came.**

Like an excited child returned from a great adventure, he began filling her head with views of the mob milling and shouting while he'd been hiding in plain view on he beach.

—*Water can be with you even when you're invisible?*

Assent. A proud dragon nod inside her head.

—*How wonderful.*

—**Yes, she is wonderful. She is my sister.**

—I know, I know.

Then Erde felt ashamed, for she knew she'd sounded snappish. He was still so caught up in the wonder of acquiring a sibling. She didn't blame him, particularly since the sibling's gifts seemed to dovetail so conveniently with his own. But she worried now that she, not he, might be the jealous one. She would just try to think of it as having two dragons instead of one. She was eager to question Water about who she thought the Caller was, and about what else she might know that Earth did not. But first, there was the question of Endoch.

—*Dragon, is Water sure this dark man is her dragon guide?*

Assent, query, puzzlement.

—*Well, I mean, he . . . I don't think he knows very much about dragons.*

Earth looked at her, then looked across the room at Endoch, who had frozen in mid-stride and stood staring at them with his mouth open.

—*Hmmm. My sister says maybe you are right.*

Chapter Seven

N'Doch knows what he's seen. He's been watching the silver one since she did her growing taller thing right in front of him, and then—in a moment shorter than an eye blink—the big guy is there beside her. Three-D and substantial. Definitely not a hologram. N'Doch notes that the white girl can actually lean her whole weight against the critter's scaly brown shoulder.

The problem is, he can't believe it. He wants to, but he just can't. He's always told himself those vid people can do anything. Hire *them* to put men on Mars, he's always said. They'd get it done soon enough, and make a good show out of it, too.

But here, in the dusty shadow and light of his favorite hiding place, his own secret kingdom, this officers' gymnasium, his credulity is tempered by the still, sane presence of the space. Here—safe, relaxed, clearheaded—he finally has to admit that he's been making up most of his explanations for the events of the last half hour, or at least stretching what he's heard to fit what he's been seeing. He's never seen a real cybercritter, only the info-shows about the cutting edge developments in special effects, shows he realizes are no more reliable than your everyday newscast. Because he *wants* them to be true, somehow they become true when he needs them to. But right now, in this calm room, away from the constant hype and hustle of his daily life, those stories are no longer working.

But he's never been without a story, so what should the new story be? The big guy was on the beach, and now he's here. Apparently translated through steel and plastic and wood within the space of a breath. Not an easy thing to explain in the world as N'Doch knows it. In fact, it's a bigger stretch than cybercritters.

And then there's the silver one with her head-invading music. The right music. *His* music.

N'Doch finds himself weak at the knees again. He's dimly aware that his arm is hurting where the short brother slashed him. He knows he should be paying more attention to the wound, getting it cleaned and covered before any one of a billion bugs take up residence. But this other matter has him too distracted.

"This is all a setup, right?" he asks the girl, one last chance at a rational explanation. "You know, for the vid?" If she's not an actress, if she's making this up as she goes along, just like he is—and her look of innocent bewilderment is almost enough to convince him she is— then what are these critters?

If not a vid-tech special effect, then . . . what?

To stave off the upswelling panic, he resorts to an exercise of logic. Either they're real, these critters, or they're not. Fine. If they're not real, he's seeing things. If he's seeing things, he's either sick or crazy. Or—he remembers the tomato—he's been drugged.

But he doesn't think he's crazy, and he doesn't feel drugged, at least not the usual way. And except for the growing heat in his arm, he feels healthy enough. He'd managed not to drink any of the sea water drenching him, and he'd spotted both critters within moments of being cut. No bug goes to work *that* quick. Anyhow, the brothers saw them, too. That's what saved his life.

Which means they're real, the conclusion he'd already reached and explained away with invented technology. But if they're real and *not* cybercritters, then what the hell are they?

This time the panic will not be kept down. Rising up with it comes a notion that defies all his attempts at logic. N'Doch tries to ignore it, but he knows where it comes from. It's the same part of him he goes to when he writes his music, where the answers have nothing to do with logic, they just appear out of his soul like magic.

Appear like magic. That was it. That was the notion he was trying to avoid. *Magic.*

N'Doch meets the great golden gaze of the larger critter and gives in. His knees buckle.

*   *   *

Erde saw the fear rush into his eyes just before he collapsed. It was like watching black water flood a ditch. Earth's sudden arrival must have frightened him. The dragon was big, after all, though not nearly as big as she'd thought a dragon should be. And he could look terrifying if you didn't know him. But why was Endoch scared now, when he hadn't been before, back on the beach? Must be he was better at covering it up than she was.

Then she noticed there was blood on the floor where he'd fallen, and recalled the vicious swipe the man with the club had delivered. She relayed the reminder to Earth, but it was Water who went to him, lowering her sleek head to nose at him, crooning gently. Endoch yelped and scrambled backward on ankles and elbows as if terrified. Erde thought Water was the least sort of dragon to be frightened of, but Endoch's terror rang in the air like a hammered bell. Erde found herself gripping Earth's neck crest in sympathy. She could sense the dragon's bemused surprise.

—*He is frightened. He does not know what she is.*
Erde nodded, remembering.

—*I didn't know who you were either, when I first saw you. I thought you were going to eat me.*

A graver negative than usual washed across her mind.

—*What, not who. He does not know what a dragon is.*

This, Erde could not imagine.

—*You mean, he doesn't believe in dragons?*

She'd met people like that, though they were rare. They usually didn't believe in witchcraft either, until someone laid a proper spell on them. But most people thought witches and dragons were the minions of Satan, which was why Fra Guill's campaign against them roused such fervor throughout the countryside. But Erde knew better, about both dragons and witches.

The question was, how to convince Endoch?

N'Doch's whole world is turning upside down.

He's too old to believe in magic, or maybe too young. His weird grandfather believes in magic, for God's sake, and he's so uncool and old-fashioned, it's an embarrassment to have him in the family. Not that you ever saw anything of him, living all alone out in the bush like he does. The old man once told him towns were bad for his health. *Well, yeah,* N'Doch recalls replying, *but so is being a hermit.*

N'Doch's fear retreats a bit before a vivid rush of childhood memories, rising like a flight of birds to distract him: the heat and red dust of the bush, the stillness at midday, the scent of parched vegetation. His mama often sent him out to stay with Papa Djawara after his father took off and she was so busy working. Jeez, the man was old even then. And weird. N'Doch feels his mouth curl in an involuntary grin. The old man did tell great stories. Sang them, really. *Probably what got me started,* N'Doch realizes, listening to all those long songs that went on verse after verse, late into the night, unbelievable yarns about powerful shamans and evil curses and spirits of the dead that enter the bodies of men and animals in order to work their will among the living. The usual old tribal stuff.

But there was that one long tale, N'Doch recalls, one that was different from the rest and the old man's special favorite. He always reworked it so it was about the adventures of a young man named Water. As N'Doch roots around trying to retrieve it from faded memory, he finds himself gazing up into a pair of liquid dark eyes that are focused on him with alarming intensity. He reads concern there, yes, but also rebuke and impatience. He remembers the song now, and the memory takes his breath away: a young man named Water meets up with a monster from the sea. Only she's not a monster, she's a magical creature, a dragon, and the whole long song is about the quest they embark on to save the world. He doesn't recall ever hearing the ending. He always fell asleep first.

A dragon?

No.

The silvery-blue critter nudges him, showing just the faintest trace of irritation. N'Doch backs away in horror.

A dragon?

He blinks, he coughs, he shakes his head. He does all the requisite things, even pinches himself, but he's been looking at this critter for over an hour and he knows she's not going away that easy. He's not dreaming, he's wide awake, his arm hurts like hell and there's a dragon in his hidey-hole.

Two dragons. And a weird white girl who acts like she's dropped in from some other planet. Who knows? Maybe she has. Why should things start getting any saner? Meanwhile, he's flat on his ass and elbows, and bleeding all over his beautiful wooden floor, the only thing in his life that's whole and perfect. N'Doch grasps at logic again: what do you do when something you can't believe is happening, actually is? Hey, you go with it. Like the first bars of a new melody, you just follow it out, see where it leads you.

So he tries to get up, but his legs won't work. And it's hot in the gym, so much hotter than usual. He's bathed in sweat and slipping in his own blood as he struggles to rise. The blue critter puts her forehead to his chest and presses him back to the floor. He's surprised how gentle she is, since she's looking so irascible. There's music in his head again, and N'Doch decides to lie there and listen, while the blue critter noses at his arm. Her inspection hurts despite her gentleness, but the pain is somehow past the edge of his current awareness, which is filled with the music. He understands now that the bugs are in his wound, the worst bugs, the really fast-acting kind, and that means he's got to act even faster. He's got to get serious about moving to his stash of anti-biotics, though who knows if he's got anything here that's recent enough to kill this bug—they all mutate so fast and his pill source is not exactly over-the-counter yesterday's formula.

His breath is getting short, a bad sign. He draws his knees up to his chest and turns over onto his side. Again, the blue critter stops him. N'Doch is amazed by the strength in that seemingly delicate neck. He struggles a bit, but the music swells in his head and then he can't recall why he's resisting so hard. Her voice is so soothing, her warm breath on his cheek so familiar, his mama's of course, why didn't he see that? She'll take him into her arms and make his hurt go away. His grip on consciousness is tenuous. N'Doch forgets why he's holding on at all, and lets go.

Chapter Eight

His fever had risen so suddenly, she hadn't seen it for what it was. He'd seemed so hale while leading them to safety, as if his wound didn't bother him at all.

Cautiously, Erde joined Water at the dark boy's side. She shouldn't think of him as a boy, he was clearly several years older than she was. But on his back and so feverish, he looked young and vulnerable. She wondered suddenly if his fever was contagious. The only sickness she knew that rose so fast was the plague. Chilled, she retreated a few steps. She saw no rashes or boils, the outward signs of plague, but she did not want to have come all this way simply to be felled by disease.

Earth lumbered up beside her. She wrapped a hand around his nearest horn for comfort as he lowered his big head thoughtfully over the stricken youth. Then she recalled how the dragon had healed the old man in the barn at Erfurt. He'd been beaten senseless and was bleeding to death from a sword cut to his side, but when Earth was through with him, he got up and walked away. And the she-goat. Earth had healed her, too, by washing her awful wounds with his big cowlike tongue.

Erde wasn't sure she should remind Earth of the she-goat, whom he'd been later forced to devour to keep himself from starving. The noble goat, of course, had given her permission. Instead, Erde imaged the old man, though he'd proved far less noble, an ungrateful coward who'd revealed their hiding place to Brother Guillemo himself.

—Dragon! Do you remember? Can you help this one too?

There was doubt and diffidence in the dragon's reply.

—The wound I can close and make well, but he already burns from within. . . .

—The fever? You can't heal the fever?

An immense sigh, like the ground shifting, then sadness, failure, a sense of inadequacy.

Water raised her head from her scrutiny of Endoch's condition. She fixed Erde with her demanding stare, and an image formed in Erde's head, which she saw exactly mirrored in the broad expanse of Earth's mind. She knew immediately that the thought came from the she-dragon. The quality of the communication differed so from Earth's blunt, honest imaging. It slid into her consciousness—not surprisingly—like water, rushing here, a trickle there, not to be denied. Insistently flowing into cracks, following the contours of her thoughts, shimmering like the ruffled surface of a lake. At times two images, or three or several, layered one over another, adding depth and richness.

Erde was delighted. With Earth as a conduit, she could speak with Water almost directly, if she could but learn to read her imaging coherently. Right now, the layering and shimmering obscured the meaning of the image. There seemed to be several narratives playing at once: one of Earth washing the dark youth's wound, one of the four of them huddling together in an earnest, conversing fashion. But surely Water did not intend the topmost layer the way it seemed, for it showed Erde with her dagger in hand, stabbing into the soft fur of the sea dragon's neck, then catching the flowing blood in cupped palms.

—Dragon! What is she saying?

Earth's horror was as profound as her own. But after consultation with the sea dragon, it faded to wonder and admiration.

—Her blood will heal the fire inside. You must give it to him.

—I? Me?

Vigorous assent.

She has shown you how. Quickly, she says. You must do it now!

Dragon's blood. The most magical substance of all, according to the lore.

Erde gripped her dagger dutifully but was stopped by the sinuous beauty of Water's beckoning head and neck. Earth shoved at her with his snout.

—Quickly!

—Oh, Dragon, I can't!

—She says you must, or he will die.

Erde forced herself the few steps to Water's side and slid her dagger from its sheath. Alla's dagger. The old woman's parting gift. Lying on Erde's palm, the fine tapered blade seemed to drink in the broken sunlight and return a steadier glow of its own. Water arched her neck to expose the most delicate underside. Clenching her jaw, Erde laid the razor edge against fine silver fur. The dragon drew away sharply, startling her. She shot a doubting glance back at Earth.

—The point. You must use the dagger's point.

"Ohh," replied Erde faintly. She could not imagine. Sir Hal would be better at this. He would know the appropriate ceremony. But at Earth's insistent urging, she gathered herself again and set the dagger point-first. This time, when she applied a bit of pressure, Water did not recoil. Rather, she leaned into the blade, and Erde took a breath and drove it in, then jerked it right out again with a cry of remorse.

The blood did not spurt from the wound. It pooled at the opening, glistening, waiting. Water curled her slim head around to regard Erde expectantly. Erde stared, then quickly sheathed her blade and offered cupped and shaking hands to the wound. Like water from a mountain spring, the blood flowed neatly into her palms. It ceased flowing when the hand-made basin was full. Light-headed with wonder, Erde carried the precious liquid to the unconscious youth.

But he couldn't have been entirely unconscious, for when she let a few red drops leak into his half-open mouth, he roused himself enough to drink in the entire handful, swallowing as greedily as if he sucked in life itself. The blood ran out of Erde's hands as cleanly as water, leaving no stain behind. With the last drop, Endoch lay back again, smiling, and fell into a deep calm sleep.

Dragon's blood.

Erde had always wondered how one acquired dragon's blood to do magic with, without hurting the dragon. Oh, if only Hal were here to see this. She stared at her pristine hands, still cupped and shaking, then back at Water.

Earth was washing the sea dragon's neck, gently closing the wound.

Chapter Nine

When he wakes up, N'Doch feels better than he has in a very long time. He knows right off that something amazing has happened.

He's got no idea how long he's been out. He's lying on one of the exercise mats—he can tell from the unexpected comfort beneath him and the slightly musty smell. He inventories his body parts carefully. There is no pain anywhere, not even in his left arm, which he recalls was slashed wide open last time he checked.

Shouldn't move, he decides, better not reveal his return to the living before he's cased the situation. He listens to the ship, the way he's learned to, for any noise he doesn't recognize that might be the mob banging about inside, searching. He hears nothing, only the gulls outside and the slap of the sea against the hull, removed by the distance of six decks between. A cautiously raised eyelid reveals even less. At first he's sure he's gone blind. Then he realizes it's night, and he's facing a wall. He has to turn somehow, at least his head. He rolls it back soundlessly and sees, in the broad, bright squares of moonlight falling from the windows, the two cybercritters crouched head to head.

Not cybercritters, he reminds himself.

Dragons.

He's still having trouble taking that one in. But he's decided it is the only explanation left, if you can call magic an explanation. He wonders what they're up to out there in the middle of the basketball court, so still and silent but looking so at ease with each other. Having some sort of dragon confab, he's pretty sure, whatever dragons confab about.

He twists his head a centimeter farther and, past them, he can make out a flat darkness in the opposite corner: the girl, asleep on another gym mat. N'Doch almost laughs out loud. She couldn't have gotten farther away from him unless she'd left the room. But then he thinks, *Well, that's good.* She's safer that way. She looks innocent, but she isn't.

He realizes that accepting the notion of dragons still doesn't give him a clue about what to do next. He's pretty sure the fishermen won't venture into this "haunted" boat at night when the dead might walk, so he's got till dawn to decide. If he got up real quick and quiet and just slid out through the locker room just to his right, he could slip past the mob alone and be away, free of all this crazy business in a flash. He wouldn't have to worry about how there could be dragons and girls from Mars. Or wherever. But then he'd never have the whole story. And think of the songs in it. It might just be his big chance in a whole other way. He's got to play it out for a little while, or he'll wonder about it for the rest of his life.

But he can't just lie there waiting for whatever's due to happen next. He's never been much for lying in bed, which is what's got him in this trouble in the first place— like, if he'd plopped down for the midday snooze with everyone else instead of going out prospecting for supper, he'd be the same old N'Doch he was this morning. But now—and this is what really concerns him, 'cause he knows it like he always knew when the first winter rains would come: inexplicably, in his gut—he knows that since the silver dragon swam into his life, his life's never gonna be the same.

N'Doch contemplates that one for a while. He's always thought he wanted his life to change. Now he finds himself hoping the longer he lies there, the longer he can keep this new life from starting. It was okay when he thought he was acting. Eventually everyone'd pack up the cameras and go home, and his life would be still his life, only better. But now that it seems that he really does have a dragon on his hands, it's another thing altogether. Because, hey, what do you do with a dragon? You don't exactly take it home with you like a stray dog. Feeding a dog is hard enough, or keeping it from being someone else's dinner . . . but a *dragon?*

On the other hand, who's to say his old life was anything worth holding on to?

This thought makes him roll over in involuntary revolt. He's surprised by the depths of rage he suddenly feels about his lot in life. He's not sure where it's come from. He thought he was getting along okay these days, apart from wanting so bad to be famous and not be hungry so much of the time.

But the rage is real, and so strong that it propels him to his feet before he can stop himself, and across the floor to glare belligerently at the communing dragons, without a clue why he feels he should challenge them with it. The abrupt motion reminds him of his arm. While he stares at the dragons, he sneaks his right hand around to check out the gash.

It's gone. He looks, steps sideways into a patch of moon, and looks again. His skin is smooth. No blood, no scab, not even a scratch.

N'Doch clenches his eyes shut, raking his memory. Did the short brother miss after all? Was he so scared, he just thought he'd been hit? No, no. He remembers the hot sear of pain, his panic about infection and the bright blood messing up his precious gym floor. He *remembers* this.

When N'Doch looks up again, the dragons are staring at him, taking no notice of his rage and confusion. The big one is a horned tower of shadow with a luminous glance. The little one is silver with moonlight and her eyes are dark. N'Doch hears a note start—long, soft, an oboe, he'd say, if he was hearing it outright instead of in his head. But it's impossibly sustained, which is why it holds him. He's waiting for the next one, for the pattern to develop, for the melody to show itself.

Instead he gets pictures, and this is where he decides he must be still asleep or maybe delirious. Either way, he's dreaming. No wonder his arm is healed and he feels so good. Well, it's been a nice dream so far, why not go with it? The pictures are like his own private video, playing in his head.

It starts with a landscape of cold, fog-shrouded mountains. N'Doch likes how the chill of it actually seems to penetrate the sodden heat of the gymnasium, cooling the sweat on his brow and the small of his back. Next he sees a big old castle, perched on a high rocky spur of these mountains, gray and forbidding, with little slit windows and lots of towers like in one of those King Arthur vids. N'Doch has no interest in white guys wearing tin suits—though his mama tunes them in whenever they're on—so he can't imagine why he'd be dreaming castles. But then this long-shot p.o.v. changes, zooming in fast on the tall front gate. He's expecting a moat and piranhas, crocodiles at least, but there's only dry rock, falling away sheer from the base of the walls and crossed by a built-up stone causeway. A stout iron grille stands between two round towers of stone. There's carving over the gate, animals of some sort fighting, but he doesn't spend time on the details because now he sees the girl, the Mars girl. She's there in his dream, on her belly in the icy mud, squeezing through a narrow slot between the iron gate and the ground. The oboe note slips behind a muffled wash of percussion, and a solo cello appears, low, grinding, urgent. When the girl struggles to her feet, N'Doch can see she is half-frozen, terrified . . . and running away.

Next thing he knows, he's in a big dark space, like a cave. He's never been in a real cave, but he's seen the pix. This dream is like some virtual reality tour where it's not his hand on the controls. The girl is there again, still terrified, and this time there's something sneaking up on her, something really huge and nasty. Only it turns out to be the big brown dragon, and N'Doch thinks he's looking kind of scared and lost himself. The cello accompaniment turns decidedly plaintive. In the way of dreams, N'Doch understands that the big guy has lost something, and the girl's supposed to help him find it. He can see how she takes to the critter right off, despite his being a dragon. He sees the awe and dedication in her eyes, as if a dragon is what she's been waiting for all her life. Like he felt about the blue critter's music, first time he heard it.

Then, in a moment of dizzying coincident vision, N'Doch sees himself at the same time he's seeing the girl. He *is* the girl, and yet he's himself, staring at the little silver dragon with the same awe and dedication. The vision is too much. The sweetness of it pierces him. It catches in his throat and he has to look away. He's not used to sweetness, or beauty that shortens his breath. He stands there, shaking in the moonlight, staring at the patterns of bright and dark cutting in such sharp angles across the floor.

He understands that he has not been dreaming.

Suddenly there's an entire story in his head: the girl's escape from her drunken father's boondocks castle, the perils of her flight into the countryside with the dragon, the hot pursuit by priests and armies, like something out of a costume drama. Is it true? Has he made it up? He doesn't know where it came from or what to do with it.

And still, there's more. The images keep unraveling. He sees the brown dragon waking to his magic gifts and understands he's being told it was magic that sealed up his wound as if it had never been. But it's too devastating to believe such things, or to believe anything with the kind of conviction N'Doch senses is lying in wait inside the silver dragon's dark stare. In his world, people die when they believe in things. People who might be related to you. They're gunned down on their doorsteps, or they vanish into prisons and are never heard from again. N'Doch has spent his nearly twenty years learning to stay fast and loose, with ties to nothing and no one. He'll do what he can to help his mama, but she pretty much takes care of herself. The only thing he believes in, really, is his music, and that he carries safely inside him. It's sustained him through the hard times like no person ever could or would.

Of course, a dragon is not exactly a person.

The images stop, leaving him bathed in a waiting silence. N'Doch looks up finally, meeting the silver dragon's gaze.

All right, he concedes. *This is really happening.*

Her music, their music, swells in his head, and the next thing he asks himself is *Why me?*

Chapter Ten

Erde dreamed that the dragon was nudging her shoulder. When she stirred, she saw him crouched beside Water across the room. The floor beneath her was still shuddering gently. Ah, she thought. One of his baby-quakes.

She allowed herself a proud smile. He was using his gifts without having to be endlessly petted and encouraged beforehand, which meant he was finally gaining some self-confidence. Despite the mob outside and the peril of their situation, she decided she could tease him a little.

—I am awake, O Great One, and at your service.

Earth turned from his huddle and stared at her. He blinked slowly, twice. In her head, Erde saw only an embarrassed blank. She giggled, and for a moment, the dragon let his big tongue loll from the corner of his mouth, as he used to in comic puzzlement. But Erde sensed it was self-parody this time, Earth recalling his former self for her amusement as well as his own, and sharing a bit of pride in his maturing. But not too much pride.

—I am not great yet, not until I have learned what Purpose I am to be great for.

Erde thought his logic a trifle circuitous and literal-minded, but she knew what he meant.

—Will you still talk to me, then, and wake me with earthquakes?

She had meant it fondly and in jest, but he blinked again, regarding her gravely.

—I will, for you will be great with me.

—I am already great. I am a baron's daughter.

It was lovely to be able to joust with him verbally. His grasp of language had grown dizzyingly. Erde mused that if human children learned so fast, there'd be no keeping up with them.

Then Water was there, flowing into Earth's consciousness, eddying busily in his mind, diverting both their thoughts like a guild master calling a meeting to order, reminding them both that they had a crisis to deal with by pelting them with images of a howling armed mob tearing an unseen something limb from limb. Earth returned his attention to her so obediently that Erde found herself wondering if the sea dragon was perhaps his older sister, since he deferred to her so readily. Or was it that, despite her having waked more recently into the world, she had more confidence than he did? She was graceful and she was beautiful, and Erde knew Earth thought himself dull, brown, and clumsy. But the sea dragon was also turning out to be a little bit bossy. Now that she'd gotten their attention, she was flooding them with images of Endoch.

Erde tried stopping up her mental ears.

—*Shouldn't you ask her about the Caller, who she thinks it is?*

—**Her first concern is the boy, to wake him to his duty,** Earth relayed. **And she needs your help. She wants you to explain things to him. She says you must use your words to help him understand.**

—*My words? I don't do words very well. I only just got them back.*

—**You must try. Please, you must. He knows how to hear the meaning in words.**

—*But, Dragon, he doesn't speak my language, and I don't speak his.*

She could feel his puzzlement, like an itch inside her brain. A hurried conference with the sea dragon eventually produced the understanding that the sounds Erde heard Earth speak in her head were an illusion of words he had learned to create in order to accommodate her human habits of communication. Earth was surprised (and interested) to learn that the sounds Erde made when she spoke did not convey meaning to the boy, and vice versa.

—My sister hears what he means. You must teach him to listen to her.
—How will she know what I mean?
—I will tell her.
—Who will tell him?

N'Doch senses the shifting of attention away from him. Then, suddenly, the girl gets up from her mat in the corner, out of what he'd thought was a dead sleep. She comes straight for him, padding on bare feet, her face purposeful. She takes his hand awkwardly—he can tell she's not too keen on the idea—and leads him to the silvery dragon's side, pressing him to sit there on the floor. The girl sits down opposite, cross-legged. He worries she's going to make him play one of those girly hand-clapping games he thinks are so dumb. Instead, she lays a feather touch on both his eyelids, closing them, holding them shut very gently. N'Doch gets the idea. He keeps them shut when she takes her hands away, figuring he can't see much in the dark anyway.

"Sehr gut," she says. Next she lightly pinches his ear-lobes and pulls them outward. *"Hören sie."*

"I got it," nods N'Doch. "You want me to listen."

She speaks slowly and carefully, as if she thinks that'll make him understand German all of a sudden, which he doesn't and won't, but he goes along with it anyway. He's glad she doesn't shout, like some people do when they don't speak your language. She keeps her voice quiet, intense.

After a while, he can tell she's repeating the same sets of words over and over. He's getting a little bored, so he shakes his head, but she reaches out again and presses rough palms flat against his temples to hold him still, then talks at him some more. When the music video starts in his head again, N'Doch realizes she's not doing this on her own. He's in for another dose of force-fed information and credibility testing.

But when he gives in and pays attention, just for the hell of it, he notices that the video and the music are repeating themselves just like the girl, at pretty much the same rhythm. An image of himself and the silver-blue dragon comes with a certain musical phrase and a certain string of the girl's now familiar but incomprehensible syllables. An image of her and the big dragon brings up different words, different music.

N'Doch has always liked the cartoon of the lightbulb clicking on in someone's head. It's exactly what happens to him now, as he puts two and two together: Brilliant light floods his brain. It's the light off the vast glowing landscape of understanding that opens up as comprehension dawns: the girl is not the only one talking to him.

"Wow," he breathes.

His eyes pop open from the shock. The girl is smiling at him in the moonlight. He hasn't seen her smile before. He's momentarily charmed by the warmth of it softening her delicate somber face. But she makes him shut his eyes again, and continues talking. N'Doch tries putting words to the images visiting his brain and as he does, he hears the girl's spoken German echoed by his own French, English or Wolof, like she's being overdubbed, with a slight delay. It's a messy, echoing effect but the delay keeps shrinking, until the overlap is a match, not perfect, but if he manages to shut out the sounds she's actually *speaking*, what he hears in his head are words he can mostly understand, though in no way fathom the source of.

"*Sei ist* your dragon," says the girl. "*Du ist* hers. You hear her when she sings?"

He nods. He's reluctant to admit it.

"You must listen to her in your head. Then you will understand everything."

That music has meaning is no mystery to N'Doch. He's just never thought of it as literal language before, and suddenly, the possibilities seem endless.

"Too cool," he tells the girl. He stops worrying about what's real and what isn't. Now all he wants to do is sit here in the dark with this blue dragon she calls *his,* and learn how to talk in music.

But first he has to ask: "What's her name?"

"Water," says the girl, as clear as daylight.

His eyes pop open again. He looks at her. "But that's my name."

She smiles knowingly. "Of course it is."

Erde recalled so well the thrill that had shot through her when the dragon informed her that its name was the same as her own. She had not for an instant considered it a mater of mere coincidence and neither, she could see, did Endoch. But instead of looking thrilled, he looked trapped and wary.

"Why do we have the same name?" he demanded, and a few echoes and relays and image-layers later, Erde understood his words, though not how to answer them. A proper metaphysical answer required someone like Sir Hal, a lifelong scholar of dragon lore. Erde thought she'd best limit herself to the practical aspects.

"You are her Guide. There are matters in the world of men that a dragon will not know about. Therefore we are here to help them."

Endoch eyed her skeptically. "Help them do what?"

He's so suspicious, Erde noted. Probably he'd been taught bad things about dragons, like the people at home. She would have been, too, but for her grandmother and her nursemaid, Alla. She felt both worldly-wise and totally inadequate to this task the dragons had laid on her. If Endoch had grown up without anyone to prepare him for his destiny, she would have to fill him in on the crucial details. It would not be easy. She was sure it was going to be a bit of a shock.

"We must help them carry out their Purpose," she replied.

He frowned. "What purpose?"

"Well, the Thing they're supposed to do."

"What are they supposed to do?"

Erde licked her lips, suddenly aware of a vast, not entirely physical thirst. Because, of course, this was the hardest part of the explanation. "They don't know yet."

"They don't . . ." Endoch rolled his eyes. "Are you for real? Is this thing some kind of gimmick after all?"

"Gi-mic?"

Neither dragon could translate these syllables. Earth couldn't recognize the image, Water couldn't put a sound to it.

"Yeah, you know, a stunt of some kind? If so, what's in it for me? Why should I go 'round risking my life for you guys? I don't even know you!"

Erde was momentarily stymied. Earth interposed his analysis.

—*He does not yet wish to accept his destiny.*

Erde sighed, sucked in a deep breath and prepared to

settle in for the long haul. "Is there a well in this stronghold?"

"A well? This is a boat, girl. There's no well in here. Don't you have boats where you come from?"

A boat? Erde glanced at Earth. Had one of them misunderstood? *No*, insisted the dragon. Scanning the darkness around her, Erde tried matching the bright-hulled craft on the beach with this cavernous square-walled room.

"Then it is a very big boat," she marveled. "Your liege lord must be very rich and powerful. Is he a king?"

Endoch furrowed his brow, then shook his head. "Man, I guess you're from Mars after all. But you know what? You're in luck." He stood up, stretching, checking his arm again as if to make sure it really was healed. "I got some okay water stashed away here."

He strode off into the darkness. Both dragons watched him go somewhat anxiously. But Erde saw in the young man's doubt and resistance something that dragons, who always knew what was real and what wasn't, never could.

—He won't leave. But he can't let himself value a thing he fears will be taken away from him.

—What thing?

—His dragon. If she is not real, he will lose her.

—Of course she is real.

—He doesn't know that yet. I think he has led a very hard life.

Endoch came back with a squarish, white jug hooked onto one thumb. He twisted its neck to remove some kind of stopper, then set it to his mouth and drank deeply. Then he placed it on the floor and slid it toward her. "Help yourself."

Erde grasped the milk-white handle. The jug wasn't as heavy as she'd expected. Its sides gave easily as she pressed her palms against them, but did not break. She lifted it gingerly and took a cautious sip, followed by a long grateful series of gulps when she found the water to be warm, brackish but potable. She set the jug down and tapped the side of it with her fingernail. It was hard like clayware, pliant like oiled leather and, now that she studied it in the moonlight, translucent like glass. But glass could never be so sturdy or so flexible.

"What ware is this?" she asked.

"What what?"

"What is it fashioned from?"

Endoch snorted. "You sure do talk funny. I hope you sound better in German—I mean, to someone really hearing German. 'What ware' . . . well, I guess it's Tupperware."

He seemed to think he'd said something clever. Erde looked blank.

"Plastic, girl. What'd you think it was?"

She fingered the parchment-thin edge of the jug's mouth. "We do not have this at Tor Alte."

"Come on! You're from Germany, right? They make all kinds of plastic in Germany. Mostly the expensive kinds."

Erde did not wish to argue with him and further expose her ignorance. Perhaps her father's provincial mountain domain was more backward than she'd realized. "I have some bread and some cheese," she offered instead.

Endoch's eyes lit up. "You do? Outstanding!"

She took that as approval and went to retrieve her pack from the cloth pallet she'd been resting on in the corner. The small loaf was nearly stale—it was hard to imagine, after all that had happened, that it had come from Deep Moor's bake ovens only a day ago. But the pungent scent of the cheese, as she unwrapped the stained oilskin, made her mouth water. She split both neatly in half and handed Endoch his portion.

He took it quickly and wolfed down half his chunk of bread before sniffing more carefully at the cheese. "You make this stuff yourself?"

Her mouth full, Erde shook her head.

"But you know it's safe?"

She returned him a puzzled frown. Did he think she would poison him?

"You know, all the hormones and drugs, and the stuff the animals pick up in their feed . . . ?"

She hadn't the faintest idea what he meant, and neither did the dragons.

Endoch looked at her, back at the cheese, and shrugged. "Well, what the hell. You're eating it. I'm too hungry not to." And he did, slowly this time and with great deliberation. "Not bad," he concluded. "Tasty."

He let his gaze swing about casually, then settle finally on her pack. Before she could stop him, he'd reached, grabbed it into his lap. "What else you got in here?"

The taste of the cheese is what gets his mind working. It's like nothing he's ever eaten before, a deep sharp rich taste that lingers on his tongue like a fading chord in his ears. He thinks, *This cheese came from somewhere else.* Fancy imported stuff. Just enough to get him *really* hungry. He wishes he had more.

It's habit that makes him snatch her pack. Normally he'd be on his feet and out of there, with the pack his spoils of the day. But he's not going to steal from this girl. He can't even seem to consider it. It would be like stealing from the dragons. But he'll take food if she's got it, and he does want some answers, better than the ones she's been giving him. Maybe the pack has some of them inside.

He dumps it out on the floor, waiting for the girl to squeal and pummel him, like the girl this morning—was it this morning?—with the tomatoes. But this one just watches. Her silence chastises but she makes no move to stop him. N'Doch unfolds the inner bundle and lays out the contents. The wrapping is a thick blanket of some kind. He shakes it out. It's a cloak, dense and gray. He holds it up to his nose. The smell is strong but indefinable, until he decides it's what he imagines sheep would smell like. Real wool, then. Amazing. There's more real wool in the bundle: a knitted cap that looks homemade. It also looks small. He does not try it on. He picks up the leather vest she'd been wearing, now neatly folded. He thinks that might actually fit him, but he lays it aside with the cloak and the cap. Next, a small metal rectangle with a lid. He opens it. Inside, a couple of flat rocks and a bunch of crackly wood shavings. N'Doch holds it up and cocks his head.

"To make fire," the girl says, as if it should be obvious.

"Why not just carry matches?" Even more obvious. "Or a lighter. Take up less room." He fingers the flinty rock restlessly. The taste of the cheese is still in his mouth, and the musky smell of the wool. Some things about this girl are beginning to fall into a pattern. He puts the tinderbox down. "Hey, look—are you from one of those nature-freak communes where they don't allow technology? Where they, like, you know, live in the past?"

He can see she's thinking it over, which probably means he's got that one wrong. Finally, she says, 'Why would one wish to live in the past?"

"Well, yeah, good question." In fact, he wonders if he can answer it. "A lotta people think it was better then."

This time she nods. "When I was little, I always wanted to live back when my ancestors fought with dragons."

She says it with such conviction, he has to grin and shake his head. "Mars," he murmurs. "For sure."

"Then I met Earth."

"That's his name, the big guy? Earth?"

She nods.

"Tell me yours again?"

"Earth."

He remembers he's hearing it in translation. "Right. Gotcha. Like you said, of course it is."

He picks up the final object in the pile, a dark box of carved wood. The girls' eyes flick down at it and away, too quickly, and he thinks, *Okay, the prize is in here, maybe her money or her credit cards.* He studies it at eye level. He'd say the style is old, but the box itself seems pretty new. It looks like a prop from the costume vids his mama watches, but he knows what vid props are like and this box is too well made. The carving is skilled and elaborate, leaves and flowers and the faces of men and women, and on the top—somehow, he is not surprised—is a small figure of a dragon.

N'Doch shakes the box gently. It rattles. "Whadja do, rob a museum?"

When she just keeps watching, he twists the little latch, raises the lid, and pokes at the contents, an old scrap of paper wrapped around something round and hard. He takes it out and the paper unravels neatly on his palm, offering up its contents as if to say, *viola!* N'Doch is taken aback, both by the uncanny presentation and by the beauty of the object exposed. It's a big red stone, set in silver. Even in the cool flat light of the moon, the stone looks like a drop of blood with a flame shining through it. On top it has, sure enough, another tiny dragon cut into the curving surface. N'Doch stares, astonished by the fineness of the detail. It's not a sparkling sort of jewel like he's used to. He can tell it's old. The weight and warmth of it are heavy on his palm. "Man," he breathes, with newfound respect. "This is some heist you pulled off, girl."

"It was my grandmother's brooch, the dragon brooch of the von Altes. She had it from her father and he from his."

"Yeah, right."

She blinks at him. "You do not believe me? Why should you think I would lie to you, Endoch?"

It's the first time she's actually used his name, or at least an attempt at it. She's probably trying to manipulate him. "N'Doch," he corrects irritably, "And I think so because anybody would and everyone does."

"No," she says back, straight as a bullet, as if she expects that'll clear it up, just like that.

"You think I'm a fool, right?"

"Of course not."

What's weird is that N'Doch does believe her, but he can't let her see that. "Like for instance, you'd lie to me if you stole it."

Now she looks perplexed. "But I wouldn't have to steal it. It's mine. It was in my family. Besides, it wouldn't let itself be stolen. It belongs to the Dragon Guide."

"The what?"

"The Dragon Guide. That's me. You. *Us*. Like I told you." She peers at him. "You really don't know, do you."

And that's what finally riles him, her sympathy so close to condescension. He tosses the big stone down and springs to his feet. "No! I don't! And you know what? I don't care! I've had enough of this shit!"

The girl looks down at her hands while his snarled words ricochet around the room. He feels rather than hears the dragons stirring behind him.

"I am sorry, Endoch. It is difficult at first," she concedes softly, "But you get used to it."

"I don't have to get used to anything!"

"But you do, Endoch. It's your destiny."

"There's no such thing! My life is what I make it! No

rich girl with family jewels tells me what to do! I do what I want, you hear?"

N'Doch's pacing brings him face-to-face with the sea dragon, shimmering blue and silver in the moonlight. Her calm, intent stare stops him cold, fills him with dread. Actually, he does believe in Destiny, but he's always said his destiny is to sing songs and be famous. This dragon business would put a serious crimp in his plans. The beast wants him, wants everything he has or is to be put to her service. He'll be a slave to her. He sees a lifetime of being bonded in some weird-ass mystical way he doesn't understand to a creature he doesn't want to believe in, pursuing some mysterious "purpose" that sounds like a wild goose chase with a crazy white girl he has the misfortune to feel protective about. If anything is proof that this dragon stuff is dangerous, that is. If he was his normal self, he'd have seduced this girl long ago. It scares him that he can't even bring himself to fantasize about taking off all those layers she's wearing and laying her down on one of the gym mats. The thought stirs nothing down there, only a chill nausea in his belly. He feels like a stranger to himself and it frightens him, more than hunger or the mob, even the sharks off the beach. More than anything. He can think of only one way out, and in his panic, he takes it.

He whirls, snatches up the red jewel from where he's tossed it down in front of her. He's at the door in a second, through it in two, and is racing down the corridors to freedom.

Chapter Eleven

The stone is hot in his clenched fist. N'Doch slams the hatch behind him, shifts the stone from hand to hand distractedly, then shoves it into the pocket of his shorts as he bolts soundlessly down the dark passageway. At the verge of the shark tank, he halts to catch his breath and survey the black, still stretch of water, his protection and his nemesis. A faint clank and rustle floats across from the far side. N'Doch freezes, cursing inwardly. In his desperate need to be free of the dragons, he's forgotten the mob of fishermen. He listens, squinting into the dark. He hears a low murmur, spots a dim, quick flickering. Okay, they've posted a watch, and the watcher is lighting up a joint.

Actually, N'Doch is glad for an excuse not to brave the shark tank twice in one day. At least he thinks it's one day. He hasn't a clue how long the fever had him down and out. How long would this mob bother to lie in wait for him, once they've had their fun? He's not that big a deal. Maybe the watcher is one of Malimba's brothers. N'Doch sucks his teeth and grins. Let 'em wait. The shark tank may be the quickest way out of this rust bucket, but it's not the only one.

He backs up along the passage, feeling behind him for the stack of metal rungs he knows are there, climbing the right-hand wall. The lowest two or three are slimy with the nameless ooze that coats most of the tanker's lower surfaces. It feels toxic and nasty, but it's never harmed him so far. N'Doch grabs hold and hauls himself upward, through the torso-sized opening, past the hatch cover blown against the side of a narrow shaft peppered with shrapnel scars. He feels the hot draft moving through the holes, but no moonlight penetrates to the shredded upper decks. It gets hotter as he climbs.

The shaft empties into the remains of Engineering and Navigation, just below the Bridge. Plenty of moonlight here. N'Doch shoves aside a pile of concealing rubble and lifts himself onto the jury-rigged boardwalk of charred plastic paneling that threads a crooked path across the intermittent floor. He has spent envious hours imagining the wealth of equipment and high-tech wonders once housed within this deck. Now it's an empty, cubicled wilderness of hanging cables and shattered glass, the usual wake of the scavengers. The Toe Bone Gang claimed this prize and refused to share it, just to make a point, even though there was plenty to go around. N'Doch recalls watching hungrily from the beach with the lesser gangs, while the Boners carried armload after armload to their waiting trucks.

He pads past a mad sculpture of twisted metal, all that's left of the forward companionway to the deck below. He tosses more rubble aside and uncovers the second emergency access shaft. All this time, he refuses to think about what's in his pocket or what he's left behind. He closes the ears of his mind to the siren music playing in his head. It's the blue dragon calling him, he knows that now, and he's told himself he doesn't care. She's calling him back and promising him nothing. Like he said, what's in it for him?

As best he can, he ignores the faint voice inside him that's offering an outrageous suggestion: "How 'bout a reason to live?" Up till now, N'Doch has thought life was its own reason, which is why he's a good survivor. And it would be inconvenient to admit he's been thinking that just surviving is getting real old. So he hears, but tells the voice to shut the hell up.

He lowers himself into the second shaft, pulling the debris back to hide the opening as he descends. He's careful on the ladder where it starts to get slippery. The bottom of this shaft ends in a watery pit that's too far up the beach to get washed clean by the tide. The stench makes him retch and hold his breath. The air itself could be contagious. N'Doch figures if the dead do walk the tanker, it's out of this dank and fetid shaft bottom that they'd rise. He leaves it at the galley level, where a small breach in the outer hull offers escape through the tanker's far side. But first he decides he'd better scope out the beach.

From a broken-out porthole a few decks above the big gap on the port side, he can survey the sand below. He peers out carefully. To his disgust, the mob is still there. In fact there seem to be even more of them. They've built a bonfire out of palm fronds and turned his pursuit into a party. A few of the men are roasting fish over the blaze. One idiot's using his precious gas ration to power a vid set with a portable generator so no one'll miss the soccer match. Jugs of home brew are being surreptitiously passed. Even out there, far from the imam's watchful gaze, the men are cautious. N'Doch's mouth waters. The thing about being a fisherman is you can just go out and catch something more or less edible, as long as you avoid the bottom feeders. He'd have learned the trade himself if they'd let him, but he didn't have the family connections. These days, you can't even surf cast on a Saturday without them getting after you, protecting their territory. N'Doch doesn't blame them, really. There's so few fish left to catch. *I'd protect mine, too*, he muses, *if I had any*.

Now there are voices raised around the fire, over the yells and catcalls from the soccer game. He hears his name being tossed about, so he settles in to listen. It seems the fishermen are annoyed. They haven't yet laid eyes on these sea monsters supposedly in the act of gobbling up their boats. Where's all the excitement they were promised? Some are calling the brothers liars. Others had clearly reached N'Doch's first conclusion, that the whole thing was a vid shoot, so they'd rushed off to the beach to take part and are sullen about missing their chance to be on camera.

The brothers—all five of them now (one has his foot heavily bandaged and keeps checking it worriedly)—are busy tapdancing, tossing out this tale and that excuse to keep the mob from turning on them. They have to shout to be heard over the game, and must have been doing this for a while, 'cause they're all going hoarse. N'Doch would enjoy this drunken spectacle, were it not that their most successful tactic seems to be exaggerating the heinousness of his own crime and hyping him into a threat big enough to throw the mob's rage back in his direction.

So now, in the short brother's mouth, N'Doch the to-mato thief becomes N'Doch the vandalizer, the armed looter and hostage-taker, N'Doch the violator of inno-cent young women.

Violator? N'Doch swells up with outrage. He grips the ragged sides of the porthole and almost yells out in his own defense. He'd *never* take a woman against her will! Most of the pleasure is wooing them and winning them over.

But the fishermen are buying it, hook, line, and sinker. They are shaking their fists and roaring because, N'Doch thinks, it's probably what they'd like to do to at least one woman of their acquaintance, and they're pissed that he got there first. He tells himself he'll get even, in the way he always has: when this nonsense is over, there'll be a whole new repertoire of nasty songs about drunken fishermen going around town.

When it's *over*. . . .

He realizes he's thinking about the blue dragon, holed up forward in the gym. He has been all along, with a part of his brain that won't set her aside. It keeps asking, will she be safe in the ship? Will this stupid mob get bored and go home, or will they keep at their drinking and roaring until they've worked up enough courage of numbers to invade his sanctuary? What will the dragons do then? Eat them?

For a moment, he thinks how much he'd like to be there to see that. Then he reminds himself forcibly that he doesn't care what happens to the blue dragon, or the brown one with the girl. But he doesn't need to check his pocket for the jewel he's stolen. It lies warm and heavy against his thigh, weighing inexplicably more than a thing its size reasonably should. Small as it is, for a jewel, it's big enough. Finding a fence for it will be tricky. N'Doch has never dealt with the Big Guys before.

Meanwhile, it's time to be out of range of the mob before its outrage whips up from passive to active. N'Doch crosses back to starboard and skins through the thin gap between two in-bent metal plates. Between the inner hull and the outer, he has stashed a tarred length of rope for just such an emergency, looped around a cross-tie. He drops the loose ends through the outer hole and lowers himself hand over hand to the sand. He jerks the rope free, coils it quickly and tosses it deftly up into the hole. He's racing away before he's sure if it's landed correctly.

He speeds along the beach without really knowing where he's heading. His brain is full, too full to think. He puts himself on autopilot, his eyes squinting to scan for debris. The moon has set, and a predawn glow is creeping across the sky. N'Doch feels vulnerable, too visible, dark against the lightening sand. The damp night air is thick with fish stink. He wonders about it until he feels the first few dead ones under his feet. Another kill, washed in with the tide. Getting to be commonplace. He shifts his trajectory, avoiding the water's edge, and slows. He skirts two small inhabited wrecks, people he knows. He sees the elder son of one family pacing the deck with a shotgun, probably anxious about all the shouting and firelight down the beach. N'Doch stays out of sight and cuts inland at the next path through the palm brake.

He spots the thicket of old vid antennas and satellite dishes sprouting from the *bidonville*, and slows when he reaches the first tents and lean-tos. A runner always looks guilty, he reasons, even if running for help. People in the camp are just stirring, the women mostly, starting their morning duties in the dull, slow way of the unwillingly awakened. Maybe the mob back at the tanker will go straight to their boats when dawn comes. Wait till they see the beach already littered with their day's catch. But they'll go out anyway, and maybe this morning, their wives will get to eat some of the breakfast they cook.

Several campfires are already burning. The starchy hot scent of boiling rice reminds N'Doch that he's now as hungry as he's ever been. The girl's little morsels of bread and cheese were just a tease. He decides he'd better head home. Whatever little food his mama might have, she's sure to give him some.

It's full dawn when he reaches her house, a cinderblock box lined up with a thousand others along a dusty road on the far side of town. The houses are small and dark, having been thrown up several governments ago during a rare moment of social oratory convincing enough to lure foreign aid. The mortar between the cinder blocks is already crumbling and the corrugated plastic roofing is brittle and cracking from the heavy, steady dose of UV in the sunlight. But it's a house and his mama is lucky to have it. She knows this. She's so aware of it that she hardly ever leaves it for fear some squatter will move in and take possession while she's out at the market. It's the only thing she has, the house and her vid set, which is as old as she is but like herself, still functional.

She's up and talking to it when N'Doch steps in the open doorway, a tall woman in a once-bright print moving slowly around her one small room, scraping up last night's cold rice from the bottom of the pot. Surreal color flickers along the cement-gray walls. His mama is shaking her head.

"I told you yesterday if you let him do that to you, you'd sure be sorry," she's scolding. On the pinched old screen, a lovely woman is weeping while an angry man throws crockery around a perfectly appointed room. It looks like no room N'Doch has ever seen.

"Ma," he says. He's sorry now that he has nothing to bring her. But wait. He has. The stone in his pocket. *She* could fence it, maybe. Say she found it somewhere in the rubble.

His mother clucks her tongue. "Anybody could have told you that, girl."

N'Doch tries again. "Ma." He does not move from the doorway.

Her eyes are fixed on the vid, reflecting the dancing image and brimming with knowledge and empathy. She turns her long back to N'Doch as she shakes the used tea leaves loose in her cup and pours in boiling water. "Well, don't just stand there like a lump, boy. Get on in and sit down."

N'Doch thinks it's weird that his mama never calls anyone by their name. A lot of the time he calls her by *her* name, which is Fâtime, mostly to get her attention. He slouches in and drops down at the scarred metal table under the window next to the door. The window's too high and narrow to see out of, but it's the only one and it does let in some light and air, to add to the breeze provided by the man-sized hole his father pickaxed through the back wall just before he took off. To cover it, N'Doch salvaged an old Venetian blind as soon as he was old enough to carry something that big. He gazes around the room, taking stock. The pocked cement floor is gritty under his feet.

"You sold the couch?"

She nods, spooning the cold rice into a plastic tub. Her eyes on the vid, she sets the tub in front of him. "Aye-esha's third is too old to be sleeping with her now. She took it. I told her she'd have to come get it herself, 'cause I wasn't gonna be dragging it all the way 'cross the street, so she did."

N'Doch pouts irritably, knowing Fâtime won't turn away from the screen long enough to notice. Now the table and the two folding chairs beside it, plus the TV on its plastic crate, are the only furniture in the house besides the loom in the corner and the broken-down cot behind the sheet on a rope that offers Fâtime a measure of privacy. The sofa was hers, after all, and it's true he hasn't been home in a while, but where's she think he's going to sleep?

"She pay for it?" he demands through a sticky mouthful. He sees the finished weave on the loom is still short, a long way until her next sale. His mama's generosity worries him sometimes.

"'A sack of relief rice, near full. Ten cans of beans, two melons, and the promise of a dozen of those big yams she's growing up right."

He sits up, impressed. "Got any melon left?" He can't think of anything that would taste better right now.

Fâtime rolls her eyes back at him briefly. "Finished the first two weeks ago. She'll bring the second when her next crop comes in."

Two weeks?' It's been longer than he realized since he's visited. He should come by more often, he knows he should. He's all she has left, 'cept that crazy old man out in the bush, his grandfather. But he hears no reproach in her voice. His mama, he knows, gave up a long time ago expecting much out of the men in her life. They're always dying or leaving.

He reaches for another fistful of rice and discovers he's cleaned the bowl out already. Impossible! He's just started eating! He tips it toward him. Sure enough, he hasn't left her so much as a grain. He sets the bowl down and flattens his palms on the table. But maybe he won't show her the jewel just yet. In fact, he can't really bring himself to take it out of his pocket, to reveal such a lovely thing in the drear light of this house.

"Ma, I didn't bring you anything this time. I was . . ." How can he begin to explain? ". . . kinda in a rush."

Fâtime shrugs, points at the screen. The lovely woman has changed one sparkling gown for another and redone her makeup. "Not a brain in her head, this one with the nails. Now that other one, with the head of hair, look, here she comes now, see her? She's a smart one. She don't let anybody by her."

N'Doch looks. The woman in the French-style gowns has been replaced by another slim beauty wearing bright festival robes and a high, elaborate hairdo, corn-rowed and braided and strung with glittering glass beads. Her skin is dark silk, flawless. She is breathtaking. Normally N'Doch would use this occasion to drift off into a fantasy about himself and this woman in a soft bed somewhere. Perversely, he finds himself staring at her hundreds of beads and tiny braids, thinking that both he and his mama could eat for a year on what that hairdo cost. Probably the jewel he's stolen wouldn't bring as much. A single hairdo!

This is an odd thought for him, not that he hasn't counted such things out before, but odd that he should feel *angry* about it, rather than merely envious. The equation is somehow shifting in his mind. He used to be glad that at least his mama had the vid and its constant diet of fantasy to distract her from being so hungry most of the time. Now there's this vague, undeveloped notion that if the hairdo wasn't eating up so much of the world's money, there'd be more of it around to feed his mother and himself. The idea sighs into his head like a night breeze and out again as he loses his grasp on it, unable to apply it in any pragmatic way to his own life.

But it leaves him looking at his mother from a new angle, actually *looking* at her, for the first time. She's his mama, but she's also a stranger, a rangy, sloppy woman who happens to resemble him, as if someone else's skin had been wrapped around his skeleton. A woman afraid to leave her house. A woman starting to put on weight, who weaves and watches the vid and expects no more out of life. A woman who's finished.

It's the resemblance that catches in N'Doch's throat. Suddenly he sees himself, a fat old man glued to the tube. It's the starch that puts the pounds on and stretches out the skin, swelling it up, then leaving it slack in the endless cycle of gain and loss. When the food comes, you eat as much as you can, storing up for the times when there is none. Rice, bread, yam. The relief people never send anything fresh like a vegetable, and who knows what brew of chemicals are laced into his mama's favorite, their instant mashed potatoes? Only N'Doch's music and the chance of fame stand between him and this horrifying vision, this endless . . . sameness. Only his music, and now the . . .

His hand has slipped unnoticed into his pocket. The red jewel is a hard, hot lump on his palm. When he closes his fist around it, the heat is nearly unbearable. Yet it draws him, like the flame tongues of a bonfire beckoning in the darkness, and he understands he'll never sell it. Could never. Not this, the dragon stone. He'll keep it, then. It'll be his secret talisman. He holds it tightly, suffering the biting heat as best he can, and hears . . .

MUSIC.

N'Doch's head whips around. Where? But it's not the television and it's not his mother singing to him, though that's what it sounds like, her low tuneless lullaby that soothed him when he was too hungry to sleep. He knows who it is, of course. It's the one he's just tried to leave behind, the other Big Chance he doesn't want to think about, the one who's gonna ask so much in return for what she'll give. It frightens him that she can touch him even here.

He stares at his mother while she stares at the vid. She's totally absorbed. How can she not hear this music, so like her own? She's lost to it, and probably lost to her own as well. N'Doch doubts she could sing to him now the way she used to. And suddenly, he can't sit like this any longer, not speaking, with her locked up in her vid world. If he'd talked to her more in his life, maybe she'd be talking back. But he hasn't, and she isn't. He has to leave, just like he always does. But this time, he isn't off to meet up with his boys or chase after some girl or pursue any one of the many scams he's usually juggling.

This time, he doesn't know where he's going. In town, the brothers will be after him. On the beach, there's the mob. They won't leave him alone as long as his supposed villainy offers them entertainment at his expense. So he doesn't know where he's headed and he's not sure when he'll be back. Abruptly, he's tired of the runaround. It doesn't seem as glamorous as it did when he was a kid, first getting into gangs. But he should tell Fâtime something if he's going to be away for a while, make up a story at least, so she doesn't worry. He opens his mouth with the beginnings of an excuse.

"Ma . . ." He stops, stumped.

She turns to him. She looks at him directly, for the first time since he came in, yet her gaze is fuzzed, like she's watching something just a fraction past him, like where the back of his head might be if she could see right through him.

She says, "If you're in trouble again, go visit Grandpa Djawara."

Then she turns back to the vid, and it's like she'd never said a thing. It's like smooth water closing over a sunken boat.

N'Doch is chilled. It's been years since she's tried to pawn him off on his grandfather. It's also the third time in twenty-four hours that the old man's come to mind. Weird. And three is a mystical number. N'Doch reminds himself he doesn't believe in omens or signs or any of that superstitious stuff. On the other hand, he didn't believe in dragons either, until yesterday. And Papa Djawara's *would* be a good place to lay low for a while.

It would also be a good place to hide a dragon.

The thought is in his mind before he can stop it. Once there, it digs in and will not be evicted, even though he opens his fist to let the jewel go, then snatches his hand out of his pocket. The stone is like hot lava against his thigh. N'Doch stares at his palm, amazed that it is not scorched and bubbling.

Her eyes on the screen, tracking the woman with the exquisite hair as she weeps over a dying child, Fâtime says, "Go to Papa Djawara."

"Ma. How would I get there?"

"Walk, if you must."

"Walk? You're kidding, right?"

"Just go. He will explain everything."

And then, the vid claims her attention entirely. Try as he might, N'Doch can get no more out of her.

Chapter Twelve

Erde stirred on her mat, sensing a change in the hot stillness of the room. She sat up in bright sunlight, even though she'd shoved her pallet into a corner. The low early rays had searched out her spot exactly, as if trying to wake her. She'd been dreaming of darkness and cold, dreaming of home and horses and men marching in snow and rain. It had been very real, her dream. As real as life. The surprise of sun was disorienting.

She glanced about groggily. What had changed? She listened for the howls and clanking of the mob outside, and heard nothing but the cries of the big white birds that wheeled in the air outside the high windows.

She peered into the far corners of the room. Empty. Then the dragons had not yet returned from their fishing expedition. Clever Water had gone first, down and out through the great hole in the middle of what Erde now accepted to be a ship but could not yet picture in its entirety. Earth had transported after her, once she'd searched out an empty stretch of beach and imaged it back to him. Both dragons had been starving. Erde wished Water good hunting, wondering if she'd been aware from the first that she'd have to deliver Earth's share of the catch directly to his landlocked feet. He wouldn't venture so much as the tip of a claw into such deep and turbulent water.

Erde sighed and stretched. After the confusion of the night and the anguish of the boy fleeing, stealing the dragon brooch, Water had sung to her and she'd slept well, except for the dreaming. She wondered if Water's singing her into so deep a sleep had somehow prompted her dream. It didn't matter. She felt infinitely more clearheaded. But her stomach was rumbling. She drank a little water from the strange jug that the boy had left behind. Keeping Hal's training in mind, she rationed it carefully. Who knew when she'd find drinkable water again, in this strange country of so much water but all of it seemingly salt.

She wondered if it was only the sun that had waked her. And the heat, though she had by now shed every layer of clothing that modesty allowed. Her woolen men's leggings and leather tunic, plus her own linen stockings, lay neatly folded inside her pack. She'd taken off her oversized linen shirt but kept it beside her while she slept. From what she'd seen so far, clothing was not very important in this country. Still, Erde doubted she could bring herself to parade around in only her shift. At least it was adequate for sleeping in.

She scanned the room again, peering into the sun-hazed shadows in the corners and under the balcony that ran along the far side. She saw nothing she hadn't seen in her careful search before she'd gone to bed.

Then someone spoke.

She recognized the voice, but not the oddly strangled tone of it. Without the dragons, she understood not a word. She reached to touch her dagger, belted neatly against the small of her back, but felt no real fear. The dragons had said he would be back and that she must try to be patient with him, and understanding. Mostly Earth had said this. Water understood it and agreed, but found the necessary patience somewhat harder to achieve.

She turned toward the voice. "Endoch! You're back!"

"N'Doch," he grumped. "N'Doch. Can't you get it right?"

Now his tone was very clear. Erde tried again. "Nnnndochh."

He snorted from the shadows. "A little better."

Annoyed, she sat up straight on her mat and pointed to herself. "Erde."

"Yeah, I know."

She set her jaw, squinting hard through the bright shafts into the darkness beyond. "Erde."

"Okay, okay. Jeez. Airda."

She shook her head. "Erde. Erde."

The shadows fell silent. Then the boy stepped out into the sunlight, one fist raised stiffly in front of him. Erde read it not as a threat but as a warding gesture. Though he was scowling ferociously, he seemed reluctant to come any nearer. He glared at her for a long frozen moment, then tossed the thing in his fist at her. The dragon brooch fell into her lap. "Erde," he growled.

She took up the brooch gratefully and gave him her most brilliant smile. "N'Doch. Thank you."

N'Doch grunted and looked away, around the room, then back again, turning his palms up in a demanding shrug.

Erde knew who he'd come back to see. "They're out hunting."

When he frowned at her, not understanding, she made exaggerated eating gestures, which seemed to satisfy him partly. Still, he did seem to need to pace, back and forth, back and forth. She wanted to tell him he needn't feel anxious, or ashamed for having bolted. The dragons understood, perhaps better than he did. But she couldn't, until the dragons returned to translate, so she sat quietly on her mat and smiled at him encouragingly.

He paced past her and stopped. "They're still out there, you know. Sleeping off all of that rotgut. But they'll be up with the heat, and mad as piss. You can't stay here."

He glared at her as if he expected a reply. All Erde could offer was an apologetic shrug. N'Doch scowled and withdrew into the shadows to pace, refusing to even look at her.

She was relieved finally to feel the familiar quickening in her head, the sense of a void being filled, that announced the dragons' return, both of them together this time, with Earth using his gift to bring his sister along with him. Erde jumped up to meet him, wondering at the smug satisfaction he was projecting, until he opened his jaw and spilled a slippery, silvery mass of fish onto the floor.

Raw fish, some still living. Erde thanked him, effusively enough (she hoped) to conceal her dismay. She wished not for the first time that Earth and his sister were more conventional dragons. Then she'd be able to roast this pile of fish in the flames of their fiery breath.

Fire. She remembered the line of thought that Water's arrival had sparked. The dragons' names, Earth and Water, had suggested a familiar sequence which followed with Fire and Air. The four Elements. Was it significant or just a coincidental word association?

But once again, the matter of N'Doch was more pressing than her own mind ramblings, and the thought slipped away as her attention was called for. Both Earth and Water had settled down facing the darkened end of the room where the young man stood, stilled with renewed awe at the dragons' sudden reappearance.

They'd done it again, damn it. He'd been all collected and ready to face the shit they'd no doubt deal him for snatching the jewel and bolting, ready to take it quietly, ready even to try to explain, ready for anything but being knocked off his feet again by his own wonder.

Dragons. Real dragons, out of thin air. What else might the world hold in store, if dragons are possible?

N'Doch thinks it'd be easier if they were pissed at him. It's what he's expected, but what he gets instead is a welcome.

The feeling inside him is not a comfortable one. His head aches with unsung music. His heart feels too big for his chest. Again, he badly wants to run away, but this time he knows that he can't run fast enough or far enough to escape this silver-blue inevitability, what the girl calls his *destiny*.

It's not just that he has nothing better to do. It's that he can't seem to do anything else. He's tried it and failed. Returning to the tanker was like being hauled back by an invisible leash. All he can do is resent it furiously, which he does, but that too is getting old. He's getting tired of himself.

Destiny. An impossible, old-fashioned notion, like magic. In N'Doch's world, chaos is the rule, the randomness of life and events. But in N'Doch's world, the impossible has recently become possible, and the only thing he can see to do now is go with it. Think of it as just another random event. Follow the melody out. See where it leads.

Once again that first step is the hardest, but then he's easily across the floor and facing the blue dragon directly, flattening his palm on her velvet brow, letting her music flow into him like water.

Water.

A dragon.

His dragon.

PART TWO

The Journey into Peril

Chapter Thirteen

S he's almost caught him this time.

N'Doch considers himself pretty much in touch with himself. He's an artist, after all, and a good song must come from the heart. But after a few moments of feeling turned inside out and displayed raw, he lets his hand slide from the blue dragon's brow. It's one thing to pour all your emotion into a song—where it's neatly packaged, safely contained by the melody. But even his sloppiest, mushiest, written-after-a-bottle-of-cheap-wine ballads never made him feel as flayed, as vulnerable, as weak-kneed in the grip of it as he feels staring into the dragon's eyes. Is this how it's always gonna be with her? He averts his eyes, backs away. He's not sure he likes it very much.

The fish are an easier thing to deal with. Remembering the dead fish on the beach, N'Doch hunkers down and paws through them expertly, to sort out the ones with parasites or diseases. To his astonishment, he finds none. This has never happened. The usual ratio is one more-or-less healthy fish to three sick ones. The fishermen toss fifty percent of their catch back to the sharks and you have to check out the ones they do sell pretty carefully. But this, N'Doch can't believe: right in front of him, dripping their salt damp and scales onto his precious polished floor, are at least two dozen fat and perfect fish.

He says, "We got an hour, maybe two, before those guys outside come to their senses. Let's eat!" He yanks his switchblade out of his gym shorts and sets to work gutting and cleaning.

After the first three, it occurs to him what a mess of fish guts he's going to have all over the place. He wipes his hands on his thighs and pads off to his stash in the gym's wood-paneled locker room. He's had many occasions already to be grateful that the Toe Bone Gang didn't bother with mundane objects like kitchenware and janitorial supplies when they stripped the ship. Returning with a four-liter bucket and a plastic tarp, he finds the girl crouched over the pile of fish with her big knife in her hand. It's the first time N'Doch has seen it out of its sheath, and he studies it with interest. It's longer and heavier than he's expected. In fact, he's thought it might be just a prop, but the bright gleam along each edge tells him this blade means business. A *man's* weapon, despite its prissy antique facade. Puts his own beloved blade to shame. He wonders if the girl knows how to use it.

He lays out the tarp, scoops the fish guts into the bucket and sets it between him and the girl. He lines up the three cleaned fish in a neat row on the blue plastic, then squats and reaches for the next one, watching the girl while pretending not to. With care and some obvious experience, she scales the fish, then slits it open and scrapes the guts into the bucket. N'Doch nods in grudging approval and picks up his pace. He'd hate to be outdone by a mere girl. Soon the tarp is covered with fresh fish fillets and N'Doch's stomach is rumbling. The dragons have retired to the far corner of the gym. He gives them a covert look as he returns to the locker room for the two-burner stove he's cobbled together from parts of the ship's galley. He's been careful to use it only when he has to, so for now it still runs on gas. He loves the little castered frame he rigged for the meter-and-a-half-tall propane tank, and his favorite find was a magnetized matchbox that stores right on the cylinder.

Well, that's not true, he decides, blowing grit out of his one dented frying pan. *My favorite is really the flipper.*

He hefts the only slightly bent aluminum spatula. It's bright and smooth, with the satisfying weight and balance of expensive cutlery. The only reason it's in his hands is that it had fallen down behind a row of cabinets. He shows it off to the girl, but she offers only a blank expectant look, so he shrugs and gets down to work. He extracts a single kitchen match from the rusted box. When he lights it, the girl gasps and recoils. He sees her doing that crisscrossy hand thing that Catholics do when they're upset. *From Mars,* he thinks again. He puts the match to the burner and turns on the gas. Thin blue flame erupts and settles soothingly as he adjusts the flow. He's proud of this stove, proud that he could make it work without blowing up himself and everything else. He turns to the girl to soak in her admiration and finds her staring at the lighted burner like she's never seen one before in her life. Now he's sure he's right about the no-tech commune. He turns the burner up and down a few times to watch her eyes widen, then scolds himself for wasting gas. He bends away to load his pan with fish and, out of the corner of his eye, he sees the girl stretch her fingers toward the flame. He grabs her wrist just in time.

"Are you nuts? You'll burn yourself!"

She stares at him, then sit back on her haunches with a puzzled, considering scowl. She twists her head slightly, as if listening, toward the dragons in the corner. "Hot," she says distinctly, in French.

N'Doch blinks. "Well, yeah. Hot." Then he says, "You gotta understand, the worst thing is not having the choice."

He's got to give her one thing, she's not stupid. She makes the leap. "Yes, N'Doch, I do understand. But you see, that's exactly what I like about it."

"Hunh," he says. "Well, different strokes . . ."

He turns away and settles the pan on the burner.

Erde watched the dark-skinned youth lay two large fillets in the flat metal dish. She knew now that she had misjudged him. Why had the dragons not mentioned, when she'd questioned his qualifications as a Dragon Guide, that this Endoch was a magician?

N'Doch, she corrected, rehearsing his name silently. She rolled the foreign sounds along her tongue and thought of the mage she'd promised to find for Earth those two long months ago, the one who'd help him remember his Quest. Maybe she'd found him after all. She knew N'Doch was a mage because he'd just exhibited a mage's most basic skill: he'd conjured fire in his bare hands, and had not been burned by it. Plus the flame burned blue, the color of magic. Now he was preparing his pots and potions. Erde settled down to observe what further alchemy this unlikely mage might produce. Soon the crispy scent of frying fish informed her that this particularly alchemy was going to be culinary, that N'Doch was *cooking* in that odd metal dish with the handle. Erde was not disappointed. She was hungry enough right then to prefer food to any kind of magic.

N'Doch climbs the tall fire ladder to the high windows, laying the uneaten fish out on the wide sills to dry in the sun. When he climbs down again, the girl and the dragons are gathered in the center of the gym, facing him with identical expectant stares. He's amazed that a dragon can make the same expression as a human, that look the girl has that says, "Well, now that we've all eaten, it's time for you to get on with solving the rest of our problems."

Or that's the way N'Doch reads it, and rebellion rises within him, swift and hot as lava, mostly for being caught up in inescapable forces that he doesn't understand—except for knowing there's something he's supposed to do. But accepting the reality of this so-called destiny doesn't mean he has to like it. He'll go along, for a while at least, but it's gotta be on *his* terms.

From the bottom of the ladder, he glares back at the dragon huddle, then slouches over and hunkers down. He is careful not to look directly at the dragon Water. He can feel her anyway, hear her inquisitive background music invading his head, but if he doesn't meet her glance, at least he can avoid losing himself once more in her scary blue stare. He doesn't worry about what language he's speaking. He knows now that somehow his meaning will get through to all parties. He says, "I think . . ." then stops himself. He traces obscure patterns on the gleaming floor and starts again. "My mother says hide out at my grandfather's. I think maybe we all could."

Silence settles into the room along with the pale dust motes falling through the sunlight from the clerestory, and N'Doch hears sounds he shouldn't be hearing yet.

"Someone's in the corridor!" he hisses.

The dragons understand right off, and the girl gets it a second later. N'Doch leaps up and sprints for the door to make sure the lock is still in place. He puts his ear to the surface and listens for a moment, then pads deliberately back to the huddle.

"We are in deep shit," he says quietly. "There's at least ten, maybe fifteen guys on the other side of that door. It'll take 'em a while to get through, unless they send for a cutting torch, but we can't go anywhere either. Sooner or later, they'll get smart and start climbing in the windows. So we're trapped, unless . . ." He pauses, then guesses wildly, glancing up at the dragon Earth. "Unless you can get us out of here."

More silence, and the banging and clanking out in the corridor gets a lot more aggressive. Then the girl says, *"Ja. Sei kann."*

N'Doch shakes his head, but this is no time to argue the terms of the agreement. He shuts his eyes with a grimace and wills himself to allow the dragon music into his head.

"He can," the girl repeats, "but he needs to be able to see where he's going."

"What?"

"Just listen! He will explain."

N'Doch is amazed how simple and instantaneous comprehension can be when you have the right interpreter.

Chapter Fourteen

Even so, when they actually make the move, N'Doch is not really prepared.

They have to move quickly, so they agree that Water should image an interim destination. N'Doch's first experience traveling with Earth should not be from the driver's seat. He pouts, thinking they don't trust him, but he's glad enough when the time comes. Any lingering doubts he's allowed himself about the reality of dragon magic are blown to bits when he shakes the dizzying tingle out of his limbs and looks around.

He's back on the beach. But not the port beach, where the broken supertanker lay, where he'd been a split fraction of a moment ago. This is a different beach, and N'Doch knows it well, recognizes its diamond-bright sand and the smooth blue water of its protected inlet even though he's never seen it like this, in broad daylight. He doesn't take the time to wonder how he's ended up there. That could be a fatal luxury. Instinctively, he ducks, then glancing up and seeing the girl just standing there, snatches her down beside him.

"Why'd he bring us *here?*"

They're out of sync again. The girl frowns. N'Doch grits his teeth, looks to Water and repeats himself.

The girl is puzzled. "She showed him and he went there."

"Then she's gotta show him somewhere else! Fast!" He's whispering, though he knows it's pointless. The spy ears are sensitive enough to hear an ant walking. "Back to the boat! Anywhere! Just get us outta here!" Better a mob of irate drunken fishermen than Baraga's bionic dogs and the men they'll bring with them. The girl wouldn't stand a chance. And the dragons . . .

N'Doch sees it, a horrifying flash. His beautiful silver-blue monster boxed up in a high-tech cage for Baraga's video zoo. Just the sort of prize the Big Man would pay top bucks for. In his former life, mere hours ago, N'Doch would've already opened negotiations, might still if his life depends on it, which it might, he recalls, if he doesn't quick-wise explain to the dragons why this apparently deserted, picturesque, and pristine beach is the worst possible place to drop in on. He grasps the girl by both shoulders, like his brother Sedou used to do when he was supposed to really pay attention. He guesses this means he's the big brother now. He only hopes he lasts longer.

"There's this rich guy lives here, you got me? I mean, *really* rich. You can't imagine how rich." He circles his arms, encompassing the miles of unbroken white curling to the north and south—not even a footprint—and the manicured grove of royal crown palms embracing the curve of the beach like a green-armed lover. He wishes he could point out something obvious, like razor wire or guard towers, or mega laser emplacements, but that's not the Big Man's style. "And this is his private beach estate, that he doesn't like just anybody wandering around on."

If the girl weren't from Mars or wherever, the sheer untouched beauty of the place would ring her alarm bells immediately. But N'Doch sees she has no problem understanding the perils of trespassing at least, so that anti-tech commune of hers must have taught her something about the standard division of wealth out in the world. He's wondering if they impressed upon her just how far some folks will go to preserve that division, when he hears the dogs. The girl's eyes widen.

"Knew it," N'Doch groans. For a wildly optimistic moment, he'd hoped dragons and girls from Mars are invisible to Baraga's blanket of sensors.

The sound is literally bloodcurdling. He could explain to the girl how the dogs have been genetically engineered to produce the loudest, scariest howl a mammalian throat can produce, so that their victims will have plenty of time, while the dogs approach, to regret their trespass. But explanations wouldn't be too reassuring, since their bodies have been engineered as well. At least she's listening, and the buzz of image and music in his head says the dragons are, too. In fact, the images are getting kind of frantic. N'Doch clenches his eyes and shakes his head uselessly against the surge of mental static.

"He doesn't like dogs," the girl says apologetically.

"These aren't your normal dogs."

"This was her fishing place . . ."

He's just figured that out. Where else could you come up with a pile of hundred percent healthy fish? Baraga stocks the bay from his own hatcheries. "'Fine, fine. Now tell them to get us out of here."

The girl smiles at him. Does he detect condescension? She's not as worried about this as she should be. "She hears you, N'Doch. That's why you hear me."

"I know that," he growls. "We got no time for lessons now."

"We have to have time." Her smile hardly wavers. "Here's what you must do: recall a place that you know in every detail."

He's looking over his shoulder, monitoring the dogs' approach. "Most of those kind of places are right here in town."

"A *safe* place. You spoke of your grandfather's . . . ?"

He shouldn't have said anything. What if he can't remember well enough? "I don't know . . . it's been a while."

"Think, N'Doch! If you can really *see* it in your mind, Earth can take us there."

She'd said this back on the tanker, but he didn't truly absorb it until the reality of instantaneous transport was finally incontestable, when he found himself on Baraga's beach. He gets it now: kind of like the old Star Trek vids without all the fuzzy lights and music. The blue dragon aimed them at the one deserted spot she could image, and there they went. Pretty neat. Not her fault it wasn't a real smart choice, but he's got to do better.

He bears down on his brain, digging after old memories of the bush. Concentrating is hard, with that uncanny howling tearing at his ears. And now, behind the dogs, he hears the resonant hum of the sleek sand sleds that give Baraga's patrols their own kind of instant transport. N'Doch tastes a bitter surge of envy, like he always does when he's reminded of the Big Man, the so-called

Media King, and of what a man can buy with all that money. There's no one he hates with such purity, such simple fervor. But it's not so simple, really. He hates Baraga because the man's got everything and can do what he likes. But N'Doch knows that if the Media King chose to smile on him, say, sign him to even a minor recording contract, he knows he'd be bought as fast as the next poor kid with a keyboard. And this makes him hate Baraga even more.

But this is an old old rage and he hasn't got time for it now. The primal yowl of the dogs is maybe five hundred yards away. The girl looks nervous. The blue dragon is pinning him to the sand with her gimlet glare.

"Someplace safe . . ." he mutters. "Don't you know what you're asking?" Things will have changed in the bush, though maybe not so much, that far out. He can recall well enough the endless miles of scorched peanut fields, and the scattered, hard-baked villages. Familiar, yes, but in his mind, there's a sameness to all those miles. Can he remember one specific field or place along the road? If they could wait until dark, it'd be a lot easier to avoid detection.

But no such luck. He can make out the individual drones of the sleds now. There are four of them coming, and these are the two-man sleds. Probably Baraga's spy-eyes have them on visual, so they already know what a prize awaits them. N'Doch doesn't want to stick around to find out, though it would be fun and a rare taste of power, however fleeting, to wait until the sleds and dogs and whatever have pulled up around them, then vanish right out from under their noses.

He lets the image dance through his mind and abruptly, the background dragon music he's almost forgotten about turns sharp and urgent. Not even his fantasies are his own any more. Dogs or no, he'd like to sulk, but the dragon will not indulge him. Hard music, a storm of music in his head presses for action. He feels like a child being punished, and it turns out that's just what he's needed to vividly recall his time in the bush.

"Okay, I got one!" The dogs are in sight. "How do I do this?"

The sensation is painless, but he feels like his brain is being vacuumed.

*   *   *

It's an odd little place, just a thicket of rocks and an old baobab tree out in the middle of nowhere. *Nowhere is good right now,* he thinks. He'd recalled it at the last minute, mainly because it's where he escaped to when he missed his mama, or his grandfather was mad at him. Uncannily, the rocks themselves—pale, wind-smoothed boulders—are piled up in the shape of a dragon. As a kid, he'd called it the dinosaur. Now he sees it differently.

He's impressed by the big guy's accuracy. First, he's brought them nearly a hundred klicks in less than a heartbeat. On these roads, that's a long day's ride on a crowded, rickety bush taxi, not counting breakdowns or hijackings. Second, N'Doch had envisioned the rock pile from a bit of a distance, trying to fit the whole of it within his mind's eye, and that's exactly where he finds himself, once again breathless and queasy, a short walk away from this almost forgotten shrine of his childhood.

"Cosmic," he murmurs. He scans the horizon, notes that the girl does, too, only he doubts she'll know what to look for. He's glad she's held tight to the water bottle he gave her. She does seem to grasp that you gotta carry everything you need if you mean to survive.

So far, the horizon is empty, just the dry unplanted fields and scrub. He remembers there used to be some untilled land out this far, but that's long gone. It's the bush in name only these days. The scrub is gray and limp, and the sky's got that sickish yellow tinge to it even here.

But he sees no telltale rise of dust, no thin trail of smoke from some midday cookfire too close for comfort. 'Course maybe nobody's got much left to cook. Still, he's pretty sure the nearest village is at least two miles past his grandpapa's. He feels the old twinge of agoraphobia that the bush always brought on but, right now, anywhere but Baraga's beach is okay with him. Once he gets everyone into the rocks, where they can't be spotted from the air, they'll be safe—for a while, at least.

Erde sensed the true isolation of this new place he'd brought them to and let herself relax a little. True, it was hot as a smithy's forge and the air was full of red dust, but as N'Doch herded them toward the rock pile, she could see shade there. The crevices between the biggest boulders were as deep as caves, and, mercifully, dragon-sized. Nobody would be chasing them for a while. She mentioned this to Earth and he agreed it would be a novelty, at least in their own recent lives. Time to settle in, time to finally question Water, and then, plan the next leg of their Quest.

N'Doch seemed to share this need, once he had the dragons under cover. Erde thought him overly concerned about the view from above—-did he suspect the very birds might give them away? But she smiled benignly to see him fuss so over Water, when a few hours ago he would scarcely acknowledge her. These wise and ancient creatures bound you by making you feel responsible for them. How silly, to think that great and magical dragons might have need of mere mortals, yet there it was. She remembered well how helpless Earth had seemed when she'd first found him—or rather, when he'd found her, at a time when her life had collapsed in ruins around her. The only thing that kept her sane and moving forward was the dragon's obvious need of her. Perhaps N'Doch's life was in a similar crisis, or was it just coincidence that they'd both been on the run when their dragons found them?

With a final upward glance, N'Doch shrugged, apparently satisfied. He took a long drink from his white water jug—Erde had been honored when he delivered one of these magical objects into her care—then he dropped down cross-legged to face her with the air of a man with a billion questions and no idea where to begin. He glanced furtively at Water, dozing behind him. He hadn't learned yet that his connection with the dragon wasn't directional and did not require eye contact. Only awareness, an inner listening.

"Okay," he began. "Now let me get this straight . . ."

"These are real dragons," he states propositionally. It's getting familiar now, almost comfortable, this simultaneous translation thing. Like talking with the vid playing. "And somehow I'm hooked up with one of them."

The girl nods. So far, so good. He knows this sounds like kindergarten, but he's got to get all this weird shit out on the table where he can see it. Maybe saying it in words will give it logic or structure, like writing a song makes sense of messed up emotions.

"Like you're tied up with the big guy."

"Earth."

"Yah. Earth." He's not sure why he avoids calling the dragons by name, except that it feels like giving in. If you name a thing, it's for sure real, but at least you retain the power of the naming, which is a kind of power over the thing. If a thing *tells* you its name and you accept it, you also accept that the thing has a power in its own right: self-determination. If he had a dog or a monkey, he'd pick a name and that would be that: The dog or monkey would be his. He studies the silver-blue dragon thoughtfully.

"And she's Water."

"Yes. Water. She's Earth's sister."

Though he hears musical agreement in the background, he makes a face. "Nah. Can't be. I mean, look at 'em. They don't look anything alike."

Instead of snapping back at him like usual when he doubts her, she seems to go off on a thought of her own. "I know. Isn't it peculiar?"

N'Doch laughs. Does this mean the girl has a sense of humor? "It's all pretty damn peculiar, I'd say."

She nods, serious again. "But you get used to it."

"Okay. So there's these two dragons . . ."

He's interrupted by a bugle of music, not urgent or angry this time, but eager, as if the sea dragon's just thought of something she'd meant to tell them all along. The girl's deadpan face blooms with amazement and delight.

"She says there are more! She remembers four! Oh, a wonder! Isn't it, N'Doch?"

"I'm having enough trouble with one."

"Oh, but *four!*" She turns to Water. "Where are they? Do you know?" The sea dragon looks glum. The girl turns back. "She doesn't know."

"You're a one-woman conversation." N'Doch wants to get back on track. "Now listen up, okay? There's these two dragons—and maybe more—and then there's you and me, and we're supposed to help them do something, only no one knows what it is."

She resettles herself, but she's having a hard time restraining her glee. "It's their Purpose. We have to help discover it. Four!"

"Yeah, okay, four. But couldn't they just, you know, *be* here, like on vacation?"

She frowns. He can see she doesn't appreciate his levity. "All dragons have a Purpose. They wouldn't be here otherwise."

"Hah," he mutters before he can stop himself. "Wish I could say the same."

Her sudden smile dazzles him. "You can, now."

"Yeah, well . . ."

She spreads her hands, palms down, like she's calming a riot. N'Doch notices how they're large and long-fingered like his own. He wonders if she plays an instrument. Maybe he could teach her one. "Earth woke from his long sleep under the mountain because Someone was Calling him to his Purpose."

"Oh, yeah? Who?"

"That's what I keep telling you! We don't know!"

N'Doch hears for the first time the big dragon speaking in his head, and understands that a further level of connection has been achieved, probably because he hasn't been fighting it so hard. The big guy's voice is not the *basso profundo* rumble you'd expect from a dragon. It's more like a young voice that will be deep when it grows up. And N'Doch can hear humor in it, a wry, self-deprecation that matches the sad-sack expression the big guy often wears. It's almost playful. Nonetheless it shakes N'Doch to his very bones and sinews to hear someone else's words forming between his own ears.

—*I did not even know my name when I woke.*

—*I knew mine.* Water chimes in busily, like the mezzo making her entrance late into the quartet. —*But I am older.*

"Gaaaghhh . . ." is all N'Doch can manage. His brain rocks with sound, words, music, meaning. He thinks he might just pass out.

"We tried to figure out who was Calling him," continues the girl, like nothing out of the ordinary is happening, "I told Earth we'd find a Mage to tell us, but we were having these awful dreams and being chased all over by my father and the terrible priest, and the Summoner was calling him all the while! If it wasn't for Sir Hal . . ."

She's stopped by the look in N'Doch's eyes. Even she can tell overload when she sees it.

He's grateful for the momentary silence, but he wants to look like he's up to the challenge. He can keep up with a girl from Mars, even though she's got a lot more words in her than he'd thought. He takes a long steadying breath. "Sir Hal?"

And she's off again. "Yes! He found us. Saved us. Taught us how to get along in the wilderness. He's a famous scholar of dragon lore, well *in*famous, really—most people don't approve of dragons, you know. And he's a King's Knight, one of the few still loyal to His Majesty."

"His majesty who?"

"Otto, High King of all the Germanies." She looks crestfallen. "Have we come so far south that you haven't heard of King Otto? Oh dear! Have you even heard of the Germanies?"

"Well, *Germany*, yeah. A way while back, there was East and West, but now there's just one. Germany." He's always amazed by how thoroughly these regression cults indoctrinate their members. "I'm no history geek or anything, but I'm pretty sure they haven't had a King of Germany for at least two hundred years."

He watches the girl absorb this one. When no trace of guile shows through her confusion and dismay, he asks her casually as he can, "So, tell me something. What year do you think it is?"

Her chin lifts, hardens. "Think? I am no ignorant peasant! I am a baron's daughter. I can read and write and tell the hours. The year is 913 and it's September." She squints out into the sun. "But I can't really tell what time it is. It's different here, somehow."

"I'll say it is." N'Doch sucks his teeth. "Well, here's the thing: You got the September part right. And you're in the People's so-called Democratic Republic of Maligambia. That's in Africa, which *is* pretty far south of Germany. But, girl, let me break it to you gently. The year is 2013."

"It is?"

"Uh-huh."

To her credit, she doesn't launch right off into one of those twisty rationalizations the cultists always trot out to shore up their most ridiculous beliefs, like how God put the fossils in the rock to test the faith of Christians. She just stares at him, and the music in his head starts sounding more like bees swarming. She's having a silent confab with the scaly duo—no, not fair—neither of them are scaly, certainly not his silky blue monster, his lovely Water. Another cliché down the drain. N'Doch scolds himself. He knows he's just feeling miffed at being left out of a conversation moving too fast for him to handle.

"Hey," he says. "Can I get into this discussion?"

The girl turns a long, long gaze on him. He can see the years themselves in her eyes. "2013? Then we have traveled far indeed."

The future was something Erde had few thoughts about, other than the most immediate variety such as, "What's for dinner?" or "What can I possibly make for Grandmother's Name-Day?" Occasionally she would wonder which baron's son her father would marry her off to or what castle she'd live in when she grew up, but such thoughts never bore the weight of reality. Not like actually *being* there, feeling the truth of it all around you.

She had no problem believing that she was indeed in the future. Magic can make anything possible. She just wished the dragon had warned her. But perhaps he hadn't known either. Dragon time was less linear than her own, she was learning. Her sense of it was that time began *now* and ended *then*. After all, didn't you live one day, then another, and so on? But for the dragons, it seemed, time just *was,* and you could go anywhere in it you wanted to if you had the right directions.

Which of course for Earth meant the right *image*.

Which meant that if, in transporting to the place they'd seen in their nightmares, he'd brought them to the future, then they'd been dreaming the future all along. Erde decided not to tackle the mystery of how you could dream something that hadn't happened yet. She supposed it was something like the gypsy women and their picture cards, or Hal's lady Rose and her Seeings. Rose claimed to be able only to See what was now, but the dragons said all of time was now, happening all at once, which would explain why Rose occasionally seemed to See the future. Erde couldn't quite get her mind around it, but the dragons were magic and they knew best, so she'd just have to take their word for it.

The notion that she couldn't ignore was that the world might not go on as it was—as she knew it—forever and ever, that the passage of time might automatically equal change. Therefore, the difference of N'Doch's world might not be due simply to her having traveled far, far south into exotic lands. Instead, the whole world, from north to south, might have changed, might be like it was here in what he called Afrika: hot, dry, dusty . . . unrecognizable. So if she went back north, there might be nothing familiar there either. This was more frightening than any breakdown in her definitions of Time. She'd always been proud to be able to say that Tor Alte and its surrounding lands had been held in the von Alte name for three hundred years. But *eleven* hundred? Suddenly she wanted more than anything to go there and see.

N'Doch was watching her carefully, as if he'd expected some desperate reaction to his news. But even if she did feel desperate, she'd try not to show it.

"Is . . . uhm . . . German-y . . . like this now?" She gestured around vaguely. She didn't want to seem to be judging his world too harshly.

"Now? As opposed to when?"

She thought they'd been through that, but maybe he wasn't listening while she discussed it with the dragons. If he didn't start making a habit of listening, it was going to be hard to keep track of who understood what.

"As opposed to when I come from." She liked the sound of that, how easily it came out. Not "where I come from" but "when."

N'Doch sighed explosively. "All right, look—enough is enough. It's none of my business but somebody's got to clue you in sometime, might as well be me. So listen: whoever's told you the year's 913, your parents, this King Otto, whoever, they're just pretending you all live in the past, 'cause they can't deal with the present. You get it? It's all a big fat lie. I'm telling you that here and now, and you just gotta accept it. Okay?"

She let him finish and then calm down a bit, for he

was getting rather heated about it. She guessed that the fact that, as young as she was, she'd been born eleven hundred years ago was a hard one to swallow.

"I don't mean I've lived that long," she reassured him patiently. "That would be impossible. Only dragons and the Wandering Jew live that long. I mean I just came from there yesterday."

She says it with such simple conviction, it makes his hair stand up on end. Not from Mars after all, but from the past. A time-traveler. And she's so sure about it, he can't think of a way to refute her. Especially when he's asking himself: If dragons can move through Space, why not through Time?

Abruptly, he's tired of it, all of it. Tired of having his brain crowded with other people's thoughts and voices and concepts, of having his reality stretched beyond all reasoning. And no wonder. He hasn't slept in twenty-four hours, except for being down for the count while they cured his fever, and that can hardly count as rest. It's only that he's eaten better than usual that's kept him going. It doesn't really matter, he realizes, if she's from now or whenever. She's here and so are the dragons, and somehow, he's got to deal with them.

"Okay, I got it. You're from the past. Fine. I'm gonna get some sleep now." He lies back and folds his elbow over his eyes, sealing out girl and dragons, the whole preposterous vision. "When it's dark, I'll go talk to Papa Dja."

Chapter Fifteen

Erde told Earth that she'd never in her life met anyone so badly brought up.

—*Ending a conversation without so much as a by-
your-leave!*

—*He's tired. He's had a lot to think about today.*
Water stirred from her doze.

—*I think we could all use some rest.*

—*But he was so rude! And we were actually talking
about something for the first time ever!*

—*Remember, you're not a baron's daughter here.
He owes you no fealty.*

—*What about simple courtesy?*

—*His definitions are different from yours.*

—*Rest now, child. I feel great things are about to
happen here.*

—*You do?*

—*Rest.*

The dragons were the ones who really wanted to rest,
Erde decided, so she'd better let them. Forcing her petulance away, she studied N'Doch as he plunged into sleep
beside her. He didn't ever seem to worry about how he
should behave. He did whatever he felt like at the moment. Erde found this both enviable and infuriating. Did
everyone just do what they felt like in this world of
2013? How did they get anything done without fighting
about it?

She resisted sleep for a while. She thought she should
stay awake and keep watch. But the hot close air in the
shadow of the rocks made her drowsy, and neither
N'Doch or the dragons seemed concerned any longer

about the possibility of attack. She stared out at the brushy horizon until her eyelids drooped. Then she seated her dagger more comfortably against her waist, laid her head on her pack and fell asleep.

When the dream came this time, it was not like the old ones. It was not on alien ground, or wracked with deafening noise and odious smells. She was home again, not a specifically known location but an easily comprehended one: a wide, frost-seared grassland backed by fog-shrouded mountains, a dark forest of pine and fir flowing over the waves of foothills down to the edge of the plain, a chill, thin river. It was early morning, just coming light, of a dull wet day. Along the meeting line of grass and trees, an army was camped.

Erde found she could approach the camp, slowly, at eye level, as if riding along the rutted path and in among the silent tents on horseback. The illusion was so real that she started in fright, in the dream, when the door flap of a nearby tent was suddenly thrown aside and a man stepped out, not ten feet in front of her.

He was solid and blond, with the hard-muscled body of a warrior but sporting a courtier's close-cropped beard. His breath made smoke in the icy air, a chill Erde could not feel. The man stretched and shivered, shrugging his wool cloak more tightly around his naked chest. He tested the wind, listening intently, then frowned and looked toward Erde. She recognized Adolphus of Köthen, and wondered if he would remember her. But instead, he stared past her, as if surprised by not seeing the something or someone he'd expected. He turned away, then glanced back again, quickly, as if trying to catch that someone in the act of being there after all. Erde knew in her dream that he could sense a presence, maybe even her own specific presence, and that this puzzled him. It puzzled her, too, since they hardly knew each other, and why should she be dreaming about Adolphus of Köthen? But she was glad it was only a dream because this formidable, intelligent man was officially her enemy, the ally of her father and the terrible priest. She wouldn't want to be this close to him if he could actually see her.

And yet she lingered, because the dream gave her the power and because, she realized guiltily, she liked looking at him, liked his interesting combination of toughness and reserve, liked how his thick, straw-gold hair bunched along his neck like pinfeathers, liked even his oddly dark brows and eyes. His alert scowl reminded her of her father's favorite peregrine, Quick, except Köthen carried himself with an easy confidence unlike the posture of any bird of prey. Much else about Köthen reminded Erde of Hal, though this was no surprise since Hal had fostered him as a lad, and by Kothen's own admission, taught him everything he knew. Erde thought it a great human tragedy that Baron Köthen felt called upon to go to war to usurp the King, thereby pitting himself against his beloved mentor. For there never was a more loyal servant to His Majesty than Heinrich Peder von Engle, Baron Weistrasse, known to his friends as Hal. Except, now that she thought of it, Köthen had invariably called him Heinrich. A mark of respect, or a way of distancing a man whom he honored far more than was convenient for him?

Now Köthen looked the other way. Armor clanked. There was a stirring of men and horses outside a black-and-green tent flying the von Alte battle standard. Her father's tent. Past it were a quartet of white pavilions, each guarded by a stout, white-robed monk. Other monks were lugging heavy pails of heated water into the largest pavilion.

Erde felt a chill at last, and a sudden urge to scurry away, as if some roving eye searching a crowd had picked her out with evil intent. She stared with Köthen, then after him, as he turned abruptly, his scowl deepening, and stalked past her, away from her father's awakening and the tents of the priest, away from the camp and the new smoke rising from cook fires, into the morning darkness under the trees.

When she woke in the thick heat of a far century, she knew it was not precisely a dream that she'd had. A profound sense of home lingered. Somehow she had *been* there, had returned to the preternaturally early winter of 913, and been privy to a true event, however insignificant . . . or probably not. Only time would tell that. But why Köthen? She scanned her mind for the dragon to tell him the news, but he was still sleeping off his bellyful of fish. She opened her eyes, slitted against the late-afternoon glare, so bright even in the deepest shadow of the rocks. Once again, N'Doch was gone.

Chapter Sixteen

On the way to Papa Dja's, N'Doch rehearses his explanation for showing up out of the blue after all these years of ignoring his grandpapa entirely. How long?—he counts backward—eight years, it has to be, and five since Sedou's funeral, when the old man walked all the way in from the bush to sing the ancient death rituals behind the imam's back. He wouldn't take a bush taxi. Wouldn't even take the public bus.

N'Doch would never admit it out loud, but he misses his older brother. More than, say, his little brother Jéjé who died so young the family hardly had time to get used to him being there. Or Mammoud, the eldest, who was out of the house and into the army at fourteen, when N'Doch was just learning to walk, and dead a year later. With Sedou, he'd actually had a sort of relationship, a rocky one for sure, with Sey always yelling at him to stick around home and mind. Sedou was the righteous one, of all his mama's sons, the one who did his schoolwork and worked extra hours at odd jobs to help feed the household. Of course that righteousness also made him pigheaded and fanatical, and got him killed for speaking his mind. N'Doch thinks writing songs is a smarter way of saying your piece then getting involved in politics. It's true he hasn't written any songs about "issues" yet, but he keeps thinking he might. He hasn't written any about Sedou either, though he's got a lot in his mind. Probably the songs about Sedou will end up being about politics, so he figures he'd better just get famous first. If you're famous enough, they pretty much let you say what you want.

There's no road the way he's going. It's a direct overland route, a mile and a half across the dry, empty fields waiting for the fall rains that have been coming later and less often every year. The soil is as dry and hot as beach sand beneath his bare feet, and the scattered grass clumps rattle like drumrolls as he brushes past. N'Doch thinks it's odd but all the same incredibly cool that he knows exactly in which direction his grandpapa's house lies. *Exactly,* as if flashing signs or a homing beacon were showing him the way, 'cept it's right there in his head and he's sure of it in ways he isn't about a lot of other things he's had to do with much more recently and in greater detail. He's even impatient with the occasional detour around brush thickets or rocks. He can sense the deviation from the straight line as acutely as he would hear a string out of tune. *Pretty weird,* he muses, but then everything is, right about now. Why should this be any different?

He decides he'll tell Papa Dja that the dragons are research clones escaped from some top secret American zoo, like in that old vid about the dinosaur island. If the old guy questions him too closely, he'll just say that's what the girl told him, he doesn't know any more. How he'll explain the girl, he's not sure, with all her bizarro clothes and speaking German. Maybe he'd better make it a German zoo. He'll just say she showed up on the beach looking for help, which isn't far from the actual truth. It just ain't *all* of it. . . .

He's there almost before he realizes. Ahead of him, just as he remembers it, the unlikely copse of thick-trunked trees, like a handful of forest tossed down among the parched scrub to spread the miracle of leaf and shade over Papa Djawara's tiny homestead. The real miracle is, there's no barbed wire or broken glass palisade along the tops of those mustard-colored walls, and N'Doch knows the gate will not be locked. When everyone else in their right mind has taken the appropriate security precautions, Djawara has steadfastly refused to do anything but adopt a pack of mangy stray dogs. N'Doch looks around, wondering where the dogs are. There must be dogs. Papa Dja always had dogs. Out hunting, most likely, good luck to them, and leaving the compound open to surprise intruders such as himself. Papa Dja always said he had nothing worth stealing, but an intact house under trees is prime real estate. Plus, the old man grows a lot of good, safe edibles inside those unassuming walls. N'Doch knows this, and he guesses everyone else around knows it, too. There must be water underground somewhere, though no well digger's ever been able to find it. If they had, Papa Dja would've lost his house long ago. But Fâtime says the locals are afraid that if they steal from Papa Djawara, he'll put a bad spell on them and that'll be that. This wouldn't hold the gangs back, but so far, they've pretty much kept to the towns and the City. So in some ways, the old coot's nutty reclusiveness works in his favor. Fâtime says he's even managed to hold on to a goat.

N'Doch approaches the gate quietly. It's that still, amber part of early evening. Entire flocks of birds are appearing out of nowhere to settle in Djawara's trees. In town, the market stalls would be going great guns again, after the midday lull for the heat. Housewives would be bartering their last pair of shoes for the evening meal. Out here, the farmers in the villages are probably setting their chairs out in the street to fan themselves a while before falling exhausted into bed. And that's just what his grandpapa is doing when N'Doch sticks his head inside, past the broken ironwork gate: sitting under a big lemon tree, fanning himself slowly.

Like the trees and the mustard-colored walls, Djawara is exactly as N'Doch remembers him. Thinner and grayer, maybe, but the same slight, erect, round-faced man in an antiquated white tunic and woven tribal skull-cap. At least he doesn't have his ceremonial robes on. N'Doch recalls asking Fâtime one time why Papa Dja wore so many clothes. She just shook her head, probably at both of them. He's always been told he has her height but his grandpapa's frame. He's not sure who shares the old man's ready but ambiguous smile. Certainly not his mama, at least not anymore. And though he'd like to think his own smile could be as complex as he remembers Djawara's, he doubts he's lived long enough for that.

The old man is smiling like that right now, easing back comfortably in one of a pair of metal folding chairs, the least bent one, facing the gate as if someone has just gotten up from a conversation and Djawara expects them back presently. N'Doch hesitates, glances behind him.

The flood of memories is a surprise to him. It's hard just to stroll in to this place so pungent with his boyhood. But he can't not go in. The old man has seen him and waves him in with his palm frond fan.

"There you are, there you are. Took your own sweet time, did you? Took a nap along the way?"

N'Doch looks behind him again. Has the old geezer mistaken him for someone else? Is he losing what's left of his marbles? "Papa Dja? It's me, N'Doch, Fâtime's boy."

"I know who you are, though it's been so long, that's a miracle in itself."

"I know, Papa, and I'm sorry."

"Sure, sure. We're all sorry these days."

The bright smile belies his grandfather's dire tone. N'Doch edges in a few steps farther, both eager and reluctant. He nods at the second chair. "You were expecting someone?"

"You. I was expecting you."

"Oh." That's just the sort of thing the old man's always saying, that earns him his reputation as a crazy man. "Well . . . how are you?"

"Very well, very well. And yourself?"

"Oh, fine, real fine. And the cousins? And the neighbors? And the goat? And the garden?" N'Doch throws himself into the old-style greeting pattern, hoping to lure this very traditional old man into the right frame of mind about him. "And by the way, where are the dogs?"

Djawara's smile barely wavers. "The family won't talk to me, what's left of them, and the neighbors are afraid to, as well they ought to be. The goat's stopped milking and the garden's just squeaking by. I'm getting too old to care for it properly." He pauses for a little cough and a breath, peering at N'Doch from under lowered brows. "But the dogs, mercifully, are hale and healthy. Only I put them inside, as I hear one of our visitors isn't fond of dogs . . . I hadn't counted on that."

N'Doch's eyes narrow. "Visitors?"

"You know, you know." Djawara tosses a casual wave in the precise direction that N'Doch has come.

"Ah," N'Doch replies, thinking of how tired he's getting of being caught entirely by surprise. "So . . . you know about the, ah . . ."

Djwara nods. "Visitors. The signs were all pointing to

it. If I'd read them more truly, I'd be better prepared. But as it is, it is. We'll make do, won't we?"

N'Doch nods with him, still second-guessing. Like, what if they're talking about two different things? Dragons and, say, the visiting relief workers, or the Frenchmen who try unsuccessfully to sell Djawara a windmill every year? N'Doch leans against the crumbling gatepost. "Well, Papa Dja, funny you should mention, since I was hoping you could take in a visitor or two for a while, only I'm not sure . . ." His eyes flick around the visible parts of the courtyard and the small thatched-roof bungalow at its center.

". . . there's room?" The old man leans back in his chair, palm fan waving. "You'd be surprised. This place is a lot bigger than it looks."

N'Doch sucks his teeth, says nothing. He's spent the whole trip from the rock pile inventing explanations for dragons, without a thought of what to say about why he's come.

Djawara chuckles. "Come in, come in, son. I'll make us some tea. Sit down and rest a bit till the light fades. Then we'll go out and bring them back."

N'Doch slouches into the welcome sweet shade of the lemon tree. He shakes his grandfather's small, dry hand, then sets the water jug at his feet and sits. He looks up and sees actual lemons hiding among the shiny dark leaves, like little suns among storm clouds. He can hear but not see the birds settling into the branches, chattering and resettling each time another flock lands. After a long silence, he gets his courage up.

" 'Scuse me for asking, Papa Dja, but how did you . . . ?"

"Know?" The old man takes a grateful swig from the jug. "Well, your mama told me, of course. But as I said, even if she hadn't, I'd been feeling it was time."

"I see." N'Doch considers this briefly. He's forgotten about the old man's irritating habit of finishing your sentences before you can even get them out. "How did she know?"

"You didn't tell her?"

"No way."

"Well, there you are. That's Fâtime for you. I always

said she could pry secrets out of a stone. I recall one time she even . . ."

" 'Scuse me again, Papa, but *how* did she tell you? You put in a phone since I was here last?"

Djawara frowns. "Phone? This is no rich man you're kin to. Even if I had the money, I wouldn't have one in the house." His hands sketch little circles above his head. "All those waves, you know . . . they get in the way. No, she told me in a dream, son. That's how the poor folk talk together."

Speak for yourself, thinks N'Doch. It's true his mama's always put great stock in dreams, but he's still not convinced he and his grandpapa are on the same page. Just doesn't seem possible. "So, ah . . . what exactly did she tell you?"

"That you'll need help understanding where to go next."

N'Doch gives up, sits back with a sigh. "Well, that ain't lying."

When it's dark, and the tea has been made and drunk—three ritual cups of the thick, sweet brew—Djawara dons a brightly printed robe over his worn white tunic and carefully brushes out the folds. They walk in silence back to the rock pile. The old man keeps pace through the night heat without complaint. They're almost there when he grasps N'Doch's wrist suddenly and draws him beneath the canopy of a thicket.

"What?" N'Doch demands.

"Quietly!" Djawara points upward.

N'Doch listens. After a while he hears the airy whock-whock of a hovercopter approaching from the south, from town. It's flying low, like it's looking for something.

"Damn, Papa! You got great ears!"

"Shhh!"

They watch it pass by to the east, the direction they're headed, and vanish into the night toward the north.

"Already!" N'Doch has figured to have more safe time. "Who is it?"

"Baraga, I'm fairly sure of it."

The old man does not ask how or why. "Then we must hurry."

The girl and the dragons are awake when they get

there, awaiting his return. He can see that this time they were sure he'd come back, which makes him feel predictable, and that really bugs him.

Papa Dja touches his shoulder as they step under the shadow of the rocks. "One moment. What are their names?"

"Didn't Mama tell you that, along with everything else?"

"No more than she taught you manners, it appears."

N'Doch wants to explain that his manners are fine, it's the damn situation that's making him so touchy. But the old man's frown can lay him out like no one else's. How could he have forgotten that?

"Umm, the big one's called Earth and my . . . the other one's Water."

"Don't be so afraid to claim what's yours, son."

Djawara's past him before N'Doch can think of a proper comeback. But it occurs to him maybe this is why he stayed away after all those extended visits when he was young: this man, half his size and weight, can still make him feel like a child. Pretending he's moving through the frames of some surrealist stop-action video, N'Doch does the introductions. To his chagrin, Djawara greets the girl in what sounds like pretty good German. She has some difficulty with it at first, so Djawara adjusts his pronunciation. N'Doch hears it, like a change of key in a piece of music. The girl nods and smiles.

"Didn't know you spoke Kraut, Papa Dja," he marvels sullenly.

"It's *Alte Deutsch*," Djawara says, moving on to gaze up at the dragons. "Old German. Not all that different, really. Knew it would come in handy some day."

"Hunh." N'Doch notices how both critters have withdrawn into the deepest recesses of the rocks so that their true shape and size is lost in darkness. Maybe they hoped not to frighten this elderly and frail-looking human, but N'Doch thinks they look scarier that way, looming up out of the earthly void like myths or nightmares, the pale ambient moonlight touching just the relevant detail: a giant ivory claw, the gleaming curve of a horn, a shimmer of velvet, and two pairs of eyes that seem to radiate a warmer kind of light. N'Doch backs up involuntarily. But Djawara seems to have a very clear idea what a man should do when faced with a brace of dragons. He goes right to them and stands with his arms spread wide and his chin high. He looks so small in front of them, smaller than the girl even, and painfully vulnerable, but N'Doch sees that his eyes are closed and his smile transcendent. Drawing his palms together beneath his chin, the old man bows to them deeply, and the dragons incline their great heads in solemn recognition.

Erde saw that this dark little man she understood to be N'Doch's grandfather knew his way around dragons, and liked him immediately. That he spoke her language, albeit a bit oddly, naturally increased her high opinion of him. That he seemed totally unsurprised by herself and her companions made her suddenly much more relaxed about the future of the dragons' Quest. If N'Doch was not the mage they sought, perhaps this old man was. He certainly looked more like a mage. For one thing, he wasn't going around half-naked like everyone else she'd seen. He even wore a hat, and soft leather sandals on his neat, ash-colored feet. Covertly, Erde searched the intricate patterning of his ankle-length, wide-sleeved robe for familiar alchemical or astrological symbols but all she could make out in the dim light were fish and birds, or maybe they were flying fish, which sounded at least somewhat magical.

She let him pay his proper obeisance to the dragons, then approached him with the formality and respect due to a learned elder and probable mage.

"We seek a wise man's counsel, honored sir."

"And his hospitality as well, I'm told." His bright, crinkly eyes were on a level with her own. "Both of which you shall have, such as I can offer, which I fear these days is slight."

Earth's urgent need cut through her own impulse toward at least a smidgen of polite introductory conversation.—*ASK HIM.*

Erde cleared her throat. "My companion asks: Are you the mage we seek?"

This seemed to surprise him as nothing had so far. His eyes flicked up at the dragon and back again. "Why would he think that?"

—*Why, Dragon?*

*—BECAUSE HE SEEMS TO HAVE BEEN EX-
PECTING US.*

Erde relayed this, and the old man smiled. "No and
yes, daughter. Never and always. Waiting for long centuries, without expectation. From grandfather to grandson.
You of all people know how it is, how it has always
been."

"Not entirely, learned sir. My grandmother died before she could explain everything to me in detail."

"Ah, then I am sorry for your loss, but you see, she
gifted you with what detail was necessary, or you'd never
have found . . ." He nodded gravely toward Earth.
". . . him. Any deeper knowledge would create an improper anticipation. Preparation, yes, but one cannot live
one's life waiting for a thing that might never happen."

*But I'd have been happy to be even as prepared as you
seem to be,* Erde thought. "I've no wish to cause offense,
honored sir, but would this explain why your
grandson . . . ummm . . . ?"

"Yes, daughter?"

"Sir, he doesn't seem to understand much about
dragons."

"Well, now, there don't seem to be many of them
around nowadays, do there?" The old man's smile
hinted at her own imperfect understanding. "But, yes,
he has been a reluctant pupil. He's grown up in a world
that has no use for the old knowledge. Yet he absorbed
what he needed, or you wouldn't be here."

Erde saw the truth in that. She glanced at N'Doch,
who had moved away into the moonlight and was staring
up into the air. Despite his ignorance and disbelief, he
had finally not deserted them. He had gotten them
where they apparently needed to be.

"Papa Dja," he called now from the edge of the light.
"That copter's coming back."

Prepared, thought Erde, *but still unpardonably rude.*
But instead of scolding the youth for interrupting, the
old man turned his way and listened.

"It is indeed."

"Think it can see us under all these rocks?"

"Heat, son. The warm exhalations of life."

N'Doch nodded disgustedly. "Damn Baraga anyway.
I won't let him get her."

Djawara's smile broadened. "No. I should say not."

Erde followed this exchange as best she could, but the dragons' understanding of idiomatic speech was loose at best. "What flies in the night sky that worries you, honored sir?"

"One of Baraga's hovercopters," grumped N'Doch.

The old man eyed Erde sympathetically. "She will not be acquainted with that particular type of bird, my boy. We'll speak of these things later," he reassured her. "First we must figure out how to get ourselves to safety without being sighted."

"You think it's safer at your house?"

"For a while, yes. We can mislead this pursuit."

"Really?" N'Doch brightened and began to look slyly around. "Well, then, Papa Dja—I think I can handle this. I'll have you back home in no time at all."

Chapter Seventeen

It's crowded in the courtyard with all five of them there, but the look of approval in his grandfather's eyes is worth any discomfort. Approval, and just the slightest trace of awe. The old man may know something about practically everything but clearly, he's never experienced instantaneous transport before. N'Doch begins to think he could get into this dragon business after all.

The dogs set up a choral howl in the house. The girl reaches to reassure the brown dragon. It makes N'Doch grin to think that any critter as well armed and armored as that big guy could be afraid of dogs. He's glad it's not *his* dragon putting up such a fuss over nothing. But Djawara goes to the door and hushes the dogs sternly. Then he says something to the girl, gesturing toward the deeper shadow beneath the trees filling the little side yard. Remembering the copter, N'Doch glances upward, then around.

"So, Papa Dja—you got some kind of jamming signal hidden around here that's gonna disable that copter's sensors?" He laughs. "Some kind of cloaking device?"

"I said 'confuse,' not 'disable,' but actually I do. The birds are my cloaking device."

"Oh, yeah, the birds." Because of course the trees are full of them. Hundreds, maybe more. "Will it work?"

"Always has before."

N'Doch wonders how often his grandfather has need of concealment from the likes of Baraga. "What if they leave?"

"I'll call them back if we need them."

"Oh." It doesn't sound foolproof, but N'Doch is distracted by the big dragon, who is looking unusually squat and reptilian as he squeezes himself under the low, spreading branches. "He'll never fit."

"He will."

And sure enough, the brown guy slowly drags his bulk inward until he's disappeared beneath the leaves. N'Doch peers under the branches and sees only shadow, a limitless darkness—and the dragon's tail vanishing into it. A chill creeps up his spine.

"Papa Dja, how . . . ?"

"Don't think about it, son. Just don't."

"But . . ." He's not sure he wants the blue dragon swallowed up likewise, but she's already on her way, leaving a trill of music in his head that sounds like reassurance. When she, too, has vanished, Djawara dusts his palms lightly and gestures N'Doch and the girl into his house. It crosses N'Doch's mind that maybe Djawara's neighbors are right to be afraid of him.

Inside, it's dark, and Djawara lights a little kerosene lamp. N'Doch is about to explain the boondocks lack of electricity in the house, and then he remembers he's the only one who'll be missing it. The dogs leap around them with interest and suspicion. N'Doch makes a quick head count: seven of them this time. Seven scrawny but otherwise healthy-looking, lop-eared, evil-eyed mutts. Most of 'em good-sized ones, too. He expects the girl to freak, since her dragon's so weird on them. Instead, she reaches out her arms to gather them and gets down on her knees among them like she's welcoming old friends. They snarl and shoulder each other for her attention, but she speaks stern German to them and calms them. Then she smiles over their hairy backs at the waiting men.

"She tells them they're beautiful," Djawara translates. "That she's never seen such clever dogs. They lap it up. Dogs are fools for flattery."

"It's good you speak her lingo, Papa Dja." N'Doch doesn't mention his doubts that the dogs speak it also. "I can't talk to her otherwise, when the dragons aren't around."

"Aren't they around?"

"No, they . . ." He realizes he knows this now, without even looking. He can tell from the silence in his head. He wonders where they've gone, and how they left from that weirdness beneath the trees. "They're off hunting, probably. They'll be back."

"No doubt." The old man is smiling one of his most complicated smiles. "Why don't you teach Mademoiselle Erde some French?"

"Well, I will . . . I guess I will, when I get around to it . . . if she's still here."

"She will be." Djawara lights a second lamp and carries it onto the cooking porch at the back of the bungalow. He sets it on a wooden slab beside a basket of vegetables. N'Doch comes to hover over the basket eagerly.

"You grow all this?"

Djawara nods. "Poor shriveled things. I can't haul as much water for them as I used to be able to. But they're all safe."

"Look okay to me." Squashes, tomatoes, peppers, a few things N'Doch doesn't recognize. He picks up a long green thing he's forgotten the name of. "What's this?"

"A cucumber. Have you never had a cucumber?"

"Not for a real long time, Papa Dja."

"Hmm. Getting bad in town, is it?"

"Bad to worse." Actually, N'Doch hasn't thought about it like that before, that it might be worse now than it was before. He's prided himself on living in and for the moment, in the cool chaos of the present, where he's like the flash of the vid image, the instant of pure data always morphing into something else and abandoning its former self in the irrelevant past. But now the past walks beside him, very relevant and immediate, in the form of a young girl and a dragon, and in a surge of childhood memories loosed by this old man and his peculiar house. He'd forgotten how peculiar. All this allows N'Doch a newly parallax view of himself, moving through time, a product not of just now, but then and now, a continuum. Which now includes a silver-blue dragon that the old man used to sing about a long time ago. Standing there thinking all this while he's staring at the cucumber, it fairly well blows N'Doch's mind.

"You all right, son?"

"Yeah, sure." He paces a little, because he has to. "Papa Dja?"

The old man is slicing a squash into a battered pot. "Mmmm?"

"You know that old song you used to sing, about the kid and the sea serpent? How'd that end? I can't remember."

Djawara ladles precious water into the pot from a bucket covered with a damp white cloth. "Don't know. You'd always fall asleep, so I'd always stop singing."

"But there must be an ending. Every song has an ending."

Djawara smiles, heading out back with the pot, toward the fire pit. "Then you'd better invent one. You're the songwriter, after all."

Outside, the chatter of roosting birds is deafening. N'Doch pursues him. It's only half a dozen steps, but it feels like he's lunging after his old grandfather. He's just realized who he can blame for all this weird shit that's fallen down around him lately.

"You got me into this, didn't you! You were . . . prepping me somehow, way back when. What's the deal? Are you some kind of alien invader or something?"

Djawara rolls his eyes. "Of course not. Where do you get such ideas?"

"I see it on the vid all the time."

"*All* the time?"

"Lotsa times."

Djawara grunts. "Consider the source."

"Whadda ya mean?" N'Doch doesn't think the idea's so far-fetched, what with all else that's been going on. "But it's you knows what I'm supposed to do, right?"

"I know what my grandfather had from his grandfather and told to me so that I could pass it on to you."

"But why me?"

Djawara kicks up the coals of his cook fire and tosses on a few handfuls of twigs. Then he straightens and faces N'Doch directly. "There is no why. Don't you see? It just *is*. You're the newest link in the unbroken chain. The why is to be ready when the time comes, which appears to be now, so you're elected. Why *not* you?"

N'Doch can think of a billion why-nots, but he knows not a one of them will satisfy Papa Djawara. "But you got me into it," he repeats in helpless frustration.

"You got into it by getting born."

"But you got to at least have an idea!" He remembers the girl's red jewel, what she called her 'dragon brooch.' "Don't you have some, uh, magic sword for me or something? Some kind of, what's it, a rune book, like in the fantasy vids?"

"This is not a fantasy vid."

"Damn right! And it's no dream either, like I kept hoping!"

A few weak flames start up and Djawara sets the pot to boil on the iron grate. "Besides, if I gave you a book or a sword, you wouldn't believe in it."

"I might."

"Inanimate objects bear only the power you yourself invest them with. You're having trouble believing in a living dragon."

"Oh, I believe in her all right. I got no choice. I'm stuck with her, and you ain't got a clue to offer me!" He's shouting now but even over his own outraged squall, he hears the familiar sound. Both men freeze and fall silent.

Whock-whock-whock-whock.

Djawara points toward the sound. N'Doch spots the five swaying pillars of light, bright pendulums slicing the night sky. He imagines a huge, long-legged spider, stalking him through the dark bush. He ducks back under the porch roof. Inside the house, the dog patter stills. The girl comes to the door, and he waves her back urgently.

In the yard, Djawara murmurs, "Don't worry." But N'Doch sees he must be a little worried or he wouldn't be whispering or listening so hard himself.

The search beams swing here, there, then approach, like sharks swimming through the darkness, pulling the copter behind them. The light flows up over the compound walls and flares across the treetops, setting off a loud chorus of bird protest. The birds lift and settle, lift and settle. One roving beam slides over the cook fire and beyond, then reverses itself and returns, blasting Papa Djawara with its icy glare. N'Doch shrinks into the shadowed corner of the cooking porch. Djawara looks up, shielding his eyes against the light, and is no longer N'Doch's mysteriously powerful relative but a pathetic old man, blinking and staring up out of the bush, caught in the innocent preparation of his evening meal. The light passes by, circles the empty courtyard, scrapes slowly across the bird-cloaked trees, and moves on.

Djawara waits until the sound has faded. Then he bends to stir his pot. "I didn't say I didn't have a clue. . . "

The old man spoons out cold rice while the vegetables are cooking, then sends the dogs outside the walls to hunt, telling them to be careful, strange things are abroad in the night. N'Doch digs into his pack and presents Djawara with some of the fish he's dried back on the tanker. The girl looks puzzled when Djawara lays out a square yellow oilcloth on the floor, places the big flat bowl of rice and dried fish and squash in the center, then settles himself down in front of it.

N'Doch is embarrassed. He doesn't mind the old style cooking so much—in fact, this rice dish called chebboujin is one of his favorites. But why can't the old coot have plates and forks and a table, like folks do in town? Some old traditions are just stupid. What's the girl gonna think?

But Djawara slides a cushion toward her feet and invites her to sit. When she does, he goes about picking out bits of fish and squash with his fingers, stacking them along the rim of the bowl nearest her. He chatters away in German all the while, explaining himself, N'Doch figures, since the girl nods and reaches with the correct hand to begin the meal. He thinks it's gross, and he's amazed that she accepts the old man's word without question, like she just doesn't know any better about old people and their uncool ways and notions. Nevertheless, he drops cross-legged beside them, knowing he'd better eat the old man's way or he likely won't eat at all.

Erde was charmed by the little mage's courtly manners, and thanked him graciously before eating the first of the choice morsels he'd set aside for her. The food was delicious, and it was an effort to sit up straight and not gobble. N'Doch seemed very shy about eating at first. Perhaps he was just making sure she and Djawara got enough before he started in on it.

It seemed like years since she'd eaten a fresh vegetable, though it was only since Deep Moor. Oddly, this tiny compound reminded her of the women's secret valley, in essence if not in physical reality. She decided Master Djawara would feel very much at home in those fertile meadows, as the women would in the heat and dust here. Immediately she felt as protective of the mage and his home as she did about Deep Moor. She studied every detail of his exotic dwelling: the rough yellow walls and baked mud floor; the flat, bright weave of the fabric hangings; the low wide benches, tossed with cushions, that hugged the walls in between shelves crammed with colorful books. Then there were the mage's alchemical lamps, whose flames rose and fell on command, like the cook fire back in N'Doch's stronghold, the castle he called a ship. And she knew true magic lurked outside, beneath those modest trees whose shade had swallowed up two full-sized dragons without a trace. When she'd looked for Earth in her mind soon after, he wasn't there. She hoped they'd gone hunting again, and would bring back a load of fresh fish to swell this good man's scanty larder. She waited until he'd eaten enough to slake his hunger, then blotted her lips gently with the hem of her linen shirt and told him of the dragon's dilemma.

He listened through to the end, only nodding now and then. He seemed unsurprised by the dragons' ignorance of their own Purpose. When she was done, he got up to make tea, a thick, sweet brew that he served in tiny, delicate flagons without handles. Only after the second serving did he return to the subject, with the suggestion that a quest after an unknown grail might be all the more passionate for being fueled by mystery. Erde could see he put great value in uncertainty. To her mind, he revered it rather too much, but she'd never say so, out of courtesy. Just as she was considering how to probe him further, she felt the dragons return, sleepy and sated.

—*Dragon! Welcome! Did you bring food for this good old man?*

—*Of course. I am no ungrateful guest.*

—*You are the very soul of gratitude, my dragon. Now, we are discussing important things. You must stay awake and listen.*

—*We spoke of important things as well. My sister has remembered something further.*

"Oh, what is it?" Erde exclaimed aloud. "Oh, Master Djawara! The dragons have news!" She translated as Water explained.

—*I said that there are more of us. Now I recall the others' names: They are our brother Fire and our sister Air. Air is the one we must find. Air was firstborn. She will know what our Purpose is.*

"Great," said N'Doch. "So now we're looking for two people."

"A person and a dragon," Erde corrected.

"Perhaps they are one and the same," offered Djawara.

"Why do you say that, Master Djawara?"

"Because it seems likely that the eldest should be the one responsible for gathering the others when the need arises."

"But what's the need?" demanded N'Doch.

"Indeed, that seems to be the question," Djawara agreed.

With their news delivered, the dragons had gone to sleep. Erde wasn't sure how much help their news had been. "I beg you, honored sir, surely there is some advice you could offer us, to further our Quest, to help us find the Summoner?"

The mage did not hesitate. "You must go to the City."

The words struck home, and Erde wished Earth had stayed awake to hear them. The City. The idea kept reappearing in different guises, in Gerrasch's reading of his bones and pebbles, in Rose's Seeing, even in Erde's own invented Mage City, with its white towers crowding a green horizon. She'd conjured it first to give a lost and despairing dragon a goal and an image of hope, but perhaps her vision represented a truth after all, guessed at by instinct or sensed by some power of Seeing she didn't know she possessed.

But N'Doch, hearing this once the old mage remembered to translate, raised a terrible fuss.

"To the City? Are you nuts? We barely got out of *town* alive! How'm I gonna go walking into the City with a dragon on either arm? Might as well send up a flare to Baraga right now!"

"Calm, calm, my boy," Djawara soothed.

"Then don't tell her such things! Look, I know you

don't want us here too long, 'cause it's dangerous for you and we'll eat you dry, but you gotta have a better idea than that! Mama said you . . ." N'Doch stops dead, hearing an eight-year-old's whine coming out of his grown-up throat.

Djawara stares him down a while, nodding and pursing his lips.

N'Doch looks away, humiliated. More quietly, he says, "Fâtime said you'd know what to do."

Djawara lets apology hang unvoiced in the air. Quietly, he pours the third round of tea. Then he replies, "You are all welcome in my house for as long as you care to make it your home. And you would probably be safe. And we would somehow manage to feed ourselves adequately—it's easier when you have help. But there is a greater need here."

N'Doch knows this. And sees that he'd hoped to avoid the urgency of it by bringing the dragons to safety in the bush. But safety is not uppermost in the dragons' minds. Not even in the girl's, despite her moments of fear and reluctance. He sees that now. He hears the music of dragon presence in his mind, pressing him to action. His shoulders droop. "Okay. So it's gotta be the City, you say. Got any idea how?"

Djawara looks to the girl, questioning her a bit like he's checking up on stuff he already knows. She tells him something that surprises him. His eyebrows arch and he nods quickly, pleased. He turns briskly back to N'Doch.

"Well, first of all, since you grew up in the City, a place-image to travel to is not a problem."

"I don't know . . . it's been a while."

"You've been there more recently than you've been here, am I right?"

N'Doch nods. Lying to the old man is hopeless.

"If you could bring them here, you can take them there, and you certainly will know your way around when you get there."

N'Doch has to admit that's also true.

"Secondly, Baraga's not the big man in the City that he is in town."

"So? It'll just be someone else after us."

Djawara dips his head doggedly. "Thirdly, your Visitors' gifts will allow them access as free as any."

"What gifts?"

"The Visitor Earth's great Gift of Stillness, which renders him invisible."

"More like a big rock. I've seen that one."

"A rock to you, who can sense his presence. Invisible to most of the world."

N'Doch shrugs. He has no way to deny this. "And the other one?"

"The Visitor Water is a shape-shifter. Didn't you know?"

"What's a shape-shifter?" But already, he does know. He sees the blue dragon in his mind, slimming to fit the close passages of the derelict tanker, lengthening to reach the high clerestory windows. "How much can she shift?"

Djawara spreads his hands in front of him, seeming to inspect each finger carefully. "Why don't you ask her?"

Chapter Eighteen

She's waiting for him when he slouches out into the dark front courtyard, full of cheb and sweet tea and questions he's not sure he wants to ask.

She's crouched catlike, facing the door, and the big brown guy is nowhere to be seen. N'Doch can't decide whether he feels like he's on some kind of weird first date or like he's facing the Mother Superior of his Catholic grammar school. He's never been alone with her before. The dragon, Water—he forces himself to think of her by name—is both winsome and officious, both animal and somehow more than human, and the real problem is not so much that he doesn't want to relate to her but that he doesn't know how.

He stares at her and she stares back. He wonders if he should think of her as a woman, if that would be a healthy thing to do, or for that matter, if it's what she would want. He's had friendships with women before, though not many, a few older women musicians he wanted to learn from. Mostly, sex got in the way. Either he wanted it, or they did, or both did but not for long. And then, the relationship was blown. It's okay with the girl—she's way too young and anyway, she wants to be his sister. With her, he's already put sex from his mind. But Water is a grown-up, and definitely feminine. So what kind of relationship are they supposed to have? He tries to imagine having sex with a dragon. Pretty kinky all right.

He's still staring at her when she begins to sing to him. Not out loud, and he's glad of that. Any song this hot would alert Baraga's sensors immediately. The beauty of it lays him out. Even the raucous birds have quieted. In the back of his mind, the bizarre thought is born that it's the dragon who should be the big pop star. And he could make it happen, if he could just get her into a studio. . . .

But in his heart, he knows this is music for his ears only. *His* music. Someday he might remember it and write it down, polish it up for public consumption. But for now, he'll just listen.

When she's done, she's still staring at him. He feels awkward, reading expectancy in her bottomless gaze. He wonders why she isn't talking to him, then realizes he's the one who's withholding. He hasn't allowed that inner letting-go that lets her voice into his head alongside the music that seems to invade willy-nilly with a power all its own. He decides he'll wait a while yet, and sing her some of his songs. It'll be like foreplay.

He starts with a lightweight piece, about a man trying to discover if his wife's been unfaithful. It's his usual opener when he plays in the market square. The shoppers don't want anything too serious while they're busy bargaining. It's better when he has his 'board hooked up, though he's done it plenty of times without, since he can't always afford to recharge his battery pack. But he likes the melody even without. It has a certain plaintive comic sweetness to it, especially the chorus, which he's really getting into, singing away with his eyes closed, when he happens to steal a glance at the dragon to see how she's taking it. He nearly stops breathing.

There, right in front of him in his grandpapa's courtyard, in place of a silver-blue dragon, is a pathetic crumb of a man, big-nosed, stooped, a little pudgy, a lovesick nerd casting his droopy eyes about in helpless suspicion exactly as N'Doch had imagined the guy when he wrote the song. He's speechless. He doesn't understand what's happening.

The image dissolves, or rather, re-forms before his very eyes into a silver-blue dragon. The process is not instantaneous and watching it makes him definitely queasy. When she's fully herself and staring at him again, he's still speechless, and without a defense left in the world.

—*Did I get it right?*

It's all he can do to nod.

—*Let's do another one.*

Her voice in his head is light and brisk, oddly familiar. Not unlike his own, but with an added undertone of Well-it's-about-time-we-got-down-to-business.

"Umm," says N'Doch, mostly to see if he can still produce a human sound.

—It feels pretty good. Hardly tires me out at all.

"Umm," he says again, then clears his throat. "Feels good?"

—You don't have to speak to me out loud, you know.

"Maybe not, but you know, I'm sort of used to it, okay?"

—Certainly. For now.

"Yeah. For now. So, um, then you're not used to doing this, is that what you're telling me?"

—How could I be, without you around to sing the songs?

N'Doch is rendered inarticulate again.

—I knew it from the moment I first breathed air. I've been trying to explain it to you, but you just wouldn't listen.

"Ummm. Oh." He knows now why her voice is familiar. She sounds a lot like his mother used to, before she gave up on him. "Sorry."

—Oh, I understand how hard it is at first. It's hard for me, too, figuring all this out by myself. My brother's not much help, you know.

"Your brother?" Oh, the big guy. "Really? Why not?"

—Well, he's very gifted, of course, and he has a very great heart. But he's still so young and he's like, hopelessly old-fashioned.

Deep inside N'Doch, absurdity finally brims over. He starts to laugh. First it's a chuckle, then a snort, then an outright belly laugh. It's what he's been needing and he lets it build and peak and still go on, like he's gonna laugh his guts out and with them, all the confusion and resentment and tension he's choked back since he first felt the dragon's hold on him. When he's finally done, he's breathless and gasping.

—It's not a joke, you know.

This starts him laughing again, but he's got it under control, barely. "You really are my dragon, aren't you!"

—What else did you think?

"I mean, the way you talk and all."

—What's wrong with it?

"Nothing. Hey, girl, nothing at all. And you know, you are so right. I should have listened to you earlier. Things woulda made a lot more sense!"

Now Water is wearing particularly self-satisfied expression but N'Doch is too relieved to care, now that he sees he's not going to have to talk the old-time talk and walk the old-time walk in order to get along with this critter he's been tied to by no will of his own.

"So. This shape-shifting thing. You wanna try it again?"

—You bet. I need the practice.

He goes with a different song this time, one of his favorites, about a beautiful woman he met once, walking along the beach. She'd just fallen crazy in love with some guy or other, and that's what made her so beautiful, passion that consumed her so much, she could spend an hour with a total stranger, telling him all about it. It was like living poetry. Totally unself-conscious. N'Doch had envied her. He wanted to be in love like that, still does and—as he watches the dragon's animal form slip and change and then reshape itself into the exact image of the woman on the beach—he thinks maybe he is. It won't be like being in love with a real woman, he knows that, but at least he has a clue about what to do with all these crazy feelings he'd been having. He wonders if this is how the girl feels about her dragon.

He lets the song finish, trailing out the last note. He can't help but sing it seductively. The beach woman smiles at him and melts away.

N'Doch grunts and averts his eyes. "I think I'm not gonna watch while you're doing that."

—Why?

"It's . . . well, it's kinda gross when you're in between one thing and another, you know? Can't you do it, like, *faster*?"

—NO. That is, not yet. I'll . . . work on it.

She's a lot less brisk than usual and he sees he's hurt her feelings. "Hey, look, it's awesome that you can do it. It's mega, you know?"

—But you don't like process, only results.

"No, I . . . hmmm." N'Doch decides he'll have to

ponder that one for a while. "How long can you hold a shape? Only while I'm singing?"

—*Maybe. I don't know.*

"And you don't get worn out or anything?"

—*Not so far.*

N'Doch nods to himself. Once again, the old codger is proved right. But he's not about to point that out to anyone. "So, tell me. Why do *you* think you're here?"

—*Something terrible is happening.*

"Where? How? O God, o God!" He laughs, 'cause her tone is suddenly so dire and serious. Then it begins to work on him a little. "Wait, you mean, to me? You're here, like, to protect me?"

—*No, jerk. Something much bigger than that. Something much more terrible, if you can imagine such a thing.*

He answers her sarcasm with a snort. "Girl, something terrible is *always* happening. Bombs, wars, plagues, famine, you name it. How much more terrible can it get? And so what? Ain't nothing you can do about it, 'cept move quick and avoid it when you can."

—*No. There is always something you can do. I wouldn't be here otherwise.*

To N'Doch, this is pure blind faith, kind of like religion and just as stupid. Which means there is no point him arguing it with her. But he can't let her off too easy. "So you're here to save the world, huh? If you ask me, which you didn't, you're way too late. But I guess you're not likely to be talked out of trying."

—*No.*

She looks at him, he thinks, a bit sadly, and despite his bravado, he feels a definite pang, a sense he's let her down.

"Hey, listen, you're into that, fine. I got nothing better to do." He's trying to lighten things up a little. "I don't know too much about saving the world, but I can take care of the little things. Like, I got it all figured out how we're gonna get you into the City."

Chapter Nineteen

Papa Djawara insists on giving the girl the privacy of the house, so he and N'Doch bed down on the cooking porch. N'Doch doesn't really mind, though he feels he has to grump a little bit so she sees it's not *his* idea to cater to her. But there are enough mats and cushions to soften the hard slab and the faint coolness of the concrete is actually a relief. And it's a novel and nostalgic pleasure to be able to sleep outside and not really worry too much about having his throat slit in the night. He figures the dogs will kick up a ruckus if anyone comes around. He'd have a dog in town, if it wasn't so hard to keep one fed. He sleeps well into the morning and is waked only by the racket of Djawara among his pots, eagerly preparing the midday meal. He's surrounded by silvery piles of fish.

"They're perfect!" he croons, scaling and gutting and laying out the fillets to dry. "They brought them this morning! Isn't it wonderful? Fish for a month! I've never seen such fish!"

"Baraga's," says N'Doch sourly. "Just hope he hasn't got each one tagged with a tracer."

The prospect of fresh fish cheb has made Djawara mellow. "Now, *that* is paranoid."

"He'd do it. He's really touchy about holding on to what belongs to him." N'Doch scratches, looks around. "So where's the girl?"

"The Lady Erde is inside, looking at books."

"*The Lady Erde?*" N'Doch mimics mincingly.

"Your companion is a baron's daughter, did you know that?"

"Yeah, so she told me. Rich girl. But hey, that was

back in 900 whatever, and she didn't bring any of it with her." Except of course, one big red stone set in silver. How come *his* dragon didn't come with a jewel? "She's no better'n me now."

Djawara smiles. "Of course not. But if you bear in mind that she's grown up being treated as if she was, you might understand her better."

"I don't need to understand her. Long as she doesn't mess with me, we'll get along fine."

"I see." Djawara lays several thick white fillets in his rush steamer and fits it on top of his biggest pot. He carries it carefully out to the cook fire.

"What's she want with books, anyway?" N'Doch calls after him from the shade of the porch.

Bending over the steamer, Djawara shakes his head. "Are you always this truculent?"

"No, I . . . c'mon, Papa, I just woke up."

"No wonder your mama didn't mind when you left home."

N'Doch blinks at him. "I haven't left home."

"Well, that'll be news to your mama."

That slows him down a little. "Yeah? Well, I guess it's true I haven't been around much." But he's always thought at least she missed him. Certainly he's liked knowing she was there if he needed someone to take care of him.

He'd like to discuss this further, but the girl comes out of the house with a stack of open books in her arms, and N'Doch doesn't see that his family problems are any of her business. She greets him politely and sets the books down on the edge of the concrete, then takes the top one out to Djawara at the cook fire and starts questioning him about it. N'Doch sees all the books are open to pictures.

"So, what's she wanna know?"

"Everything."

N'Doch laughs. "Guess we'll be here a while after all."

Djawara studies the page she's held up and answers her in detail. She nods thoughtfully and goes back for another book. Djawara says, "She's trying to find her footing in an unfamiliar world, my boy. Seems she's not had much help from your direction."

"Yeah? Well, I'm doing the best I can."

"I'm sure you are."

Stung, N'Doch turns away into the house. Already, he's searching instinctively in his head for the dragon. He's pretty sure she'll be glad to see him, even if no one else is.

Waking early, Erde had found herself surrounded by the mage's extensive library. She studied the books from her pallet on one of the cushioned benches. They were not at all like the books she knew and she longed to touch them. But one did not just go fingering a mage's books, it wasn't wise, so she kept her distance until she heard Djawara puttering about outside. Then she went out to greet him respectfully and ask if one of his magical tomes might contain a searching spell to help them locate the Summoner.

The old man laughed gently. "There's no magic in these books, daughter. Only the magic of knowledge." He led her back inside, then picked out a fat one and handed it to her.

Erde received the shiny, colorful object in reverent hands. The bindings were hard and smooth but worn, she could see, with serious and important usage. It did not seem to be made of leather, but it did have a pretty design of leaves embossed in fading gold on the top cover. She glanced at Djawara and when he nodded permission, opened the book carefully. Bright illuminations greeted her, exotic fruits and flowers and trees, full of fine realistic detail without a trace of brushwork. Turning page after page, she sighed in wonder and admiration.

"That's a natural history of the region," he explained. "It describes the local plant life."

Erde nodded. His herbarium, then. Every mage must have an herbarium.

He pulled down another, larger volume. "This one's an atlas. Maps of the world." He flipped through the pages. "Ah, yes, here we go." He took the plant book from her and laid the big atlas in her lap. "This is modern Germany."

At first, the page in front of her was just a maze of colored blocks and lines. She couldn't even recognize it as a map. Then he traced out the long sinuous snaking of the Rhine and asked her to name a few familiar places. The first one they located was Köthen.

The dragon calls him to come join her, she's under the trees, but N'Doch won't go into that place after her. It's just too weird. She says it's too hot and dry in the yard for her, so each stays where they are and N'Doch sits down in the less mysterious shade of the lemon tree and sings his songs to her until Djawara calls him for the midday meal.

When they're seated once more around the communal bowl, with the dragons listening in from the trees to translate and N'Doch's mouth is watering so from the sweet smell of steamed fresh fish in tomato sauce that he can hardly concentrate, Djawara announces that he knows someone in the City who might be able to help them.

It's news to N'Doch that his old uncool grandpapa knows anyone in the City at all.

"It's been many years since we were in touch, but we were good friends then and she was a gifted woman of great promise."

"Good friends, eh, Papa Dja?" N'Doch grins at him, trying for a moment of male bonding.

Djawara smiles. "Not that kind of friends, my boy. Her interests lie elsewhere. At least, they did at the time."

N'Doch nods. He knows what that usually means, but he wonders if the girl does. He wonders if they had women who love women back in 913. He hopes so, 'cause if not, he's not sure he wants to be the one to explain it to her. Like, what if she's that way herself and doesn't know it? He wouldn't want to get caught making any kind of value judgment. Not that he minds it himself or anything. *Chacun à son goût*. He just considers it a waste of good women.

"What is her Gift, Master Djawara?" asks the girl earnestly, and once again N'Doch finds himself wishing she'd lighten up for just one damn moment. He's seen her smile, but he's never heard her laugh like she really meant it.

"She speaks with the spirits and with the wandering shades of the ancestors."

Now, *this* is the Djawara N'Doch remembers. Spooks and spirits and omens and what all.

"Is she a saint?" asks the girl. N'Doch rolls his eyes.

"No, Lady Erde. She is a human woman."

"All the saints were human, Master Djawara, when they lived. But then they were touched by God." Her thin face sobers even further, but N'Doch thinks she looks hopeful. "Is she a witch?"

Djawara chuckles. "I'm not sure what she might be calling herself these days. Then, she was my father's brother's wife's sister, and didn't call herself anything except her name, which is Lealé."

"If it's been so long, how do we find her, Papa Dja?"

The old man looks momentarily bemused. "As it happens, I know where she lives . . . I think." He gets up, crosses to one of the bookshelves and takes down a slim green book. From it, he extracts a postcard. He hands it to N'Doch.

N'Doch reads it, crinkles his brow, then reads it aloud. " 'D.—When the Time comes . . . you see she's put a capital 't' . . . 'this is the place: 913 Rue de l'Eau. Kisses—L.' " He looks up at his grandfather. "Sure this is her?"

"Oh, yes."

"*Water* Street? 913?" He looks at the postmark. "When did you get this?"

"A week ago."

"After how many years?"

"Mmm . . . nearly eleven."

N'Doch lets out a low whistle and cocks an eyebrow at the girl. "Things are getting weirder and weirder."

"Or," says Djawara, "things are exactly as they should be."

Chapter Twenty

Erde worked hard to convince Earth that she needed at least one more day in the mage's library, to absorb information that might be critical to their Quest. Then she spent her best efforts that day trying to get Master Djawara to accompany them to the City.

He talked with her tirelessly, while N'Doch practiced shape-changing with Water. He told her everything he could about the new world she'd come to, but refused again and again to go with them. She even tried tears—he remained sympathetic but steadfast.

"It is not my journey." Djawara tossed the cushions from one of the benches and lifted the lid. Inside was a riot of pattern and color: piles and piles of neatly folded fabric. "It is your journey and dragons' only. Others can and will help you along the way, but they cannot go along. Let's see now . . ." He lifted out a pile and sat with it in his lap.

"But Master Djawara, it's so much easier with you around!" Erde flopped down beside him girlishly, but somehow the fact that, even sitting, she was taller than he was undermined the effect.

"Oh, he'll come around. He's a good boy. You'll see." His round face was smooth and calm as he sorted through the fabric, pulled out a few brightly printed bundles and set them aside. "Did you ever think that perhaps you lost your voice for a reason?"

He knew her whole story by now, and it was hard to get around him. Still, Erde was embarrassed that he'd guessed so easily what she thought was so difficult. "No, I lost my voice because . . ."

"I know, I know, child. Your heart was broken. But

THE BOOK OF WATER   149

think about it a little further. Maybe you were going
to need to know how to communicate under difficult
circumstances."

Erde brightened. "You mean, it was . . .
preordained?"

"A big word. Perhaps too big, but . . ." Djawara nodded and shrugged. "Who knows about such things, eh?
Only the gods."

She knew that she should think of the mage as a dangerous heretic because he always spoke of the Deity in
plural terms. More than one God meant pagans and idol-
aters, at least in the Bible. But Djawara's gods and god-
desses sounded rather more approachable than the stern
Jehovah of the Christian Church. For one thing, you
didn't need a priest every time you wanted to talk to
them, and Erde had no cause to love priests after her
recent experience with Brother Guillemo. And saying
something was "God's will" implied being subject to arbitrary and personal whim, like the King's will or her
father's. Not that King Otto's will was ever arbitrary,
but her father's certainly was. "Preordained" made
things sound much more orderly and under control.

So, if it was important to the Quest that she put the
skills learned through two months of being voiceless to
work on getting through to N'Doch, she would accept
that burden. The mage had explained that certain concepts and ideals that she grew up with, such as Honor
or Duty, no longer had much currency. (On the other
hand, he pointed out, being a woman no longer meant
being the chattel of your closest male relative, so some
of the changes over the years were positive.) The main
thing was, she must learn to take nothing for granted.
N'Doch would truly dedicate himself to the Quest only
when he decided he wanted to.

"I understand now, Master Djawara. And though it
certainly would be more pleasant if you did come, I accept that you cannot. You are very wise."

"And you, child, are a shameless flatterer. Now, look
in the book and see if you can make this piece of cloth
look like the picture when you wrap it around yourself."

She shook out the length he handed her and gave a
soft gasp of admiration. The fabric was soft, with a
graceful drape, and of a deep indigo printed with cream

and burgundy. She'd never been allowed to wear such rich colors as a child. "It's beautiful! Are they snakes with wings? I can't quite tell."

"I don't know. Perhaps they are dragons. Try it on."

She gave it a few serious tries and thought she was just getting the knack of it when she head N'Doch laughing from the doorway.

"Papa Dja, when I said we oughta get her some real clothes, I didn't mean dress her up some hick from the villages!"

Djawara stood back from Erde at arm's length. "Why, I think she looks wonderful! This was your grandmama's best."

"Yeah, Papa D., it's cool and historical and all that, y'know, but . . ."

"And I thought it would make sense if she dressed like a villager, so the City people won't be surprised when she doesn't behave like they do."

Erde watched N'Doch rein in his mockery. More gently, he said, "But Papa, she's a white girl. She ain't gonna fool nobody."

"Oh."

Even Erde had to smile. The old mage had explained to her about the different races of humans and how it mattered to some people what color your skin was. But in her case, he seemed not to have noticed, or at least to have momentarily forgotten. Now he pursed his lips, fussed a little with the folds of the material and said, "Well, I guess you're right. She would be rather an anomaly."

N'Doch let go a sigh of relief. "Yeah. I thought maybe let her go like a tourist—Eurotrash, y'know? Which is why she only speaks German. There are still a few brave ones coming around, especially in the City. They're mostly really rich folk, but she should know how to play that role all right, eh? We'll just say she's slumming. Granmama must've had some town clothes, yeah?"

Djawara nodded and gave the lustrous fabric a final organizing pat. "A shame, really. It looks so good on her."

N'Doch is not really happy with what they've dug up for her to wear. He lays it all out in the sun on the back porch: thirty-year-old jeans with no decent patches and only four pockets, and a T-shirt so uncool it actually has sleeves and something written on it. But he figures they can barter this for something less embarrassing when they get to the City. The girl doesn't seem to realize how dumb she's gonna look, truly *flat,* but at least it's more in step than what she was wearing before. He can see she likes the idea of wearing pants—apparently women didn't do that in her day. She rejects the sensible open sandals that Djawara offers her, insisting on keeping her soft, calf-high boots. N'Doch lets her. A tourist from the colder (but not so much, these days) North might wear something silly like that without knowing any better.

"As long as you look like you pay *some* attention to your image. Otherwise, you'll really stick out." He sends her inside to try it all on.

"Surely no one can afford to worry about such trifles any more," Djawara murmurs.

"Trifles? Cool has no price, Papa."

But in fact, when the girl comes back outside with the whole getup on, N'Doch thinks she looks pretty good. The jeans fit her well. He can see she's got a shape to her after all. He may be spending more time than he's counted on just keeping the guys off of her. He glances down at his own naked torso and ragged shorts.

"Um . . . Papa Dja? You got anything I could wear?"

They settle on one of Djawara's ankle-length tunics, a light blue one he says he doesn't wear any more. On N'Doch, it comes to just below his knees, but the girl seems relieved when he puts it on.

"Oh, my, that looks very good on you, N'Doch."

Already, he's itching and feeling confined. "I'm gonna hate this."

But he has to admit, it'll help him blend better with the day-to-day crowds. For the first time in his life, anonymity sounds like a good idea.

The dragons are eager. The blue one is at the end of her patience, which, N'Doch is beginning to suspect, is never very long to start with. But he likes that about her. He's impatient, too, except when it comes to making his music. Like now, he's as ready as he's gonna be, and he's been hearing copters in the air again, Papa Dja says more often than usual, so maybe they better get gone before they get the old man into trouble he didn't start.

Except, in a way, he did. But N'Doch's not going into that again, not now at any rate.

The girl has told him about this big shed kind of place she hid out in back in her time, and he thinks it's not a bad idea to start them out in the old industrial sector.

"There's lots of empty buildings out there," he explains. "Big old factories and warehouses, all closed down."

Djawara clucks sadly. "It was a thriving district in my day."

"Yeah, well, that was before they started getting everything from China and Brazil. It's one big junkyard now. Our main problem'll be finding a big enough place that don't already belong to squatters. Papa, you got anything around by way of weaponry?"

Djawara sits up a little taller. "Only my cooking knives, my boy."

This is what N'Doch has expected, but he thought he'd try anyway. "Never mind. I'll manage. But here's the hard one. You got any money?"

"You mean, cash?"

"Yeah. Only, no paper. It's worthless, y'know?"

Djawara disappears inside for a while and comes back with a small handful of coins.

N'Doch looks them over. "Not a bad stash. I know it'll be hard for you. Just give us what you can."

"It won't be hard on me. Any kind of cash is useless out here these days. If you can't eat it, drink it, or wear it, it isn't worth anything to anybody."

"Okay." N'Doch holds out his hand, then says, "No. Give 'em to her. She'll keep 'em for emergencies. So. I guess that's it. We'll be on our way now."

He doesn't really want to leave the cool shade of the lemon tree. The night before, as he lay on the cooking porch awaiting sleep, he realized that it'd been an hour, maybe even two, since he'd last scanned for copters, or reflexively searched the shadows for the lurking knife. A whole hour of feeling safe enough not to listen—what a luxury! The thought came to him, just before he dropped off, that he could live out here and be happy enough. Certainly he'd be healthier, helping the old guy dig and carry water for the vegetables, hunting with the dogs in the evenings out in the bush. But that thought was drowned out instantly by the habitual panic. Out here, he'd be nothing, everyone would forget about him, no big recording contract. He'd never be famous. He'd sing his songs, but no one would ever hear them, 'cept one old man and a few washed out villagers.

No, it was better to be going to the City. Life was in the City.

But, he told himself, when this dragon thing was over, he'd make sure to come visit Papa Djawara more often.

Chapter Twenty-One

They waited until midnight, then bade farewell to Master Djawara and went on to the City.

Erde thought it oddly familiar, to be dropped precipitously into the dark corridors of another strange town, so familiar that she expected (without reason) the ice and cold of the brickyard in Erfurt. Instead, the City was hotter than any place so far. There was a roaring all around them, like the rush of great winds or falling torrents, and the air smelled of . . . Erde's only thought was that it smelled like Death.

Earth coughed, a raw convulsive sound. Erde felt Water warning them to silence. She pressed a little closer to her dragon and stroked his cheek.

—*It smells like our dreams.*

—*Yes, Dragon. It surely does.*

N'Doch sniffed, peered into the blackness, and murmured, "Well, folks, the honeymoon is over."

He's chosen the big parking lot beside the derelict rubber factory. He figures they can land two dragons there without running into anything, and also, it's likely to be deserted at this time of night. There's hardly enough working cars or trucks left in the City to fill up a lot this size, and those that there are, won't be out here in the Wedge.

And he's guessed right. The wide stretch of broken tarmac is clear of anything but dried weeds and rubble, with a few burned-out wrecks along the periphery. He'll steer clear of those: even charred black, a truck cab is good cover for a single squatter, armed and dangerous. The long low warehouses are scattered, this far out. Lots of open space between. Plenty of copters prowling the skies, but they're all off a ways, over where he can see streetlights, where the buildings get closer together, in town toward the point of the pie-slice shape that gives this neighborhood its name. And past that, the broken profile of Downtown spreads its colored glow on the horizon as if the whole town is on fire. *And sometimes it is,* N'Doch reflects sourly.

But power to the Wedge was turned off long ago, like with most of the outlying sectors. Not enough of it to go around any more. N'Doch is used to moving around his own town on the blackest nights, but even he is hesitant about charging off into the unlit streets of the City.

"Man, it's dark out here," he mutters.

—I can help, you know.

"Yeah? What d'ya have in mind?"

Water's tone is faintly superior, but N'Doch backs off his irritation, since he's found she can usually deliver on what she promises, and at the moment, he needs all the help he can get. She doesn't answer him right off. Instead, he feels this strange sensation, like she's caught hold of him from behind his eyeballs.

"Yow." It doesn't hurt exactly, but for a moment, he's got double vision. He must have staggered, 'cause he's stumbling into the girl, and she's grabbing his arm for support.

"Yow," he says again, then he and the dragon are in sync and he can see with a clarity that takes his breath away, like in broad daylight except it's all black and white, and all the surfaces of things seem to be alive with tiny wormlike movements. N'Doch knows he hasn't chewed or smoked anything lately, and the moon didn't just come out all of a sudden. Besides, he's pretty sure it has nothing to do with his eyes. It's like he's *hearing* the shapes and spaces around him: the dragons, the girl, the nearby hulk of the rubber factory with every broken window and cracked cinder block picked out in awesome detail. He makes himself start breathing again.

"Wow. Radical. It's like . . . *sonarvision!*"

"N'Doch, are you well?" asks the girl.

"Yeah, fine. Just had my eyeballs turned inside out, that's all."

"I beg your pardon?"

"The dragon . . . Water . . . she . . . Hey, can your guy, like, you know, make you hear like your own ears never could?"

"No." She thinks for a moment. "But he teaches me the scents of things that I never even knew had smells."

"Huh. Like Papa Dja used to say about his dogs: They read the air and the ground like he reads his books. But you can't, like, see in the dark?"

"Oh, no—right now I'm as blind as you are."

"But I'm not, you see. This critter has ears like Baraga's spy-eyes."

"You mean, Water?"

"She can turn sounds into images, and transmit 'em right to my eyes. So I *can* see in the dark. Cool, huh?"

"That could be very useful."

N'Doch laughs, looks at her, then laughs again. She's serious. He can't believe this girl's total lack of irony. "Well, yeah, it could. Okay, first thing is, find us a proper hidey-hole."

"Shouldn't we go in search of the Mage's friend while it's still dark?"

"Safe digs first, girl. Wandering around the City at night is asking for it unless there're a lot more of you or you're a whole lot better armed than we are."

"But in the light, we will be seen."

"In the light, we'll blend into the crowds, or at least, that's the idea. Besides, Mme. Lealé wouldn't take well to us banging on her door in the middle of the night. In the City, no one goes out after dark, girl, unless they've got trouble in mind."

With his new sonarvision, N'Doch cases the outside of the rubber plant, looking for squatter-sign: newly boarded-up doorways or broken windows conveniently shaded with tarps. The really dumb ones, or sometimes a family that's newly homeless, make the mistake of letting some lantern-light show or leaving a telltale bit of clothing hanging out of a window to dry. N'Doch doesn't detect any of that, but he does spot a heap of recently dumped rubble just below an open shaftway a few stories up. He snorts softly and shakes his head. Whoever's got the factory is careful, but not careful enough.

"Let's move on," he whispers. They haven't been absolutely silent. They may have been spotted already, and they're carrying valuable food and water that he doesn't want to lose this early in the game. "This way."

He leads them away from the factory, through the dry weeds and shattered asphalt. He's thinking of a place he crashed at once, with a guy he knows won't be there unless he's come back from the dead. It took some getting into then, but once you did, it was big inside and pretty secure. It's not far, so he heads that way. The girl is stumbling on the asphalt chunks, rattling the scattered litter of metal shards. She slows, knowing she's making too much noise, but she doesn't have his magic new Sonarvision—he thinks of it with a capital "S" now, like some new product he's invented—so he takes her hand and guides her through the worst of it. The dragons, he notices, move along in utter silence. He doesn't even bother to ask how they manage that one. He's beginning to take dragon miracles pretty much for granted.

They pass a cluster of collapsed warehouses, no sign of habitation. He recalls just in time that there's a particularly nasty toxics dump up ahead. One drawback of his new vision: it doesn't help him read caution signs in the dark, unless the print has dimension off the surface. Besides, he's willing to bet there aren't any signs. The government-of-the-moment is too busy staying in control to worry about the public welfare. He takes a detour around the site, then continues onward.

Now and then, one of the snooping copters swings a little too close by for comfort, and N'Doch makes everyone duck and hide, just in case. But since he's got them moving so slow and careful, in the interest of silence, he also takes the opportunity to use his Sonarvision to scout for salvage. He sees everything's been pretty much picked over already, and the sigh comes up from somewhere deep without his even knowing. He can never quite let go of that old scavenger's dream—even though he knows it's unrealistic—that some day he'll light upon a huge and entirely unspoiled cache of prime bartering goods. Then his fortune'll be made, and he can buy those big amps and that new keyboard that'll make him a star.

Farther along, he catches a big whiff of the dead smell, over to the left, and leads his gang away from it. If it was light and he was alone, he might investigate, just see if anyone's been along yet to shake down the stiff. He hates doing it, but what's dead is dead, he figures, and he's turned up some valuable stuff that way. Tonight, however, he'll move on.

The girl's caught the scent, too. Her grip on his hand, light and impersonal, tightens. "Is it . . . Plague?"

"Which plague's that? AIDS? Cholera? Typhus? Bubonic?"

"Are there so many? What have the people done to make God so angry with them?"

N'Doch snorts. "God hasn't anything to do with it."

"But the Plague is God's punishment, N'Doch."

He stops short. Even before he opens his mouth, he knows his response is over the top, and some part of him wonders why. He grips the girl's shoulders, not kindly this time, and it's all he can do to keep from shouting. "Girl, let's get this straight: Diseases come from germs, not some god idea. This ain't 913 and even if there was a god then, he sure ain't here now unless he's a world-class sadist!" He can see, with his hearing eyes, that she's gazing at him astonished, a little frightened. Is it him she's scared of, or what he's saying? He gets hold of himself, lets her go, then dusts her shoulders off in comic apology. But he doubts she'll buy it as only a joke. "You believe in God, huh?"

She nods mutely, as if she can't imagine an alternative.

"Well, sorry," he murmurs. "I just hate listening to that god stuff. I grew up with the imams and the mullahs and the ayatollahs throwing their weight around, and it didn't do nobody any good but them, far as I could see. Lining their pockets, just like everyone else, 'cept they expect to be treated special."

Soberly, she nods, like she understands him now. "God is not always well represented by his representatives on Earth." She takes his hand conciliatorily. "But we don't ever have to talk about God if you don't want to."

N'Doch sees this is as far as he's going to get with this issue for now unless he wants a raging argument on his hands, which would likely attract all sorts of unwanted attention from the shadows around them. "Fine," he says. "This way."

The place they finally come to is an old peanut processing plant that fell in on itself after being gutted by fire. N'Doch suspects it wasn't very well built to begin with, but apparently the basement was, because it's still intact, beneath a protective and concealing layer of charred steel and construction debris. He locates the entrance, a narrow fire stair covered up with the same battered sheet of corrugated metal he recalls from before, lying there as if thoughtlessly tossed aside. *Man,* he thinks, *hide in plain sight. It sure seems to work. Course there could still be somebody down there, as clever as me. . . .*

He crouches a distance from the concealed stair, pondering his next move.

—There is nobody down there.

He starts, remembers he's not alone in his mind anymore. "How do you know?"

—Easy. If there were, I could hear their breathing and the beating of their heart. Oh, and my brother wishes me to add: he could smell them.

"You're sure of this, now. . . ."

—Of course I am! Why say so otherwise?

Hasn't she ever heard of bravado? Maybe dragons don't need any ego boosting. Anyway, he decides he'll trust her, on the basis of what her awesome hearing has managed already. He grasps the metal sheet and slides it to one side as quietly as possible. A receding darkness yawns beneath, but the air flowing up out of the hole doesn't smell any worse than might be expected.

"Doesn't seem like anything's died down there recently," he mutters. "I'll give it a try."

—You will lose your night sight down there.

"Yeah? How come?"

—What I can't see, you can't see.

He'd swear the blue dragon is smirking at him. "Fine. I'll do it blind."

"Wait," says the girl. She fishes in her pack and unwraps a squat stub of candle. She offers it to him as if it was edible.

"Way to go, girl," N'Doch crows softly, reaching into his own pack. He's got plenty of matches but nothing to light. "What a team."

Clutching the candle stub, he eases himself into the hole. The girl makes a sign to follow, but he waves her back. It's tricky going. The steps are crumbly with broken concrete gravel. He doesn't shift his weight onto his

leading leg until he's very sure of his footing. He stops
at the end of the first flight, where the stair takes a turn
and the dragon will lose the line of sight. His head is
below ground level, so he risks the brief flare of the
match through his cupped hands and lights the candle.
The stained cinder block walls close in around him. The
stair feels suddenly airless, narrower in light than it did
with his sonarvision. He sniffs carefully but smells only
the usual metallic tang. With his free hand, he reaches
for his switchblade.

It gets cooler as he descends the long stair. At the bottom, the smashed-in fire door has been yanked half off
its hinges. N'Doch slips through the opening and his
footsteps start to throw back echoes. His rat phobia is
sending warning tingles up his spine, but he reminds himself how the blue dragon has already cured him of one
major killer bug, so she can probably handle a rat bite,
even a sick one. Still, he listens real hard, sure he's heard
a quick scuttle and rush off in the corners of the basement. He holds the candle high and moves into the cavernous interior, testing the musty, still air as he goes. The
dusty hulks of boilers and air-conditioning units crowd
along the walls like parked cars. A maze of pipes and
ducting, bristly with char, hangs in the darkness above
his head. Despite being twenty feet underground, he feels
vulnerable here. But he recalls a smaller storage room,
dry and empty, across the basement somewhere to the
right. If he recalls it right, it has some kind of grating
that lets in air.

Again he hears a rustling sound. He whirls, candle out-
stretched in one hand, switchblade in the other. The
flame catches in something bright, reflective, quickly
moving, like a weapon or someone's eyes. Then it's gone.
Too tall for a rat, too short for a man. Now he hears
nothing but the rush of blood and adrenaline in his own
ears. He's getting the real creeps now. He's got to find
that room and call the dragons down. He steels himself
and turns away, though he feels the itch at his back like
he's being watched. He locates the room, pretty much
where he remembered. At the open doorway, he sniffs
again, real cautiously: ash, stale machine oil, a faint sour
tinge, nothing rotting. He's worried that his fantasies will
have enlarged and improved this hidey-hole unreason-

ably, but it is as he'd hoped—a big cement rectangle with one lockable door, a high ceiling, a dry coolish floor, and a faint drift of air past him at the door toward the invisible outlet above. The place has been cleaned out and appreciated by at least one man he knows. He wonders if anyone found it since Habbim died. He studies it carefully, then lets the dragon into his mind so she can transmit the image to the big guy. With her there, he feels a little bit steadier.

—*I could have shifted and come with you, if you'd asked me. You were never in danger.*

"Yeah?" His voice startles him, erupting into the silence. "I don't know. I'm sure there's something down here."

—*Impossible.*

"I dunno. . . ."

The two dragons and the girl wink into existence around him. N'Doch lets out a breath he didn't know he was holding.

"What do you think is down here?" asks the girl.

Now his fear embarrasses him. "Oh, nothing. Y'know, an animal or something."

This doesn't seem to bother her too much. She shudders and shrugs like she's used to having that sort of trouble around. But N'Doch knows there's hardly any animals left in the City except rats and men. Fact is, he's not sure what it could have been, but he's pretty sure he didn't imagine it.

—*Yes. You are right. Something was here.*

"You mean, it was here just now and it left? How'd it get out? There used to be only one way into here."

—*Well, it's gone now, whatever it was.*

The dragon seems to think that should be the end of it, but N'Doch is glad this hidey-hole has a lockable door. Meanwhile, they might as well get bedded down. He sees the girl already looking around for her spot.

"You take the far corner," he says, gearing up for an argument. But she's cool with that, and he relaxes. He stopped running with gangs once he became a teenager, so he's not much used to moving about in groups. He'll feel better if he can control the layout. But he does let the dragons scope out their own territory. "I'll hang here by the door." He closes it and locks it, though it makes him feel more trapped than safe. Then, to the right of it, where the door can't swing against him if somebody bashes it in, he tosses down his pack. "Okay, rest up. Come morning, we'll go looking for Lealé."

He settles himself on the concrete with his pack for a pillow, and blows out the candle. Darkness encloses him like a shroud. The dragon must be asleep already. He knows she's there, not ten feet from him, but he still loses faith in her existence if he can't actually see her. He'd hate to sound like some little kid whining in the night, so he figures it's time he tried the mind-calling thing the girl talks about. She says you just shape your thought like an arrow and send it. N'Doch wonders if she's seen a real arrow. Maybe she has. Maybe they still use such things back in 913. He feels himself drifting and pulls himself back.

—*Dragon? Hey, Dragon! You there?*

—**Of course I'm here. Where did you think I was?**

—*No, I knew you were here, but I, like, called you, y'know?*

—**Yes . . . ?**

—*Well, y'know, I never did that before, so I . . .*

—**You woke me up.**

N'Doch is miffed. She didn't congratulate him or anything. It was pretty easy, he has to admit, but she could have at least noticed.

—*Okay. Got that. Now, since you're awake, you sure you'd know if there was something alive down here?*

—**Absolutely.**

—*You'd, like, smell it or something?*

—**Or hear it.**

—*What if it wasn't making any noise?*

—**I'd hear it living. Go to sleep.**

He tries to, but just before he does, he hears the rustle again, muffled this time, like there's something moving about out in the main basement. He gets up and checks the door, which is latched and sturdy. But then, because he's come to trust the dragon's word on things, no matter if he questions her as if he doesn't, he finds himself thinking, well, then, maybe whatever's out there isn't technically *alive.* . . .

And that keeps him awake for way longer than he likes.

Chapter Twenty-Two

Erde lay awake for a while, tucked against Earth's foreleg, listening to the deep bellows-rush of his breathing, always more like a movement of air than an actual sound. Usually it lulled her, but tonight it seemed less soothing. She decided he was not asleep after all, only pretending to be, and not doing a very good job. *In fact,* she thought, *none of us is asleep. That's why the room feels so . . . full.* Probably they were all thinking about the next day and what it would bring. She had heard her father's knights use the same tone the night before a battle that N'Doch used when he talked about going into the City.

—*Dragon? Are you sleep?*

—**No.**

—*I didn't think so. Me neither.*

—**Good. That means you're not talking in your sleep.**

—*Do I?*

—**You used to, when you thought you'd lost your voice.**

—*But I did lose my voice.*

—**You didn't lose it. You just couldn't find it.**

—*Oh, really? And tell me, Dragon, do you know how many angels can dance on the head of a pin?*

—**What's an angel?**

—*What's an . . . well, angels are . . . never mind. It's an expression. Alla used to say that to me when I continued an argument to too fine a point.*

—**It's not too fine a point if you think about it. You actually did have your voice all along. You just** *couldn't use it, except when you were asleep and didn't know any better.*

—*Now, Dragon, I did not lose my voice on purpose.*

—*Purpose is a complex thing to define, is it not?*

—*You sound like Master Djawara. He said . . . Wait. Did you hear that?*

Erde stiffened against him, listening.

—*What?*

—*Do you smell anything out there?*

—*Out where?*

—*Out there, in the bigger part of the cave.*

Earth's body stilled. His breathing quickened. Erde waited while he did his search.

—*No. I smell nothing but unliving smells. Fire smells and the smell of the forge. And the smell of those things the boy calls machines.*

N'Doch and Master Djawara had explained about "machines," but Erde thought it sounded like alchemy all the same: burning certain precious substances in order to make the inanimate move. Just as the thing they named "electricity" was clearly strong air magic: calling down invisible power from the sky.

—*I'm sure I heard something. Remember, your sister said . . .*

—*She said something had been there and was not now. I think you are tired and should go to sleep.*

—*Well, I'll try.*

And she did, for a while, but she failed.

—*Dragon?*

—*Mmmm?*

—*Have you heard the Summoner at all since we left Deep Moor?*

This time, she detected anxiety in his reply and instantly regretted the question.

—*I have heard nothing. I have waited and listened. Perhaps I am listening too hard.*

—*Don't worry. I'm sure we're on the right path. Don't you agree?*

—*I am eager to find Mistress Lealé.*

—*So am I.*

—*Good night.*

—*Good night, Dragon.*

Finally, having shared her doubts, Erde fell asleep.

Almost immediately, she was dreaming.

She was home again, not home at Tor Alte but in her home time, in the chill mud and sleeting rain of a battlefield. It was early evening. From her vantage on a low hill, she could see the men and the carts moving about, hurrying to pick up the dead and the wounded before dark, butchering the dead horses to feed what was left of the armies.

In her waking life, Erde had never been to a battlefield, had certainly never seen so many dead in one place or had to listen to the moans of the dying. Their agonies filled her ears. The rutted mud was black with their blood. She wanted to turn away, but the dream would not let her.

Now a man stood in front of her on the hill. The same blood and mud stained his silken tunic and spattered his fine mail. A boy in blue-and-yellow livery raced up with linens and a steaming pitcher, and the man bent to scrub the mud and blood from his face and beard. This time, Erde was unsurprised to recognize Adolphus of Köthen, but she was sorry to see, when he turned toward her, how haggard he looked, how sad and bitter. She had assumed a warrior enjoyed fighting. Again, she thought he would speak to her, as his angry glance was so direct, but again, he looked past her and called out to someone farther along the hill. She turned and saw her father, equally battle-worn, standing beside two of his vassal barons, with a tattered parchment map stretched out between them.

In the dream, she understood she was seeing her father as Köthen saw him: florid, a bit too pudgy for a true fighting man, overly proud of his mane of prematurely silver hair, brave enough but not very bright. She understood also now that Köthen was using her father to further his own ends, but that he was no longer sure that he was getting the best of the exchange.

An early darkness was falling, thick with cold mist and cloud. Köthen signaled the boy to pour more heated water into his cupped hands. He drenched his face and beard, scrubbed hard, rinsed again, and toweled off. Out on the plain, the laden carts drew together, conferred, then split off in two directions, one group across the hill where Erde stood, the other up the longer slope on the far side of the field. Following Köthen's pensive glance, she picked out a scattering of men and horses, one flying the royal standard, another the deep red of the King's Knights.

That red—the familiar red of Hal's leather jerkin, worn despite all dangers to attest to his unswerving loyalty to the King. Seeing it, Erde sensed emotion stirring, and saw how cruelly dispassionate she was in this dream, as if she had left all feeling behind to make this journey back to where the battle had finally been joined between the King's armies and the forces of the usurpers. Men had fought and died, and Erde did not know if Hal or Rainer or King Otto himself still lived. She wished she stood on the opposite hill, instead of with her father and Köthen. At least she would know the worst. But then, she realized, she'd be wondering about Köthen.

Why was this man so often in her dreams? Not only dreaming about him, but almost as if she was him. She turned back to watch as he tossed the bloodied, dirty linen to the boy.

"See to my lord of Alte, that's a good lad."

The boy bowed and hurried off toward the gathered barons. Köthen followed more slowly. Erde's father looked up as Köthen approached. He waved away the boy with the water and lifted a corner of the map to jab a finger at it.

"What's left of them will fall back and join Otto's main force somewhere around here, I figure."

Köthen nodded tightly. "Peasants. Farmers. Tradespeople. Hardly a fair contest, wouldn't you say, my lord?"

"Ah, but if we meet up with nothing more than peasants, we should catch up with the King in three days' time, and that should be that." He let the corner drop and took Köthen's elbow, drawing him aside. Köthen eased out of his grasp but moved with him to avoid insult. "The good brother has his men spreading rumors in the villages," Erde's father continued quietly. "Once Otto is dead, Prince Carl can be accused of trafficking with witches, and gotten out of your way."

Köthen shook his head. "No. Call him off. I don't want the boy harmed. He shouldn't have to pay for his father's mistakes."

"Brother Guillemo says no bishop will crown you King while Otto's heir lives. The people, at least, require a semblance of legitimacy."

"That foul priest does love the fire." Köthen's jaw tightened. "No, von Alte, there'll be no burning the Prince. House arrest will do fine. Carl doesn't want to be King anyway. If he did, I'd put him on the throne and rule as his regent. Call Guillemo off."

"Brother Guillemo is not mine to call off, even if I might wish it otherwise. You know that as well as I do." Von Alte took a long look at the younger man before continuing. "A little late for scruples, my lord of Köthen, is it not?"

"Never too late, my lord of Alte. There'll be no burning."

Von Alte's glance slipped aside. "You may not have the say on that, my lord. . . ."

"And why is that?"

Erde's father turned, called out to the men behind him. "Bessen! Get over here and report to Baron Köthen what you heard just now."

A skinny, scrub-bearded younger knight hurried toward them. "Concerning what, my lord?"

"Concerning Prince Carl."

The man's worry lines deepened. "Right. The Prince." He faced Köthen breathlessly and bowed.

"Come on, Bessen, out with it," growled Köthen.

"An escape attempt, my lord. This morning, while you were showing yourself so valiantly on the field . . ."

"An 'escape'? As you may recall, Bessen, the Prince is a guest in my tent, free to come and go."

"As long as he doesn't go very far," put in von Alte.

Bessen nodded eagerly. "And that's just it, my lord. The Prince took advantage of your . . . generosity and tried to flee. The White Brothers foiled his attempt and brought him back."

Köthen lunged at him, grabbing huge fistfuls of his tunic. "What have they done? Is he alive?"

Bessen cringed in his grasp. "Of course, my lord baron. The Prince is safe in Brother Guillemo's custody."

Köthen shook him like a rag doll. "SAFE? You call that safe?"

Von Alte levered an arm between the two men, to pry them apart. "Get a hold of yourself, Köthen. Poor Bessen's only the news bearer."

"And that's what I'm surrounded with! Everyone reports! No one sees anything! Yet what remarkable detail they all bring to their accounts!" Köthen shoved Bessen away in disgust, then tugged his tunic straight. "My lords will excuse me while I go rescue Prince Carl from his 'rescuers.' "

"You might want to reconsider that," said von Alte.

Köthen turned back sharply ."I beg your pardon?"

"The good brother thinks the Prince is better off in his hands. You had better go well-armed and well-accompanied if you think to change his mind."

Erde felt rather than saw rage boil up inside Baron Köthen. She also sensed how well he controlled it—unlike her father, who would have raved and thrown things. Köthen's rage spoke only through a certain stiffening of his spine, a narrowing of his glance. He stared at von Alte a moment, then nodded brusquely. "I see. So that's how it is."

"That's how it is." Though her father's reply sounded smug, Erde read the terror in his eyes. The awful priest still held him in thrall.

And then she was drifting away from them, as if someone was tugging on her arm. Other voices were calling her. She resisted, wanting to hear what Köthen said before he turned on his heel and stalked away. The voices, insistent, urgent, drowned out his reply. She wanted to stay to find out what would happen to Prince Carl. She wanted to know if Hal was all right. She . . .

"Wake up, girl!"

. . . was aware of her body again. Someone was shaking her, hard. She didn't want to come back to the heat and darkness.

"C'mon, now, wake up!"

—Breathe! You must breathe! You cannot leave now!

Erde let go of Köthen and her father, let herself relax, let her chest heave to draw in the hot, smelly air. It made her cough.

"There she goes. She's okay. She's awake now."

Strong hands hauled her up into a sitting position.
"Whadda ya say, girl? You awake?"

—*Are you returned, Lady Erde?*

—*I am here, dragon.*

Erde flexed her hands, rubbed her face. Her body tin-
gled, as if the whole of it had gone dead numb and was
reawakening. N'Doch leaned over her, a darker shadow
in darkness softened by the faintest scatter of light filter-
ing down from above. She gripped his arm to steady
herself. "I was somewhere else."

His laugh was relieved. "I'll say you were."

"I went home."

—*You went there without me. Do not do it again.*

That's what was so strange, Erde realized. She and
the dragon had always shared their dreams since they'd
been together, but not these recent ones of home and
her father and Baron Köthen.

—*It just . . . happened. How will I prevent it, unless I
stay awake?*

—*I will keep watch. It is the priest who draws
you.*

"No!" she cried out, aloud.

N'Doch jerked his arm away. "You talking to him
or me?"

—*Yes. I believe this is so. My sister agrees.*

—*But how, why would he do that?*

—*How, I do not know. Why, because he seeks to
separate and thereby weaken us. He is learning new
powers. As ours grow, so do his. But I am alerted
now, and will keep watch.*

Now the waking, fetid darkness would be a sanctuary
from the perils of her dreams. Erde slumped in dismay
and felt N'Doch watching her.

"You with us, girl? You all right? It's time we got
moving."

"I am fine, N'Doch. Thank you." But when she got to her
feet, it was a struggle. The dream had left her weakened and
trembling. "Will we break our fast before we go?"

N'Doch laughed.

"Yeah, we'll eat up, for sure. Don't want to be carrying food around in the City, not where anyone can see
it, at least."

N'Doch breaks out the water and some of the fish and vegetables that Djawara packed up for them. He's hoping to actually buy bread and cheese with the cash the old man's laid on him. And wouldn't some coffee be radical. . . ?

It might be the dimness of the light falling through the grating above, but it strikes him that the girl is looking really flat out right now. He hands her an extra section of cucumber. "You wanna stay here, like, rest? Let me scout out Lealé?"

"No!" she comes back fast, like she doesn't want to miss this trip for anything. But he's worried now that she might slow him down.

"Won't he, y'know, be lonely?"

It's a nice try, but it doesn't work. She lays a caressing palm on the big guy's flank. "He will be with me, even while he's here."

He understands that she likes that part, the constant lurking presence that makes him feel crowded. "Hunh. Okay. Ready, then?"

She nods, a little too brightly to be convincing. He turns to the blue dragon. "What about you? All set to boogie?"

—*Remind me.*

N'Doch chuckles. "Sure thing, girlfriend. Here we go, then." He does a few soft bars of the song they've agreed on.

—*More.*

"You forgetful or what?"

—*I like listening to you.*

The pleasure this brings surprises him. But hey, why not? An audience is an audience. He sings a bit more, starts to get into it, and finishes the verse. He's moving on to the chorus when he spots the girl gazing at him in wonder and admiration. He finishes the chorus directly to her, then grins and sketches out a little bow.

She claps her hands, delighted. "Why, you sing very well, N'Doch! Like a true bard!"

"A *bard,* huh? You mean, like one of those guys who used to go around the place singing about Robin Hood?"

She looks sort of blank, but she nods. "Sometimes the bards do travel, yes, if the weather's good and the roads are passable. Mostly, they sit by the kitchen hearth and make up songs about doomed lovers and great battles, at least that's what my grandmama's bard Cronke did. And then he'd sing them for her in the great-hall on feast days. His songs always made me sad, though."

N'Doch finds himself smiling. The picture is there in his mind, and he understands he's getting it from her through the dragons—like a window opening onto the past. He *sees* the long room, hazed with smoke from the great stone fireplace that takes up one whole wall. He feels the need to stoop away from the low-slung ceiling beams, dark and rough and as big around as his thigh. Women in long skirts are moving about in the dim light, hauling pots and kneading dough, and an old man sits in a corner, scrunched up over a stringed instrument that N'Doch doesn't recognize, 'cept he knows it's an old one. He wishes he could hear the music. He's sure it would be plaintive and sweet. But there's no sound in this memory.

"Can you sing one of his songs?"

It's as if the idea had never occurred to her. "Oh, no. I could never *sing*."

"Why not? Everyone can sing."

"They can?"

"Sure. Don't you ever, like, sing in the shower?"

N'Doch can't remember the last time he was near a working shower, but he figures there's probably still plenty of water where she's come from. But she gets that blank look again that reminds him they're speaking different languages in more ways than the obvious one. "Never mind. I'll show you one sometime."

Meanwhile, behind her, the blue dragon's been going through her transformation, and he's been distracted so he didn't have to watch till she's just about finished. Even though this is the one they've practiced most of all 'cause it's easiest for her to maintain, it still gives him a chill to see his song come to life like that: there right in front of him, his little brother Jéjé, as he imagined he would have been if he'd lived to be nine or ten. N'Doch is glad he's warned the girl ahead of time.

" 'Kay, man. All set," the apparition squeaks.

N'Doch swallows hard. "Gotta work on the voice a little."

"Sure, guy. Anything you say." Now she's taken up a higher, lighter version of his own voice, which makes more sense for a ten-year-old kid, but doesn't go too far helping N'Doch feel any less weird about the whole business.

But the girl's smiling at the thing, her hands clasped in glee. "O excellent, Mistress Water! O wonderful and marvelous! What shall we call you?"

"Not Jéjé," N'Doch puts in quickly.

The boy/dragon pouts. "No? Then how 'bout . . . L'Eau?"

The girl picks up the game. "Or *Wasser!* I'll call you *Wasser!*"

N'Doch tries it. He can get his mouth around the syllables easy enough, so it seems as good as any made-up name except that anytime he hears it dragon-wise, in translation, he's gonna hear his own name, which is just about as strange as hearing his own voice. He shakes his head hopelessly. "All right, we're off, then. Stick close and keep your eyes open every minute."

The boy child salutes him saucily. The girl giggles. N'Doch pulls up short at the door. He has a sudden heart-stopping image of his younger self razzing Sedou. Now he's glad he never got around to writing songs about his older brother. "Look, this ain't no picnic, you got me? Hang tight, don't attract attention, or you get left behind."

The girl touches his arm. "She will behave, N'Doch."

His mouth tightens. He nods. He's forgotten for a moment that he's yelling at a dragon.

Chapter Twenty-Three

Up on the surface, it's already hot, though the sun has barely cleared the broken eastern skyline. N'Doch would have preferred to emerge in darkness, so as not to give away the entrance to their hidey-hole, but that chance is past and besides, he doesn't see anybody about when he peers cautiously over the top of the stair well. He gets the others out, the hole covered, and them well away from it before he halts for a reconnaissance.

There's not much left to look at, out here in the Wedge. Collapsed, burned-out buildings, rubble, dust. N'Doch picks out the distant profile of the Diouf, a half-built soccer stadium. Ran out of money after the last coup, so they never did finish the seating. The soccer team belongs to Baraga now, and plays in his private stadium for the cameras and five hundred of his most intimate friends, but on-the-rise rock groups use the Diouf if they can afford the security. The really hot groups don't play live gigs any more. Too much risk of getting blown up or shot, or having the so-called fans riot and trash the place, then having to pay up the damages. When you get big, you gotta go remote. It's the one thing N'Doch figures he'll regret about being famous, not being able to perform live any more.

The apparition stands beside him. "Move it or lose it, bro."

N'Doch curls his lip. "Who taught you how to talk?"

"You did."

"No way." But it makes him wonder. Is that what he sounds like to the girl?

He leads them away from the wrecked processing plant, cutting across parking lots, keeping to the wide-open spaces as much as he can. In the early daylight, the buildings and the lots and the unpaved roads are all stained the same dry, hot red of the dust. N'Doch sees a few souls stirring here and there, bent over, languidly picking through the rubble, probably the same rubble they've picked over a million times. He keeps his distance and moves on.

The main road into town is still paved, but junk-strewn, full of potholes and sifted over with a fine layer of red silt.

"Not many trucks through here lately," N'Doch remarks. Lots of footprints, though. Lots more than you'd expect, given how deserted everything looks. He hears a few copters off in the distance, and waves the boy/dragon over to him. "You hear any of those gettin' close, you let me know, okay?"

The apparition nods. Being out in the open seems to have sobered it considerably.

The girl is doing what he said, sticking close, gazing about like she's trying to memorize everything. "Was there a war?" she asks him finally.

"Nah." Then he reconsiders. "well, actually, yeah—a lot of little ones. But really it's, y'know, the climate thing."

She gets quiet a moment, in the way he's familiar with now, waiting for the dragons to puzzle out a particularly opaque translation problem. Finally she says, "You mean, the weather?"

"Ha. It's much bigger than weather. I mean, the weather's the *result,* but . . . well, the way the vid guys say it, all our bombs and factories and cars and stuff have really screwed everything up, which means the air and the water and even the dirt, y'know? The whole gig." Now that he's into trying to actually explain this global warming thing, N'Doch realizes he doesn't really know what the hell he's talking about, just the garble he's heard on TV. But it's okay, 'cause this girl's not gonna know any better. He could tell her it's all a space alien conspiracy and she'd buy it just as fast. At least he's got the basic idea. "So it's getting hotter all the time and we don't get the rain any more when we should, while some other part of the world is being flooded out, which means the farmers can't hardly grow anything in either place. And then, half the time, what they do grow is full of chemicals and all kinds of toxic shit from the ground, so you shouldn't eat it even though you're hungry enough to eat the toxics raw if they was right there in front of you."

He takes a breath. She's staring at him, wide-eyed. He thinks, just in case she is picking up on some of this, maybe he should feed it to her slower, 'cause it's a big one, maybe the biggest. If she really doesn't know what "climate" means, doing a major core dump on her all at once is gonna be a waste of time. Plus get him all riled up, since nothing makes him madder than the notion of some day soon not being able to eat, drink, or breathe. But it does occur to him that he'd better start keeping her out of the sun. Pale as she is, she'll burn up like an old scrap of paper.

"At any rate, it ain't good, and it's getting worse."

Her brows knit. "People have made this happen?"

"That's what the science guys say. Course, with them, you always gotta ask who's paying their salary."

Her frown deepens. "But . . . why would you do this?"

"Hey! It wasn't me, all right? I just live here. Besides, nobody did it on *purpose.* Lotta times, you do things, you don't think about what else's gonna happen because of it."

"And when they knew what was happening, they stopped it?"

"Well, no, not exactly." He realizes now that the science part of this isn't the toughest part to explain after all. "Like, for a long time, nobody believed it, and then the scientists were scared to say anything 'cause fixing it was gonna cost so much money. Now I guess everybody just thinks it's too late."

"At home," the girl says slowly—she's mulling it over hard, and beside her, the apparition is wearing a pensive expression that Jéjé never would have. "At home, we are having wrong weather, too, except it is the opposite: it is too cold and wet. It snowed in the middle of August."

"Sounds like paradise."

"Oh, no, N'Doch. Our farmers can't grow enough either. The grain was thin and blighted. The fruit trees hardly ripened. And the kitchen gardens were blackened by frost just when they should have been producing their best."

"Hmm. Sounds bad." N'Doch is distracted by movement up ahead, a couple of thin dogs snarling over some lumpy thing in the road. He doesn't want to tangle with them or their lump. Where there's two, there's usually more, and who knows what the lump might be carrying. "This way."

He veers off the road and cuts across a dusty field that used to be a playground for the factory workers' kids. He recalls a few big metal-frame swings and a beaten-up slide, but all that's left now are the poured concrete emplacements that held their legs. The clarity of the memory surprises and disturbs him. He speeds up, as if he could walk away from it. The girl has to pick up her pace to stay even with him.

"But, N'Doch, at home we have none of these things you talk of, these . . ." She tries to reproduce the French she'd heard, having no word of her own for "bomb" or "car" or "factory."

"But you burn stuff, right? You're wearing that fancy knife, so you must melt down metal somehow to make the steel. And if it's so cold, you're probably cutting down every tree in sight just to keep warm."

"No, N'Doch, it is not like it is here. There are many trees everywhere. There are always enough trees."

"Yeah? Well, some day there won't be." But he can see she can't imagine it.

"But still, the weather is perilous. The priests say . . ." She glances his way. "Please do not be angry, N'Doch, but the priests *and* the people say it is God's will. That the snow and the ice in August is God's punishment for their sins."

N'Doch decides to be patient about the God thing for once, since the girl obviously doesn't know any better. "So what's everyone done in 913 that's so sinful?"

That kind of slows her down, like maybe she hasn't thought about it. "All the usual things that God says are sinful, I suppose—Envy, Sloth, Gluttony . . "

He notices she leaves out the Murder and Adultery parts. "Gluttony. Now there's a sin I could really get into right now."

"It's not a joke, N'Doch."

"C'mon, girl, be real! The whole concept of sin is a joke!" He didn't expect his patience would last, though he's not sure why her innocence riles him so much. "There's no such thing as pure good and pure evil. There's only life, and getting along in it as best you can."

She stops, with the dust of her own footsteps rising around her like smoke, as if the ground was on fire. Her eyes are dark and serious, and N'Doch feels pinned to a wall even though there isn't a wall anywhere in sight. "There is true evil, N'Doch. I have met it in person. And there is true good. How can you say otherwise when you have known a dragon?"

Now that's interesting about the dragons. She says it without a trace of doubt in her mind, but when N'Doch sneaks a backward look at the image of his dead brother trotting along behind him, he knows he's not so sure. Pure good, in his book, should not be so fuckin' weird. But to get her moving again, he says, "Yeah, I'm sure you're right. We'll talk about it later."

In the far corner of the field is a big tree. The old men used to hang out in its shade, drinking their endless little cups of sweet tea and arguing politics. Sometimes Sedou would be there, N'Doch remembers, arguing with them. There's no one sitting under it now, and the tree itself is scarred and leafless. But N'Doch decides to take advantage of its thin shadow for old times' sake. When he was little, venturing forth in his first kid-gang, this tree marked the end point of the Wedge, where the factories and warehouses—often the goal of the gangs' scavenging forays—blended into the blocks of walled residential compounds and the narrow streets of the commercial districts. He leans against the tree, surrendering to the memory, then shakes himself alert. He can't get caught standing around out here in the open. Having safely passed the dog pack, he heads back to the boulevard, which will take them through the DMZ into the City proper and the comparative anonymity of the daytime crowds. The address Djawara has supplied for Lealé is in one of the more stable, conservative neighborhoods, which means he'll have to play the role and blend, if he doesn't want to get stopped.

He surveys his little entourage for a final reality check before they hit the inhabited zone. The girl looks pretty convincing, now that she's sweated up a bit. Except, of course, she's white. The apparition would convince anyone but N'Doch. Or his mama. Amazing how something like a song can conjure a person so totally—with details, even, that he didn't know he remembered, like how Jéjé's skin was the lightest in the family, so much that Fâtime's girlfriends teased her about who the father might be. It occurs to N'Doch that with his own dark skin, the pale girl, and the apparition in the middle, they might be taken for a family. Which is an okay cover, after all. He wonders if the girl will mind. Maybe she won't even notice.

The low-slung buildings are closer together here, lined up more or less regularly along the dusty street, with alleys and empty lots between. The DMZ is the buffer between the full-out war zone of the Wedge and the residential districts of the sometimes working poor. N'Doch leads his group past used furniture stalls, junkyards and car repair shops, all boarded up now, plus a couple of derelict gas stations. One still has its chain-link intact and some dogs inside, plopped in the shade but ready to spring on any intruder. It might be doing business now and again, if the owner has a buddy in the current government or can luck into a black market score to fill his tanks.

Past the DMZ, things begin to come to life—a few people are moving about, mostly men and conservatively dressed, but real people with homes and televisions, not squatters. They're doing their day's chores before the midday heat settles in. Watchers, N'Doch calls them. He divides the world into the Watchers and the Watched. The Watchers live only vicariously. The Watched live on television. He counts himself as being Watched-in-waiting, and hopes he doesn't have to wait a whole lot longer.

Along the ragged curbs, the single-story shops are still mostly closed, their once-bright facades sun-bleached to pale yellows, pinks, and salmons, their carefully hand-lettered signs chipped and faded. But here and there, a steel accordion gate is half-open, a corrugated metal blind is raised, even an awning is partly extended. No merchandise hangs around the doorways. Nothing is displayed out front, nor for that matter inside, N'Doch suspects. In this part of town, you just have to know who's selling what and when they might have it, as well as be pretty well known to the seller, or he won't even let you into his store, never mind do business with you.

"We'll just move on through here," N'Doch urges as the girl starts to lag, wanting to peer inside the shadowed doorways. "Folks aren't gonna like you staring like that."

"Like what?"

"Like a tourist." Which is what she is, N'Doch reminds himself. He'll know he's into the real City when everybody they pass doesn't step aside to avoid them or stop to glare after them as they go by. He's encouraged to see a water seller's stall that actually has a customer, and two old men under a scrawny tree playing checkers with washers and lug nuts on a curling paper board. Finally they move through a gang of small boys kicking a much-patched soccer ball around in the middle of the street, and N'Doch relaxes his pace a little. People actually live here, Watchers for sure, but still, people who won't immediately try to rip him off. They live in boxy cinder block houses with tiny concreted front yards, invisible behind high stucco walls with steel mesh gates. N'Doch lived in one himself for a while, half a mile or so away, before things got so bad, before Sedou was killed, before . . .

He'd known that's how it would be—like it was going back to the bush and Papa Dja's, only worse—the flood of memories he'd rather not be swimming in, struggling to keep himself afloat.

"Damn!" he says softly.

"S' up?" asks the apparition.

He gives it a look, and the way it hauls back from him tells him the look was not kind. The girl sees it, too.

"Is something wrong, N'Doch?"

He's not used to it, having his feelings work him over like this. He feels like a boxer on the ropes. To cover, he grabs at the apparition and cuffs it playfully. "Nothin's up, kid. Nothin' at all."

Erde sensed that something was still not right between N'Doch and his dragon, but because she had bonded so instantly with Earth, she had little advice to offer them. They'd have to work it out on their own, as she was sure they would.

Besides, she couldn't concentrate on N'Doch and Water—or Wasser, as she had dubbed Water's shape-shifted form. She could only look around and around, trying to soak in all the newness and make some sense of it. Entering this strange town, this City, was like step-ping into the intricately painted pages of her grand-mama's illuminated Bible, where every leaf or flower, even the stones in the walls of the ancient sacred cities of the Holy Land, looked exotic and unfamiliar, nothing like the lands around her father's castle. Not the ruddy dusty street, not the pale, petal-colored crumbling walls or the sparse, dry vegetation or the dark skin and bright clothing of the inhabitants. And, of course, there was the heat, the constant heat. Perhaps it was the unrelent-ing sun that made everyone's skin so dark. Perhaps if she stayed here long enough, she would be burned as black as N'Doch.

As they moved deeper into the City, there were more people in the streets, and the buildings got taller. Soon they were tall enough to cast a shadow along one side of the road, and of course everyone chose to walk on that side, so it began to feel like a crowd, almost like the crowds in the towns at home on festival days, except this crowd was neither joyous nor rowdy. Erde thought this particularly strange. Except for the children, or their parents disciplining them, all these people were rushing here and there in total silence, keeping strictly to their business. No one stopped to greet an acquaintance or exchange a bit of gossip, perhaps because there were so few women about. As the crowd thickened, the men even shouldered and shoved one another, and no one stopped to apologize. If one of them pushed her hard enough, Erde worried, she might stumble and be tram-pled by the throng. Or get separated from N'Doch, who was slipping between the moving bodies with the speed and ease of an eel through swamp grass. She'd be left behind and he'd never know he'd lost her until it was too late. Of course, Earth could come instantly to rescue her, but Erde could just imagine what sort of terrible panic that would cause, if even a half-grown dragon ma-terialized in the midst of this crowd. She snatched at N'Doch's arm, but he shook her off surreptitiously.

"Not here!" he hissed. "Hold on to the kid if you want. Nobody'll mind that."

To his surprise, she gets it right off.

"Is it improper?" she asks.

He nods. "In public. In private, men and women do whatever they want together." He glances back, grinning, but she's looking both shocked and curious, and since he's not hot to be the one filling her in on the facts of life, especially right here and now, he lets it drop.

"We're getting close now," he says, but she's already distracted. She's stopped dead in front of a barred-up shop full of televisions. The window actually has most of its glass left. Only one row of the vids are on, a big enough expense but the least a shop owner can get away with and still expect to sell anything. One of the early morning series is playing. A couple of teeners have stopped to watch. The girl is being shoved this way and that, but she's staring at the bright line of repeated images like she's never seen a TV before. Remembering where she's come from, N'Doch realizes she probably hasn't. Hard to imagine such a thing. A few guys pull up to stare with her, in case she's spotted something they don't want to miss. N'Doch doubles back through the crowd to stand beside her before she and the apparition get 'napped right out from under his nose.

She doesn't have to look up to know he's there. That dragon thing again. It keeps unnerving him. She reaches for his arm, then stops herself halfway, so her hands gets left floating in the air.

"What magic is this?" she whispers.

The older guys glance at him, check themselves in the cracked window glass and move on. The kids are glued to the tube, and ignore them. N'Doch can see the girl is scared. "Only electronic magic. Remember I told you about electricity?"

She nods dubiously. "How are the people in the windows made so alike? Are they golems?"

"Those aren't windows. And those guys aren't really there. It's only a picture."

"Someone has painted them?"

"Not exactly . . ." He can see this is gonna be a hard one.

"But they move. They're so . . . like they're alive."

"Well, they are, only not there in the box. Somewhere else." He tries to see the vid images the way she must be seeing them, as something alien and inexplicable. He fails.

"What's it for?" she asks finally.

"To watch. Whadya think?"

"Why should we watch what other people are doing? Isn't *that* improper?"

"They're actors. They get paid to be watched."

"Why?"

For a moment, he's at a loss for words. "Look, um, the vid . . .those boxes . . . they show all the daily series, and you can hear all the big groups play, and see the sports, y'know?" His voice trails off. She doesn't have a clue, though he can see she's trying hard to get one. He has a sudden vision of his mama, alone in her little cinder block house with the box going all day long, the steady reassuring background noise of her life. "It tells you stories," he says finally, "and keeps you company."

"Oh," she says wonderingly. "Stories."

She lifts her hand toward the window, as if to reach through the bars to touch the dancing images. N'Doch grabs her wrist.

"Unh-unh. Might bite."

She recoils, stares at him, then back at the screens as if she expects the vid characters to leap out at her, teeth gnashing.

"I mean, you might set off the alarm, that's all." He sees he's freaked her a little, but since she doesn't know what's what, it won't hurt to have her thinking twice before she goes around laying her hands on things. "Let's move, okay? You'll see plenty more vids around. Everyone's got 'em."

She follows, but her brain's obviously on overdrive. "Master Djawara did not keep one of these companions."

N'Doch laughs. "Papa D. thinks the box is evil."

"He does?" She stops to stare back at the shop again. "Why? Is it *black* magic?"

He motions the apparition to pull her along faster. He's impatient now, tired of having to explain things all the time. He wants to get on with finding Lealé. "Depends on who you ask."

"If it was black magic, the Church wouldn't let it be shown out like that, in public daylight."

He likes that phrase, "public daylight." As if there was any other kind. "The church ain't got nothing to say about it. This here's the Land of the Prophet."

"You mean, like Isaiah or Ezekiel?"

"Mohammed. You never heard of Mohammed?" He grins, 'cause he's never been devout, only so much as he's needed to get by the imams. "You a pagan, girl."

Instead of the laugh he expected, he gets a frown. She turns pensive. "Brother Guillemo says so, too. He called me a witch."

"You keep time-traveling and running around with dragons, what d'you expect the brother to think?"

"I know," she agrees seriously.

"Hey." He shoves her gently. "It's a joke. You really oughta lighten up, girl. I mean, this is some old guy way back when, right? You're here, in 2013. Whadda you care what he thinks?"

She shakes her head. "He's there now, even as we speak. He haunts my dreams. He'll be there, still after me, when I go back."

N'Doch can see that this Guillemo guy is a real bad thing in her life. "How do you know you gotta go back?"

She blinks at him, opens her mouth, then shuts it again.

"Bingo. Never thought of that, didja?"

She licks her lips, then purses them. "No, of course I will go back. I must go back, when the Quest is fulfilled. I am sure of that. But . . ." She tosses him a sidelong little glance, impish almost, the closest thing to humor he's seen in her so far. "Perhaps in a country where there is so much magic all around, it is not so terrible to be called a witch."

Chapter Twenty-Four

When he finally locates Water Street, and the address that Papa Dja has given him, it's a narrow side lane, rutted and unpaved, with the usual walled yards and cinder block boxes at the back. No names on the gates, only faded numbers, but the street is pretty clean, not much litter around. N'Doch rings the bell at Number 913.

The gate is solid sheet metal, scarred as if someone had been beating on it with a sledge. A little sliding panel is set at eye level. N'Doch rings for several minutes without result.

"Gotta be patient," he assures the girl. "Just gotta wait 'em out."

The apparition is scuffing his feet in the dust, his hands shoved deep into the stretched-out pockets of his shorts. N'Doch remembers these shorts now, except they were *his* shorts, not Jéjés, and were particularly prized for being the match to a pair worn by his favorite pop star at the time. And that's what weirds him out. The time was ten years ago and he hasn't seen those shorts since. Or the pop star.

"She ain't in there," says the apparition.

"I said, you gotta be patient. People don't just come racing out to see who's knocking. They might be watching their show. They might feel safer not being home."

The apparition shrugs. "There's someone in there, yeah. But it ain't her."

N'Doch's fists ball up on his hips. "How the hell do you know?"

The girl looks right and left. The street is empty. She

lays a warning hand on his arm. "Surely you've seen by now . . . if she says she knows, she knows."

Damn! He's forgotten again. Of all the shapes the dragon could have pulled out of his mind, it had to be this one? N'Doch guesses he should be grateful she's not walking around looking like his mother. Or Sedou. This last notion leaves a hollow ache in his gut that he'd rather not have to deal with. He resolves to stop thinking of the apparition as his brother Jéjé. He reaches to ring again. "Gotta at least find out if she lives here."

The little panel jerks open on squealing tracks, just a crack. "Who is it?" demands a voice.

It's a woman's voice, despite its gruffness. N'Doch assumes his best public persona, the one that always charms the ladies. "We're looking for my grandpapa's dear old friend, Mme. Lealé Kaimah. Is she at home?"

"Yeah? Who's this grandfather?"

"He is M. Djawara N'Djai."

"And who are you?"

"I am his grandson, N'Doch N'Djai."

A pair of crow-footed dark eyes scrutinize him through the narrow crack. "Lealé doesn't live here anymore."

"Excuse me, but my grandpapa received a postcard from her just last month giving this as her address."

A short pause on the other side of the gate. "What do you want with her?"

N'Doch lets a whiff of the bush spice up his performance. "We're just into town, my family and I. First time, y'know? Papa Dja asked us to look Mme. Lealé up, see how she's been all these years."

"Huh," scoffed the voice. "Looking to sponge off her, more likely, now she's found something steady for herself."

N'Doch lets his shoulders droop. This woman wants abject humility. "No, no, Madame. In fact, my grandpapa was not even sure that his old friend was still living until he received her card."

The voice chuckles. "Oh, she's living, all right."

"Then I may report to him that she's well?"

"You can go see for yourself. I guess you sure are new in town, 'cause it's no mystery to anyone local where Lealé's living these days. You know where's the Marché Ziguinchor?"

"No, but I'll find it, I'm sure."

"Yeah, well, you go down there. Ask for the house of the Mahatma Glory Magdalena."

"The what?"

But the panel slams shut as N'Doch leans toward it. He almost rings again, but he's pretty sure he's gotten all he's gonna get out of this woman.

"I think she means 'who,' " notes the girl. "The Magdalene was . . ."

"I know, I know." He doesn't, but he's tired of being informed all the time. He stands chewing his lip for a moment. "The Ziguinchor. What's Papa Dja doing knowing someone who lives there?"

"Then you do know it?"

"Oh, yeah. But I wasn't about to tell her that."

"Why? What is it?"

"A part of town where rich people play, but not the kind like Baraga. He's bought himself some respectability, at least. The Zig is where the rich and famous go when the old money won't have 'em around." He doesn't know how to say it to the girl, but he's wondering if Papa Dja's old pal has made her success working in a pleasure house.

"Is it far?"

He shakes his head, but he's thinking that the Zig is the sort of place he'd rather go by himself, not dragging some white girl and a kid after him. He'll have to turn down offers for them right and left, and somebody might get argumentative. But he's got nowhere he can stash them meanwhile, so he'll have to risk it. Better in the morning than later on. At least a tourist will be less of a novelty there. He's never seen the Zig by daylight. It's the one part of town that doesn't even get started until after dark.

He leads them back to the main drag, and all the rush and bustle on the boulevard. They're just crossing to the shade on the north side when he hears sirens coming. His first thought is, *Run!* But he can't, with all this new responsibility. He hurries the girl and the kid onto the sidewalk, against the charred wall of a boarded-up house. The crowd stops and lines up along the curb to stare at the oncoming vehicles.

The girl moves in close, looking up at him wide-eyed. "What is it?"

N'Doch bites back an impatient reply. Probably she saw him tense up, and it worried her. It's not her fault she doesn't know anything, but he's just not cut out to be a tour guide. "Somebody famous."

"A powerful lord?"

N'Doch laughs. "You're thinking, like your daddy, hunh?"

"No, N'Doch. My father wasn't very powerful. I used to think he was, but that's because I was a little girl. Now I see that he wasn't as powerful as he wanted to be, and that's why he allied himself with Brother Guillemo. To get more powerful."

He blinks at her. This story of hers is beginning to sound interesting. Maybe there's a song or two in it. "Well, that's the way of it, isn't it? Power and money." He stands up tall to see over the heads of the men in front of him. The lead pair of motorcycles have just run the signal at the intersection, their headlights flashing. Behind them are four more, rolling along two by two, a stone's throw ahead of the limo. Behind the limo, more flashing lights and the sirens of the rear guard. N'Doch lets out a low whistle. What blows his mind is not the numbers or the noise, but the style and splash.

The six lead cycles are bright cherry red. All their chrome parts are polished gold. The riders are uniformed in opaque black helmets and glossy black boots, and skintight gold bodysuits set with bits of mirror, so that each is shaped by darkness top and bottom and by edgy, dancing sparkle in between. The limo itself is mirrored gold all over, even the windows, and entirely anonymous. No logo, no flag, no banners, none of the usual personal advertising. Not even an initial.

"Who is it? Who?" the crowd murmurs.

The hot air is full of guesses and pronouncements. Even N'Doch finds his cool ebbing away. The sirens fill his ears and set his blood pounding. The bright heavy sun, rising toward the midday heat, pales to insignificance before such brilliance, such blinding spectacle. He imagines the frosty interior of the limo. He smells the soft leather of its seats, the sensual perfume of the woman next to him as he rides across town to the studio to shoot his latest music vid. Maybe it's two women, and they're chatting softly while he, aloof, gazes through the gold-tinted window at the people who've lined the streets to stare at him with fascination and envy. And then a new thought enters his fantasy: Will he remember where he's come from, when that day arrives? Will he remember that it was him once, lining the streets? He'd like to think he would, but . . . hey, why should he? Nobody else does, once they've made it.

The limo slides silently past. Behind it are another six cycles, roaring and flashing. When they've all gone by, the street seems vastly empty. The crowd mutters and complains.

The girl is entranced. She cranes her neck after the taillights, clapping her hands in glee. "Oh, a golden carriage, oh wonderful! Is it a king?"

"You think everyone rich is a king? We don't have kings here, you get it?" Like the crowd, N'Doch is left aroused and dissatisfied. "Don't know who it was, anyway. A publicity stunt of some sort, maybe. Who'd go to all that trouble and expense, otherwise; without telling you who they are?"

He's aware now of a low keening sound in that place between his ears where the dragon music has staked its claim. He looks around, realizing he's lost track of the apparition. He spots the kid balled up in the corner of a gated doorway, shoulders hunched, his hands pressed hard to his ears. "Oops," says N'Doch.

He slips through the dispersing throng to catch hold of the kid and help him to his feet. The girl is there instantly, wrapping her arms around the boy-thing, crooning to him soothingly. This time, N'Doch thinks, it's she who's forgotten the kid's really a dragon.

"Musta been the sirens," he offers. "Hurt his . . . her ears." He assumes it's pain. What's a dragon got to be afraid of?

"No," the girl replies. "Well, yes—mine, too . . . but not only. Mostly, it was the badness, she says."

He finds himself staring at them, this alien white girl with her arms around *his* dragon. "So why can't she say that to me?"

The girl looks up at him. "But she does. She will. She wants to. But you have to listen."

"Hunh," N'Doch says. They've been this route before. But he thinks maybe he'll just give it a try, for the hell of it. See what it's like. "So, remind me—how do I do that?"

She cocks a dark eyebrow at him reprovingly. "You know how, N'Doch. Just like you do it to understand me. Like you do it when you want to. Only you also have to do it when you don't want to."

"Hunh," he says again, but then he's more interested in something else. "What'd she mean, the 'badness'?"

"It was a feeling she got." She releases the apparition and urges it gently toward him. Sounding just like Papa Dja, she says, "You ask her."

N'Doch lets out a breath, feeling already like he's conceded something. "So. What did you mean?"

The apparition shimmers, seems to swell and shrink with its own breathing. N'Doch throws up both hands, palms out.

"Not here! You can't! Don't change!"

The apparition shakes its head, shivers and settles back into a steadier reality. "Sorry. Just kinda threw me there, y'know?"

"Umm . . . no. I don't."

"In the car, I mean. Not bad, exactly. Something . . . wrong."

"Yeah . . . like what?"

The boy-thing shrugs, as if its panic had never happened. "Don't know, bro."

N'Doch lowers his hands. "Great. All that fuss for an I-don't-know."

"It's a warning," says the girl.

"Right. 'It's a sign! It's an omen!' You sound like Papa Dja."

"You could do worse," notes the apparition. "At least he gets it right some of the time."

Unfathomably irritated, N'Doch rounds on him. "Whadda you know? You never even met him!"

Now the apparition looks truly offended.

"Of course she did," puts in the girl hastily.

N'Doch presses both palms to his temples and squeezes hard. Yes! What was he thinking? "Sorry! Sorry. Okay?

You two are making me crazy. Look, it's time to move. We gotta check out this Mahatma Glory Whosits while it's still daylight."

"Magdalena," say the kid and the girl together.

N'Doch sighs. "Whatever."

Chapter Twenty-Five

They're still on the outskirts of the Ziguinchor when N'Doch begins to see the signs. Posters in shop windows and pasted on the walls. A billboard, erected hastily on the roof of someone's house, alongside an old satellite dish. Even little stickers, brand new, in all the colors of the fluorescent rainbow, blooming on the faded doors and gateposts. He's used to having political broadsides and government proclamations plastered up all over the place, but this is different. These are almost . . . decorative.

He points them out to the apparition and the girl. Carefully, the girl sounds out the words.

"Glow . . . rye? Sorry, the letters are funny. Glowree? Glory!"

Impressed, he nods. "It's her. That's the place we'll find Lealé."

The image is the same everywhere: the dark face of a woman superimposed on a bright four-pointed star. It's shaped like a compass rose, like he's seen on old maps in the history vids. The woman is smiling beatifically. "That's all it says, 'Glory,' but it's gotta be where that woman was talking about." He's kind of relieved, 'cause this face don't look like it's selling sex or kinky games. Still, you never know. "Maybe Lealé's joined some kind of religious cult."

The girl shudders. "Oh, I hope not."

"Why? You know your Bible stuff, sounds like. I'll let you go ask her where Lealé is."

She eyes him sideways. "But, N'Doch, I do not speak her language."

He snaps his fingers, an oversized gesture. "Damn! Right again!"

Her brow creases, then smoothes. Her eyes lighten and she grins, sketching a little bow. "Ah ha," she says, then nods for him to lead the way down the street.

N'Doch thinks, *Now we're getting someplace.*

The stickers and signs soon become elaborate arrows pointing the way. N'Doch just follows them.

"That Water Street woman sure was right about this place being no trouble to find," he remarks. But the closer he gets, the uneasier it makes him. This Glory person doesn't look to be leading a very private life. There's sure to be lots of people around, and awkward questions about the kid and the girl. He wonders if he can manage to hunt up Lealé without getting tangled in this Mahatma's dubious business.

They come around a corner finally and there in the wide square is the ramshackle four-story pile of crumbling yellow stucco that houses the Marché Ziguinchor. N'Doch thinks of the coins Papa Djawara has given him. He thinks of cheese and bread and oranges. Oranges! Maybe even a tidbit of chocolate, that fabulous luxury of luxuries. But the market is closed, and the ring of outside stalls as well. It's nearing noon. Both vendors and customers have fled the heat. Those with no place to go have staked out niches in the shade. The bundle of rags tucked in each corner is a person napping. N'Doch's timing is off again, but it's no disaster. He's hoping, despite his disclaimers to the woman at 913 Water Street, that Lealé will be good for at least one full meal in the Glory woman's kitchen, and a cooling siesta in his grandfather's name.

Besides, now that he thinks about it, he's glad the stalls are closed. He wouldn't want the girl to have to see some of the stuff they sell in there besides food. But he oughta find shade for her pretty quick, he sees. She's damp and flagging, and paler even than usual. She may not know to drink enough, though N'Doch notices the apparition is sure putting a big dent into the water bottle he made it carry.

Still, he lingers by the south entrance to the market, staring pensively at the big, barred wooden doors. Litter has blown up in piles against them, like they haven't been open in a while. There used to be showers of neon here, people night and day, and music blaring into the streets. A resourceful kid could always find what he lacked at the Zig. All sorts of deals going down, lots of biz, the very center of biz, even in the hottest noons. Maybe at night, it still is. N'Doch hopes so, 'cause right now, it's looking real drab and down on its luck, falling apart like everything else.

The apparition taps him on the arm. N'Doch turns, and there's the place.

"Yee-ow," he murmurs.

It's a big stone building, a mansion really, filling one entire end of the market square. It has white columns and an upper gallery with wrought iron railings, like from colonial times, even to the magenta riot of bougain-villea cascading from the balcony. N'Doch recalls there was some kind of hotel here before, but he doesn't recall these elegant columns or that lacy iron gingerbread, or the ornate but massive gates in tall white walls topped with razor wire. The place even has its own driveway. He especially doesn't remember the mammoth light-box sign over the front portico: the beaming woman in the golden four-pointed star. Above, her name in glowing block caps: "GLORY." Underneath, a legend: *In this sad world, a bridge to the next.*

N'Doch eyes the impressive guard house between the motor gate and a smaller pedestrian gate beside it. He supposes an entire system of locks, screens, sensors, alarms, and monitors—and armed bouncers.

"I guess Lealé's come up in the world, all right," he mutters. "If she's in there. Question is, how're we gonna get *us* in? Probably need a password and our own per-sonal bar code."

"Go knock on the door," says the apparition.

"Sure thing, smart mouth. You got 'rich boy' stamped on your forehead?"

"It says 'Welcome.' "

"Where?"

The boy-dragon points. Sure enough, over the pedes-trian gate, in gold letters. *Bienvenue.*

N'Doch fights through a twinge of resentment. The

real Jéjé never lived long enough to learn how to read. "Well, it don't mean us, you can bet on that."

"You won't do it, I will."

And before N'Doch can stop him, the kid is sprinting across the square. The girl starts after him, swaying a bit in the sun, then looks back. *"Kommen sie nicht?"*

"Huh?" The damn kid's fallen down on the translating job. N'Doch holds his ground a moment, then groans softly and follows. Got to get the girl inside before she drops. Besides, he's just noticed the shiny new street signs on the mansion's corners: *Rue de la Terre*.

The kid waits for them at the walk-in gate, then just as N'Doch is catching up, he raps on it sharply. It swings open to his touch. N'Doch can see that the gate itself is a metal detector, but the smiling guard in the bullet-proof booth waves them in like the host at some swank garden party.

And inside the walls, that's exactly what it looks like—the aftermath, at least, of a really *big* do.

A shallow, tiled yard runs the width of the building, dotted with fancy fruit trees in big ceramic tubs. People are lying about everywhere, curled up beneath the trees, asleep on the stone benches in between. At least, he assumes they're asleep. Smiling too peacefully to be stiffs, even on their hard beds of tile and stone. Maybe the place is a pleasure house after all. But the sleepers look to be sleeping normally, not napping off a high of some sort.

The girl nudges him. At the far end of the yard, several slim young guys in white robes are wandering about watering the bright, lush flowers overflowing the bases of the potted trees. One is picking up scattered bits of clothing from the tiny oval of green inside the circular driveway. N'Doch stoops and rakes his fingers across its manicured velvet. "Unnh. Real grass . . ." He wants to get down and roll in it.

But he sees the girl eyeing the white-robed guys with serious suspicion. He doesn't think any of them looks like much to contend with, but he waits anyway, to be spotted and told to get the hell out, like all the other times he's been told the likes of him don't belong in someplace he'd really like to be.

Instead, the guy scavenging the clothes bundles up his

armload and comes over, smiling. "My, my, aren't we up early? Hello, I'm Jean-Pierre. How can I help you?"

N'Doch is tongue-tied for the split second it takes for the apparition to pipe up.

"We'd like to see the Mahatma Glory Magdalena."

"*Danke,*" adds the girl hastily.

The guy's brows lift. "Oh, I'm afraid it's much too early for that. She won't be up for hours yet. But you're welcome to wait. The line starts around the corner to the right. Of course, there are . . ." He waves a languid hand at the litter of sleepers. ". . . a few petitioners in front of you already, but it shouldn't take much more than a few days. Will it be cash or credit?"

N'Doch eases himself forward. "For what?"

The guy takes N'Doch's measure and pumps a little more warmth into his smile. "For your Reading, of course. You are here for a Reading?"

N'Doch judges that the same charm he puts to work on the ladies might work with this Jean-Pierre. He smiles back, heavy-lidded. "Well, no. Actually, we're searching up an old friend of my grandpapa's. At the last known address, they told us to look here."

The guy's warmth dims perceptibly. "Ah. An elderly gentleman, then? We have no elderly gentlemen working here. Perhaps your informant meant he is on line, awaiting a Reading. You are welcome to look around, but I do hope you won't disturb any of our guests unnecessarily. They all need their sleep."

N'Doch smiles ingratiatingly, though it pains him to do so. "I'm sure they do. But it's not a gentleman we're looking for. It's a lady, and not so elderly. I'd guess she'd be in her fifties."

"She's here," says the apparition suddenly.

N'Doch turns. "Hush, now."

The girl catches on. She slides restraining hands onto the apparition's shoulders. N'Doch gives her a little nod, already turning back to the young man. "Her name is Lealé."

The guy's face goes briefly blank, and then his smile returns. N'Doch imagines a robot checking a data file, but he knows that look: the momentary shutdown of the bureaucrat who's just received a piece of information he doesn't know what to do with.

"What was that name again?"

Bingo, thinks N'Doch. He conjures up a pleasant innocence. "Lealé Kaimah."

The guy backs up a step. "Well, now. Let me see. Why don't I just go on inside and check the records for you? Anyone waiting in line will have signed the reservations book. Perhaps your friend has already been and gone, happily enlightened."

"My grandfather's friend, she is. From long ago."

"How lovely. And what did you say your grandpapa's name is?"

"I didn't. It's Djawara."

"Yes. Well, then, I'll just go check." The guy escapes up onto the colonnaded porch and into the house.

"Sure lit a fire under him, didn't we?" crows N'Doch. He's not used to people being polite to him, for whatever reason.

"A toady," scoffs the apparition. The girl nods, like she knows all about it.

Erde sank gratefully into the shade of a column but kept herself alert. Despite the exotic and unfamiliar setting, she recognized in this white-clad man the tone and body language of a courtier. This was not like any court she had knowledge of, but instinct told her that she must not take anyone or anything at face value. Politics, flatteries, and subterfuge had ruled at Tor Alte, even during her grandmother's more open reign. Erde wondered what the Mahatma Glory Magdalena had done to acquire the kind of power that the presence of courtiers implied. She knew it meant the woman could be dangerous. If not dealt with properly, she could stand between them and finding Master Djawara's friend Lealé.

When the young man in white had vanished through the broad double doors of the manor house, N'Doch said quietly, "Stay put. I'm gonna have a look around. Drink some water, huh? You look awful." He started away, then halted. "Listen, if the guy comes back, let the kid do the talking. Speaking Kraut to 'em will only make 'em think we got money."

Erde nodded, uncorking her water jug. She'd finally figured out that N'Doch spoke a kind of Frankish, some future version of the language she'd heard from visitors riding into Tor Alte from west of the Germanies, in the same way that the German that Master Djawara spoke was a future version of her own. She didn't speak much Frankish, beyond the few polite phrases of greeting and farewell that would be expected on formal occasions from the daughter of a noble house. But she was sure she could learn it.

She watched little Wasser scuff around the white-paved driveway, and opened her conscious mind to her boon companion waiting a morning's walk away in the war zone.

—*Dragon, how are you?*

—**I am sleeping.**

—*You are not. You are awake and translating.*

—**The part of me that is not awake is sleeping.**

—*Brilliant Dragon! Part of you can sleep while another part is awake?*

—**Yes. Only now, all of me is awake.**

—*Poor Dragon. I'm so sorry.*

Erde's smile, repressed mentally, came out physically. She caught Wasser grinning at her mischievously.

—*Well, Dragon, answer my question, and then you may go back to sleep, however much of you wishes to.*

—**Yes?**

—*Will your sister teach me this Frankish tongue that is spoken here?*

—**Ask her. She is awake.**

—*Dear dragon, I cannot, unless I ask her in German, which her current boy-form does not speak. Therefore, you must stay awake to translate even if I do ask her myself.*

A giant dragon sigh rumbled through Erde's mind like the echo of a distant avalanche. Still grinning, Wasser nodded.

—*She says, yes, she will teach you, if you will teach her.*

So, while N'Doch had his look around, the lessons began.

Expecting to be stopped and strip-searched at every step, N'Doch wanders the grounds in a way he hopes looks sufficiently casual. But his notion of stumbling across some secret sector proves bogus. There are people sleeping everywhere he turns.

The right side of the mansion has a row of tall curtained French windows opening onto a wide flowered terrace. The stone is white, the flowers are pink. It's all like some kind of vid set, except for the sleepers. Here, where there's shade from a few ginkgo trees, they're lined up back to back, head to toe, like in some sort of fiendish dormitory, or like one of those makeshift morgues they throw together after some war or natural disaster. It gives N'Doch the creeps, looking at them just lying there like that.

At the end of the row of windows is a big door with a canopy as long as the terrace is wide, all draped in gold and white fabric, something glittery with sequins. N'Doch goes up close. The sequins are shaped like four-pointed stars. He doesn't know much about fancy fabrics, but he's beginning to get the drift here. He tries the massive and elaborate brass handle on the shining white door. Locked. No surprise there. It's even less of a surprise when he continues around the back, where there are more tall, curtained windows facing a graveled car park and a six-car garage. Out on the gravel, two of the white-robed young guys are hosing down the mirrored gold limousine.

Even though it's not a surprise, N'Doch has to work to stay casual-like. He's gonna actually get close to the thing, maybe get a look inside. The gravel is dark with many priceless gallons of perfectly good water. He can see it's clear coming out of the hose. Course, that doesn't mean it's safe. N'Doch guesses the flashy motorcycles have had their wash and are already stashed in the garages.

He slouches over diffidently. "Want some help?" He knows a little lightening of the work load can often be bartered for information.

But the guys in white stare at him like he should only dream of being allowed such a privilege. One of them smiles, though, the same even smile N'Doch has seen enough of already in this compound. It's beginning to make his teeth itch.

"Oh, no, sir, but thank you. The Mahatma would never wish a Guest to soil themselves for her sake."

N'Doch thinks: *With all that water, you'd end up being cleaner than you arrived.* "Oh," he says. "I see. Okay for you to, though, huh?"

His offer of worker solidarity falls on deaf ears. "We don't mind, sir. As her devoted disciples, such onerous tasks are our honor and our duty."

"Natch," says N'Doch. If the Mahatma Glory won't be up for hours like the guy at the door said, who was it out parading around in her limo? He'd like to hang and check out the fabulous car, but probably it wouldn't do to look too curious here. "Well, see ya."

"Our best wishes for your Reading."

"You bet."

He follows the driveway out of the car park, across the back of the house and around the left side. He finds a little grove of trees, some thick-leafed tree he doesn't recognize, rising out of a carefully mowed square of lawn. N'Doch slows, studying it. Here, there is not a sleeper in sight. Weird. That soft grass under those heavy trees looks like the coolest, most comfortable place for a lie-down in the whole compound. He sees no fence or keep-out signs, no guard post or dogs. Somehow anyone coming here just knows to stay away from this spot. He'd expect at least a scrawny pigeon in the grass, the one or two that haven't already been netted and eaten. This should be a perfect refuge for 'em. He gets a little chill, staring into this silent green emptiness. It reminds him of the weirdness beneath the trees at Papa Dja's. At least there, there were birds.

He stores his search data in a corner of his brain and goes off to find the girl and the kid. They're hunkered down in the shade on the front steps, tight as you please, playing some sort of word game in two different languages. It takes him a while to realize it's a two-way vocabulary lesson.

The girl looks up. *"Bonjour, monsieur N'Doch,"* she chirps proudly.

N'Doch grins. *"Mais, bonjour, mademoiselle."* Pretty neat. No dragons between 'em or nothing. *"Ça va?"*

She throws a quick one back at the apparition. The kid nods encouragingly, like a grown-up.

"Oui, monsieur," says the girl. *"Ça va très bien, merci."*

N'Doch applauds, and she blushes. "She's a fast learner," he tells the kid.

"I'm a good teacher. *Sprechen Sie Deutsch*?"

"Oh, no, you don't. Leave me outa this."

"But why, N'Doch?" asks the girl. The dragon translation program has kicked in again. "It's fun!"

"Schooling's never fun. I know what I need to know, y'know?"

The minute he's said it, he hates how narrow it sounds, but he can't take it back. It's a show of weakness to second-guess yourself.

The girl's brow furrows. "No, I guess I don't. Don't you always want to be learning new things?"

"If it's useful stuff, sure I do." He's digging his hole deeper, he knows it. He can't seem to stop himself. Seconds ago, he was delighted to hear her speaking his language, but something about her dead earnestness just needles him badly. "Wouldn't want to waste my time otherwise."

"It's a waste of time to be able to talk to me?"

"Hey, we're talking now, ain't we?"

Her frown is deepening. "I mean, to each other, without the dragons."

N'Doch looks away, yawns. "I say, if it ain't broke, don't fix it."

The girl tips a handful of white pebbles from palm to palm, says nothing. The apparition leaps up and sticks its little Jéjé nose right in N'Doch's face, scowling.

"You're mean, big brother, that's what you are!"

"I ain't your brother."

"So much the worse for you!"

N'Doch sees the apparition's outline waver, and panics. "No! Don't do it! I'm sorry! I didn't mean it!"

The girl catches at the kid's hand. "Wasser, please. Let's not fight. We've more important things to worry about."

Erde heard an echo of herself in N'Doch's petulance, the younger self who rebelled against her father's arbitrary dictates. But it was Earth, now waked fully by the sharp turn of the conversation, who offered an explanation.

—*He is rebelling, too.*

—Against what? No one here's telling him what to do.

—In a way, you do. By setting a superior example.

—He doesn't think it's superior. He thinks I'm stupid.

—He thinks you think it's superior. He doesn't quite believe it's who you are.

—Well, this is very mixed-up, Dragon.

—Yes. Especially since he also suspects he's given up something in order to become as clever as he is about survival, something he suspects you still have.

—What?

Earth maundered about a bit, rumbling gently in her mind, as if he wasn't so sure of this grand theory of his after all. But their philosophical reverie was broken by Wasser's sharp little elbow digging into Erde's ribs.

"Hsst!"

"Listen!" N'Doch agreed.

There was a commotion inside the house. A woman's voice raised in querulous demand, and a hubbub of lower voices explaining, placating, apologizing. In the tiled front yard, the young men in white set down their watering cans and eyed each other anxiously.

"Sounds like Her Gloryship is awake after all," N'Doch murmured.

The front doors burst open, both of them, in a great sweep of gleaming paint and polished brass that scattered several of the young men who had gathered to eavesdrop on the argument inside. A tall, ebony-skinned woman strode out in a flurry of color and motion, yards and yards of glimmering white silk and bright, multicolored scarves and beads, hundreds of strands looped about her long neck and her bare, dark arms and woven into the intricate architecture of her hair. She halted on the top step, the back of one hand pressed to her brow, her eyes closed, her back gracefully arched. The young men in white rushed to gather about behind her like angels in the heavenly choir.

Erde wondered if she was meant to curtsy. Out of pure habit, she almost did.

N'Doch stared up at the woman openmouthed. "What an entrance!" he breathed.

"They're here!" declaimed the woman, who had to be the Mahatma Glory herself. There was no mistaking her from the images plastered on every fence and doorpost, like the Virgin Mother's on her holy Feast Day. "They've come, as I predicted. The doubters laughed, but I said they would and they have come to me!"

She opened her eyes and turned her fiery glance on her visitors in order of height: N'Doch first, then Erde, and lastly, little Wasser. Her gaze lingered there and narrowed. The boy-dragon shivered and shrank against Erde's side.

"They tried to keep you from me, said you weren't important. The foolish ones! What do they know about the world and eternity, ah?"

Erde thought of raving priests and white-robed henchmen in another time and place. She shifted an arm and hugged Wasser protectively.

Then Glory spread her own arms with a tinkling of beads and little bells hidden within the shimmering folds of her robes. She offered them the blinding, beatific smile of her painted image. "Come to me, children. Your journey is ended."

"I hope not," the apparition muttered, his voice muffled by Erde's T-shirt.

N'Doch said, "This could be interesting."

PART THREE

The Call to the Quest

Chapter Twenty-Six

Erde had been schooled in courtly manners and presentation from the earliest age. Her elders had drilled her constantly, for she would naturally be the focus of much attention, being a baron's daughter and probable heir. She'd felt about it the way she felt about learning to dance: a series of moves designed to produce a given outcome, a collection of predetermined masks she was required to put on. She'd resisted her training, and had often been punished for it.

The Mahatma Glory Magdalena's presentation caught her entirely by surprise. She had never laid eyes on such a woman: so grand, so spectacular, so histrionic, all arms and hands and braided, beaded hair flying in every direction. Dignity and decorum were the basis of court behavior, seen at its best in the dignity of Erde's beloved grandmother, the late baroness, a woman of no small presence herself. But to stand in the Mahatma's presence was like standing in a gale. Every word she uttered, every move she made called attention to itself. A welcome from this woman was writ in capital letters, given with tears and sighs and lightning flashes of her brilliant smile. Entirely undignified. And yet, Erde admitted, her charisma was such that you gladly let it buffet you in the face, even if it threatened your balance. You just HAD to watch her, to see what outrageous thing she would do next.

And what she did next, after she'd finished declaiming about the foolishness of her overzealous protectors and the perfidy of anyone with the temerity to doubt her predictions, was to swoop down on her three visitors with the same grandiose flashing of tears and smiles. She

enveloped each of them in a smothering hug, finishing
with Wasser, who was trying so hard to be invisible behind Erde's right hip that she was sure the boy/dragon
had actually shrunk in size. Wrapped in the silken folds
of Glory's robe, Wasser looked five years younger than
the putative ten-year-old who'd walked through the
gates. Erde hoped the dragon knew what she was doing.
It wouldn't do to draw attention to herself by exhibiting
unusual abilities.

"Precious children!" Glory exclaimed, though Erde
did not see how the woman could think of N'Doch as a
child. "Brave children! Come all this way to see Glory!
Glory hallelujah!" She glanced around at her slack-
jawed acolytes and threw up her arms. "I said, glory
hallelujah, brothers!"

"Glory hallelujah, sister!" they chorused, though none
of them looked very happy about it. "Amen, amen,
amen!"

Glory's hot-ember eyes narrowed. "For I have seen
the light. . . !"

"Oh, yes, sister! Amen!"

"And with God on my right. . . !"

"Amen!"

Roused by the noise, a few of the sleepers groaned to
their feet and shuffled over to join in on the chorus.
Glory's smile brightened, like a fire fed by the addition
of kindling.

"There is truth in my sight!"

"Amen, sister, amen!"

Beads and bells tinkled as Glory lowered her arms
and pressed her palms together. "Amen," she repeated
with obvious satisfaction, then turned back to her visitors. "Now, dear and blessed, dear and foreseen travelers, rest from your trials, from your terrible journey."

It wasn't all that terrible, Erde would have reassured
her, if she'd been further along with her lessons in
Frankish. But Glory seemed to be enjoying her own version of their story. The light in her eyes, Erde saw now,
was not unlike the hot glint that filled the bard's eyes at
home, old Cronke, when he was deep into the recitation
of a favorite tale.

"So, enter this humble house, good children! Bring to
Glory's hearth the heavy burden of your terrible tidings,

and lay it down! Glory hears all! Glory sees all! Glory will ease your load!"

And Erde wondered: *Which particular terrible tidings does she have in mind?*

N'Doch has felt the sudden gust of chill air expelled through the doors as the Glory woman flung them open. It makes him eager to get inside even though he has his doubts about the wisdom of venturing into what is clearly a crackpot's lair. But he's never been into an air-conditioned space that he didn't immediately get thrown out of. He'd like to know what it's like, this rich man's luxury. Maybe it's no big deal, really, but he thinks it probably is.

So against his better judgment, against all the accumulated cunning gleaned from a life in the streets, N'Doch lets the Glory woman take his arm on one side and the girl's on the other—he sees the girl's got the apparition well in tow—and sweep them up the shallow white steps like a small herd of sheep. Or whatever. N'Doch has never seen a sheep, but he knows their reputation for going willingly to the slaughter.

The white-robed toadies fall over each other in their haste to haul open the massive double doors, so that Glory and her guests pass through into the house without a break in stride. N'Doch sees only darkness inside, and pulls back a bit. Glory urges him inward. The doors, as tall and wide as any he's seen, breathe closed behind him with barely a whisper.

He's in a dim, cool hall, so dim he can't be sure how high or wide. He wants to stop, wait a bit for his eyes to adjust, but Glory is drawing them down along thick carpet he can only feel. His strongest impressions are sensual: the plush carpet; the caress of perfumed air cooling his skin, wicking away his sweat; the soft murmur of voices in other rooms, like the steady wash of the sea on a calm night. It's a spooky thing. He'd like to be *seeing* a lot more than he is.

"Hey, girl . . ." he ventures casually, into the darkness.

"I'm here," she replies. "And Wasser, too."

He feels a little better, though Glory's grip on his arm is disturbingly strong. He wonders briefly if his usually unerring instinct for gender has played him wrong. But he's seen the womanly curves of her body shaping her robes and now can't help but notice her rounded hips and full breasts as she holds him tight to her side. Experimentally, he leans into her a little so her breast rubs against his chest. Her nipple is hard. Apparently she's enjoying this scene she's creating in more ways than one. N'Doch is more curious than ever, but the oddness of it makes him doubly wary. Like, maybe it's fear. He's seen that. But he can't say that this woman looks like she'd be afraid of anything.

Finally his eyes adjust, but by then, they're at the end of the hall in front of another set of double doors. N'Doch barely has time to register the polished hardwood paneling, outlined with a glint of gilt, when the doors are drawn aside by white-sleeved arms and are swallowed up into the thickness of the door frame. N'Doch is freed as Glory raises the arm that held him, moving into the room and signaling behind her without looking.

"Water! Warm water, soap, and towels for Glory's guests! Then food and drink! Quickly! Hurry now!"

She flies about the room, beads jingling, hands and arms in motion, and a small battalion of toadies swirls after in her wake, drawing drapes and shades, flicking on lamps, plumping pillows, pulling giant upholstered chairs and ottomans away from the walls into the room. N'Doch takes up a position at the epicenter with the kid and the girl, like in the eye of the storm, watching and wondering just what the hell this is all about.

Shimmering white tablecloths are spread. Water is brought in big white porcelain bowls. A soft white towel is put into N'Doch's hands. Because he can't think of any reason not to, he dips a finger into the nearest bowl. The water is warm and clean. It doesn't smell or sting. N'Doch rinses his hands, then his face and neck. Now he's really aware of the cool air, chilled at such inconceivable cost. It's actually raising goosebumps on his forearms. N'Doch is amazed. He thought that only happened when you were scared shitless. He asks himself, has he ever been this cold before? He thinks he would remember if he was, and can't.

He watches the girl, sees how easily she falls into being waited on, how her cool brief smiles and calm nods look

almost professional, like he's seen actors do it on the
tube. He sees the apparition observing her carefully,
doing exactly what she does. The toadies and acolytes
seem surprised, like they're not used to being treated graciously. He figures he'll just give it a try. He's gotta be
at least as good an actor as the girl is.

The Glory woman washes, too, though N'Doch can't
imagine that she needs to, seeing as she supposedly just
got up, plus took the time to get dressed to the nines like
she is. She's got three attendants dancing after her like
their lives depended on it, one holding a bowl, one the
soap, and the third a whole pile of towels. She seems to
notice them about as much as she would the furniture.
She's in motion all the time and they have to stay alert
to keep up with her without slopping suds and water all
over the ankle-deep carpets. N'Doch wonders why she
won't sit still, if maybe she's nervous or something, or
like, did she take in too much of the precious white pow-
der when she woke up this morning?

He thinks of the sleepers on the ground outside, and
imagines the whole compound seething with people
charging about at the speed of the Mahatma Glory Magdalena. It makes him laugh. But when he hears voices
down the hall, a deep man's voice pitched to carry above
others, and he sees Glory go on the alert, N'Doch realizes
she's been listening, real hard all along, and part of her
nonstop movement is simple wariness.

She goes to the door, trailing attendants, and calls
down the hall, promising an immediate arrival. N'Doch
notes the trill of coquettishness that brightens her voice
and offers just a hint of submission. Then she whirls back
into the room, tossing her towel aside without looking
to see where it might land.

"Children, dear children," she declaims, circling, her
eyes still drawn to the door. "Forgive your naughty Glory
for abandoning you so soon after your arrival. But she
won't be long. She just *must* bid a very special Guest
good-bye, and then she'll be back to you in an instant!"
Gathering her skirts, she wheels out the door and away.
The attendants gather in the hall like storm refuse and
stare after her.

So now, of course, N'Doch is dying to know who's

this "special guest," this guy with *cojones* enough to make this astonishing woman hop to so fast.

"Wasser is not happy here," murmurs the girl at his elbow.

"Can't he speak up for himself?" N'Doch is enjoying the spectacle. He doesn't want his curious adventure brought to a premature end by some little kid's failure of nerve.

The girl gives him an odd, impatient look. "She's only warning you. There is something unusual here."

N'Doch snorts. "You don't think I can see that? You think I spend my life in air-cooled mansions with fresh water and servants at my beck and call?" No, but I'd like to, he finishes silently.

"Not that kind of unusual," she whispers. "Dragons don't notice human comforts. Or discomforts, for that matter. It's like what she said about the golden horseless coach. There's something . . . wrong."

Dragons. Right. Distracted by luxury and longing, he'd once again forgotten. He tells himself he really cannot afford to keep doing this. "Okay. Warning taken. Let's play it out, though. Sees where it goes."

She nods, dipping a corner of her towel into her basin. She pats delicately at her pale, sweated forehead. The towel comes away red with dust.

N'Doch grins. "Better just stick your whole face right in there, if you want to get that off." But he knows she won't. It wouldn't be . . . ladylike."

At last the washing ritual is completed. The basins and dust-ruddied towels are whisked away, and a regal spread of bread and fruit and cheese is laid out on the shining tablecloth. N'Doch thinks it looks like an advertisement. He checks it out pretty carefully, to assure himself it's real and safe and no one's pulling a fast one. He sees the girl holding back and tells her to go ahead, who knows when she'll ever see another meal like this one. When a steaming pot of coffee is wheeled in on a silver cart, he's sure he's died and gone to heaven.

"Eat, children. Help yourselves." Glory swoops back into the room like a gust of hot wind. Her brilliant smile and mobile hands urge them toward the table. "You must be dry and famished from your long and arduous travels."

To N'Doch's disappointment, she offers nothing further about her "special guest." Instead, she hovers briefly, pointing out delicacies, watching them as if to make sure they eat. She even grazes the food herself a little, commenting on the quality of this or that, and he wonders sourly if he's seen the extent of her, if she's like so many other star performers: all bombast and stupid small talk. He promises himself he will not be like that when *he's* a star.

Then suddenly, she's off again, shooing the remaining acolytes from the room. "Leave us, leave us! Glory knows you're eager to hear the message they bring us, but first, you must let the dear children eat and you must let them rest!"

It seems to N'Doch that the young men all give him a look and go reluctantly, like maybe they don't trust him with her or something. And he's not too busy piling food on a plate not to notice when Glory locks the doors behind the last of them. She does it quietly, so quietly and carefully that N'Doch would be worried if it weren't for the fact that somehow he just knows it's the people on the *other* side of the door she wants to keep from noticing. When she's slid the bolt home, she rests her forehead against the rich wood for a long, still moment. He sees that she's breathing hard.

When she finally turns, she's no longer the flamboyant Mahatma Glory Magdalena. Her smile is gone. Her eyes look weary, haunted. Gathering herself, she glides swiftly to the table and past it, murmuring, "Say nothing. Not a word." She gestures them to gather up their food and follow. She's dropped the mask so suddenly that N'Doch is left a little dizzy. The girl, however, seems relieved, as if this new Glory is a more expected one.

"Lealé?" she whispers.

Still in motion but without all the arm-waving, the woman agrees less with a nod than with a roll of those haunted eyes, a look that also tells them to hurry, that no real conversation can be had until they get to where she's leading them. At the same time, she's muttering to herself, "I didn't know, I didn't know."

N'Doch thinks she looks confused, but he's more concerned right then with his own humiliation. How'd the girl figure it out so quick? It was the dragon told her, he's sure of it. *His* dragon. He elbows the apparition urgently. "You could have clued me in first, kid."

The boy/dragon blinks up at him, echoing Lealé. "I didn't know."

"Yeah, sure."

"Really."

"Yeah?"

So maybe the girl's more on the ball than she looks. This is a hard one for N'Doch, but he figures he'll learn to live with it. Meanwhile, he reflects, the confusion of identities in this caper is really getting out of hand. He decides to think of the woman as Lealé, since she's the one Papa D. sent him looking for.

And now she's saying in her regular "Glory" voice, "Bring your food and drink, children. We'll go in here where we can be comfortable." A deep archway in the far wall divides the big room from a smaller alcove where there are soft couches, big enough for sleeping or making love, and low tables and some kind of music N'Doch can't quite make out. He guesses this little area doesn't have the hidden mikes and cameras she seems to be worried about. It looks comfy and all, but when they're all there and setting down their plates and glasses, and N'Doch is getting ready to really tuck into his food, Lealé eases past, touching each one of them on the shoulder. When she has their attention, she mouths silently, "This way."

She moves back to the archway, leaning one hand against the wall beside it, then makes an abrupt turn to the left and vanishes.

The girl and the kid follow right her after like it was nothing. N'Doch swallows, but knowing what he does about surveillance sensors, he understands he better not react visibly to what he's seeing. And he hates the idea of leaving all this good food behind. So he palms an orange off his plate and assumes an easy slouching pace across the alcove until he's under the arch and able to see the slim opening where the paneled thickness of the arch has swung noiselessly aside. A dark narrow passage yawns. A hand, Lealé's, reaches out and snatches him inside.

Chapter Twenty-Seven

Waiting in the dark for N'Doch to join them, Erde squeezed Wasser's hand. It was chill, she noted, and the palm slightly damp, but what else would one expect from a dragon named Water? She was delighted by this new turn of events: the sudden shifting of identities, the magical appearance of a secret passage. Wonderful omens, each of them. Signs that the Quest was finally on its way again.

"Is this what was 'wrong'?" she whispered eagerly to Wasser. "Things not being what they seem to be?"

"No." The boy/dragon shivered. "Nothing ever is."

"True enough. But some things are even less what they seem . . . or more. Oh, I don't know. Anyhow, have you any better idea what it is, what you're afraid of?"

"I'm not afraid. Who said I was afraid? I'm . . . horrified."

Erde silently considered this mysterious difference.

"Same body language, I guess, different emotion."

"Oh. Horrified by what?"

Wasser gave an impatient snort. "By the wrongness, of course." Erde could hear him scuffing his feet in the darkness. "Maybe the right word is 'outraged,'" he concluded.

"Hurry now, children. It won't be long before they notice. Up ahead is a place we can talk."

With N'Doch in tow, Lealé propelled them forward. The passage was pitch-black and wide enough for only one body at a time. Erde was forced to lead the way with a hand braced against each enclosing wall. But now she noticed something ominous. Reaching behind her, she drew Wasser close to murmur in his ear. "It's gone awfully quiet in my head all of a sudden."

"Yes. I felt it as we stepped through the door. Wherever this place is, it isn't here."

As little sense as that made, she knew exactly what he meant. "He'll be worried," she whispered.

"He'll be frantic."

"You're doing very well translating on your own now."

"Yes." Erde could hear the boy/dragon grin. "I am, amn't I."

"Aren't."

"I knew that."

"Did you really know we were coming?" asked N'Doch behind them.

"Wait," Lealé replied. "Until we get there.'

"We're between the walls, huh?" he marveled.

"Yes," Lealé murmured, but Erde thought her tone a bit doubtful.

"Your surveillance rig isn't high-tech enough to reach inside the walls?"

"Not this wall."

"Cool. Lead shielding, eh?"

"Not exactly."

Erde took in their conversation with half an ear, partly because she was worried about Earth, now totally isolated in his underground burrow, and partly because Wasser's German had only recently been lifted from her own head. It did not include words for much of what they were discussing. More important, she was distracted by a peculiar but somehow familiar sensation. Feeling her way along this lightless passage was not exactly the same, but certainly reminded her of how it felt when Earth transported her someplace. The same feeling of "otherness." A kind of deafness within an echo, a tingling kind of numbness. Only, instead of being instantaneous and then over, before you were really aware of it, the sensation went on and on like a dull ache, not rising or falling in intensity.

"Hsst!" Wasser jogged her arm.

A square of green light shone ahead—how could she not have seen it before?—an enlarging square rather like an open window. She seemed to be moving toward it, but at an oddly unpredictable rate. For a while, it would grow steadily, then it would stay the same for what seemed like minutes, though Erde knew she had not slowed her pace. Occasionally she would glance behind her, unthinking, to check on the others even though it was too dark to see anything. When she looked ahead again, the square would have suddenly enlarged, and she would be sure she was almost on top of it, ready to burst through into whatever mystery lay beyond.

"You could at least tell us where you're taking us," N'Doch muttered.

"To the only safe place. Everywhere else, I am watched. It's the price of fame. But this place no one knows about except . . ." Her voice faded, then as quickly recovered. "I call it my 'Dream Haven.'"

"Say it again?"

"It's where the Dreams come to me."

"Hunh. Seems like everyone's having dreams lately."

Erde knew Lealé had stopped short when she heard N'Doch's soft explosion of breath as he ran into her.

"You're not the Dreamer, surely," Lealé said.

"Sure, I have dreams, I guess. Doesn't everybody?"

"I mean the dreams you remarked upon."

N'Doch was silent a moment. Erde tried to will him to keep his silence, tried to nudge Wasser to still him before he said too much. "No," he admitted finally, "that would be her, I guess. Mine are pretty ordinary. But she's been having some real humdingers."

"Yes," Lealé replied slowly. Erde could almost feel the woman's eyes boring into her through the darkness. "Yes, I know. And I am meant to warn her against them. I see that now."

"So you did know we were coming."

"I must tell her not to listen to them. Except . . ." She broke off, as if changing her mind or suddenly losing her train of thought.

"Don't think that's gonna be necessary," N'Doch went on, oblivious. "She's already . . ."

"Wasser," Erde murmured, "Ask her if she saw us in her dreams."

But N'Doch's ears were keen. "Hey, girl, how 'bout me? I can do that now, remember, just as good as him."

Erde doubted it, but she could see how much it meant

to him, so much that he'd forgotten (or conveniently
ignored) the fact that it was thanks to Wasser that the
translations entered his head in the first place. He didn't
even seem to have noticed that there was currently one
less link in their communications chain.

"Then you must do it," she said to him. "But don't
tell her about my dreams, ask her about hers. Did they
tell her about us? What did they say? Why does she
need to warn me? Ask her if . . ."

"Whoa, slow down, girl. I'll get to it."

His insistence on always appearing casual was, Erde
thought, his most irritating characteristic. After all, some
things were more important than others. Some things
were worth getting excited about. But N'Doch had to
behave as if nothing in the world mattered at all.

"So that's how you knew we were coming, Sister
Lealé, from your dreams?"

But Lealé did not answer, and just then the passage
widened and they were in a tiny empty room, lit only
by the watery light from a wide doorway directly in front
of them. This was the elusive green square that had led
Erde through the darkness. It looked out on a bright
grove of slender, smooth-trunked trees. Three broad
steps of translucent stone led down to a flawless lawn
that looked but did not smell like it had been fresh-cut
minutes ago with a very sharp scythe. And there was
something odd about the trees. A prickle up her spine
made Erde halt just inside the opening. The others gathered beside her.

N'Doch spoke first. "So, are we there?"

"Yes," Lealé murmured. "This is my Dream Haven."

"Pretty weird lookin' trees out there."

"They're all the same," Wasser supplied.

"Yes," said Erde. "How remarkable. Every one of
them, exactly alike."

"Cloned, must be," N'Doch remarked. "This is kinda
like your little park out back, 'cept those trees are,
y'know, normal."

"I see you've been exploring already." In a brief flash
of humor, Lealé deftly parodied his answering shrug,
then turned serious again. "I think it is sort of my little
park out back, but whenever I go in there, I never end
up here. It's very confusing."

"What happens when you go out there from here?"

"I never do."

"There's someone out there," Wasser said quietly.

"Oh, no, dear," Lealé assured him.

"There is."

N'Doch eased forward. "Let's go find out."

Lealé grabbed his arm. "No! You can't!" When he looked back at her in surprise, she let go but her eyes begged him. "Really. I never go out there. He wouldn't like it."

"He?" N'Doch gave her a sly look. "Aahh. The guy down the hall."

Lealé laughed. "Oh, no. Not him." Then she sobered and fell silent. Her moods were so mercurial that Erde was unable to make sense of them. The pale green light from the grove flowed over her anxious face as if it had substance, like smoke or water. *This is how it would feel,* Erde mused, *if you could live at the bottom of a clear lake.* She noticed how oddly steady the light was, as if every branch and leaf in the entire grove was utterly motionless. As still as the grave, she found herself thinking, then made herself stop, because of the chill it gave her. She remembered certain spring mornings at Tor Alte when the castle on its barren crag was wrapped in fog, and the sunlight seemed to come not from above, but from all around, as if trees and rocks, everything, even the fog itself, were aglow. *This place,* she decided, *is not of this world.*

"Then who is it you're so worried about?" N'Doch prodded.

"When I do my readings," Lealé offered finally. "I call him my spirit guide. My clients prefer to be able to envision their contact with the Infinite. Actually, I don't know what he is. I just know when he's here."

"Here? You meet him here?"

"He speaks to me here."

"Only here?"

"Yes. He calls me and I come."

Erde's ears pricked up at her use of the word "call" but N'Doch only nodded.

"Seems obvious to me—it's him out there, whoever he is."

Lealé shook her head. "He doesn't speak to me from out there. He's . . . somewhere else."

Watching the grove, Erde saw a flicker of movement. "Wait!"

Lealé started. "What? What is it, dear?"

Erde pointed, then let her hand fall. "No, it's gone."

N'Doch shifted his weight onto the first of the white stone steps. "You saw something?"

"It's nothing. That's how it always is," Lealé said. "Especially lately. I'm sure I'm seeing something, but he always tells me to pay no attention, and there's never anything out there really."

But Erde knew she'd seen something. "Did you see it, Wasser?"

The boy/dragon shuddered. "I felt it. We're very near now. . . ."

"Near to what?"

"Knowledge."

"I tell you, it's nothing," Lealé insisted.

"How do you know," countered N'Doch, "if you never go out there and look?"

"Please. Don't."

The fear that had been building in Lealé's voice finally drew Erde's attention away from the grove. Looking back into the darkness, she noticed that it was no longer so dark, and that the room was a little larger than she'd thought. She could see the walls now, paneled wood below and an intricately repeating pattern of some kind above, like a tapestry, only smoother and more abstract. It didn't seem to have any particular color. It just reflected the watery green glow pouring in from the grove.

"He doesn't want me to go there," Lealé continued. "He's been very clear on that score. And he's . . . not very pleasant when he's crossed."

N'Doch made a broad show of looking around. "I don't see any gate here, no bars or signs or nothing."

"I know. It's . . . like a test. He asks very little of me, but if I disobey him, he won't send the Dreams to me."

He folded his arms. Erde could see stubbornness rising in him like sap. "Okay, but he's not sending me any gigabillion-dollar dream scam, right? So you just stay put like you're supposed to, and I'll go have a look around."

Lealé grabbed him again, and a flare of the Mahatma's

fire burned in her gaze. "Listen, it's you who've shown up like beggars on my doorstep! I don't even know who you are! Now, I've been generous because you invoked the name of my friend, but I'll not have you calling my Dreams a scam! My Dreams are true ones!"

"I thought it was you who sent for us," N'Doch retorted.

Lealé held on to him even more intensely. "Who are you? I don't even know why I sent that card! I need to understand why . . ." She broke off again abruptly and drew her hand away. "Forgive my rudeness."

"Hey, no problem. And my name's N'Doch, just so you know. Try to remember it. Someday you might see it plastered all over town just like yours."

"N'Doch, then. Is that why you think I'm a fraud? Please understand, then: It's not the fame I crave. I do have to promote myself in ways I'd prefer not to, but that's to get the people in. To get their attention, so they know there is hope for them. To support this house, this place of peace and safety, so they can come here and be helped. People need truth in their lives!"

N'Doch avoided her earnest stare. "Don't get me wrong. I'm all for turning whatever gimmick you got into making your name and fortune. I hope to do that myself real soon. But this spirit guy, he's your thing, not mine. My thing's something else at the moment, a lot of questions that need answering, and one of them just became: What's out there?"

"No! You mustn't! You can't!" Lealé's hands began to lift and fly about her in random fitful movements. Erde saw finally that simple envy was making N'Doch misbehave. In his desire to win, he was ignoring what was sensible. She stepped between them.

"Remember that Master Djawara sent us here to listen to Mistress Lealé, not to frighten and insult her."

"Aw, girl, this is stupid! We're here, why not just check the place out? It's just a bunch of trees."

"You know better than that by now, surely?"

"What is she saying?" asked Lealé.

Wasser turned away from the grove for the first time. "Anyway, we certainly shouldn't go out there without telling my brother. I don't want to leave him stranded, in case we . . ."

"So tell him!"

"I can't."

"Why the hell not?"

For a moment, even to Erde, Wasser seemed tall and threatening in the eerie green glow. "Listen."

N'Doch blinked, and listened. "Yeah? So?"

"Listen *inside*."

N'Doch lowered his eyes, then quickly raised them again. "Hey. Where'd he go?"

His smaller self again, Wasser replied, "I don't think he went anywhere. Question is, where did *we* go?"

"Hunh." N'Doch's shoulders slumped. "Okay. You win. But, Sister Lealé, it seems silly to bring us here if it's so risky for you."

Lealé had been watching their exchange with narrowed eyes. Erde wondered what she'd made of it. "It's less risky than everywhere else."

"Right, so you said. The listeners. So who's listening?"

Lealé took on an entirely new face, world-weary and amused. She waved a dismissive, bright-nailed hand. "Oh, that's a whole other story. It's not really fit for children, and it certainly doesn't concern you."

"It does if you can't feel good about us talking where they're listening."

She gave him a quick, seductive smile. "It's just a jealous man, you know?"

N'Doch's sly grin bloomed in reply. "Ah! Now we get to the guy down the hall."

"Yes." Her smile turned faintly bitter. "Keeping track of his investment. Really, it's not your problem. I just don't want him knowing about all this." She gestured around the dark recess and outward, toward the grove. "Where my dreams come from or this . . . other business."

"The business of the card you sent Papa Djawara."

Lealé's nervousness returned. "Yes."

N'Doch glances around the cramped dark space. He sees low cushioned benches set along the wall that he hadn't noticed were there. In fact, if you'd asked him, he'd have sworn there was no place to sit before.

He sits. "Okay. You wanna talk. Let's talk."

The girl and the apparition join him. The kid grabs

the seat nearest the door, probably so he can keep an eye out for any goings-on in the weird park thing. Lealé does not sit. She paces, not the smoothest thing to do in a space that small. N'Doch can see she's as nervous as a cat.

"I need to start at the beginning, if the story's to make any sense at all. You see, Djawara and I grew up together. We were distantly related." She turns to face N'Doch. "He is truly your grandfather, Djawara is?"

Her doubting makes him huffy again, but the girl is watching him, so he nods in a way he hopes looks noncommittal.

"I should have guessed it would be someone close to him. But I recall him mentioning, when we were still in contact, that he'd lost a grandson or two."

"Three. I'm the fourth, the one he wasn't close to, for a while at least."

Still pacing, she stops in front of the apparition, her face softening like women always do around little kids. "Is he your grandpapa, too?"

The apparition shakes its head.

"What's your name, then?"

"Wasser. It means 'Water.' "

N'Doch is still not happy with this name, has not once yet used it.

Lealé turns to him. "An interesting coincidence. Your name in Wolof is also . . ."

He nods. "Water."

Lealé looks to the girl now. "And yours, my dear?"

"Erde," the girl says, just a bit late.

"A lovely name."

The girl nods. *"Danke."*

"It means 'Earth,' " says the apparition, his child's eyes narrowing on Lealé. N'Doch wonders if the kid means it to sound so much like a challenge.

But Lealé brightens. "Ah. Like my little boulevard outside. Then it must be right." She starts up her pacing again. "I'll go on with my story.

"So, as we were growing up together, Djawara and I, we discovered we shared interests that set us apart from our other friends and relatives. Interests in the past, in history, in the old myths and customs. Djawara, particularly, was a gifted storyteller. He could expand his tales indefinitely, until they became entire sagas based on the adventures of some mythic hero. Later, when I did a little study myself, I discovered that he'd invented most of what he'd held us so enthralled with. When I put it to him, he admitted it readily enough, even seemed pleased with me for finding him out. Then he swore me to secrecy and confessed that he did it to distract himself—and us— from his growing obsession with the one tale that he hadn't invented, at least not consciously, the one tale he just somehow *knew*."

"The boy and the sea monster," N'Doch murmurs in spite of himself.

"Yes. The very one. He told you?"

"He used to sing it to me, when I was little." *Before I decided he was just too uncool to be with,* N'Doch reminds himself ruefully.

"It frightened him, I think," Lealé goes on. "This tale that would not leave him alone, whose central figure— the keeper of the ancient ways—he finally realized was himself." She stops in mid-pace and lets her gaze drift to the floor. "I had my own . . . dilemmas . . . at the time. I was having strange, well . . . visitations. Dreams and visions I couldn't explain. So when Djawara came to me—hoping, I'm sure, for a dose of healthy skepticism— I met him instead with encouragement and belief. I thought, well, if my much respected friend was being overtaken by some inexplicable fate, then my own bizarre experiences might be valid too. So, you see, each of us became the other's proof of sanity, and thus we were bonded for life."

She sighs and leans her head back, smiling, and she's beautiful again. N'Doch can tell she's picturing the young Djawara in her mind, and wishes he could be there to see him, too. "Later on," she continues, "When the events of our lives led us apart, we promised to be available for each other whenever our spiritual lives reached a crisis. For many years, they never did. Then I began having a kind of dream I'd never had before."

For the girl's sake, N'Doch asks, "When was that?"

"Two months ago," the girl puts in abruptly.

He frowns at her. "Let her tell us, huh?"

Lealé asks, "What did she say?"

"She said, two months ago, but that's just . . ."

"That's right. She's exactly right." Slowly, Lealé turns and looks at the girl, like she's seeing her for the first time. The girl smiles, like she's trying to look helpful, but Lealé shudders, moans a little, then drops right down in the middle of the floor cross-legged and buries her head in her hands. "Oh dear oh dear oh dear!" she wails, rocking back and forth. "I knew it I knew it I just knew all this was much more complicated than it seemed at first, much more than he said it would be! Oh dear oh dear oh dear!"

N'Doch sees tears and all, but he's not quite convinced—the change came on her so sudden. But the girl jumps up right away and kneels at Lealé's side, and puts both arms around her like she's known her forever. *Women can do that,* N'Doch reflects. And here comes the apparition now, only he goes around the front and sits facing Lealé, taking her hand more like a woman would do than a little kid. N'Doch thinks maybe the two of them are getting a little carried away, and he stays put, waiting for his part in it to come clear to him. Lotta times, since all this began, he's felt more like a glorified tour guide than this so-called "dragon guide" he's supposed to be. Like, where's his converted armored personnel carrier with the bullet-proof viewing windows, so he can say stuff like, "and on your right, ladies and gentlemen . . ." He's heard the patter. For some weird reason, the tour APCs broadcast it over their exterior speakers as they troll along the city streets and byways. Maybe they're trying to prove those rich foreigners riding in there in air-conditioned comfort are actually learning something useful.

Meanwhile, the girl is saying, "There, there," and other meaningless stuff made even more meaningless by the fact that she's saying it in German, like she's forgotten that Lealé's not a subscriber to the dragon comnet. But the apparition is translating softly in its little-kid voice, and to N'Doch's surprise, all this fuss seems to be having some results. At least Lealé has stopped her wailing.

"There, there," parrots the apparition, its small hands soothing Lealé's knee. "It's all right."

Lealé takes a breath, a long shuddering one, then lets it out in an even longer sigh. "No, you don't know . . .

it's not all right! I should never have told him about Djawara and our pact. I never expected it to come to anything, you see, but now . . ."

"Tell us, Mother Lealé," urges the apparition while the girl murmurs and pats. "Tell us about your dreams."

"I can't!" She hunches up, whispering suddenly. "Not here! He might hear me!"

"Seems like you got overhearing problems wherever you go," N'Doch comments sourly.

"Mother Lealé," whispers the apparition, "surely if he can call you into this room, he can hear you wherever you are."

"Yeah," N'Doch agrees. "So it doesn't really matter, does it, and that's supposing he's listening at all."

Lealé eases herself back onto her heels. She looks a bit cornered but maybe a little comforted and, N'Doch could already tell, always willing to accept an excuse to talk about herself.

"Well, okay, but I refuse to say anything bad about him." She palms tears from her cheeks. N'Doch can see her preparing for a long recital. "Before, you see, my dreams were entirely random. I'd have one every now and then and there'd be someone in it I knew, so I'd go tell them about it and interpret it for them. And I was often helpful to them about some problem they were having, which made me feel good, like I wasn't going through all this weirdness for nothing. Then word got around, though, and people I didn't know came by looking for readings, and sometimes these people would offer me money, and we were poor, so I'd take it."

She shifts a little, her eyes wandering to the walls. N'Doch notices she's placed herself with her back to the door and the still green grove outside. "But then I felt they shouldn't go home empty-handed, so I looked them over as hard as I knew how, and made stuff up best as I could, to satisfy them. Yes!" She slaps her knees lightly with both palms and stares her challenge all around. "I've said it! I used to take money for fakery. But, children, if you understand the world at all at your tender age, you know that all people really want is an exciting performance and close personal attention to their mundane little problems. One way or another, I *always* gave them their money's worth! But then . . ."

Lealé takes another deep breath, steadier this time, and flicks a glance at the girl. "But then one night, about two months ago just like you said, I had this new kind of dream. It was a very specific dream, full of very precise information about some guy I'd never seen before in my life, like watching a vid-doc on the tube or something. I thought it was odd at the time but I didn't worry myself too much about it until later that day, the guy himself— the *exact same guy,* no doubt of it, I could tell you what he looked like even now—he knocks on my gate over on Water Street asking for a Reading.

"Well, needless to say, I gave that guy the Reading of his natural life, and he went out of my house and made a whole lot of money in some business deal, the crucial detail of which had been revealed in my dream! When I heard that, it gave me a chill. Then I had second dream like that, and again the stranger I dreamed about showed up right after, and it kept on happening. Then word really got around fast, and . . ." She stops, breathless, then looks around at each of them as if for sympathy, and shrugs.

"And *presto!*" N'Doch supplies. "You're the Mahatma Glory Magdalena."

Lealé nods as if she can't quite believe it either. "Except that it's not me doing it. Oh—I dreamed this house myself and made it so. Or rather, I learned how to make it so. He taught me."

"This spirit guy . . . ?"

She laughs full-out this time. "Oh, no. Sorry. The *other* one. My investor. I dreamed him once and he showed up."

"And saw you had a gift could make you both a handsome living."

"Yes."

"Which now you don't want to let go of."

"Do you blame me?"

N'Doch stretches his legs. "No way. I'm in awe of your achievement, sister." But it seems to him there's one big detail missing. "So the spirit guy . . . when did he put in a personal appearance?"

Now Lealé hesitates, licking her lips and searching the corners of the room, as if even to speak of him invited his unwelcome presence.

"Please, Mother Lealé," begs the apparition on cue, even though now it's looking just as scared as she is. "Tell us."

"One night I dreamed about me, finding my way to this hidden place. When I woke up, I went and found it, just as the dream had told me. While I was there, I grew drowsy and must have dozed. He came to me then. It was . . ." She's talking so quietly that N'Doch has to lean in to hear her. ". . . after my second dream about Djawara."

"What'd you dream about Papa D.?"

"At first it was just . . . about him. Later, it was about the visitors he would have . . . you. Only not you, exactly. I never expected he'd be sending children. . . ."

N'Doch thinks she's called him a child just about once too often. "What *did* you expect?"

She shrugs uneasily. "Just that there'd be more than one, and that one would be a Dreamer . . . like me."

The girl's been real quiet for a long time, listening, but now she starts murmuring into the apparition's ear.

He says, "Erde asks if you are sure your dreams of Djawara came from your spirit guide? If it was he who sent the dreams, then he must have known all about Djawara already. If he didn't know, he couldn't have sent those particular dreams."

"You mean, they were just . . . dreams?"

"Perhaps," says the kid.

"But they were true dreams, or you wouldn't be here."

"Why should that surprise you? You are, after all, a Dreamer."

N'Doch jumps in. "Anyhow, you haven't betrayed Papa D. after all, so you don't have to worry."

Lealé glances at him, then away. "It isn't Djawara I'm worried about. Djawara is a man of power. He can take care of himself. It's . . ." But she can't quite bring herself to say it, so a silence falls in the dim little room.

"It's us," says the apparition finally. It gets up and walks to look out the green, open doorway. "Isn't it."

Lealé nods. "He wants you . . . done away with. And I was supposed to do it. When you got here."

The apparition smiles at her gently. "I thought you said he didn't ask very much of you. . . ."

But N'Doch's had enough. "Who is this guy anyway?

What's he got against me? I don't even know him!" He knows it's nuts, taking death threats from spirits seriously when he doesn't even believe in spirits, least he didn't used to. But that was back when he didn't believe in dragons either. "Sounds like a major raw deal coming my way, and for nothing!"

"Be cool, my brother," the apparition advises from the doorway.

"*You* be cool," N'Doch snaps back.

The kid turns, standing taller and older, silhouetted against the livid green. "You're surprised only because you've forgotten who and what you are, what I am, what we are, and what we must do."

Lealé watches with a mixture of awe and agitation, so that when the kid comes toward her again, she recoils, leaning back on one hand, twisting herself defensively to one side.

"Mother Lealé," the kid says in a soft voice that fills the room. "It is absolutely vital that you tell us everything about this 'spirit guide' of yours. What he says, how he looks when he comes to you, *everything*."

N'Doch is watching, too, and not real happily, 'cause the older the apparition makes itself appear, the more it looks like Sedou.

Lealé shivers, staring up at her pint-sized inquisitor. "Who are you? *What* are you?"

N'Doch thinks, *Well, I guess the gloves are all off now, aren't they?*

Chapter Twenty-Eight

Erde had observed Wasser's handling of Lealé with admiration, but she did wonder how much his/her true nature the boy/dragon thought was safe to reveal. Something that Lealé had said provoked this display of strength. Apparently Wasser had decided that the woman had information he needed to know sooner rather than later.

"What kind of spirit might this be that visits Mistress Lealé?" she asked, thinking to gentle the moment away from confrontation.

"There are no spirits," Wasser replied gravely, with his eyes still fixed on Lealé. He looked as though he might pin her to the ground if she but moved an inch.

"No spirits?" Lealé managed. "But I . . ."

"There are only Powers, and humans with a gift. I am one such, and I wish to know what other seeks my end."

It was a tone she had never heard out of Wasser or even Water, before. Quiet, but full of intimations of ancient strength and grandeur. Erde backed away a step and sat down along the wall. She saw N'Doch do the same, both of them leaving the floor to what both of them knew was a dragon with a serious purpose in mind.

"First, describe this 'spirit' to me. Don't leave out the smallest detail."

Lealé's brow creased. "I don't see what . . ."

"Not the smallest detail. I do not ask without reason."

"What if he hears and comes after me?"

"I will protect you."

Lealé grinned weakly. "I think you'll have to grow some before you take him on."

"If it will make you feel more confident." And right

there in front of her, he did, each moment looking less and less like a little boy and more like a man. Erde saw N'Doch ease himself backward along the wall.

Lealé stared, caught between terror and curiosity. But she was not undone, having already lived much of her life with the miraculous and inexplicable. "What is your gift?" she asked shakily.

O clever dragon, Erde thought. *Offer a choice of truths and let the hearer make the wrong one.*

"I have many. Tell us about your dream-giver."

Lealé blew air softly between pursed lips. "Well, he is very vain . . . he'll probably love hearing me describe him. He's very handsome, you see. . . ."

"He's human, a man? He comes to you as a man?"

"Oh, yes, he surely does. He's tall and broad-shouldered, with perfect ebony skin and the flashing golden eyes of a warrior."

"He's got gold eyes?" N'Doch asked dubiously.

Lealé was caught up in her description now. "As gold as the rising sun. And his voice is very deep and resonant."

"Of course it is," muttered N'Doch. "And he's able to leap tall buildings in a single bound."

"How is it that I look as I do?" Wasser reminded him quietly. "There are humans with the gift to take on the aspect most desired."

N'Doch glared at him. "You are certainly not what I most desired."

"Consider it further, my brother."

Erde was grateful when N'Doch folded into a thoughtful silence for a while. It was clear to her, as it would have been to any woman, that Lealé's relationship with this "spirit guide" was rather complicated. She seemed now to be consulting her inner portrait of him, or it, and her expression had grown definitely dreamy.

"He has very big hands with unusually long nails, which he keeps up very carefully. In fact, he paints them."

"Yes," replied Wasser softly. "Long nails. Anything else?"

Lealé giggled briefly. "Oh, he won't like me telling you this, but it's his choice, so he must think it makes him look good." She lowered her voice to a breathy gossip's whisper. "He always wears a lot of gold jewelry. All sorts of it, anywhere you can imagine! Places even I wouldn't have imagined!" She sat back with a pretense of offended modesty. "Isn't that peculiar?"

N'Doch started to chuckle but Wasser only grew grimmer.

"Ah. Golden eyes, golden metal," the boy/dragon said tightly, turning to gaze out on the grove again. "What color does he paint his long nails?"

"Gold! What else?" Lealé leaned forward intimately. "And detailed with exquisite miniatures of beautiful naked women, a different one on each nail—I mentioned he was vain, didn't I?" She grinned as if it were a great joke, but Wasser's tense back told Erde that it was not.

"What else?" The boy/dragon now seemed the reluctant one, and Lealé the eager raconteur, spurred on by N'Doch's appreciative laughter.

"He has a right to be vain, beautiful as he is, but he's also very proud. He's always boasting of how powerful he is. And he has a terrible temper!"

"What does he do?" asked N'Doch.

"Oh, he can't actually do anything physical, but he can take my Dreams away and make my life completely miserable!"

Wasser turned. "He cannot manifest?"

Lealé shook her head.

"A Power, then, surely," Wasser concluded. "It's as I feared."

But N'Doch looked enormously relieved. "Then he's not gonna be, like, jumping out of bushes to slit my throat or anything."

"Not him, no."

"So what does it matter?"

Lealé's mouth tightened. "You can't imagine how much it matters. His tongue is as lethal as any blade."

". . . as corrosive as acid," murmured Wasser from the doorway.

"Yes," she said to his back. "Exactly."

"O, I fear, I fear," he whispered, as if to himself.

N'Doch shook his head. "Not me, man. I'm real glad to know some spook who's said he wants me dead can't actually make it happen."

Wasser sighed, as if exhausted. "Anything more you can tell us?"

Lealé shrugged. "Well, let's see . . . he smokes."

N'Doch laughed out loud. "You got a spirit that smokes?"

"No." Wasser turned toward Lealé, his face darkened by shadows and foreboding. "He comes in smoke. He comes wreathed in its tendrils, as if accompanied, and perhaps here and there a touch of flame."

"Yes," breathed Lealé. "How did you know?"

"You know who this is," Erde murmured.

"I have an inkling now, oh, yes, I do, a terrible inkling. But perhaps this is his idea of a prank, a way to make his presence known and demonstrate his superiority at the same time."

"A prank?" repeated Lealé, sobering. "No, I don't think so. Not when I tell you how many ways he'd figured out that I could murder you. If he's who you think he is, would he want you out of the way so badly?"

"If he's who I think he is, he is capable of anything."

"Hold it . . ." broke in N'Doch. "I thought you said he couldn't . . ."

"If he can't manifest a physical presence in this plane," said Wasser impatiently, "he has only to coerce a human agent into doing his bidding. By giving them gifts, and promising great wonders."

Staring down at her hands, Lealé nodded.

N'Doch snorted, scanning the dark walls, the invisible ceiling. "Wow. So maybe bringing us here is one of the ways, huh?"

"No," said Lealé mildly.

"And why not?" Wasser inquired, just as mildly.

Her bittersweet smile seemed to be admitting to a fatal weakness. "He didn't tell me it'd be killing children. I guess I just don't have it in me."

"I am glad of that, Mother Lealé."

"But you know, he'll only find someone to do what he wants. And, of course, I will be ruined. I should have known things don't come this easy." She thought for a moment, then frowned gently. "He got one thing wrong, though. He told me to expect four of you, not three."

This seemingly minor bit of information seemed to drain the last gleam of hopeful doubt from Wasser's eyes. He hunched, let out a soft moan. His whole outline seemed to waver.

N'Doch leaped to his feet. "No! Don't do it! Not here!"

Erde moved to comfort him, but the boy/dragon caught him/herself and steadied. "It's time we got out of here. I must warn my brother." He started down the receding dark passage, then threw over his shoulder angrily, "My other brother!"

Chapter Twenty-Nine

When they get back to the alcove, N'Doch sees the food's still sitting on the plates like nobody's touched it. In fact, his coffee's still hot, which makes him wonder about how much time they'd actually spent in that weird dark place. Maybe not as long as it seemed.

And now there's a lot of knocking on the door out in the main room. N'Doch checks behind him to see if they'll have some explaining to do, how they went in with a little kid and came out with a full grown man. But the apparition has returned to kid form. N'Doch breathes a sigh of relief.

Lealé motions them toward the sofas in the alcove and mimes eating. "Rest, children, and we'll talk later," she says in her Glory voice. "I must return to my duties." She draws heavy, embroidered drapes across the archway and lets herself out between them. N'Doch can hear her unlocking the big double doors and exclaiming in full-blown Glory persona, "My goodness, what *is* all the fuss about?"

The reply is murmured and unintelligible.

"What did you think?" Glory comes back. "Of course I'm ready! Are the afternoon candidates assembled? I hope you remembered to . ."

The thick wooden doors shut behind her. The big room is silent. N'Doch gets up to sneak a peek through the drapes, and feels the now familiar itch inside his head. He turns to reply out loud, but the apparition quickly raises a finger to its lips.

—*We'll take no chances.*

N'Doch nods. It'll be an effort, him not being real experienced at it, but he's beginning to see real advantages in this silent communication. As soon as he goes to the right place in his head, he feels the big guy's presence there again and hears his rumbled greeting. He's surprised how glad it makes him.

And now he guesses it's safe to ask:

—*What'd you mean, your* other *brother?*

—**Our brother Fire.**

—*And he's, y'know, like you? A dragon?*

—**Of course.**

Her voice in his head is irritated, and in front of him, the apparition frowns. But its gaze is oddly distant and N'Doch's almost sure it's frowning at the possibility of Fire and not at him at all.

—**And if Fire were to take a human form, it would likely be as Lealé has described.**

The girl's voice chimes in, softer than her spoken voice.

—*Surely not, Mistress Water! A dragon works only for good!*

—**Whatever gave you that idea? Brother, perhaps it's time to relieve this child of some of her illusions.**

The girl looks dumbstruck, and Earth's reply, when it comes, is humble.

—**I did not recall what our brother Fire was like until just now.**

—*We gotta go talk to this asshole, then!*

N'Doch turns to the hidden archway, where the paneling had swung inward so readily at Lealé's touch. He presses on the wall and nothing happens. He feels around a bit, searching for a seam or crack to tell him where the hinges are. Nothing.

"Damn!" he murmurs. He tries to picture exactly where Lealé placed her hand just before she vanished, and feels around some more. Still no luck. The apparition joins him but stands back after a while.

—**We will look very suspicious to anyone monitoring the surveillance system.**

N'Doch shakes his head. He's beginning to understand why they need him around after all. He's like their technical expert.

—*From what she said, I got the idea there was only sound sensors in this part of the room.*

—**That doesn't seem very thorough.**

He wonders how much detail he's gonna have to go into.

—But look at all these big plush sofas and things . . . maybe the big bankroll himself wants a little privacy in here from time to time . . . you know what I mean?

The girl looks back at him blankly, but N'Doch feels Water's knowing assent in a whole new corner of his mind, a place apart from where all four of them spoke together. He hopes the images that ran through his mind along with the thought of the bankroll on the sofas have stayed in that special corner as well. He figures they must have, or the girl would be blushing something fierce. What's odd about all of this is he's just recalled what Papa Djawara implied about Lealé preferring women. Maybe when he said her interests lay elsewhere, he meant she was hot for some other *guy.* Certainly now that he's watched her operate, N'Doch's inclined toward that explanation. He realizes now that Lealé's a hard one to read. She's like a whole lot of people rolled up into one.

—So we can't get back in there till Lealé tells us how. What'd you wanna do, then? You think she expects us to just hang around here?

N'Doch looks longingly at his plate still mostly full of food. He sees the girl has edged herself closer to her own plate in order to pick at it surreptitiously.

"You hungry, girl?" he asks aloud.

She nods, and N'Doch grins. It's beginning to feel like she really is his baby sister. "Then, first things first, I say. Let's eat."

It's just about the best meal N'Doch can ever remember. He tries not to stuff himself so much it'll slow him down, but it's hard. His reflex is to eat when the food's at hand, 'cause it'll likely be a while before you see it again, especially food like this—safe, fresh and delicious, with such a variety of tastes and textures all at once. He's not used to being able to choose to eat *this* instead of *that* simply because *this* might taste better.

After a while, he looks up. The apparition is waiting none too patiently in front of a full plate.

"Eat up," N'Doch advises. "You don't get it much better than this."

The kid makes a little Jéjé face, entirely out of sync with the voice in N'Doch's head.

—I can't eat in this form. The parts aren't all in the right place.

N'Doch doesn't know why, but it makes him laugh.

—You mean, if I sliced you open right now, it'd be a real biological surprise?

—Wouldn't be a pretty sight.

—Kinda like it isn't when you're changing, huh?

—Probably so.

Sitting cross-legged on the edge of the sofa, struggling not to get lost in cushions too deep for his small body, the apparition's really looking like his dead little brother. It makes N'Doch remember stuff he'd forgotten, moments of stupid kid-jokes, moments of shared conspiracy, the few moments they'd had to feel like brothers before Jéjé was gone. Moments sort of like this. He grins across the girl's dark head, bowed over her plate.

—Whadda ya say, think we oughta go exploring a little?

The apparition nods, and the girl looks up. She's been listening in.

—As soon as is possible, we must find some place for Earth to join us.

She's right, of course. N'Doch gives it some thought.

—There's a big garage out back.

—What about the park you and Mistress Lealé spoke of? Is there cover?

—Not much. Besides, I got a weird feeling about that place.

The apparition hops to its feet.

—Let's go take a look.

The girl's been eating slowly. N'Doch waves at her to keep at it.

—You stick close and hold the fort, case Lealé comes back.

Her eyes widen in protest.

—She won't expect you to talk to her or anything. Just keep an eye on her, y'know? Follow her around like you're glad for another woman's company.

He thinks it's a pretty clever ruse, but the girl nods so pensively that N'Doch suspects he's touched a true nerve. It makes him wonder about her a little. Like, maybe she's got a mother somewhere worrying about where she is, like his mother worried about all her sons, and lost them anyway, all except him. What would it do to poor Fâtime, so worn and numbed by loss, to see the spitting image of her youngest standing right in front of her the way the apparition's there in front of him now, ready for an adventure? He thinks it might just finish her off.

He jerks his head at the kid gruffly, the way older brothers get to do, and lifts his hand to the girl.

—*You can always just pretend you're asleep. And if you need us, just give a yell. We'll come running.*

She nods. She doesn't look all that worried, actually. She knows, as he does, that she can monitor them every step of the way through the big guy.

N'Doch turns and parts the concealing draperies with a finger. He surveys the outer room, counting a camera port in every corner.

—*No way we're gonna get outa here without them seeing. Better just look like we know where we're going. I'll go first, see if I set off any alarms.*

He pushes through the heavy curtains and wanders across the room to the food table. It's all still there, laid out like a gang leader's funeral supper. Though he'd been sure he couldn't possibly cram in another bite, N'Doch finds a few things he hasn't tried and starts nibbling. It's a good enough cover, and so far, he's heard no bells or sirens, no Jean-Pierre flapping down the hallway, screeching like some big white bird. Course, all the most expensive systems give silent alarms: some bright red readout below a bank of sleek monitors in an office somewhere full of fast guys with guns.

The apparition joins him and pretends to pick at the food for a while. Neither of them have any trouble producing the right body language of two bored young men tired of being cooped up inside.

—*You ready, bro?*

The apparition grins at him. As one, they turn and head for the door.

Chapter Thirty

It was odd, Erde thought, the lassitude that came over her when she was left alone in the alcove, enclosed by its thick draperies and its strange furniture, as softly cushioned as a feather bed. The cool air smelled faintly of perfume, and the light was dim and golden, like a dying fire but as miraculously steady as the sun's own light. This, she supposed, was Master Djawara's "electricity", which she had not yet seen close up. The lanterns that made it were tall and thin, like brass bells turned upside down on the top of pike poles, and did not flicker. For the first time since arriving in this world of 2013, she was not hot and sweaty, she was not uncomfortable or dirty, and she was not hungry. She thought perhaps she should be a bit more nervous than she was about being left on her own in a strange house, but the rich food and the sudden comfort were making her irresistibly drowsy.

—*Dragon, I need to sleep a little. Will you watch over me and wake me up within the hour?*

—**I will, as best I can from such a distance.**

—*Not so far, really, and they will find a place here for you soon.*

—**I am eager for that.**

—*As am I, dear Dragon.*

Erde settled herself into the deepest cushions, in the farthest corner. Perhaps if someone looked in here, they wouldn't even notice her. Her last thought, swimming up through the layers of drowse just as she fell asleep, was: I hope I don't dream.

But of course she did.

* * *

She thought she woke in darkness, but then the darkness showed a dim light through a crack across from her bed. A lantern in the outer room, she decided sleepily.

—*For shame, Dragon! You've let me sleep far too long.*

She yawned and stretched, awaiting his reply, his expected excuses about how badly she needed her sleep. But the dragon's answer did not come. Then she realized that, stretching, she could not feel her body. She tried to sit up and had no awareness of limbs. No sensation at all except a creeping dread. She was not awake. She was dreaming, and the air in the room was damp and chill, and full of the snap and groan of wind among tent ropes.

She watched the lighted crack, her only anchor in the blackness, and understood she was looking through a slit between lowered tent flaps. Outside, the light dipped and flared in the breeze. Torches, then. One at least. And no other sound but the wind.

Suddenly, as if she'd arrived in this dream just at its moment of crisis, she heard the soft thud of running feet, feet trying not to make noise, encumbered by the weight and rattle of weapons and armor.

She heard a frightened voice cry, "Halt!" and heard it just as quickly hushed, followed by a hurried conference, low and urgent.

The tent flap was snatched aside.

"My lord!" A half-dressed squire, painfully young, stood in the opening. "My lord baron! Are you awake?"

"What? Yes!" growled a voice so close to Erde's side that the shock alone nearly woke her up, a voice shaking off sleep like a dog shakes off water. "Yes, fool, I'm awake. What is it?"

The boy hissed to the man behind him, then took a torch from him and stepped aside. A tall and burly soldier stooped into the tent and went down on one knee. The torch at the opening lit his mud-spattered face and heaving chest, and the grim rage in his eyes.

"Wender. What . . . ?" The man on the cot came up warily on one arm. The edge of the torchlight touched the rough gold of his beard, and Erde could confirm what she already anticipated: Adolphus of Köthen.

"My lord, they've taken the Prince."

"What? We had men guarding his tent."

"Dead."

Köthen sat up, swinging his legs to the ground. "All?"

"Throats cut, all three of 'em, with the Prince's own dagger, my lord, conveniently left behind."

"What of the priest's men?"

"A showy mess of surface wounds, but all likely to recover, probably by morning if circumstance doesn't intervene. I'm tempted to let it. Each claims to have seen the Prince fighting 'like ten thousand demons.' "

"Ah, Carl, poor lad." Köthen ran angry hands through his sleep-matted hair. "Is there a trail?"

"Two, my lord. The one we're supposed to find, and then the other. I sent six of our best to follow the second, and came to fetch you."

"All this without arousing notice?"

Wender smiled, and Erde pitied the man who got on his wrong side. "Aye, my lord."

"Pray they find him. Pray six will be enough. Have you horses ready?"

"In the copse."

"Tell that silly boy to douse the torch before he announces us to the entire camp. His little fire should be enough to keep the dark away." Köthen heaved himself out of bed. "Help me dress."

Before the torch could be extinguished, Köthen walked into its flickering light. He was naked. Erde tried to look away, but the dream-state did not allow her the luxury of modesty, and in the slowness of dreams where a few seconds can seem an eternity, she found herself made breathless at the sight of him. She'd never seen a grown man naked. She thought men were probably ugly without their fashionably form-altering clothes. Even Rainer, that fine figure of a young man she'd convinced herself she was in love with, even in her most romantic fantasies she'd always pictured him fully dressed.

But this man was beautiful, naked or clothed. She could not help but notice his efficient grace, or how the muscles moved under his skin as he bent to snatch up his clothing, or how the failing torchlight glimmered gold on the hair of his arms and chest and thighs. The intimacy of the moment shamed her. Surely Baron Köthen would be appalled if he knew. But she could not look away. She thought she could look at him forever.

Then he moved out of the light and threw on his shirt and undertunic. Erde was released from her disturbing fascination and had a moment to consider the dire news about the Prince. She wondered where her father's hand was in this latest plot.

Wender shook out Köthen's mail and held it high for the baron to shrug into, easy enough as he was at least a head taller than Köthen and several stone heavier. "It seems this priest will make you King, my lord, whether you like it or not."

Köthen laughed sourly. He slipped on his blue-and-yellow tabard, then bent to pull on his boots. "And when Otto and his mysterious champion are dead on the field, and I've rallied the people around me with the promise of victory and peace, how long do you think I will survive?"

Wender grunted. He turned away and came back with Köthen's sword and dagger. Köthen took them wordlessly and buckled them on.

Outside the tent, the torch had been upended in the squire's little campfire. The two men hesitated, straining through the high sighing of the wind to pick out other, man-made noises. The moon was bright. Köthen squinted at it suspiciously.

"Back to bed with you," he murmured to his waiting squire. "Or at least pretend to be, as if I were still inside asleep as usual. Have you your weapon handy?"

The boy shivered and patted the long knife on his hip.

"Good lad. Protect yourself if the need arises." Köthen nodded to Wender then, and followed him off into the night.

The horses were waiting with another dozen men in a copse of aspens out of hearing of the encampment. With the moon to light their way, they quickly picked up the trail of those who had gone ahead along the muddied road.

"He hopes they'll mingle with the track of ordinary travelers," noted Wender. "But only brigands and soldiers travel in a time of war."

Köthen grinned. "Well, we know which of us are the soldiers. . . ."

Erde found herself galloping through the moonlit darkness as if she were a hawk on Köthen's shoulder.

She could almost forget she was dreaming, but for the rock and rise of Köthen's body on his racing horse, in such sharp contrast to her own smooth surreal flight.

But cushioned as she was by the unreality of the dream, she could not shrug off the lurking dread. Köthen's presence somehow held the dread at bay. She recalled how he had protected her from the priest in the barn at Erfurt, even though she was a stranger and the ally of his enemy. Being with him flushed her whole body with warmth and a sense of well-being. But she knew that this strange euphoria was but a thin tissue between her and the terrible things she sensed were about to happen, and could do nothing to prevent. The dread was real and could not be avoided forever.

They rode hard for a good while until Wender judged they might be closing on the men he'd sent ahead. The ground was half mud, half ice, and pocked with puddles frozen just enough to make a noise when horses' hooves crashed through them. Where the trees folded over the road, straining out the moonlight, Wender slowed them to pick their way along more quietly, listening ahead. Soon Wender pulled up, his hand raised for a halt. Köthen rode up beside him.

"A light, my lord, though the trees off to the left."

Köthen cocked his head. "No sounds of battle."

"No. We'll go in on foot, in case our men are yet waiting to engage."

The baron nodded. He seemed to have no difficulty taking direction from an older and more experienced adviser. "Quickly, though, in case they've been taken unawares."

The company dismounted silently and left two men behind with the horses. Köthen drew his sword. Several of the soldiers armed their crossbows. They left the roadside and crept into the trees, seeking the quietest path through the sodden leaves and matted underbrush, avoiding the brighter patches of snow and ice where a man's footfall would sound as loudly as a shout.

Those ahead did not seem to be making any great effort at silence. They'd lit two torches already and soon a third flared to life. Erde could hear horses milling and snorting, and voices that were restrained but not muffled. Wender waved his company forward, signaling one man to Köthen's right and taking up the left-hand guard himself.

They were well within range when a voice ahead sounded an alert and the torches were doused in an instant. But that single word of command told Wender what he needed to know. He signaled his men down, then whistled sharply, three ascending notes and one falling.

"That's Hoch," he whispered. "I'm sure of it."

A whistled reply came back immediately, the same four notes in reverse order. Wender rose and moved on ahead.

They came down into a snow-swept clearing, broad enough for a circle of moonlight to make its way through the overhanging trees. Hoch's men relit the torches while Hoch came forward to meet them. Erde saw in the man's eyes the dread she'd been shoving aside. Köthen saw it, too.

"What is it, Hoch? What have you found?"

Hoch had a thin, intelligent, worried face. Erde thought he looked more like a guildsman than a soldier. He swallowed nervously but looked his baron in the eye. "The worst, my lord."

"The Prince?"

Hoch dropped his glance, nodding.

"Dead? Already?"

"Dead, my lord. Within the hour."

Köthen swore and looked away. Then he glared around at the waiting men as if searching out someone to blame for this outrage he'd been so sure he could prevent. His men stood their ground silently, their heads bowed, absorbing the heat of his rage and giving him back their trust. It moved Erde deeply that Köthen, even as he was at that moment, a dangerous and angry man swinging a naked blade so that it flashed in the torchlight, would never turn his rage on his men. Her father's men would have retreated well out of range, as far as was possible with honor, in such a situation.

Prince Carl dead. Murdered, she supposed, and she had no doubt by whom. The mad priest's plot was proceeding. Was it possible that he—and evil—would somehow win the day?

Finally Köthen took a breath, lowered his sword, and sheathed it abruptly. "Show me," he growled.

Hoch offered a slight bow. He motioned to one of the torchbearers, and led the way.

The young Prince lay crumpled at the foot of a big tree. He was small for his age, having not inherited his father Otto's height. His feet were bare and battered. Not at all the figure of a King or warrior, Erde mused. He'd been a studious boy, she recalled Hal mentioning. Her heart went out to him: a scholar, doomed by birth to be a pawn in the vicious games of men more powerful and ambitious than himself. He was dressed in the soft robes he would have worn for retiring to bed. Clearly, he had not been armed. One torn end of a long sleeve had been folded back to cover his face.

Erde searched for blood or wounds. There were none anywhere on his slim body, except on his torn and muddy feet. Then she noticed the rope disappearing beneath the covering sleeve. Hoch took the torch in his own hand and raised it in order to illuminate a stout overhanging branch of the tree. Another length of rope dangled there, its loose end hastily slashed.

Hoch cleared his throat. "We cut him down not five minutes before you came, my lord."

The men in Wender's party shifted and muttered.

Köthen stared up at the offending rope. "He will call it a suicide and discredit the whole of Otto's line. Why? This Prince was not his enemy. Are there no depths to which this man will not sink?"

No, Erde wanted to shout at him. *Not a one! I could have told you that! Hal tried to tell you in Erfurt, but you wouldn't listen!*

Köthen raised his voice to be heard around the clearing. "Let not a man of you believe that the Prince died by his own hand!"

Wender laid a feather-light hand of warning on his baron's sleeve.

Köthen shrugged him off brusquely. "Yes, yes, Wender, I'll be quiet. For now, at least. But later . . ." He knelt beside the body and briefly lifted the concealing sleeve. "Forgive me, my Prince. I tried to keep you safe as best I knew how."

Wender waited, sucking his teeth, then said quietly, "We could undo the shame at least, my lord."

Köthen gave his lieutenant a shocked look that slowly turned to bleak acceptance. He rose, flicking the sleeve back into place. "Do it," he said, "then swear the men to secrecy."

"Aye, my lord."

Wender sent the men scurrying—to untie the rope from the tree, from the Prince's neck, to burn the evidence and scatter the ashes, and finally to do the necessary violence to the corpse. Köthen moved away, out of the gathered circle of torches, away from the busy clot of men. He moved like a man in physical pain, sorry for the death of an innocent, Erde thought, but also deeply disturbed by the sacrilege of this pragmatic desecration. Köthen would go to confession and do his penitence, and still carry this guilt on his soul forever, even though he had allowed it for all the right reasons, to honor a monarch he himself was trying to usurp. Watching him brood, she ached for him. Her desire to reach out to him grew so intense that she could almost believe it was possible, by sheer force of longing, to walk out of her dream-state and into Köthen's reality.

This was a new idea, and even as swept up as she was in dream-induced fantasizing, the fact that she was considering it seriously quite took her aback. Her intention shifted a bit more toward the rational with her sudden realization that she had information that might ease Köthen's guilt: If what Hal and Rose had surmised about Rainer's parentage was true, a rightful heir to the throne might still exist, that is, if Köthen and her father hadn't already killed him off unknowingly. But she had heard Köthen's brief reference to Otto's "mysterious champion," and was sure it could be none other. If Rainer lived, and if he was the true Prince, Köthen could forget all this needing to be regent in order to keep the country together. He could join Hal and establish Rainer as Otto's heir, and this alliance would crush the offending priest like a bug. And then they could all run the country together. Erde thought it a grand and glorious vision, a future one could look forward to. It was nearly—minus Rainer—what Köthen himself had offered Hal at Erfurt.

It was a perfect plan and would solve everything. The hell-priest would at last be defeated.

She was very aware of being without substance in her dream-state, but her other senses were fully intact. She could see and hear and smell. Perhaps she could simply speak to Köthen without leaving the dream at all . . . why had she not thought of this before? And what harm could it possibly do to try? She focused on him very hard and thought of speaking, as she did when she spoke with the dragons.

—*My lord of Köthen. . . .*

Her dream-voice was like the whisper of night wings. She could hear it . . . but could he?

A thrill shot through her when she saw his head lift slightly and his eyes sweep the darkness in front of him as if listening. She had never expected to make contact so easily and now she was almost tongue-tied. What should she say to him? How should she introduce herself, a person he hardly knew, his enemy? How explain to him what was happening? She recalled how long it had taken N'Doch to accept the joining of minds. Köthen, she suspected, considered himself a rationalist, a pious man but not much given to superstition. How could she put words into his head without him thinking he was losing his mind?

—*My lord of Köthen . . .*

It sounded so formal. Then she remembered what Hal had called him.

—*Dolph . . .*

His head jerked this time. His eyes widened. She watched a faint flush of fear race through him. She decided she would not introduce herself at all. It was not her identity that mattered, it was her message, and now she realized she must convey it quickly. Even in her disembodied state, she suddenly felt faint. Each effort to bridge the gap between Köthen and herself sucked energy out of her like water down a drain. It was a greater gap than she'd imagined. She had to tell him her message before she lost the strength to do it.

—*Baron Köthen . . . Dolph . . . a Prince may live still . . . find Hal and ask him. . . .*

Köthen shook his head hard, then pressed his temples

with both hands and let out a strangled cough. "Hal?" he murmured.

A sentry's whistle off to the left distracted him. Quickly, Wender joined him at the edge of the darkness, and Köthen was once again all business.

"Visitors, my lord."

"Indeed. How convenient. Have you done what you must?"

"We have."

"Prepare His Highness for transport, then, with the honor due his rank. And, Wender . . . don't be too quick about it, eh?"

"Will he come himself, do you think?"

"He expects to find his Christmas goose still trussed and hanging."

Wender grinned his flat, dark grin. His eyes flicked off through the trees toward the road, where the approach of men and horses was no longer a suspicion. "Sounds like he's brought a whole regiment. And enough torches to light a town."

"Or burn it. Better send some of the men into the woods to cover us, in case in his madness, he decides to murder us all and lay the blame for Carl's death on me."

"What head will he have left then to crown, my lord, having so long ago lost his own?"

Köthen's laugh was a short bark. "Why, I suppose von Alte's next in line, poor fool."

Wender snorted and went off to prepare the body. Köthen drew his sword, set its point to the frozen ground, and leaned on it gently, awaiting the priest's arrival.

Now Erde's terror stirred in earnest. From the time her dreams of home began, she knew Fra Guill would enter them sooner or later. Even in his absence, his black aura pervaded them. Her dream-state connection with Adophus of Köthen, her supposed enemy, was a mystery and a surprise, if now increasingly a pleasure. But from the day the hell-priest first presumed upon the hospitality of her father's court, from when his thief's eyes picked her out and followed her everywhere, when in the barn at Erfurt he had sniffed her out of hiding despite her disguise, she knew that her fate was entwined with Guillemo's in some grim and awful way. In fact, if there was any way she could manage to wake up, now was the time to do it. But she was unable to wake herself from these dreams as she had learned to with ordinary nightmares. So she withdrew inward as best she could, and imagined concealing herself in Köthen's shadow.

Even so, when the first of the white-robes appeared, pale ghosts moving between the black columnar ranks of trees, each with its own huge torch, she thought of the lost souls wandering in torment, the souls these white ghosts had put to the torch at Tubin and the other "witch-ridden" towns. And she wondered if it was possible to die of terror while dreaming. Only the thought of the dragon waiting for her a thousand years away gave her the strength and the reason to master her fear, the way the man beside her was mastering his loathing and outrage in order to gain control of himself, and the situation.

The priest's forces fanned out as they entered the clearing, a long arc of hooded men in white, mounted on tall white horses. Köthen did not move from his casual pose, but his eyes took them in, counting. Erde counted twenty, and was relieved not to find her father among them. Apparently he was not included in this particular conspiracy. Did that imply that Josef von Alte was losing his usefulness to Brother Guillemo? Erde feared for her father's life if he was.

A space left in the center of the ranks was filled at last by Fra Guill himself, unhooded but wearing a full soldier's breastplate over his white monk's robe. His tonsured hair was no longer the madman's rat's nest it had been when she'd seen him last, but his face had grown gaunt and sallow. His eyes receded so deeply into their hollows that they appeared as two shards of ice glimmering in wells of shadow.

He spurred his horse forward. "Abroad so late, Köthen? Or is it early?"

If Köthen noticed the lack of honorific in the priest's greeting, he did not show it. Erde took this as a frightening sign of how far the tables of power had already turned. It occurred to her to worry for Köthen's safety as well as her father's.

"Late, Guillemo, much too late, in fact. But so are you, it seems."

"The battle against Satan knows no clock. Late is early, is it not? And so, what finds you here?"

Köthen tossed a nod behind him. "A little business. What finds *you* here?"

"Our hardy pursuit of that Satan's minion, Otto's treacherous spawn, who's made a bloody and murderous escape this night."

Köthen leaned on his sword hilt a little more heavily and replied dryly, "He'd hardly have been trying to escape, Guillemo. He's barefoot and in his bedclothes."

The priest's eyes narrowed until their light was virtually extinguished. "You have news of the villain?"

"I have news of the Prince, if that's who you mean."

Erde wondered if Köthen was hoping to make Guillemo beg. He was goading the priest, for some hidden reason or because he could not restrain his hostility completely. Either way, she wished he would stop. Was she the only soul in Christendom besides Hal Engle who understood how venomous Fra Guill really was? When she'd faced him last, in Erfurt, he'd seemed wily but entirely mad. Now he appeared to have regained possession of himself. Erde was unsure if this was better or worse.

"You've caught up with him?" Guillemo sat up ever so slightly to peer past Köthen toward the huddle of men on the far side of the clearing.

"In a manner of speaking."

"What's the news, then?"

"Your heart's desire, Guillemo. The Prince is dead."

"Ah." Instantly, the priest crossed himself and bowed his head. A moment later, twenty white-robes did likewise, sending a rustle of wool and rosaries through the damp, still air. "Did he confess his dread villainy and call on his Savior before being given his end?"

Köthen seemed to be working a bad taste out of his mouth. "I doubt he was given the chance. He was dead when we got here."

The banked glimmer in Guillemo's eyes flared up again. "Ah! Distraught, then, with the weight of his bloody deeds, as a ray of goodness pierced his heart and made him see his . . ."

The priest had an infinite supply of self-serving rhetoric, as Erde clearly recalled. But Köthen had had enough. "Carl was murdered, Guillemo. By brigands, one supposes, unless you have any better ideas."

"Murdered? You've seen it . . . him . . . yourself?"

"You know me, Brother. I never take anyone's word for anything."

"I'll go to him, then. To offer whatever poor words might be allowed to intercede for his tarnished soul."

Köthen cocked his head, still leaning on his sword. "Be my guest."

The white-robes remained in their long array as their leader rode across the clearing. The torches made way for him, and a man-at-arms leaped forward to hold his horse as he dismounted. As he moved into the crowd of soldiers, Köthen jerked his sword out of the ground and strode after him.

Wender met him just outside the circle of light, stooping to pick up Köthen's hurried murmur.

"I don't like it. He's taken it too quietly."

"Grace in the face of being outmaneuvered, my lord?"

"Not even a possibility. Stay by me."

They found Guillemo on his knees beside the Prince's corpse, peeling back the wrapping of cloaks and oilskins with his own too-eager hands. Hoch and Wender had artfully arranged the layers to allow exposure of the Prince's wounds with a minimum of effort. Guillemo wished to see a little more. He yanked and burrowed until he was satisfied, and all Köthen could do was stand and watch. Erde wished he would move off a bit. She had little stomach for being forced to observe the poor mutilated body at such close range. But she did note how all evidence of Carl's true cause of death had indeed been erased by Wender's careful butchery.

Guillemo studied the wreckage carefully. He touched his finger to a ragged gash, then smoothed the blood between finger and thumb, sniffing at it cautiously.

Wender muttered at Köthen's side, "More like a chirugeon than a priest."

Köthen watched and waited, and soon had his answer.

Guillemo sniffed his bloodied fingertips again, rubbed them together and sniffed again. Abruptly, he cried out and sprang to his feet.

"Water! Ho, water! Quickly, on peril of my soul!"

A man-at-arms grabbed a waterskin off the nearest

horse and ran over, shoving it at the priest with both hands in frantic bewilderment.

"Pour it for me, fool! Quickly, on my hand! Or else we'll both be damned!"

The nervous soldier drenched Guillemo's hand, water spilling everywhere, even on the Prince's body. The priest then raised that hand, dripping, and held it out from himself like it carried some treasure or disease. "A torch, now! Bring me a torch!"

A torch appeared, and Guillemo directed the man to angle it toward the ground so that the flame swelled and leaped upward, overfed with fuel. With slow ceremony, Guillemo passed his wet hand through the dancing flame, several times, back and forth, until the soldiers murmured and gasped and took a step or two backward, away from him.

A mere carnival trick, fumed Erde, yet see how it amazes and subdues even these hardened fighting men.

At last, Guillemo withdrew his hand from the flame and held it up to show how it remained unsinged and unscarred. "A virtuous man has no need to fear the purifying flame," he remarked. Then he turned slowly toward Köthen. "But you, my lord baron . . . what unlawful devil's ritual have you been enacting here?"

Köthen went entirely still. Erde could see he was suddenly and exquisitely aware of the trap that yawned before him, reeking of brimstone and the black smoke of the stake. If he told the truth, his earnest sacrilege would be for naught. Poor Carl would have only an excommunicant's grave in unconsecrated ground. To deny the deed would mean lying to a priest, God's representative on Earth, and there were a dozen men present who might not be so willing as he was. A moment later, Köthen relaxed. Either he'd found an opening, or he was simply brave enough to fake it.

"Since when is it unlawful to bring a King's son home for burial?"

"You wish me to believe that you found him like this? With the devil's own sign cut into his mortal flesh?"

"What? Where?"

Guillemo pointed. "There!"

No sane man, nor an honest one, would have traced

out a pentacle among the crisscrossed wounds on the Prince's chest.

"I don't see . . ." began Köthen. He turned to Wender. "Do you see . . . ?"

"Of course he doesn't, for foul magic has hidden it, from all but a wary and knowing eye!" Guillemo met Köthen's furious stare for the length of a breath, the gleam in his own eyes already victorious. Then he rounded on the nearest man, the frightened one who'd brought him the waterskin. "You, my son, for the salvation of your immortal soul! You tell me what's gone on here! What terrible unholiness has this godless man led you to commit?" Without looking, the priest raised his arm and pointed at Köthen.

"This is nonsense, Guillemo," scoffed the baron, but Erde could see he knew it wasn't. "We have more important tasks in front of us."

The priest turned, his head high, shoulders flung back. His eyes seemed to have found their former life, and filled the hollows below his dark brows with flash and danger. "My lord of Köthen! What could be more important than a man's immortal soul?"

Just lie to the man, Erde pleaded desperately. Had she been there in reality, she would have flung herself at Köthen whatever the peril, and begged him not to pursue this futile debate. Like his mentor Hal before him, he refused to believe that the craft inspired by lunacy could win out over the craft inspired by reason. But Erde was sure that he'd soon learn, as Hal had, how easily men are swayed by superstition and terror.

Wender had apparently reached the same conclusion. From the moment the debate was joined, he'd begun to ease himself backward through the cluster of men. Now he moved casually along the outside as if trying for a clearer view of the action, grasping certain elbows, prodding certain backs as he worked his way around the circle. He got concealed nods in return, and those men, four, six, seven of them, keeping the rest of the onlookers between them and the long line of white-robes across the clearing, backed off slightly and quietly readied their weapons. Their eyes strayed to Hoch, who would give the order. When Erde looked for Wender again, he was gone. Slipped off into the woods, she guessed, to alert the hidden reinforcements.

Meanwhile, Köthen was saying, "Nothing is more important, good Brother, unless it be the bringing of peace and order to the land, so that its people have time and security enough to tend properly to their spiritual well-being!"

Guillemo rolled his eyes and groaned as if hearing the worst sort of blasphemy. "Oh, dear Savior! Forgive the day your loyal servant agreed to an alliance with this unbeliever!"

"You go too far, priest! How dare you question my faith?"

"Who better to question it than a man of God?"

Köthen spread his hands and turned to the men around him, seeking a show of their support, a sign that they knew where Fra Guill's posturing was leading and would have none of it. Erde felt a moment's pity for him. Hal had said that men's willingness to follow him was Köthen's greatest strength. He'd risen to power on their loyalty and support. When he searched their faces now and saw loyalty ebbing away, as she did, he would know he had lost them, and losing them, had perhaps lost everything.

But would the realization be enough? Or would he keep flailing away at the priest's apparently invincible juggernaut of unreason? She must tell him to forget reason, forget honor! Tell him he must back out of the trap while he still had a chance, for once closed, it would open again only as the flames rose up around him at the witches' stake!

She *could* tell him. She was there, at his ear. . . .

—. . . *Run, my lord baron!. . . you must save yourself!* . . .

Köthen shook his head, a negating shudder.

—. . . *Listen to me! You must flee!* . . .

He brushed the air dismissively with his hand.

Guillemo gasped and pointed. "Ah! See! See how the Dark One speaks to him even now! But you cannot put off Satan so easily, can you, my lord baron, as if you were swatting a fly!" He lifted both arms and bellowed, "O, down on your knees, Adolphus of Köthen! Confess

to the Lord your vile sins of trafficking! Throw yourself
on His mercy, for it is infinite!"

Köthen was breathing in the tight, measured way of
a man readying himself for desperate action. His gaze
remained fixed on the priest, though Erde was sure he'd
rather be scanning the dark woods for help and rescue.

—. . . *Dolph, behind you! Your man is behind you! . . .*
She had little strength left for this urgent speaking
across centuries. She gathered herself for one last try.

—. . . *Now, Dolph! Run! Or I swear, HE WILL
BURN YOU!. . .*

Guillemo froze, both arms still raised toward the cold
night sky. "What?" he whispered.

And Erde learned that she had not lost all bodily sensation in her dream-state: She distinctly felt her blood
run cold.

He took a step toward Köthen. "What do I hear?"

"You hear nothing!" Köthen snapped.

"Do not deny it!" Guillemo hissed. "She is here!"

This time Köthen did not have to feign bewilderment.
"What 'she'? There is no 'she' here."

The priest edged another step closer, sniffing like a
dog on a scent. His blazing eyes searching the air around
Köthen's head. He seemed to have forgotten the rapt
audience he'd been playing to so fervently a moment
before, but the sudden change in him only frightened his
listeners more. Erde noticed to her horror that, deep in
their hollows, his eyes were the same green-gold as the
eyes of a snake.

"Is it possible," he murmured to Köthen, "that you
do not know?"

"Know what, priest?"

"The witch-girl. She speaks to you. It's her voice you
hear in the night sounds. . . ."

Köthen's nostrils flared. "No. . . ."

"It is." Guillemo moved closer, within a pace. "What
does she say to you?" He slithered sideways, circling,
his voice pitched low and far too earthy for a cleric.
"You hear, witch? He minds you not. Come, speak to
one who's worthy of you!"

Erde shrank from him in panic, as his aura invaded
her dream space.

—*Wake! I must wake! Dragon, help me!*

—He cannot, witch.

The hell-priest's mouth had not moved. His voice was in her head.

—And you never shall wake. . . .

—I will! I will!

But there was smoke twined in his hair and tiny flames danced around his body, and his green-gold eyes pinned her like prey. He was the hell-priest and he was not. He was something more, something Other. He would swallow her, eat her alive, he would snuff her, smother her, he would . . .

—HELP ME!

She grabbed for Köthen and felt the hot shock of contact. He felt it, too, and moved at last, jerking himself aside as if to confront the one who'd touched his shoulder. But his hand by instinct stayed to his sword hilt, and Guillemo sprang back, bellowing.

"To me! Ho, to me, knights of God! We are under attack!"

The Other in Erde's head lost hold. Her dream-self shot off like a stone from a catapult, careening away, away, toward blackest emptiness, toward the void. But just before the void, something caught and held her, something soft and strong and infinite. And a voice spoke to her, as light and as large as the stirring of air.

—He cannot help you, but I can. . . .

And then she was ever so gently repulsed from the edge of the darkness and sent back toward the light, drifting slowly. She could not propel herself back to the clearing. She hadn't the strength. She could only float helplessly and watch from a distance as . . .

Hoch's order rang out. Köthen's head turned to the sound of horses behind him just before the charge of the white-robes drowned it out. He drew his sword and with infinite trust in his lieutenant, backed off in the direction of Wender's approach. Hoch's men were already halfway to their horses, preparing to meet the charge. A few of the remaining soldiers got hold of themselves and backed away with Köthen, leveling their own weapons at those who remained undecided.

Köthen yelled to the stragglers, "Come on, think, you fools! Since when does a madman speak for God? Come now, while you can! He'll show you no more mercy than he's shown me!"

The priest raced in among them, screeching hellfire. Most of them broke and ran, terrified. Hoch drew his horsemen up in a line between his baron and the priest, and the white-robes were almost upon them when Wender swooped down out of the woods with a big gray horse in tow and lifted Köthen bodily into its saddle.

"Two to one's my count," he shouted over the clash of steel and hooves and leather. "Do you wish to fight another day?"

"I do, indeed," Köthen rasped, reining in his horse so that it danced and circled. "I've been fool enough for one night! Get the men out of here!"

Wender signaled Hoch to pull the men off and retreat.

"Wait!" Köthen yelled. "We must see to the Prince!"

Wender snatched at the gray horse's bridle before Köthen could turn back. "Already seen to." He pointed as two men raced past, one with Carl's swaddled body slung over his horse's shoulders. "Quick, my lord! He'll have them after us!"

"Only for show. I'm more useful to him now as a living threat of witchcraft than a dead one!" Köthen urged his horse forward anyway. "Wender!"

"My lord baron?"

"Name your reward!"

They were moving away from her now, a dozen men low over their horses' necks, ducking branches, fleeing through the dark woods faster than Erde, in her weakness, could follow.

"A speedy escape, my lord!" called Wender, "And after that, the hell-priest's head."

"That you'll have to stand in line for. But I'll use my influence, if I have any left!"

Their voices were fading. She wanted to go with them, to share in the euphoric bravado of the escape, to know that they were safe. But she only drifted. . . .

"But first we shall deliver this sad Prince to his father."

Even this did not catch Wender by surprise. "Aye, my lord, we shall."

And then she heard only the thudding of hooves as they faded beyond her hearing entirely, and beyond her consciousness.

Chapter Thirty-One

Waking up was a surprise, almost as if she hadn't expected to. But she had to be awake, or she wouldn't have been so painfully aware of her body. She was as weak as a newborn and ached in every joint, as if she'd been put on the rack. She was lying facedown with her limbs sprawled as if she'd fallen or been tossed down from a height. She flexed her hands. Her fingers clutched something prickly-soft. She managed to turn her head and lift it slightly. She was lying on grass.

Grass! For one joyous moment, she thought she had ended up at Deep Moor. But this grass was much too short. Tiny even blades, each one the exact copy of the next, and entirely without scent. Unnatural. She pressed weakly against the ground and it gave a little like ground should. But it released no rich, dark smell of loam, no bright sweet-green pungency of a sunny valley mead.

Erde struggled to pull herself up. When she called for the dragon and got no response, she knew exactly where she was. No, not exactly. She knew where she was . . . she just wasn't sure where *that* was.

Just sitting up left her breathless. She remembered the dream, every moment, and recalled how this weakness had come upon her, how every word she had murmured in Baron Köthen's ear was like breathing her life's blood into the wind. She fell back on one elbow and looked around: perfect green lawn stretching as far as she could see, endless receding ranks of the smooth-trunked trees that N'Doch had called "cloned."

How ever did I get here? she wondered.

She pondered her catapult journey to the edge of the void, and decided that not all of her travel had been a dream-state illusion. Just like she had actually *touched* Baron Köthen's shoulder. That had been real, certainly. She could recall the sensation as if it was imprinted on her fingertips: the silky feel of the tabard sliding over the hard mail beneath, the smoothly jointed links close-textured like her grandmother's beaded purse, and warm from the heat of Köthen's body.

Erde blushed, thinking of him. She missed him already. It was absurd. It was ridiculous. How had she allowed this to happen? She knew that young girls were meant to be romantic, but this was worse than falling in love with Rainer even though she'd thought he was dead. At least Rainer was only nineteen. Köthen was at least thirty, he barely knew she existed and he lived a thousand years away. She'd never even had a conversation with him. The one time she'd met him in person, she'd still lacked her voice. Perhaps she was merely homesick. The raw dangers of 913 were at least more comprehensible than the mysteries and complications of 2013. She hoped that when she grew up, she'd finally become sensible enough to fall in love with someone she could actually spend some time with.

Meanwhile, here she was in Lealé's "Dream Haven." That she had come from a dream to here warranted thinking about. She wished the dragon were there to discuss it with her. She wondered how much time had passed while she'd been dream-shifted to her home time, and was anybody likely to be looking for her yet?

What she needed to do was get up right away, if she could manage, and find the doorway to Lealé's little room. Then she could follow the passageway back to the house. Standing up was difficult, but not impossible, though once she got there, her balance was unreliable. She was, she realized, enormously thirsty. Hungry, too, although eating would require far too much energy. She staggered a little, turning step by step to scan the odd forest in all directions for a sign of where the door might be.

When she'd completed her circle—though it was hard to tell exactly, with identical views at every angle, if she really was back where she'd started—she steadied her balance and thought she had better try it again. At her next sideways turn, she let out a small shriek of surprise.

A small table stood in front of her, right there on the grass where she was sure there had been no table before. It was a delicate sort of table, with a single carved central pedestal and a short, lace-trimmed square of snowy linen covering its top. Not at all the sort of object she would have missed the first time around, especially as it contained a clear glass pitcher full of water, a plate of lemon slices, and a dainty glass tumbler, all set out on an oval tray of finest silver.

Erde stared. Having just come from 913, the world of the hell-priest, she wondered if this was some sort of a trap. N'Doch, she recalled, never drank water unless he knew where it had come from. But she had a feeling about this water . . . a good feeling. A feeling that emanated from the forest around her, as if someone was whispering in her ear—as she had whispered in Köthen's—that she mustn't worry, everything was perfectly all right . . . at least for now.

But if it wasn't a trap, it could still be an illusion. She was questioning reality now the way N'Doch questioned the safety of anything he put in his mouth: by habit. In the world of her growing up, reality had not been in question. Everything was real, even witches, magic, and dragons, all things that N'Doch's world had decided not to believe in. Lately, even she had questions about witches, having been labeled one herself, and most of what she called magic, Master Djawara called "science." The only thing she was really sure of was dragons.

So to prove that the water was real, she drank it. She felt a lot better for it afterward. Almost up to putting her mind to the problem of not having seen even a hint of a door, or anything but trees, the same tree, over and over and over again.

When they get past all the sleepers, most of them up and about by now, N'Doch and the apparition head straight for the odd little park. It's the only place he's seen so far that might be big enough to hold a dragon. He can feel the big guy in his head, but not so clear as he can when the girl's around. He's a little worried that she's fallen asleep and they're letting her, even with this thing about, like, *going in* to her dreams. But they're the dragons, he figures. They gotta know what they're talking about.

They walk along slow, so's not to alert one of the "flappers." This is how he thinks of Glory's henchmen in their flowing white gowns. He's teaching the apparition how to saunter, how to do it with authority, so you don't get bothered on the streets by just anyone thinking you might look like a mark. The kid's not real good at it yet. Sauntering doesn't really suit its dragon nature. But N'Doch thinks it's worth a try anyway.

At the edge of the park, the apparition stops along the gravel path and stares into the trees like it was reading a book.

"What?" asks N'Doch. He figures it's okay to talk aloud out here, with no one around to listen. He doubts if the big bankroll's likely to be bugging the woods.

The apparition points toward a corner of the park, where the trees are the thickest. N'Doch looks, then shrugs.

—Look carefully.

N'Doch sighs and looks again. And then he notices that, everywhere else, he can see the far surrounding wall through the straight smooth trunks. In that one corner, he can't. *The trees must be thicker there*, he thinks, though he sees no change in their spacing.

—I'm going in there.

"Sure, okay. Let's go."

The apparition shakes its head, puts a finger to its lips.

—You stay here at the edge and watch me. Keep in constant contact and tell me when you lose sight of me. If you lose contact . . .

—I'll be right in there after you, don't worry.

—No! Tell my brother Earth, if you can hold that connection, or go wake up Erde immediately and tell them both what has occurred. If you come in alone, we may both be lost.

"Easy, man. Glory ain't gonna let the punks and muggers hang around where they could be hurting her business, y'know."

—Do as I say!

N'Doch sulks, but when the dragon gets this tone on, he knows he's gotta pay attention. He scuffs the gravel, looks around for something to lean against.

—I'm gonna look like some terrific kinda guy, letting my small bro wander off into the bushes by himself.

The apparition turns just inside the first row of trees and flashes him a grin.

—Just tell 'em I went in there to pee.

N'Doch watches, trying not to look like he's watching, in case *he's* the one being watched. The apparition pads off purposely through the trees, exactly like it's looking for a likely spot. N'Doch smiles. *This kid's all right,* he thinks. Maybe Fâtime won't have a coronary when she sees him, if N'Doch prepares her right.

The trees don't seem to be closing in around the apparition as he goes, though by now he's already farther in than he should be able to go, judging from where the wall is everywhere else. N'Doch checks it out to either side and checks back. The kid's still walking. N'Doch thinks maybe the wall takes a big jog out there where he can't see it. No reason, after all, why the lot has to be square.

And then, between one step and the next, the kid is gone. Like, in a heartbeat.

"Yo!" N'Doch sputters. He takes a few long steps forward, and then remembers.

—Hey! You there? You all right?

—Yes, of course. Why?

—You disappeared!

—Really?

—You didn't, like, step behind a tree or something?

—No. Wait a minute. Keep watching.

An instant later, he's there again, waving through the trees like some kind of tourist. He vanishes again, reappears, vanishes, reappears.

"Awesome," N'Doch murmurs.

—What does it look like from there?

—Like you're switching yourself on and off like a light. What's it look like from there?

—Come ahead and find out.

N'Doch scans the view in both directions. One flapper by the garage putting the final polish on the Glory Car's headlights. Whole bunches of "guests" moving about in the front yard, paying him no mind whatsoever. N'Doch saunters into the trees. Before he gets to him, the apparition vanishes again.

—Hey!

—Just walk straight. You'll get here.

He stops, glances back at the house. Hardly seems like he's covered any ground at all. He shrugs and keeps going. Ahead of him is nothing but trees, and he's thinking he's gone wrong somehow when all of a sudden, he's there.

The trees open out into a big grassy clearing, shaded by overarching branches. In the middle of it sit two dragons. N'Doch looks behind him again. The house and grounds are right there, not a hundred yards away.

"Total bizarro," he remarks, and turns back to the dragons. It's kind of a leap for him, seeing her in dragon form again. He was just getting used to the apparition. But he can't help but notice all over again how beautiful she is.

"Lookin' good, girl," he muttered.

They're both sorta grinning at him.

"Guess you guys figure you're safe here. . . ."

—As safe as any place around here, and a lot more comfortable.

"You're pretty glad to be out from underground, huh?" he says to the big guy, who flexes his muscular neck, looks around and seems to shrug in a pleasantly ironic fashion.

—My name is Earth. I was born underground.

"Oh. Right. Sorry." N'Doch has to admit it's about time he started calling the big guy by his actual name. It's just, well, it sounds weird going around referring to someone as "Earth." Of course, it's no weirder than everyone calling *him* "Water."

—You weren't born underground.

—I was. Under the mountain.

—No, that was later. We were all born together, at one instant, out of elemental matter. You don't find that under any old mountain.

Earth looks both interested and mournful.

—You are wise, my sister. You recall so much of our beginnings.

—Not enough, or I'd have some idea what our brother Fire thinks he's up to.

"What's his problem, this brother of yours?"

—He was always the most volatile.

"He's like his name, huh?"

—As are all of us.

N'Doch considers, and has to agree. "Can't wait to see what *his* dragon guide looks like."

—If he's awake, he must have heard the Summons. Why would he be plotting against us?

—Did I mention he was also the most devious?

—Sister! A dragon would never be devious!

Water pulls her sleek little head back as far as her long neck will allow, and stares at the big guy as if he's from Mars.

—No wonder that girl of yours has such anti-quated notions!

N'Doch just has to laugh. "She awake yet?" he asks Earth, sort of to let the pressure off him. This Water gal is beautiful, but she's not too long on tact.

—I have not wanted to wake her. Perhaps I should ..

—We were going to make a quick food run, is what he means. You already got to eat, remember.

"Hey, go for it. I'll take a walk back and check in on her. Listen, you think Glory . . . I mean, Lealé knows about this place, y'know, what it does in here?"

—It would explain why she thinks it's the same as the wood outside her "Dream Haven."

"Is it, do you think?"

—There are intriguing similarities, but until we've gone there . . .

"Yeah. Who can tell? Okay, you guys go eat. I'm heading back."

He intends to check on the girl all right, but what he really has in mind is a closer look inside the house. Now he's got himself free of all his recent encumbrances, he figures he can do it pretty quick and pretty thorough. Never know what he might find in there.

He looks for a back way in, but there's only the front door and the big ceremonial side entrance for the "guests," and they're lined up two deep out there, winding all the way around the neat stone terrace a few times and ending up down on the lawn.

Got her hands full this afternoon, he thinks. He wonders if her spirit guide gives her a Dream each for every one of these poor suckers, how he could possibly have the time, especially if he's busy plotting against his siblings. If he is this Fire guy, that is.

Another dragon. N'Doch wipes his brow on his forearm. That's all he needs.

He finds the front door unlocked but not unguarded. Two flappers are sitting up beside the columns in lawn chairs, fanning themselves. N'Doch opts for sheer chutzpah, and strolls right by them with a smile and a little wave. They nod at him, none too graciously. Apparently the word's gone out that he's here at the Mahatma's invitation.

He's glad to be back in the air conditioning again, though the central hallway is so dark, it really does give him the creeps. Maybe the Mahatma's trying to save money on electricity. He puts his hand to the first big brass knob he sees. He turns it quietly, expecting resistance, but it opens easily into bright, even light and the sounds of keypads, cooling fans, and drive hum. Under that, work chatter. An office. Well, if he'd had light enough out in the hall, he could've read the sign on the door. He backs out silently. No point disturbing the daily maintenance of the Mahatma Glory's financial empire. Now he wishes he'd had the nerve to ask Lealé how much it costs for one of these Readings of hers.

The next door down is already open. N'Doch peeks into a long dim room full of sofas and draperies and china lamp bases, sort of like the alcove off the dining room, only richer and more formal. Huge vases of flowers decorate carved ebony tables so polished you could see yourself in them. There are dark paintings with heavy gold frames and their own hidden spotlights. It smells like leather and cigar smoke and, well, money. It's exactly how N'Doch imagines the rich people live, except this room doesn't look much like anyone lives here. More like it's for people to come to now and again, and pretend that they do.

He thinks he'll just try it on for size himself, seeing there's no one here trying to stop him. He goes in, strolls around a bit. He sees a newspaper, actual printout, sees that it's about everywhere else in the world but here and passes it by. He picks an oblong silver box, looks it over longingly, then opens it a crack. Out flows the heady thick aroma of expensive tobacco. He's tempted. He's not much for smoking cigars, but the barter value on the street is astronomical. He sets down the box, exactly as he found it. It won't do to go getting acquisitive this early in his stay. Plenty of time when he's leaving to lift the odd little treasure or two.

He strolls around a bit more. He spots a minute silver coke spoon on a tiny silver tray. This really tempts him—it's so portable. But he moves on, feeling virtuous, until a glimmer of crystal and amber draws him toward a shadowed corner and a whole tray of decanters and glasses, the big round kind with the stubby stems. N'Doch whistles low through his teeth and selects a decanter at random. He lifts the diamond-shaped stopper, and an even headier scent curls out and around him like a finger beckoning. This summons he cannot refuse. Besides, who's gonna know? Isn't that what it's here for? He pours a few inches of the golden liquid into a glass, then replaces the decanter as carefully as he did the cigar box. He carries his prize around a bit, just liking the bulbous smooth feel of the glass in his hand. Then he spots two big leathers chairs with high backs flanking a brick fireplace. There's a coldflame log burning cheerily in the grate.

He eases himself down into one of the chairs. The leather groans under him as sweetly as a woman. He kicks off the horrible plastic sandals that Papa Djawara made him wear into the City, and digs his toes into the deep pile of the carpet. He is memorizing every sensation. He tries to convinces himself otherwise, but deep in his heart, N'Doch does not really believe he'll be rich someday, some fantastic overnight sensation. He knows that's a line he's bought from the media, 'cause he had no other line available to him at the moment, no other way out he could believe in. He raises the glass to his lips and touches his tongue to the liquid, then leans back, savoring the deep bite, the honey that burns to the back of his throat and sends its sweet heat up into his nostrils.

Tears come to his eyes, and he tells himself it's the

liquor. He doesn't brush them away. He stares at the dancing fire that produces no heat, and slowly consumes the entire glass, the finest Armagnac. When it's gone, he carefully sets the glass down on the table beside him, and falls asleep.

Chapter Thirty-Two

By accident of repetition, Erde discovered that the little table with the water on it was only there after she had consciously thought about it. She'd look for it and find it gone, then turn back a moment later, and there it was, the lovely slim pitcher filled once more to the brim with sparklingly clear water. And the glass was newly clean and dry each time.

There is something in this wood, she decided. Logically, it was the same something that both she and Wasser had caught just a glimpse of from the doorway to Lealé's dream room. *And it knows that I'm here,* she concluded. *It hears me thinking somehow.* Since it offered her water when she was so thirsty, it must be a benign presence.

"Hello? Are you there?" Her voice echoed softly among the trees, less like a ricochet than as if her call was actually being repeated over and over. A faint rustle among the leaves made her turn, but there was nothing there. Would it put in an appearance, this presence? If she thought of food, would it feed her as well?—for as her strength began to return, she really was feeling hungry. Ravenous, in fact.

And lo, as she kept turning, there it was: another, larger table, full of food. But this table had a more familiar aspect, as if its mysterious conjuror had plumbed Erde's own memories to produce a feast such as might have been laid in sunnier days at Tor Alte. For there was the lustrous pewter table service, and the dragon-embossed gold goblets that her grandmother the baroness had used on ceremonial occasions. And there, the tall gold carafe that matched the goblets, a gift of His

Majesty King Otto, to whom the baroness always raised a toast whenever the wine was poured. Erde reached a tentative finger to its rim. Perhaps it would all just disappear. But the carafe remained, smooth and weighty to her touch. She stroked the crisp, brown curve of a rye loaf, still warm as if snatched mere moments ago from the bread ovens and rushed up the long stone stairs to the banquet hall. . . .

No! I am not at Tor Alte. You cannot make me think I am.

She stared around at the endless progression of copy-cat trees and identical blades of grass.

"Who are you? What do you want with me?"

The leaves stirred like a sigh. Erde's short-cropped hair ruffled, as from a gentle caress, and was still. She felt an overpowering urge to eat, and could not come up with a good enough reason to resist.

What a comfort were the familiar smells and tastes and textures of home! Though it was odd that she could eat so much and not feel as stuffed as she did at home every feast day. She wondered, if the dragon was here, would the weird wood produce a brace of sheep for him, or a nice fat goat? He must be very tired of eating fish.

The thought of the dragon brought her out of her reverie. She was much better, much stronger now, really she was, even though the meal felt so strangely light in her stomach. What had made her think of Earth, when she'd been so lost in nostalgia? It was almost as if someone had called his name to remind her.

"Was it you?" she asked rhetorically.

Again came that odd, faint stirring of the leaves. Erde felt it then, the Presence. Calm, huge, unthreatening, but beyond her understanding.

"Please tell me. Who are you?"

There were no words, yet she knew she'd been answered. And what she heard was a call for help.

He wakes with a start and thinks he must still be dreaming: a fireplace, big leather chairs, rich carpet underfoot? *This ain't my life.* And then he shakes off the rest of his sleep, and remembers. The empty glass is still there on the table beside him.

But it was the noise that woke him. The old, clipped

"wock-wock-wock" of a copter, coming in close. Out in the hall, doors are opening. Habitually hushed voices are heating up to an anxious pitch. A whispered conference convenes right outside the door of the long parlor. N'Doch strains to catch a word over the racket of the copter, but nothing he hears makes any sense. Flappers come and go down the hallway—he hears the nervous snap of their long skirts rather than the soft pad of their footsteps along the carpeted floor.

His first, not-entirely-rational thought is that the copter is coming for him. It's what he's always thought, when the pursuit was on and he happened to be nearby, that he was the quarry. And sometimes he was. But he's been taking a pretty raw look at himself, and he can't muster that old fantasy anymore. It used to make him feel important, alive. Now he's had a glimpse of how egotistical paranoia really is.

On the other hand, the copter is damn well coming closer. He can hear it right over the house, hovering, its rotors agitating even the air inside the room, inside his lungs, the very blood in his veins. The paranoia is an old habit. He'll be caught in a place he does not belong. N'Doch shrinks into his chair and thinks hard about what to do. Break and run is the obvious thing, but it's probably too late for that. And then, there's the girl to think about. And the dragons.

The dragons. It's like someone stuck out a hand with an offer of help. N'Doch lets a little of the panic go. He's not alone in this venture. He's got a couple of powerful friends, after all.

So he feels around in his brain for that still unfamiliar spot. It's like when he was learning to play, how his hands had to search out the right notes, only it's harder 'cause he can't be looking at the inside of his brain like he could cheat and look down at the keyboard. But he knows when he's found it now, at least. It's shaped just right, like his inside-self is a key fitting into a lock. Only this time when he tries it, the dragon isn't there.

Damn, he thinks. *Still out stuffing her gut.*

But the fact that she could be back any minute keeps him from falling back into the panic, lets him listen to the roar of the copter's descent like he just *knows* it's coming for someone else. Like, maybe Lealé hasn't been keeping up on her protection payments, so the militia's staging a little raid to teach her a lesson.

Outside, the copter settles, somewhere out back on the grass. The high turbine whine chokes back to a steady growl, then the engine cuts off and it's only the rhythmic swish-swish as the rotors slow down. N'Doch thinks you could write a whole symphony with the range of sounds that a copter makes. Whoever it is out there is planning to stay for a while.

The bustle out in the hall has quieted down, too, but N'Doch expects that's because they've all run outside to deal with this latest unexpected arrival. Judging from the way they treat him, he guesses the flappers don't much appreciate random events dropping in on them. Now might be as good a chance as any for him to move around, find a better place to lay low, maybe check on the girl. And he's just about to do it: he's bid good-bye to the best chair he's ever sat in and he's up with his sandals in his hand, gliding across the dim room like the shadow he's often been called by both his friends and his enemies, when the front doors burst open, and light and people and noise stream into the hall. N'Doch hightails it back to his tall-sided chair by the fireplace, where he makes his lanky body as small in it as he knows how to do.

"You need help, is that what you're saying?"

It was like that night above Tor Alte, when her small, quiet life was changing forever and Erde found herself faced with a creature out of ancient myth, demanding to be fed. She felt powerless and ignorant and in no way up to the task.

But the Presence had given her food and drink, and those had revived her, so the least she could do was find out what sort of help it thought it needed. At least she had some experience at this sort of thing now. She thought of Rose and Deep Moor, and Rose's "Seeings." She settled herself down on the grass and cleared her mind.

"Speak to me, then, however you can."

But nothing at all came to fill up the mental space she had cleared. Instead, the leaves rattled, and the wood became suddenly animate. Things began to happen around her. A tiny brown mouse scuttled across her feet and pounced on a grasshopper. A swallow swooped right past her nose and snatched up a gnat. A spider spun its web in the grass.

Erde took all this in very thoughtfully. Then she ventured, "Something is after you?"

The leaves stirred a bit more loudly. Erde would swear she heard negation in their dry rustle. Then a large ginger cat with yellow eyes bounded out of the woods with the brown mouse held delicately in its jaws. It crouched in front of Erde and set the mouse down between its paws. The poor mouse darted this way and that, desperate for escape, but the cat's paws were everywhere it looked.

"Ohh, I see," murmured Erde. "Something already has you."

Prey and predator vanished. The wood stilled. Calm again. Gratitude. Assent.

Erde couldn't imagine how anything could hold this Presence a prisoner. It was so huge and open and . . . well, but it was true, she had to admit. It didn't feel powerful, at least not as she'd learned to define the word. It didn't feel strong or aggressive or overbearing. Still, it must *have* power. It had conjured up food out of thin air . . . or had it? To Erde's surprise, she heard her stomach grumbling again. Could it be? Had her wonderful feast been only an illusion?

Around her, the trees lifted their branches and sighed with regret, and then they renewed their wordless plea for rescue.

The front doors hiss shut. The hubbub flows down the hall.

"Jesus H., JP, I can't see a goddamn thing in this place! Why don't you people get some light in here?"

It's the bankroll, N'Doch is sure of it. He remembers the voice from earlier, the sort of voice that's always louder than anyone else around it, a voice used to giving orders and speaking for attribution. The bankroll himself, heading N'Doch's way.

"Least you know how to keep a decent temperature! Christ, it's hot out there!"

N'Doch hears Jean-Pierre, the head flapper, doing an

apologetic tap dance at the same time he's trying to use all these low, calm tones calculated to make the bankroll shut up and listen. N'Doch can't believe the idiot thinks it'll work.

"Of course she's busy!" the bankroll retorts, "She better be busy! She's gotta pay for all this! She's got expenses! One of them is your goddamn salary, and you don't want to be losing that at a time like this. So get your ass in there and tell her I need to see her . . ." He pauses, and N'Doch can almost hear a sharky grin spreading across his face. ". . . as soon as she can make her charming self available."

They're right there at the parlor doorway. N'Doch curls deeper into his chair.

"You know, monsieur, I'll do everything I can but when the call is on her, she . . ."

"I know, I know. She's 'apart from this world.' Isn't that what you always tell them? Kind of like being asleep, isn't it?"

"Not unlike that, monsieur."

"Fine. If she was asleep when I came, what would you do?"

"I'd wake her up, monsieur, of course."

"Well . . . ?"

"Monsieur, I'm only doing . . ."

"Your job, I know. Look, JP, here's the story. I'm a good boy. I make appointments. I come here on time, when I'm scheduled. I could just as easily make her come to me—I'm a busy man and the world's in crisis. But I don't do that, do I?"

"No, monsieur . . ."

"So when something exceptional comes up, I expect a little respect, you know what I mean?"

"Yes, of course, monsieur. I've sent . . ."

The bankroll sighs. "Don't send, JP. Go. You go. Now. You get me?"

N'Doch can't hear Jean-Pierre's reply. He figures the guy's mouth's gone too dry to manage even a syllable. N'Doch has about zero sympathy for the flapper flunky. *You get,* he quips silently, *what you get paid for.* He hears the bankroll come into the parlor, trailed by placating voices.

"Please have a seat, monsieur."

"Would you like a drink, monsieur?"

"Perhaps you are hungry, monsieur?"

"The PrintNews is right here, monsieur."

The bankroll snorts. "Get it away from me. I got enough problems already without having to read about 'em. Give me a big brandy and a little privacy. I don't plan to be staying long. Come to think of it, I'll take the privacy first. Get out of here, all of you. I'll see to myself."

A flat, deep voice says, "Sashsa and me'll be right outside, sir."

The bodyguard, N'Doch surmises.

"Thank you, Nikko. Sasha, if Marco calls, I'll take it in here."

The bowing and scraping and whining dies down until all N'Doch can hear is the bankroll pacing about at the other end of the parlor.

"Jesus Christ!" he exclaims again, and lets out an explosive sigh.

N'Doch smiles, picturing the bankroll's tension dissipating into the room in radiating lines of cuss words and insults to the staff. This dude he can almost feel sorry for. Then the pacing turns purposeful and heads N'Doch's way. He tenses. But it stops partway, replaced by sounds of glass clinking and liquid being poured. N'Doch's just dying for a peek at this guy. He figures he could sneak a look now, while the dude's busy at the bar. He eases his body forward just enough to peer around the high winged back of the chair, but the leather creaks and he's gotta make like a statue before he's moved far enough for the full view. All he sees is half a dark, slick-haired head on the well-tailored, medium height shoulder of a man in a business suit. European or mixed. Ordinary enough, as far as it goes.

Finally, there's Lealé's voice, trilling down the hall. The bankroll moves back toward the door with his brandy to meet her.

"Oh, hello, Nikko. Is he in there?" She rounds the corner. "Ah, darling! Back so soon? You should have warned me—I'd have sent the car." It sounds to N'Doch like Lealé's thrown herself bodily into the bankroll's arms.

"Stow the car. Haven't you heard what's going on? Food riots at the Ziguinchor, right outside your door!"

Lealé takes on a pouting tone. "Oh, dear. Again?"

"Your man out front was smart enough to lock the gates."

"I hate that! You know I hate that!"

"This is no joke, Glory. Word got out somehow about the next price hike, and the shit hit the fan. Why'd you have to pick this neighborhood, right in the middle of everything? There're plenty of safer places."

"Oh, darling, it couldn't be any other place! You know what the dream told me. It'll be over soon out there, like it always is. I come from there, remember? People must just stand up and shout about things every once in a while, but they'll settle down again, once they remember that shouting doesn't do any good."

"This time, I'm not so sure . . ."

"Ooo, you're so grumpy! You didn't come all this way to be grumpy. Come here. Oh!" Lealé giggles. There's the small clink of a glass being set down, then the rustle of her robes and a moment of heavy breathing. "See? You just couldn't wait to hold your Glory again. Here, let me close the door."

"Now, none of that. I don't have time. Besides, you'll make Nikko nervous. He's feeling jumpy today."

"Awww, what is it? Another bomb threat?"

"There are always bomb threats. There's not enough explosive made to supply all the bomb threats we get in a month."

"Poor darling . . ."

N'Doch is sort of relieved there's gonna be none of "that," just a mini-lecture on the perils of doing business. Sitting over here in the dark is like watching the daytime vid when only the sound is working. But the news of the food riots crowds into his mind. *Close call,* he thinks. *We were just there. It must've all started when the marché opened up again for the afternoon.*

"Look, Glory, I just had the damnedest dream."

"Now, darling, what has Glory told you about sleeping in the middle of the day?"

"That's what's so damn peculiar. I wasn't asleep."

Lealé laughs, low and throaty. "A daydream, was it? Was Glory in it?"

"Yes. You were." But there is no intimacy in his reply.

"Excuse me, sir." A soft male voice chimes in at the door. "Mr. D is on the line."

"About time. Ask if he's seen the numbers this morning. No, give it here . . . Marco! You seen the . . . yeah! What's the deal? All of a sudden, they're killing us! . . . yeah . . . no, I'm at . . . I'm in a meeting right now. Shouldn't be long . . . well, get on it, man! I'll be back to you."

Now N'Doch gets his first real twinge of envy for the bankroll. Before the music thing grabbed him so hard, and he was running with the Needles Gang, he'd had a phone for a while. Some deck jockey had fixed it so it fed off a random selection of purloined access codes. He could call anywhere, for as long as he liked. Now, *that* was power. He can still feel the lightness of it in his hand, like it was nothing, but that phone was more lethal in its way than any hand weapon. Then one day he up and sold it to buy his first set of amps. It seemed like the right move at the time, but since then, there's been times he's wondered. *Hindsight's twenty-twenty,* he tells himself, *so meanwhile, back to the soap opera. . . .*

"Sasha, here! Get this thing outa my sight! And hold the calls now, got it?" The bankroll paces a bit more. N'Doch guesses that Glory's just sitting there watching, waiting for him to work it out. "It's a bad time, Glory, a bad time. You better be making enough to support the two of us."

"Oh, darling . . ."

"No bullshit, Glory, and to tell you the truth, it's not just me. Things are about to fall down around our ears, I can feel it. And then there's this damn dream! It was . . . like the ones you have."

"Kenzo, dearest, you're not supposed to be having that kind of Dreams . . . let Glory do that for you! She'll take the worry out of it."

Kenzo? N'Doch's not sure he's heard her right. He supposes there's more than one "Kenzo" in the business world, but . . .

"Fine," the bankroll growls, "but I had it anyway."

"Then you better just sit down and tell Glory all about it."

As the bankroll spins out the long and torturous

dream-strand that's shaken him so badly, N'Doch listens hard, not to the words, but to the voice, which he is now trying like crazy to identify. But he can't quite be sure, and finally he knows he's got to risk it. He *has* to get a real look at this dude.

He moves as slowly as he knows how, tries to time his moves with the rhythm of the bankroll's speech, so the voice'll cover the creaking of the damn chair. *No good spy,* he thinks, *would ever sit in a leather chair.* He gets his head and shoulders twisted around, then leans out over the arm of the chair. He gets a clean shot, a full-face view of the guy with his hands in the air, sketching a particular detail in his narrative. Once the input from his eyes reaches the processing part of his brain, N'Doch nearly stops breathing.

Omigod. *Baraga!*

Chapter Thirty-Three

Now that she knew the truth about her less-than-substantial meal, Erde was no longer so confident about how recovered she felt, or about the apparent comfort of her current situation. If the Presence was a prisoner in this wood, could that not mean that she was also? If she couldn't leave and couldn't eat, starvation became a real possibility. And how could she even be sure the Presence was telling the truth about itself? Perhaps it was holding *her* prisoner.

Certainly, she needed to talk to it further, but an in-depth discussion was going to prove difficult if the only way the Presence could communicate was by making the wood and its creatures act out each intended meaning. There was a game at home something like that, intended for long winter afternoons by the fireplace. But Erde didn't feel much like playing games, even in the interests of communication. It seemed that the Presence could manage to convey its emotional state, particularly assent or dissent. It just wasn't very good at actual information. So perhaps if she asked only questions with yes or no answers, she might make more progress.

For instance: "Do you know a way out of this wood?"

The leaves rose and fell, rose and fell. Negation.

"Does that mean I'm a prisoner, too?"

A definite stirring. Negation.

Erde pondered the apparent contradiction. "You mean . . . I can get out, but you can't?"

A stillness, tinged with melancholy. Assent.

Perhaps it would tell her about its own situation. "Are you a prisoner because of something . . . you did?" she asked carefully.

A sudden rotating gust snatched at Erde's clothing and tousled her hair. Fistfuls of leaves detached and threw themselves in her face.

"Please! Please! I'm sorry! I apologize!"

The gust died as if it had never been. Fallen leaves were nowhere in sight.

"If you have all this power, why can't you just leave?"

No response at all. Not a yes or no question.

Erde chewed her lip. "I can't say why, but I believe you. And of course I'd like to help you, but I don't see how I can." She found herself thinking about the dragons again, both of them this time, and recalling how Earth had at first been able to talk to her only in mind pictures. Finally, an understanding bloomed.

"Is it the dragons' help you want?"

Not a leaf or blade in motion. Total assent.

She couldn't figure out a way to shape, "How did you know about the dragons?" into a yes or no query. If the Presence had known she was thirsty and hungry without her saying so out loud, probably it had learned about the dragons the very same way.

"I'm sure they would help you if they knew, but they're never going to unless I find a way out of here."

The silent wood came alive again. The ginger cat, the brown mouse and the blue swallow all appeared from different directions and met on the grass at Erde's feet. Once there, all three of them promptly settled down and went to sleep.

Erde stared. This really was like a child's game. "Is it something about sleeping?"

Assent.

"You need to sleep now?"

Negation.

"Ummm . . . you think I need to sleep?"

Assent.

"But I don't want to sleep! I want to get out of here!"

A long silence. Assent and reassurance.

And as she watched, the three sleeping creatures woke up, not as animals usually do, instantly on the alert, but stretching and yawning like humans. Then, as one, they looked up and about them, as if in realization, then jumped up and took off joyfully, each in the direction it had come.

"Oh, dear," said Erde. "I think I understand. I'm still not awake yet, am I?"

Assent, softened with sympathy.

"So, to get out of here, I have to go to sleep in my dream, this dream that I'm still in, then I have to wake up, and hope that I've woken up for real this time."

Assent. Assent. Assent.

She had said she didn't want to sleep, but suddenly, she did. The urge was so overpowering that even she knew it wasn't her own. She wondered if the Presence understood that the chances were about even: She could end up in 2013 with the dragons, or a thousand years earlier. She thought of Köthen, and decided it didn't matter. Either would be preferable to starvation for an eternity in this weird, weird wood.

As she lay down and tried to prepare herself for any eventuality, she noticed a queer thing: A long line of soldier ants were picking out a very eccentric trail through the velvety grass. They were . . . Erde yawned. Sleep was approaching faster than she'd expected . . . spelling out letters? Words? Why not? In a dream, anything was possible.

She lifted her head the barest inch, all she could manage as sleep rushed toward her. Words, definitely words.

They read: RESIST TEMPTATION.

He flattens himself back into the deepest part of the chair. At first, he can't even think.

Baraga. *Here.*

His heart races. He stares into the fireplace, sees only darkness.

Baraga. *Baraga!*

But the roof doesn't cave in, and the man at the other end of the parlor continues his recitation as if nothing has changed, and finally, N'Doch gets hold of himself.

Kenzo Baraga, the Media King, the man he now and forever most loves to hate, is sitting not thirty feet away from him. The slick-black Asian hair of Baraga's Japanese mother might have clued him in if he'd been thinking, but . . . whoever would have thought? Kenzo Baraga, in person, right in this room. And what's he doing? Not forging dreams and deals or ending careers and hopes, like he's supposed to be, no—he's complaining about some stupid dream he's had! N'Doch can't believe it.

Not that he supposed the Big Man wouldn't have problems. But they should be world-class problems, and Baraga should be eating 'em for breakfast, not be sitting there pouring his heart out like a schoolboy to some fawning woman! But in a way, N'Doch likes it that the Big Man's got a soft side. It humanizes him.

"I'm on this road," the Media King is saying, "and it's hotter 'n hell, and dusty. The road is crap, like it was paved once, a very long time ago and never kept up. And I'm alone, and walking, can you imagine? My . . ." He stops, and in the still room, everyone listens as sirens wail past outside the gates. "So my clothes are all torn, and all I can see, everywhere around me, is burned-out buildings."

"There, you see?" Lealé soothed. "It's just the riots that have you worried."

"I had this dream *before* the riots started. And besides, this place looked like a city, or what's left of one, but I knew .. in the dream, I knew it was really my life, my business, all of it. Everything! Everything I've built, gone up in smoke!"

"I know you've been very anxious lately, darling, but . . ."

Now N'Doch's brain is working overtime. He recognizes opportunity when it finally comes knocking. It may take some pondering, but he'll be damned if he doesn't figure a way to turn this bizarre coincidence to his advantage.

Briefly, he reviews his options. First, he could just go up and introduce himself to the Big Man as Lealé's . . . as Glory's dear friend of a dear friend, then work the conversation around to asking for an audition. N'Doch's mouth twists. Yeah, right. Probably the next thing he'd see would be the business end of Nikko the bodyguard. The Media King's not known for being free with his time to unknowns like N'Doch. Besides, if he's as jealous as Lealé says, he might jump to the wrong conclusions and think his woman's taken a younger lover. That would about finish his chances right then and there. No, the only way is, he's gotta figure out some pressure he can bring to bear. Which means, entirely powerless as he is

compared to Baraga, that he's gotta either have something the Media King wants, or something he wants to
keep from everybody else.

N'Doch hears other copters in the air outside, and the
occasional crack of a sniper's rifle. Probably chasing the
rioters out of the square. If things get worse out there,
Baraga will probably bolt for his safe-hole on the beach,
but meanwhile, the recitation continues.

". . . suddenly there's this guy in front of me in a
spotlight, all decked out in gold, with this huge wall of
flame behind him—great pyro, you know? And this
amazing looking woman . . ." Baraga pauses. N'Doch
hears him take a sip of his brandy. "In fact, he's pretty
amazing looking, so I think he must be one of my groups,
but the guy's not wired or anything, and I don't see his
backup anywhere. I can't even hear them—it's like the
sound's gone dead—and I really want to, 'cause what if
they're *good*?"

"I think it must mean that you will hear them," offers
Lealé. "Perhaps very soon. And they will be good, and
your worries will be over."

"That'll take a lot more than one group."

"Lealé laughed. "I know, darling. We all need people
to start making some money again."

"The hell with that. I need a better way to make 'em
spend what they already got on me now! I need a miracle! And even that it looks like somebody's got to ahead
of me . . . !"

Yup, nods N'Doch. Salesmanship or blackmail. His
only choices.

But the catch is, he's got nothing to sell but his talent,
and that ain't worth anything until Baraga gives him a
chance and an audition, which he's not gonna bother
with unless he knows it'll be worth his very valuable
time. N'Doch sees opportunity slipping away already.

He takes a gingerly look at the blackmail angle. He's
done it before once or twice, mostly for food, real small-
time stuff, when he was really desperate. Trying to blackmail Kenzo Baraga would be raising the stakes into the
stratosphere. But if his information is good and he can
hold on to his nerve . . .

He knows the dream-reader angle is nothing. All the
big business types check in with their tarot lady or astrol-

oger or feng shui master before making the big decisions. But, for instance, N'Doch knows—the whole world knows—that Baraga is married to the vid mega-star Francinetta Legata. Does the spectacular Francie know that her husband hangs out with the Mahatma Glory Magdalena for reasons other than sound business advice? Does he care if she knows? What would she give for the information? N'Doch sighs. He'd probably be fool enough to just let her take him to bed. None of this is sounding like much so far, he's gotta admit.

And then, because all along he's been listening with at least half an ear to the conversation at the far end of the room, his brain's autopilot registers a word that drops out of the sky like his next shipment of manna.

". . . dragons . . ."

The desirable Francie is backburnered in an instant. N'Doch switches over to full manual and listens with all his instruments.

". . . or something that looked like dragons. I saw 'em on the tapes myself when they rolled it back for me. And two kids with 'em. Ask Nikko, he was there. And six of my crack beach patrol. Can you believe it? Some asshole's managed to gengineer dragons, and he's keeping it a secret!"

Again, Lealé's throaty, sexy laugh. "You mean, he's not telling *you* about it."

Wait a minute, N'Doch realizes. This isn't his dream anymore. This is us. He's talking about *us!*

"I had all the labs checked. Only a handful of people left who could pull off that kind of work since the university closed down, and I own most of 'em. Or did. I fired 'em all this morning. Dragons! Can you imagine the market share for real live dragons? Nikko! Get in here!"

"Yessir, Mr. B."

"I'm telling her about the dragons."

Nikko clears his throat. "Saw 'em with my own eyes."

"Well, where are they?" Lealé laughs.

"Lost 'em," says Nikko.

"But were they big? Really dragon-sized? How ever did they manage to elude the beach patrol? And those terrible dogs!"

Baraga pauses, and N'Doch knows exactly why. He's

just at the part that's gonna be real hard to explain. "Well, that's the thing. They just disappeared."

"Oh, into the water?"

"No. On the spot. Right out from under the noses of six sober, tough-minded men. And the damned dogs. Two dragons, two kids. They were there and then they weren't. I got that on tape, too."

He's got us on tape. N'Doch realizes he's chewing his knuckle to shreds. *I can't put the touch on him—he'll know me for sure.* At first he feels exposed, trapped, but then in a little breathless moment, it occurs to him that he's just been handed the tools he most needs and was sure he did not possess: something to sell and the status necessary to get the Media King to listen.

The grin comes shooting up out of the depths of him, fastens itself onto his face as if of its own accord. He has no control over it. He has a hard enough time choking back the laughter that wants to rise up with it. Terrified, exultant laughter, filling him until he's sure he'll burst if he can't let it out somehow. But he can't. Not right now. 'Cause, of course, *this could be it.* Right now could be that chance in a million he'd just finished convincing himself he wasn't ever gonna get. That's the exultant part. The terror part is, if in dealing with Kenzo Baraga, he doesn't play his cards just right, he could end up even worse than he was before. He could end up dead.

First thing is, he's got to talk to the dragons. A few special appearances? Shoot a few vids? Maybe even a series. What's the big deal? He's sure they'll go for it. And if they don't, well .. he'll just have to cross that bridge when he comes to it.

PART FOUR

The Meeting
with Destiny

Chapter Thirty-Four

Baraga takes up his dream narrative again, and doesn't seem ready to end it any time soon. Eager now but still bound into the enforced idleness of his hiding place, N'Doch starts plotting out a dragon-based miniseries in his head. All he has to do is tell the story of his own adventures with the dragons, right? Featuring his shape-shifting blue beauty, of course—that'll really wow 'em—and then he'll write songs to go with it. A musical miniseries: a brand new concept! The Media King'll love it!

He's distracted as the intermittent sniper fire out in the market square changes abruptly to the chatter of automatic weapons. At the other end of the room, Baraga breaks off his recitation to listen, then grunts pensively and calls in his bodyguard.

"Nikko, send someone to check with ground security, make sure the place is fully sealed off. Sasha, get Amahl on the line, see what you can find out about this."

"You might want to think about wrapping it up here, Mr. B.," remarks Nikko.

"Nah. We'll wait till we know there's . . ."

The floor shudders, twice, like a cough. Two dull thuds sound in the distance.

"Huh," says Baraga. "How far, you think?"

"Coupla miles," Nikko replies smoothly. "Southwest."

"The Presidential Palace?"

"Could be."

"Well. That'll teach the old bastard. Security, Nikko. The gates."

"I'm on it, Mr. B."

N'Doch hears the tinkle and rustle of Lealé's robes.

Her cheery bells and beads sound more anxious than seductive now. "What is it, Kenzo? What's happening?"

"A little more than somebody expected, I'd say." Baraga moves around restlessly. "Why wasn't I told about this?"

"I have Mr. Kemal on the line, Mr. B."

Listening to the secretary's breathy uninflected voice, N'Doch pictures him in slippers and long hair neatly tied back in a bun.

"You talk to him. Glory, get me an update from Print-News. They better be on top of this, or they're history tomorrow."

"Mr. Kemal says he's getting mixed reports from the copters," the secretary murmurs. "But there does appear to be action in the area around the Palace."

"Don't give me appearances," Baraga growls, "Give me facts! Tell him to get someone in there to find out what's going on! Jesus! What do I pay these people for?"

N'Doch gets a tingle of anxiety himself. The energy is rising in the room as Baraga moves into gear. It's like someone turned up the volume and it's contagious. Normally, during military actions, N'Doch just heads for the deepest ground he can find. He's not sure if being around Baraga when the bullets are flying makes him safer or more of a target.

"We're as sealed off as we're ever gonna be in this place," reports Nikko from the door. "I still think you oughta consider getting out of here, Mr. B."

"Taken under advisement."

"Someone might have seen us come in, y'know . . ."

"Nikko, I hear you."

"Yessir, Mr. B."

"Mr. Baraga!" The secretary has finally been shoved off his even keel. "Shore Patrol just intercepted mortar fire!"

"What? They're shelling my house? Get birds in the air and clean 'em out!"

"They're already on it, sir."

"Shelling my *house*? Who the hell do they think they are?"

Lealé hurried in rattling a sheaf of facsimile. "Here you are, darling. Not very good news, I'm afraid."

Baraga grabbed the stack. A strained silence thickened

the air while he read. "So that's it," he muttered finally. "Glory, clear your people out of the office. I'm gonna be needing it. Right now. Nikko, Sasha, come with me."

N'Doch waits for the silence to settle in again at the other end of the room before he peers around the back of his chair. Empty. Free at last. He hops up and goes straight for the PrintNews that Baraga's scattered behind him as he left the room. PrintNews is expensive. He doesn't get to see it very often. It's also the only real source of straight news there is—all the vid news programs have evolved toward news as-you-want-it rather than news as it is. N'Doch doesn't see any problem with this. Real news isn't high on his priority list. Actual events in the world, or even in other parts of town, don't affect his own life directly, and by the time they affect it *in*directly, it's too late to do anything about it anyway. He gets his news on the street.

But suddenly it seems kind of important to know who's bombing MediaRex Enterprises in the middle of an ordinary coup attempt, and why? He gathers up the printout and scans through it. Phew! So dry! Like reading an upgrade for software he's never laid eyes on. Names he doesn't know, factions he's never heard of, like the whole thing is written in code. Only he knows it isn't, not if you're caught up on the basic information. It makes him feel insignificant, reading about all this plotting and politics he wasn't aware of, and that makes him huffy. He tosses the papers aside. If Baraga ever needs the latest on street barter values and local gang infighting, N'Doch knows who he can turn to.

Someone's turned on the bright lights out in the hallway. Anxious flappers shuttle this way and that, plus a couple of what have to be Baraga's security guys. One or two glance at N'Doch through the open doorway, but since no one stops or comes in after him, he decides it's safe to mingle and move about, as long as he keeps out of Baraga's line of sight. Or maybe the bodyguard Nikko's.

He goes out into the hall, eyes the crowd jammed in around the door to the office, and heads the other way, toward the dining room. If the girl is awake, she won't have a clue what all the noise is about. And, holy shit, what about the dragons? When they went off to eat did they go back to Baraga's beach? He knows they're magical and all, but he doubts they're immune to a well-placed mortar shell.

He slips into the dining room, snatches a few bites as he cruises past the food table, and pushes through the drapes into the alcove. The girl is tucked away in the farthest corner, tossing and turning and gasping for breath as if she's fighting with something in her sleep. He sits down beside her and nudges her gently.

"Wake up, girl. Easy now. You gotta wake up."

She thrashes around, whimpering and panting, but she doesn't wake. N'Doch remembers the first time she had this dream trouble. This time it looks like she's losing her battle. He grabs her up in his arms and shakes her hard. She cries out and gulps in air. Her eyes pop open, and she stares at him mindlessly for a moment, then throws herself shuddering and heaving against his chest. Her arms tighten around his waist like she's keeping from being pulled away from him.

N'Doch lets her hold on. He pats her back awkwardly. She's talking at him in Kraut, long breathless murmurs broken by sobs. He keeps patting until finally she gets her breath back and quiets down. Meanwhile, he's searching around his mind to see if the dragon's come back on-line yet. Probably not, or he'd be understanding what's all this the girl's so unhinged about.

Suddenly . . . yes! There! In a rush, like doors and windows flying open, light flooding in. Connection, comprehension, all at once. N'Doch feels like he's been plugged in direct to the socket.

—*'Bout time, girl. Where you been?*

—*Are you safe?*

—*For now, at least. Are you?*

—*My brother had to fix a small wound in my side.*

To N'Doch's surprise, something like a fist tightens around his heart.

—*You got hurt?*

—*On the beach, there was metal flying through the air. I'm fine now. But because the healing uses up his strength, we had to search for more food. But everywhere else, we found death in the water. All the fish are dying.*

Another red tide washing in, N'Doch thinks. *Must be*

a really bad one. He's worried now. His dragon has been wounded. What if the big guy hadn't been around? Would she have died? Maybe Baraga's right. Maybe the world really is falling apart. He remembers now what Water had said, under the trees in Djawara's courtyard. That she was here because *something terrible is happening.* N'Doch is beginning to believe it.

—*The girl's been dreaming. I think she had another bad one.*

—**Yes. She's telling my brother about it now. She needs to be near him now. Can you bring her out to the Grove?**

—*Sure, no problem.*

Actually, it is a problem, since he sure ain't walking her out the front way, past Baraga's eagle eyes. But N'Doch is glad for a task. He's feeling helpless among all these high-power shenanigans, outside the gates and in Lealé's office. He gets the girl up and mobile, though she's refusing to let go of him for more than a few seconds at a time. So he lets her take his hand and he leads her into the outer room. Passing the food table, he thinks twice and stops.

"We ought to stock up."

The girl is ready and willing. In fact, she's putting as much food in her mouth as she is into the big linen napkin he hands her to tie up as a carry-sack.

"Whatcha been doing in that dream," he kids her, "to make yourself so hungry?"

Her eyes get round. She shudders and shakes her head, and he knows when she lets it out, it's gonna be a hell of a story.

At the big double doors, he pauses to picture the plan of the house in his mind, lining up the rooms he knows inside with the entrances he's seen outside. He guesses the ceremonial side entrance must lead into a room that's right across the hall, but when he cracks open one of the sliding doors, he sees only a blank wall opposite. It makes him skip at least one little breath when he notices, under the newly brightened lighting, that the wallpaper is patterned with dragons. *How much,* he wonders, *does Lealé know that she's not telling us about?* He sticks his head out farther.

At the very end of the hall is a small door, so small it

looks like a closet. N'Doch points it out to the girl and
raises an eyebrow. She shrugs and nods.

"Okay. Let's go for it."

He makes her walk slow and steady, so she looks like
she knows where she's going. When they get to the little
door, it's locked. But it's an old-fashioned key lock, as
old as the house is and never updated. N'Doch thinks
fast, scanning the list he carries in his mind of every
object currently available to him and their relevant uses.
He needs a shiv and doesn't have one on him. His knife
blade is too thick. He starts down the list of what he
knows the girl's got, and stops at the image of the big
red jewel she's got pinned inside her jeans. He'd wanted
her to leave it at Papa Dja's, but she wouldn't hear of
it. *Good thinking, girl.*

"Quick!" he whispers. "Gimme the dragon thing, you
know, the jewel . . . your grandmama's pin!"

She blinks at him. He mimes fiddling with the door,
and she gives him back a steady, searching look while
she pulls her right-hand pocket inside out and unpins the
red stone. He sees her overcoming heavy reluctance in
order to hand it over to him. He smiles at her. "You'll
have it back in a minute."

In less than that, he's used the pin's long-pointed fastener to pick the lock. They're inside a narrow inner hallway, lined with doors. The blood red stone is warm in
his palm. He remembers how he'd felt sure it was alive,
when it was stolen and resting in his pocket. As jewelry
goes, the thing's unnatural, but he finds that comforting
now, and lets his thumb trace the miniature dragon
carved into its polished surface. He hands it back without
a qualm. "That did the trick, huh?"

Now her eyes are full of admiration for his cleverness.
N'Doch laughs. She's an easy mark if she's wowed by an
easy piece of juggling like that. But it makes him feel
good anyway. He starts checking behind doors down the
hall. Most of them are closets, filled with the long white
tunics that the flappers wear, and shelves full of linens
and candles and boxes of incense. But the door at the
end leads them into a small antechamber, hung with soft,
sound-absorbing draperies, and from there through a curtained arch into darkness.

They both stop short at the archway. They are in a

huge, domed room. It's the deep blue of the zenith just after sundown, and it sparkles with a thousand electric stars. In the center, a big golden throne waits in a lavender spotlight.

"Oooh," marvels the girl, turning to stare all around her.

"Look later." N'Doch has just noticed the ring of chairs set one next to the other all around the wall. There's a "guest" seated in every one of them, sitting, dozing, staring in meditative poses, or chatting with neighbors. He grabs the girl's hand and makes a beeline for the outer door. He's almost there when a "guest" rises to stop him, a youngish woman who lays a pleading hand on his arm.

"Will the Mahatma return to us soon? Will I have my Reading today, do you think?"

"Er . . . she's busy right now," he replies helplessly.

She grips his arm harder. "Please, ask her to hurry. I do so need her to tell me what to do about Mama."

"Do whatever you feel like," N'Doch wants to say, and finds that he actually has. He doesn't know why but he's unreasonably pissed at this woman. "Go out into the streets. See what's really happening. Go read a PrintNews."

The woman stares at him. Cautiously, she draws her hand away. N'Doch moves on.

Outside, the light and heat are blinding, even though it's getting on toward late afternoon. The sky is a lurid yellow, thick with dust. He hears sirens and gunfire from several directions now. Copters race and hover like birds of prey, and off to the south, twin plumes of oily black smoke curl up from the Palace district. Another coup, no doubt of it. Since none of the past coups have ever seemed to change anything, N'Doch can't see why this one should get Baraga in such an uproar. Can't he just lay low like everyone else until one side or the other runs out of ammunition?

N'Doch suspects now that the answer could be found in a detailed and daily reading of PrintNews. He has that sinking feeling he gets when he's understood something big enough to make him realize how little he knew before he understood it.

On the terrace outside the door, groups of "guests"

are gathered around the vid screens built into neat stucco pillars here and there. He takes the girl over to look, certain for one insane moment that the vid stations have seen the light at the same moment that he has, and are broadcasting actual news of the coup. But the "guests" are watching one or the other of the late afternoon series with total absorption, as if completely unaware of the chaos outside the gates. N'Doch finds himself angry at them, too, and he drags the girl away quickly to avoid a scene he's not sure he would even be able to explain to himself.

He leads her around toward the back, sticking close to the house, staying under trees and behind bushes where he can. He makes her trot briskly across the open lawn and gravel driveway between the house and the grove. A few shots ring out, but they are distant, random fire. N'Doch slows once they've reached the trees, but the girl runs on ahead of him, following the call of her dragon, eager to see him after so long. Of course, it hasn't been so long, just since the morning, but even N'Doch will admit it feels like an eternity. By the time he's made it to the clearing, she's already got herself pressed up against the big guy between his paws, with his great horny snout bending over her protectively. But she looks up at N'Doch with a wondering gaze and exclaims, "He thinks I've heard the Summoner!"

Water shifts and stretches her neck.

—I think she's heard someone else entirely.

N'Doch senses the dragons' restless, edgy mood. *Don't want to rush this,* he thinks. *I gotta sell it to 'em right, or they're not gonna buy it.*

He smiles, he hopes ingratiatingly. "Well . . . when you're done arguing about her story, I'll tell you mine."

Chapter Thirty-Five

"**B**ut what temptation could it have meant?" the girl is asking.

N'Doch is stretched out on the soft thick grass. One part of his brain is wondering why it's so much cooler in this clearing than it is outside. The other is watching the girl for a sign that she's kidding, because he just can't believe she doesn't know the answer to her question. Of course, she can't see what her face does when she talks about this dude back when. She thinks she's telling out her dream story like it could've happened to anyone, like it's just some coincidence she's dreaming about this guy, but if he could hand her a mirror to look at, the glow in her eyes might just about blind her.

N'Doch considers her question answered, and wants to move on to the next one, which is, *what's wrong with her being tempted*? This Köthen sounds like a courageous dude and he's straight with his men and all, and him being a baron like the girl's father should make him just about right for her, at least as far as N'Doch sees it.

So he says all this, and the girl shakes her head, then blushes furiously and clams up. Both of the dragons stare off into the trees that rise around in an oh-so-perfect circle, pretending like they're not even involved in this conversation, so for a while, there's a silence so big you could drive a couple of APCs right through it. Instead, N'Doch sits up, and drives through it himself. Might be a leftover from his irritation with the Glory-guests, but he's suddenly tired of coddling the girl like she's in nursery school. Time she grew up a little.

"So what's the deal? You hot for this dude, or not?"

An instant later, he wishes he could be the girl hearing

Water's relayed translation. First, she looks blown-away astonished. Next she gets stony mad. Her whole body pulls itself up and gets taller.

"What'd you say to her?" N'Doch's just sure the blue critter's got a smirk hidden somewhere.

"In my father's court," the girl gets out finally, "such insulting remarks would not go unpunished."

N'Doch spreads his hands. "Where's the insult? You like a guy's looks, what's wrong with that?"

"To imply that I would have such base thoughts, such . . ." But she can't even say it out in words.

"C'mon, girl, don't get all huffy. It's just sex. It's no big deal."

Water finally decides to lend him a hand.

—It is a big deal if it's what she's supposed to be resisting.

N'Doch is dogged. The girl is still stonyfaced and looking away from him, but he won't have one of his favorite pastimes being labeled base or insulting. "It's not the sex that's the big deal, y'know what I mean? The sex is just the bait. The question is, why is the trap being set?"

—Point taken.

"Yeah, it's pretty simple, don't you think? Something wants her back there, so it puts this cool handsome dude in her path. She said herself it might be the loony priest calling her into these dreams." N'Doch is surprised to hear himself discussing all this as if it's a series of rational events with your normal type of cause and effect. Maybe he's starting to take this "Quest" thing seriously.

The thought of the priest makes the girl set her high-toned anger aside. "Yes, it could be. He was there in my head and he said I would never wake . . . Oh. I can't ever go to sleep again."

—I will watch while you sleep.

—Watching may not be enough, brother. Whatever Power is doing this, it seems sure it has found a weakness worth exploiting.

—But surely, sister, I can protect my companion. . . .

—Can you? I wonder. I am inclined to suspect our brother Fire in this also, using the priest as he would have used Lealé. He will know our secrets

*and our ways. Our companions will be vulnerable
to him.*

The big dragon rose up on his haunches and dipped
his horned head. For some reason, N'Doch thought of a
great tree tossed with wind.

*—You are too free with your accusations, sister!
You offer no proof of Fire's involvement but your
own suspicions.*

*—You will recall, brother, that I remember him
and you do not.*

Earth draws his head into his shoulders until his neck's
nearly disappeared. Making himself like a rock, N'Doch
notes. Stubborn. But N'Doch likes him for wanting to
believe the best about this other brother he has no memory of. So maybe he's dead wrong, but you gotta hand
it to the big guy for trying. N'Doch would never stand
for someone dumping all over Sedou.

"If it is Fire, who saved me from him?" asks the girl.
"And who is the prisoner in the wood?"

—It's the Summoner. It must be!

*—Whatever saved your companion's life fought
off a dragon. The only power capable of thwarting
a dragon is another dragon.*

*—That's assuming it was Fire who threatened
her, but . . .*

*—Who would know to seek a dragon's help but
another dragon?*

*—Sister, listen! I recognize this Presence from my
companion's report, this Voice that is not a voice.
It's the One who's been calling me since I awoke!*

*—But, brother, you don't think it odd that our
sister Air has not been heard from?*

N'Doch has learned a thing about dragons: They love
to argue. Particularly in ways that seem to lead the debate away from the obvious solution, like they wouldn't
want all the fun to be over too quickly. N'Doch has no
patience for this. He figures they should be doing it on
their own time.

"Why can't it be both?" he demands loudly. He's glad
to have the fourth dragon brought into the mix, 'cause
then he won't have to be waiting for any more of 'em to
turn up.

Both dragon heads swivel to stare at him. The girl,

bless her, actually giggles. N'Doch guesses she'd prefer
answer to argument also. So then it's another one of
those APC-sized silences, during which N'Doch notices
for the first time that he hasn't been hearing the sirens
or gunfire from outside, even though, looking through
the trees toward the house, he can see torn shreds of
smoke rising from the streets beyond the compound wall.

He gets up. "You guys just give it some thought, eh?"
He turns away and walks into the first row of trees. The
air around him feels very . . . well, *blue*. He still hears
nothing, but then, as he moves farther in, faint sounds
come to him, more like cap pistols and mosquitoes than
gunfire and copters, even though the house is no more
than two hundred yards away. He backs up a few steps
into silence, moves forward back into the zone of sound.
He grunts and returns to the clearing. Everyone there is
in exactly the same position they were in when he walked
away. "You know," he says, "there's something weird
about *this* wood, too."

The suddenness with which the debate was stilled told
Erde that N'Doch had hit upon a true understanding. He
did have a gift for cutting to the simplest explanation. It
was not a gift the dragons appreciated, as fascinated as
they were with the subtle and the complex and the ambiguous. But this time, his answer was so compelling, he
got no argument.

Earth's inner rumble was hopeful.

—*Could it be? Our sister Air is the Summoner?*

—*There is logic to it. She is the eldest.*

Water fastened onto the idea as if it had been her
own.

—*But who could hold her prisoner?*

—*I think why is the only unanswered question,
brother.*

"If you go into the wood, maybe she can tell you,"
Erde offered. "Maybe she just couldn't speak to me."

"We oughta go back and check it out." N'Doch wan-
dered restlessly, obviously ready for action. "We'll have
to really work on Lealé to get her to let us in again."
He paused. "But first . . . are you ready to hear why
that might be even harder than it should be?"

Erde thought she might have sensed reluctance in him,

but told herself he was just pausing for effect, the way Cronke the bard used to do at a particularly critical point in a story. "Of course," she said, to hurry him along.

N'Doch smiled, but not his usual easy smile. It was something much more complicated. "Most times, this'd be about the worst thing that could happen. But now I'm not so sure. I got an idea that might turn it in our favor. Guess who Lealé's rich boyfriend is . . . ?"

It would have been safer and more sensible to stay behind in the grove with Earth, as N'Doch suggested, but Erde felt that Duty refused her such luxuries. Besides, if she stayed behind, she'd have nothing to distract her from the disturbing thoughts that N'Doch had put into her mind about Baron Köthen. To think she might be in love with him was one thing—young girls did that sort of thing all the time. It was perfectly proper. But the possibility that she might be having . . . lustful thoughts? The very idea shamed her. Surely she was better brought up than that. Yet N'Doch seemed to think such thoughts were natural, as he put it, "no big deal."

So the strange noises and tension outside the grove seemed preferable to the strangeness inside her head, even though N'Doch did warn her that it might be getting dangerous out there. She understood that a battle was being waged, not with crossbows and lances but with the terrible weapons called guns. N'Doch described their magic to her: They shot many arrows without shafts and they could kill at a very great distance.

Water would come with them of course, so once again, N'Doch sang the song about his lost youngest brother that enabled the dragon's transformation. Erde thought he sang it even more poignantly than before, and she was delighted to see little Wasser again.

N'Doch took the lead on the way out, cautioning them both to stay alert and move quickly. With shame, Erde recalled how she had once questioned his worthiness as a dragon guide. She hadn't then understood how very different this new world would really be, how different would be the knowledge and skills required for survival in it.

He stopped as they emerged from the deepest part of the grove, just where the outside sounds became audible. "Here's where they start being able to see us again." He hunkered down to survey the compound. Erde could feel that heat radiating toward her in waves. A few more steps forward and it would close around her again, making the sweat rise on her instantly and filling her lungs with dust.

N'Doch touched her arm suddenly and pointed. A thing shaped like a dragonfly sat on the grass at the far end of the grounds. As they watched, parts of it began to rumble and rotate.

"Someone's leaving," N'Doch murmured. "The Big Man himself?"

Several men sprinted from the side of the house toward the dragonfly thing. Wasser counted under his breath. Just as the men disappeared into the machine's belly, a series of loud pops came from over the compound wall, like the noise of ice breaking up on a river in spring.

"Ha! Missed!" N'Doch's wide mouth curved into a tight grimace that was almost a smile. "Hard to tell, but it looked like him to me. Damn!"

Erde glanced at him sideways. She would have thought he'd be relieved if his enemy Baraga was leaving. Now he wouldn't have to employ the elaborate ruse he'd described, by which he could protect them all by turning this terrible man's greed and self-interest to their own advantage. It had sounded like a very risky proposition to her, largely because it did involve putting themselves into Baraga's hands. Earth had not liked this scheme overmuch. He remembered the dogs at Baraga's beach. So Erde was glad that the man was leaving. Not having to deal with him at all seemed by far the most preferable situation.

But N'Doch was crestfallen. As the dragonfly lifted into the heat-shimmered air and glided away into the smoky yellow sky, he watched after it as if it had robbed him of some priceless treasure.

"Damn!" he said again.

"It will be easier to talk Mistress Lealé into helping us now," Erde reminded him.

"Yeah. For sure." But his tone was so dispirited, she

couldn't even ask him why. He waited until the dragonfly was out of sight, then waved them to their feet and
forward. When they cleared the last of the trees, he
made them speed up for a run across the open lawn to
the house. Again, Erde heard that odd, sharp crackle in
the distance, like embers popping in a fire. Gravel
sprayed up a few feet to her right.

"Keep low!" N'Doch hissed. "Head for the bushes!"

Gravel and dirt spattered Erde's cheek, from the left
this time. Wasser sped forward. N'Doch grabbed Erde's
hand, nearly yanking her off balance.

"Move! They're shootin' at us!"

He ran, she ran, then he shoved her hard down behind
a thick row of bushes hugging the side of the house.
Wasser was already there.

"From the south, I think."

N'Doch nodded, catching his breath. "Didn't expect
this quite so soon." Together they scanned the rear of
the compound: the long low building that stabled the
riding machines, the high wall behind it, and the crumbling facades of the buildings that crowded up against
the wall and gazed down into the grounds, Erde imagined, with envy.

"The roof, over there?" N'Doch pointed.

"Likely."

"We'll go around the other side, then, out of their line
of fire."

"Why are they shooting at us?" Erde asked. "We are
not their enemies."

"They don't know that," N'Doch retorted. "They're
shootin' at anything that moves. You ready? Let's go."

Erde crept after him in the shadow of the bushes until
they reached the front corner of the house. N'Doch
stopped to reconnoiter. Erde saw the "guests" all huddled up against the compound wall in groups, or crouch-
ing singly behind the wide stone bases of the planters.

"Good." N'Doch chewed his lip nervously. "They've
left the doors open a crack in case anyone's brave
enough to make a run for the house."

Wasser said quietly, "Looks like someone already
tried."

Out on the little grass plot in the center of the gravel
drive, a woman lay sprawled on her face, moaning.

Blood leaked from her upper back. Erde moved instinctively to help her, but N'Doch caught her and yanked her back hard. "No!"

"But she's down, she's hurt. Surely they'll let us retrieve the wounded?"

His look seemed to pity and envy her simultaneously. "What kinda wars you been fighting in, girl?"

Just then, the front doors opened wide, and two of Lealé's white clad acolytes raced out across the gravel and grass to haul the woman to safety.

"Now!" N'Doch grabbed Erde's elbow, dragging her with him as he leaped up onto the columned porch and shoved through the open doorway. "In, woman, in!" he yelled at Lealé, who was standing beside the door. "You're in range!" He bundled Erde and Wasser inside after her, then held the door as the acolytes retreated inside with their bloodied burden.

N'Doch is impressed with Lealé's calm. No womanish fainting away at the sight of blood. For that matter, the girl's not either, though she does look a little shell-shocked by the sudden violent turn of events, all blown up around her like a thunderstorm. Probably she's not used to stuff happening this fast.

Lealé hovers over them briefly. "Children! Children! I looked and you were gone! Are you all right? I'm so glad you're safe!" And then she's off down the hall, directing the flapper rescue team into the dining room. "In here. Lay her on that other table! Quickly! Call Millet!"

"Stick close," N'Doch warns the kid and the girl. He trails after Lealé, moving through milling knots of anxious flappers and guests who have fled inside. The cool perfumed indoor air is heating up with the rank smells of sweat and fear. He passes the doorway to the long parlor and shoots a glance inside. More guests, crowds of them, some talking in frightened whispers, most of them huddled around vid screens that were hidden before behind the fancy wood paneling.

For the second time in one day, N'Doch entertains the wild fantasy that what they're so riveted to is the news of the coup, and once again, he's proved wrong. The late afternoon series is playing on all screens. He studies the faces of the watchers for a moment. The Watchers. Their eyes stare like they're drinking in the screen, like if they stared hard enough, they could be in there, a part of somebody else's story instead of their own. Why aren't they worried about what's going on at home, whether their house is being ransacked, whether their wives or husbands or children are being shot in the streets? *Probably they are,* N'Doch thinks, but it's like they've forgotten how to do anything about it. All they know how to do is watch.

Suddenly he knows there's something *he's* gotta do, and he drags the kid and the girl back down the crowded hall to the office. The door is closed but not locked. He ducks inside, hauling the other two with him. "Close the door," he whispers to the girl.

This seems to be the only room that hasn't been invaded by "guests" and panic. The head flapper Jean-Pierre is there with a few others, all of them busily clicking away at various keypads, muttering figures and names at each other. They barely glance up as N'Doch comes in. A last-ditch effort, he imagines, to reroute Lealé's business dealings around changes resulting from the coup. He sees there's PrintNews scattered everywhere. It's overflowed the output bin at the terminal. The service is working overtime, and here are a group of people who may actually read it. The business people. The money people. The people who know the real meaning of power. N'Doch is amazed he hasn't understood this before.

He parks the girl by the door to keep watch, for what he's not sure, but it makes him feel better as he ventures into this cool, white, alien space. The apparition shadows him as he goes straight to the PrintNews terminal and takes the latest sheet as it peels out of the slot. As he reads, the apparition reads over his shoulder.

What he sees shocks him. It makes denial rise up in him like the instinct to run, but he guesses he's got to believe what he's reading. If this ain't the truth, the truth ain't to be had. But it tears away the foundation of a notion he didn't even know he'd relied upon until he sees it crumbling. He knows things are bad. It's all around him, every day. But still, there's this notion he's buried inside himself, that things aren't really as bad everywhere else in the world as they are where he is. That somewhere, even though he can't get there, things are better, there's still hope.

If PrintNews tells true, there isn't. It's just another fantasy like every other fantasy he's been sold, 'cause there's bad shit coming down *everywhere*. He's got it right in front of him in black and white.

Half of Europe underwater, for instance, and the Amazon basin, and parts of Asia he's never even heard of. Huge storms everywhere, and crop failures, item after item, a long list of national emergencies and requests for relief, desperate cries for help muffled by the dry news service prose. He sees stuff about countries moving their capitals to higher ground, about the tides of refugees rolling inland, about governments collapsing under the strain. Revolution, violence, repression, anarchy. The weight of this steady progression of disaster bears down on N'Doch until he has to look away.

"Jeez . . ." breathes the apparition.

N'Doch's impulse is to grab the nearest responsible person and shake them until their bones rattle. He wants to scream, "Why didn't you tell us?" But there's no one in this room worth grabbing. The responsibility lies much higher up than skinny head flapper Jean-Pierre, and what's worse, it lies within himself as well. N'Doch sees he's been wrong all this time to think of himself as one of the Watched, or even Watched-in-Waiting. He's a Watcher, just like everyone else, taking what he's given as information and image, and buying right into it, same as his mama does. His particular fantasy is different from hers, is all. It's still a fantasy.

He leans his forehead against the terminal and lets out an explosion of breath. It seems to come from the bottom of his feet, an exhalation of pure rage and frustration.

"I used to razz Sedou," he tells the apparition. "Say he was living in a fantasy world if he thought he could change things by messing in politics." N'Doch saw himself as the pragmatic realist, the artist and independent loner, out for what he could get from the world. But what's coming clear is how he's been taught to want only what the world thinks is good business to sell him, assuming he ever gets rich enough to be able to afford it. The world, and by "the world" he's beginning to mean Baraga and those like him, the real power brokers—they don't want him to want freedom, they want him to want things, comfort, fame. They'd rather he didn't have a true awareness of how fucked up things really are, so they trained him not to want it.

But knowledge is power, or so it seems to N'Doch as he stands with just that sort of information held slack in his hand. What burns him the most is that this realization has probably come too late. He's never sidestepped the current of life like he thought he had, not even for a moment. He's right there in the torrent, caught up in the tide of events, tumbling head over heels along with everyone else.

"Hey, bro?" murmurs the apparition. "You okay?"

"Yeah," he replies curtly, but he isn't. His mind is a seething mess. He's blind with rage and panic and humiliation.

"I think you're not . . ."

N'Doch thrusts the paper in the kid's face. "Well, look at this!"

"I know. I did."

"Doesn't it make all your 'quest' shit look pretty silly when laid up beside the end of the world as we know it?"

The apparition blinks at him with the dragon's bottomless dark eyes. "Not if preventing the end of the world is the object of that Quest."

N'Doch thinks, *Man, haven't we been through this already?* " 'Saving the world' is just a phrase, kid. It means you're a do-gooder, which I know you are, and that's fine. But you can't take it literally."

"I can. I do."

"I mean, it doesn't mean you gotta try to do it single-handedly."

"It might."

"What?" N'Doch really has to laugh. "You?"

"Us. Not as we are but as we will be."

N'Doch feels the conversation spinning off from the crisis at hand back toward the realm of the unreal, where as far as he sees it, no solution lies. *These dragons are as bad as Baraga.* "And what will we be?"

"Eight, eventually. Four dragons, four companions. A synergy of power."

"Great. One dragon you can't find and the other one's trying to kill you."

The kid's brow furrows like he's having a complicated thought. "That must be part of the Work."

"What is?"

"Overcoming the obstacles. Solving the mysteries. All leading toward the awakening to power."

"We don't have time for all that!" N'Doch grabs up another sheet of PrintNews and shakes it like a club. "What's it got to do with today and tomorrow and how we're gonna get ourselves out of this mess?"

"Everything! Have you been listening to me at all?"

In his head, N'Doch hears/feels a blast of music, a gale that almost knocks him flat. He sags against the Print-News terminal. He's breathless and shaking. He understands that the dragon has just lost her patience with him. "Okay, okay. Okay. We'll do whatever you want."

The apparition sighs. "I want to do what you said, before you let revelation sidetrack you."

N'Doch is exhausted. He glances at the girl, still guarding the door. She watching him, and her eyes are soft with sympathy. "And what was that? Remind me."

"Lealé."

"Oh, right. Lealé." His brain feels pummeled, but another piece of his new analysis has just clicked into place, and he sees a direction, at least, in which a solution might lie.

They collect the girl and shove their way back along the long hallway, more crowded even than it was before, and into the dining rom. A group of flappers, plus an older woman N'Doch hasn't seen before, are gathered around a long table at one end, working on the gunshot wound. He sees another "guest" lying on the floor, wrapped in a tablecloth. He can't tell if the guy's dead or alive, but he figures no one would've risked life and limb to drag him in if he was gone already.

Lealé's pacing in small circles at the other end, talking rapidly into a phone like the one Baraga'd had with him. N'Doch is glad she's smart enough to stay clear of the windows. Above the drawn draperies, the windows arch in a clear half-moon of divided glass. He sees thick sunset colors in the light, and gathering darkness in the sky above. He has a momentary inspiration for a song he could write about darkness gathering all around the world.

Lealé finishes her call when she sees them coming. Her eyes land on the apparition and stay there, so N'Doch lets him take the lead. It's his party, anyway.

The kid doesn't beat around the bush. "Mother Lealé, your help is needed. We must return immediately to your 'Dream Haven.' "

She waves her arms as if warding him off. "There's no time for dreams now. Don't you see what's happening?"

"I do. All the more reason."

"No! He'll find out! You'll ruin me!"

"Events outside seem to be conspiring to do that already."

Lealé turns away, a Glory turn, and shakes her mane of beaded hair. "Nonsense. This goes on all the time. Once the new leaders have settled in, everything will be business as usual."

"Mother Lealé." The kid's tone is low, almost conspiratorial. "Do you really believe that?"

Panic flares into Lealé's eyes. N'Doch can see her trying to dampen it, but it still makes her hands flutter around too much and her voice unsteady. "Of course I do."

The kid takes her arm. "We need to talk."

Probably because he's so small and childlike, Lealé doesn't resist as he leads her toward the alcove. N'Doch beckons to the girl, and follows. As he draws the curtains behind them, he sees another shooting victim being carried in. This time, it's a head wound, and it looks like a bad one. The snipers' aim is improving.

The kid sits Lealé down on a couch, then sits beside her, holding her hand. "Now listen. You had a dream, Mother Lealé, that caused you to write to an old friend you hadn't seen in years. That dream told you to expect travelers. Was it a good dream?"

Both his formality and his question seemed to puzzle her. Lealé considered. "Yes . . . I recall being very excited. I felt something wonderful was going to happen."

"But later, you had visits from your spirit guide directing you to . . . well, disable the travelers . . . permanently."

Nervous, she answers, "Yes."

The apparition nods, and N'Doch sees the nod of an old wise woman, slow and serene. "And you also dreamed of a particular place, a house that the dream led you to acquire. What was that dream like?"

Lealé looks around her like she's costing out the furniture. "I didn't dream of the house, actually. I dreamed of that grove of trees out back and felt I had to have them. When I inquired, I found the house came with them."

"A dream of trees." The apparition has a triumphant gleam in his eyes. "And then the idea to make a business there was . ."

"Suggested by my . . . my investor, who I had helped so much by bringing him dreams in the past." She frowns, remembering. "He told me I should cut the trees down, build a new wing on the house to quarter my staff. It was our first argument ever."

"Why would he want you to destroy something so lovely? Surely it adds to the value of the property?"

"It is peculiar. He spends huge sums planting trees around his own house and grounds."

"So it must be something about this *particular* grove of trees. That he doesn't like."

"I don't know. Why does it matter?"

"Because I think I do know." He urges N'Doch and the girl in closer with his eyes. "You are a gifted receptor, Mother Lealé. There are not many such available. So, more than one entity wishing to communicate might be led to take advantage of your gifts. I believe that not all your dreams come from your spirit guide. The two we mentioned, for example: They came from somewhere else, and later your dream guide saw to it that you reinterpreted their instructions."

N'Doch is sure Lealé wouldn't appreciate the image he has of her now, as some sort of psychic ventriloquist's dummy.

"Dreams from someone else?" she asks, right on cue.

"Someone I have seen and Erde has seen, and you have seen as well, and been told to deny. The presence in the wood."

Lealé gazes at the apparition unhappily, then stands up and begins to pace.

"We must try to contact it," he continues, letting his voice follow her around the alcove. "It has been your true Work, which your spirit guide has tried to disrupt, to bring us here for that Purpose. And we must accomplish it quickly, before he succeeds in stopping us. Even this fighting now, I believe, is part of his plan."

N'Doch moves into the archway, so he can stop Lealé in case she decides to pace herself right out of the room. He wants to get this act over with and be on to finding a place for them all to lay low that isn't ground zero. He sees her eyes flick up to the top of the arch, just a flick and back, he almost didn't catch it. But now he knows he's missed a camera port in his initial survey of the alcove. He checks it out. Sure enough. Damn! But he doubts, with all this chaos going on, that anyone's bothering to keep an eye on the monitors.

Watching Lealé pace and wring her hands, Erde felt sorry for her. Unlike herself and N'Doch, Lealé had a perfectly good life that she was putting at risk. Or at least she did until the fighting broke out.

Erde considered that coincidence. War here, war at home. Could the fighting at home also be part of someone's dire plan, a someone that Water insisted must be the dragon Fire? Why would Fire wish to disrupt the Work, whatever it was, that all the dragons were being called to perform?

"Think of Djawara," little Wasser was saying, "who sent us to you in trust and full faith that you would do what was needed. . . ."

"But I don't know what that is!"

"Yes, you do."

"All right! But I won't go in there with you this time. I won't face him if he comes to punish me!"

"I don't think," replied Wasser, "that he will dare show his face while I'm around."

N'Doch bent his head to Erde's ear as Lealé palmed the wall and the paneling hissed open. "Don't forget to tell the big guy we're going off the radar."

Wasser led the way this time, down the unlighted passageway. Because he could move so surely in the dark, they were there before Erde had time to admit to herself how scared she was. What if it was Fire, and he did dare to show himself?

The dim little room was the same as it had been before, only warmer. The air was thick and close, and tinged with smoke. Wasser sniffed thoughtfully. "My brother leaves his calling card."

N'Doch grinned. "Trying to scare us off?"

Wasser approached the wide, empty doorway leading out to the wood. "More like he can't resist the chance to show how clever he is. Wherever he is physically, this room is the connection between his reality and ours. He wants us to know he's in control of it." He moved carefully into the doorway, then out onto the first wide, white marble step. He'd eased down onto the second when Erde darted forward and grabbed his arm.

"Don't go down there without some kind of lifeline, a rope or something! The door will vanish, I know it will, and you'll not find your way back again!"

Wasser retreated to the top step and stood staring out into the wood. The same trees, the same grass. Erde shivered and sat down on the edge of the step. She remembered it all too well.

N'Doch leaned against the doorway, waiting. "What d'you think, bro?"

Wasser turned. "I think . . . that's exactly what he wants. The object of this entire exercise: Lealé's dreams, the wood, everything. If I am trapped here, as perhaps my sister Air is, I cannot carry out my Purpose, the Work that is our collective Purpose."

Erde spotted movement then, among the trees. Her head jerked to follow it, but it was gone.

"You saw . . . ?" Wasser asked.

She nodded.

"Me, too." N'Doch came forward and pointed.

"No," said Erde. "It was over there."

"It's everywhere," Wasser concluded. "It's trying to attract our attention."

"To speak to us," added Erde.

"Or just trying to lure you out there where it can take control .." worried N'Doch.

"Here." Wasser extended a small hand to Erde. "We'll make a chain. Brother N'Doch, you be the anchor."

Erde took his hand and then N'Doch's, and stepped down onto the bottom stair with Wasser. N'Doch wrapped his free hand around one of the columns flanking the doorway. When they signaled that they were ready, Wasser let himself down onto the velvet grass and . .

. . . disappeared. All but his hand, which remained tightly clasped in Erde's. The pull on her was light and irregular, like a fishing line bobbing in a slow moving stream. It was easy to maintain her grasp. She smiled over her shoulder at N'Doch, who said, "You know what? It's getting real hot inside this little room."

And, yes, she saw that he was wreathed in smoke. There was even a faint ruddy flicker down the passage-way behind him. "Oh, dear. What if the house is burning?"

N'Doch raised an eyebrow. "Don't even think about it."

Suddenly her hand was yanked roughly, knocking her off balance and nearly breaking both holds. But Wasser hung on hard, and N'Doch quickly redoubled his grip. Erde righted herself and hauled back against the pressure.

"Pull, girl, pull him in! Throw your weight into it!"

The wood came alive with movement, always just out of her line of sight. The smoke in the room seeped out from the doorway in darkening curls. Erde felt like her bones might separate at every joint, she was being held so firmly and hauled on so hard.

N'Doch began to cough. "Gonna have trouble breath-ing in here before long! Pull, girl, pull!"

A breeze sprang up, a sudden tiny whirlwind that shredded the smoke into wisps but did not stir a single leaf or blade of grass. Abruptly the pressure gave from the wood side. Wasser came flying back into view and slammed against Erde, sending her sprawling on the stone step.

"Quickly!" he gasped, grabbing at her, missing, and stumbling. "Out! We've got to get out!"

N'Doch snatched them both to their feet. The door-way behind him was a wall of hot black smoke.

"Take a deep breath and run for it," Wasser ad-vised. "Now!"

"We'll fry!" N'Doch objected.

"Better that than an eternity in between!"

"What?"

Wasser scrambled up the steps. "I'll explain later. Come on!"

As he reached the doorway, the whole room burst into flame. He threw out his arms to hold the others back. He retreated a step, and the flames came after him.

"Trying to drive us into the wood," N'Doch yelled.

Then Wasser planted his feet. "Wait!" he cried. "Wait!" His small form wavered darkly against the sear of flame. "I am . . . I am . . .

—WATER

A roaring filled Erde's ears and eyes and consciousness, and swept her up and into darkness, a long tumbling passage where she wasn't sure if she was breathing or not, whether it was air or water filling her lungs. She felt the weight of heat and light behind her, driving her forward, down and down through darkness, rivers and oceans of darkness, until she gasped and was spat out by the flood onto the thick wool of Lealé's carpets.

"Hit the deck!" N'Doch bellowed, and Erde cowered, awaiting the conflagration that would finish them when all that heat and fire behind them came exploding out of the passageway. Instead, she heard Lealé wailing and pounding on the wall where the opening had been until it delivered them from instant incineration as if from the mouth of Hell itself.

"What have you done?" Lealé screamed and wept and pounded. "What have you done?"

"Where's the kid?" N'Doch croaked.

Erde raised her head. She was back in the alcove, dripping wet like everything and everyone else around her, but otherwise unharmed. There was no fire. Not even a lingering wisp of smoke. Only a blank, wood-paneled wall that no longer yielded its secrets to Lealé's pleading touch.

"Where is he?" rasped N'Doch again.

"Here." A whisper, barely audible, from the corner, nearly drowned out by the renewed crackle of gunfire outside. Wasser was smashed up against one of the couches like a discarded doll. Erde crawled toward him. N'Doch got to him first and turned him over, ever so gently unfolding, surveying his limp and twisted limbs.

"Nothing broken, little bro. You okay?"

"No . . ." His voice was weak and scratchy.

"I thought you said this asshole brother of yours couldn't hurt anyone."

Wasser stirred. "Are you hurt? Is she . . . ?"

"No, no, lay still. We're both drenched but we're in one piece."

"I . . . made water? Real water?"

"You sure as hell did. It was awesome, and it saved our lives. That dude's fire was real enough also, except . . ." N'Doch glanced up to frown at the wall where Lealé huddled, getting hold of herself.

"Except his fire couldn't leave his reality. Good thing, huh?" Wasser coughed and groaned and tried to lift his head. "I can't move . . ."

Glass shattered in the outer room, once, twice. A woman screamed. N'Doch ignored it. "What is it? What happened to you?"

"Weak . . . so weak . . ."

"Then you'll just have to rest up, little bro." He gathered the small slack body into his lap, trying to arrange it comfortably. He looked to Erde, his eyes troubled. "What's wrong with him?"

She leaned close and kept her voice low. "The magic she . . . he made cost all his strength. I think he found more power than he knew he had. If he's like Earth, he'll need food and rest, the really deep sleep that renews the life forces." In her head, she heard Earth confirming her guess.

N'Doch's mouth tightened. "He can't eat in this form."

"We must carry him back to the grove."

He shook his head. "Listen to it out there. We'd get cut to ribbons the minute we stepped out the door. Think of something else."

She gazed back at him helplessly.

"There's gotta be something!" he insisted.

"Sing to me . . ." Wasser murmured.

"What? Now?"

"Sing to me. Sing me your strength. Sing me . . . Sedou."

N'Doch feels the ache rise up in his gut. He tries to press it down, back down there where it's been all along, where he needs it to stay.

"I don't have a song about Sedou."

"Yes . . . you do . . . I've heard it in you."

You've no right to ask this, he thinks, *no right*! But the small body on his lap moves him beyond measure. A moment ago it was a magical being of awesome power. Now it needs him. It *needs* him.

Still, maybe he can fool it.

"You mean the one that goes like this?" He hums a few soft bars of a raunchy little ditty he and Sey used to sing together. It catches in his throat, but he gets it out at least.

"No . . . not that one."

The ache's still there, pressing on his ribs, pushing upward against his lungs and heart. It won't go back down like it always has before. N'Doch understands that the kid is right, the song is there. The ache *is* the song, and it'll come if he lets it. It'll be right there on his tongue, words, melody, everything, formed way back down over the years he's denied it. He's reminded of a woman's pain in childbirth, and wonders if it could ever be as bad as the agony of this bearing forth. He gives in to it and lets the song open his mouth.

It's a hard song and a sweet song. It jangles and growls, and then cuts away swiftly to soar on high pure notes of light, only to swoop down again, hawklike and ruthless, and plunge into darkness. He's real shaky on the first verse. The song is still drying its wings. But as the wings unfold their dark, crystalline brilliance, the singer unfolds with them, revealing the black knot of loss that he's carried inside him like a stone he swallowed and could never pass. In the light of day, the stone crumbles and lifts, each dark shard a rising note.

He's aware of his small audience—the girl, Lealé, a few others who have nosed through the draperies to listen. He can see that he has them enraptured. He's aware that the shuddering of the ground and the rattle of machine guns outside is the perfect thematic baseline for the story he's weaving. Most of all he's aware that, as his voice clears and strengthens, as he moves into sync with the song and with his feelings, the small body in his lap is enlivening, enlarging, transforming, until it's no longer the slim weight of a child that presses against his knees, but the solid burden of a man.

N'Doch clamps his eyes shut. He doesn't dare look down.

But the song has an ending, a dark inevitability he doesn't want to reach, and have to live through twice in one lifetime. The weight on his lap stirs and lifts away from him. A large hand grips his knee.

"That's a great song, bro," says Sedou's voice. "Let's end it right there."

He does, within a breath, before the inevitability. He opens his eyes and stares into his brother's smiling face.

"Sey . . ." is all he can manage.

"No," the apparition reminds him gently. "But almost."

N'Doch surprises himself with a nod. No hot flush of rage that this well-loved face before him isn't really Sedou. He's content just to see it again, alive and whole, and know that seeing it means the dragon's back in working order.

"Hey, big bro . . . good to see you," he says, and smiles.

Somebody at the archway starts applauding. Others join in. N'Doch wonders what they think and how much they've seen, and how much of that they could possibly understand. But the applause dies quickly as explosions shake the walls, leaving only one pair of hands offering up a precise and heavy syncopation with the chatter of the machine guns. Out of the corner of his eye, N'Doch sees Lealé rise from where she'd settled in raptly to listen. The apparition's chin lifts, his smile dies.

"Making music while the city burns?" crows Baraga cheerfully. "A man after my own heart!"

N'Doch just manages not to leap to his feet in panic. The Big Man herds the other spectators away and draws the drapes tight, dusting his hands together with satisfaction. "Well, Glory! You been hiding the local talent from me?"

Now N'Doch stands up. The apparition's rise beside him is even slower and more collected. N'Doch senses a new power in the dragon, filling his brother's already powerful body with an even greater strength and presence. This dragon-form he resolves to call by name. Sedou would be honored. Baraga's eyes are on the singer, but they stray again and again to Sedou.

It's easier to face Baraga with Sedou standing behind him, easier to look into those predatory eyes, and not wince and stutter.

"Glad you liked the song," N'Doch says, amazed at how calm he sounds.

"The song and the singer." The Big Man is actually shorter than N'Doch, but wider. Big shoulders, thickly built. His glossy black hair is artfully streaked with silver. His skin is clear and Mediterranean. He's stripped off his expensive suit jacket somewhere and rolled up his silk sleeves. He holds out his right hand and gives N'Doch a broad smile. "Kenzo Baraga. You've got talent, son. What's your name?"

N'Doch shakes the Media King's hand, something he's always dreamed of doing. "N'Doch N'Djai."

"Good name. You can always change it."

Not on your life, N'Doch thinks. Naming has always been important to him. "Sure could," he replies brightly. "Oh, ah, this is my friend Erde von Alte." He's proud that the first time he has to say her whole name, he gets it all out right. "And my brother Sedou."

Baraga responds to the girl's old-fashioned little curtsy by catching up her hand and touching it lightly to his lips. To N'Doch's surprise, she seems to accept this as an appropriate greeting among strangers. But he notices that the Media King is a little slower to shake the hand that Sedou offers. Intuition grips him.

—*He knows.*

—**He suspects. But he's not sure.**

—*He recognizes me, from the tape.*

—**Perhaps. And he has a touch of Fire in him.**

—*What do we do?*

—**We have no choice. We'll hear what his offer is.**

Shots ring out and more glass shatters in the dining room. Baraga tilts his head to listen, then shrugs and smiles. "Hell of a time to do business, eh?"

N'Doch says carefully, "Is that what we're doing?"

"Think I'm going to let a talent like you slip by me because of some minor coup? No way. I need a kid like you right now. Real star potential, with the right promotion and development."

Star potential. N'Doch has waited all his life to hear those words. And now that he does, all he can do is smile and nod like some rube from the bush. He hates himself for it. "That's real kind of you, Mr. Baraga."

"Kind, schmind. You know my rep, right? You know 'kind' isn't a word anyone applies to Kenzo Baraga. Business is business. We work out a deal, you and me, then I *own* you, 'cause it'll cost me big to make you big. But you turn it around and make me money, I'll treat you right. So. You ready to talk?"

Lealé glides forward and slips her arm around Baraga's elbow. "Dear Kenzo, give the boy a chance to think."

"It is a little . . . sudden, Mr. Baraga." Too sudden. Even an overnight discovery is supposed to have to work a little harder for it than just one song. He knows he should be suspicious, but he's so, so willing to let the Media King convince him.

"It sure is. I don't like it either. But we're smack in the middle of a goddamn revolution—got no time for the niceties of courtship. I'd like to get myself to high ground. You want to talk turkey or not?"

It's out of his mouth before he can stop it. "I . . . yes, of course I do."

"Good! Good! So, first thing we do is find ourselves some place safe to talk. I sent my guys out a while ago to bring back some secured ground transportation." Baraga glances around the alcove, seeming to court noses. "How 'bout an unplanned beachside vacation while we wait for all this to blow over?"

N'Doch can't believe it. Safety *and* his chance for the Big Break. His own scheme exactly, as if he'd laid it out himself for Baraga's approval. But beside him, he feels Sedou shift with what feels like disapproval.

Lealé laughs her Glory laugh. "But, darling, I thought they were shelling your beach house!"

"Oh, we wiped them out hours ago. A hornet's nest, nothing more. We . . ."

A huge explosion shakes the crystals in the chandelier, and the lights flicker. Two more softer thuds follow, then a burst of gunfire. The girl gasps and lets Sedou wrap his arm around her. Lealé's hand flies to her mouth to hold back a scream. The soft background hush of the AC dies into silence.

Baraga cocks an eyebrow. "Huh."

Abruptly the bodyguard Nikko shoves through the

draperies, a phone clutched in one hand and a semiauto-matic in the other. "That was the gate, Mr. B. We're down to emergency power, and our ground transport's been held up trying to get in through the front."

"How long can we hold the house?"

"Minutes."

"Risk it and call in a copter?"

Nikko shakes his head, brandishing the phone. "Base says everything's getting shot out of the air. These bas-tards are very well organized."

"Your suggestion?"

"Only chance is to work our way to the rear and let ground transport come through the back and pick us up there."

"Okay, let 'em know." Baraga thrusts his chin at N'Doch and Sedou. "You men stick with me. Nikko, keep an eye on the ladies."

"Yessir, Mr. B. Got your vest on?"

"Always." Baraga yanks open the drapes. The dining room is a haze of smoke and dust rising in the ruddy light of sunset that pours through the shattered windows. "Let's move."

N'Doch feels Sedou's hand on his shoulder as they start after Baraga. The familiar touch about cracks his heart open. He turns, meets his brother's eyes, and sees the dragon in them, trying to act like a man she knows only from his memories.

"What's on your mind, bro?" Sedou murmurs.

"Gettin' outa here."

"Listen. Only listen."

—*We've only to get to the back door. My brother Earth can pick us up there and we'll be away from here.*

—*But Baraga will protect us, especially if he thinks he's got a live dragon he can put on his network. Where else can we go? Anywhere in the city's a war zone. We go out to the bush, we put Papa Dja in danger. Baraga'll keep us safe. He's got the money and the power to do it.*

—*And the money and power to make you a star, is that what you're thinking?*

If it wasn't the dragon's usual voice in his head, N'Doch would swear it was Sedou talking. It's not just the good things he's remembering now. "It's on my mind," he says aloud. He shakes off his brother's hand and moves ahead, but Sedou's voice stays with him in his head.

—*We cannot be dancing to Baraga's music! We have our Work to do. We must find Fire and learn why he's turned against us.*

N'Doch takes a breath.

—*Okay. Then you go. I'll go with Baraga and distract him, while the big guy takes you and the girl wherever you want to go. Then you'll all be safe, and I'll still have my chance. It's a good plan. Think about it.*

It's a while before the dragon replies. There are bodies sprawled on the floor of the dining room. N'Doch nearly trips on one. No one is attempting to rescue them now. Broken glass is scattered everywhere, mixing with blood and a dusting of ceiling plaster. Sedou catches up with him at the door.

—*It's not a good plan. I can't go without you.*

—*Sure you can. You'll do fine.*

He's glad he's not trying to say this aloud. He's not sure he could do it. He's just got Sedou back and he's giving him up so soon?

—*No, I mean, we can't. Three is not four. You are needed.*

He tries to make a joke of it.

—*C'mon, it can't matter that much. What if I died?*

—*We fail. Without you, without any one of us, the Quest will fail. If the Quest fails, my existence is purposeless.*

—*Existence is never purposeless! Life is its own purpose!*

—*Not for a dragon.*

—*So then what?*

—*I will cease, as will the others. You are needed, Dragon Guide.*

N'Doch remembers when the realization first came on him, standing in the gym in the supertanker, of the burden this "destiny" was trying to dump on him. The same hollow panic grips him. Before, he'd thought it was rage and rebellion, but now he sees that it's actually fear, fear of losing his freedom, of losing his self.

—*No! I don't want it! I didn't ask for it! What about*

*what I need? I got the chance of a lifetime here! This is
my quest! You only get one chance like this one!*

Sedou looks back at him steadily. N'Doch understands
now why this brother's shape suits the dragon so much
better than Jéjé's. It's not just an issue of size. Sedou
and the dragon have a lot in common: The same hard
righteousness lights both their gazes.

—*Remember the message offered in the wood?*

—*The girl's, you mean? Yeah, so?*

—*Take it to heart, my brother. It was meant for
you.*

Chapter Thirty-Six

Erde supposed she was meant to feel safer with the giant Nikko right at her back, but she didn't. She didn't like how his eyes slid past her face, lingered on her body, then dismissed her altogether. Or how he used his burly body as a prod, herding herself and Lealé through the smoke and destruction in the outer room. Broken glass crunched underfoot. The long table loaded with food had been tipped over sideways in front of the ragged openings that are all that's left of the windows. Several people huddled behind it, a few of them looking more dead than alive.

They'd almost reached the door when the light in the room flickered again, as if even this magic of electricity was subject to wind and warfare. The bodyguard barked a warning to Baraga ahead of him, and then the room went dark. Lealé moaned softly and reached for Erde's hand. Her grip was moist and hot, like the thick damp air invading the house through its broken walls. Light fell in through the holes like light into a tunnel, enough to see by but barely, a red smoky light that raised the hair on Erde's neck. She sent images to the dragon anxiously waiting in the grove, of the ruddy shadowed room littered with glass and bodies.

—*Like our old dreams, Dragon! What does it mean?*
—*That we are meant to be here.*

Earth would think this was offering her comfort, since being where Destiny intended him to be was all he required of life. Erde hoped for a little more, and from now until they were safe again, she'd be unable to think of quests and purpose or anything else but survival.

—*Sometimes I think we're in Hell. Are we, Dragon?*

Is it a punishment for my wicked deeds and unclean thoughts?

—You mustn't fear, child. Fear is a temptation to give in to Weakness.

—Fearing and giving in are not the same. I can do one without doing the other.

—I am glad to hear it.

Baraga listened at the door, then slid it open just enough to slip through. N'Doch and the new dragon-shape called Sedou followed him. Nikko herded Erde after them, his hands on her and on Lealé in places she was sure they didn't need to be. The hall was dark, and thick with jostling, sweating bodies. Nikko palmed a small cylinder that suddenly gave forth an intense beam of white light. Erde recoiled from it, and then wished she had one. But Nikko used it as a club, flashing its brilliance into frightened eyes, forcing a path of fear down the crowded hallway.

By the little door at the end of the hall, the head acolyte Jean-Pierre was fumbling with the lock while he balanced a pile of metal boxes in his arms. He squinted into the spear of light.

"Got it all, Mr. B."

"Good man." Baraga grabbed the key while Nikko aimed his light. They piled through the door into the lightless narrow passage on the other side. Nikko came last, ejecting a handful of acolytes who tried to follow. He slammed the door and slid the heavy deadbolt home.

"Go dark, Nikko," warned Baraga from the curtained antechamber. "We got a crowd in here." Nikko doused his beam, plunging the hot little room into blackness as suffocating as the grave. But Erde felt a tickle behind her eyeballs, and grainy shapes and shadows swam up out of the black as Water extended her night vision to her human companions. N'Doch edged up on one side of her, Sedou on the other.

—Say nothing. Your safety may depend on appearing helpless.

Erde blinked, and gave her eyes over completely to the dragon's control. By the arched entrance to Lealé's Reading-hall, she could see Baraga and his henchman listening at the draperies. Baraga reached and drew Lealé to him.

"How many, you think, Glory?"

"Could be as many as a hundred."

"Laying low, hoping nobody'll notice 'em." Nikko lifted the metal thing she knew was a gun and seemed to be weighing it. "I'll notice 'em, if they get in our way."

"They are my 'guests,'" reproved Lealé's Glory-voice. "They'll let us pass if I tell them to."

"Will they let us hop into a tank and leave 'em all behind?" Baraga retorted.

"Yes. I think they would."

From what she'd seen around the compound, Erde agreed. Besides, what N'Doch would call "the Glory thing" seemed to be their only chance to get through. She didn't really believe that Nikko's gun could fend off a hundred people, and as far as she knew, it was their only weapon.

"Should she go first, Mr. B.?"

"Yeah, then you, with the light. Ceremonial-like, you know? Like the power's just blown and we're dealing with it. I'll follow with the others."

—Setting up the order of sacrifice.

Erde felt dragon energy thrumming through the body of the tall stranger beside her.

"Nah . . ." muttered N'Doch.

—Putting himself in the middle, where he's covered.

—He'll cover us, too, like he's covering Jean-Pierre. We could make him millions.

—He'll dump anyone he thinks is extra weight.

—There's no extra weight here. Three isn't four, remember.

—Baraga doesn't know that.

—Or perhaps he does. . . .

Earth's weighing in to the conversation signaled to Erde his acceptance of Fire's treachery.

—What d'you mean?

—As my sister said, he has a touch of Fire in him.

"Oh, god," N'Doch whispered, and then told them of Baraga's dream.

—Given up on Lealé to move on to more fertile grounds ..

—He's only got to get rid of one of us to satisfy

his dream-lord's demands. The rest he can keep for himself.

—No one could hold onto one of you guys by force, not even Baraga!

—You think so? Fire seems to have done it. For all we know, he's been giving the Man lessons.

—Yeah, but look: All Baraga knows is, he's got three people. One of them he's suspicious about, but he's still not sure who he needs and who he can do without. So we're safe until he knows.

—So you're saying: Lay low, my brother.

Erde saw the flash of N'Doch's smile.

—Yeah. I sure am. None of your dragon pyrotechnics.

—Not me. That's the other one.

Erde recognized the tone: the banter of men before battle. The dragon did so well in this new shape. Even for Erde, the lines were blurring between the big man beside her and the voice in her head. She could only imagine how N'Doch must feel about it, who knew them both so well.

"Ready, Glory?" Baraga chucked Lealé under the chin as if she was a child. "Show 'em your stuff."

Erde was sure Lealé was more frightened than she was letting on as she squared her shoulders and tossed her head, gestures made only to herself in a lightless room. Nikko drew back a thickly embroidered drape, then flicked on his magical light and let Lealé walk majestically into its beam.

An amazed murmur rolled around the dark, cavernous hall, like a gust of wind through grass.

"Glory! Glory! Gloreee!"

Lealé smiled and lifted her arms in salute and benediction. The hard white light caught on the beads in her hair and on her robe, making her sparkle like a jewel, shooting tiny flashes into the darkness to reflect in the adoring eyes of her invisible worshipers.

"Glory! Help us! Glory! Save us!"

"Children!" The Glory-voice rang out like a bell, chasing its own echoes around the unseen dome. "My dear children! You must stay calm and quiet until this crisis has passed. The power is off for a while, but I'm sure they'll have it back again soon."

The ground rumbled and shook, calling her a liar. But the petitioners only sighed and called her name.

She answered them, and as she talked, she moved into the huge space, out across the polished marble as Nikko's beam illuminated a path for her. Some petitioners were standing, most were seated in groups on the still-cool stone, pressed together for comfort. Lealé picked her way gracefully among them, bestowing a smile here and a touch there. Baraga trailed her, in the light bearer's shadow, with Jean-Pierre behind him, clutching his precious load of boxes. Erde had no choice but to follow. She noted that Sedou took up the rear, scanning the unlit vastness with the interest of one for whom the dark is no obstacle. She hoped Baraga was too focused on his own escape to notice.

As they progressed grandly across the hall, more of the petitioners stood up. They pressed in closer and their pleadings became more desperate. Lealé's pace slowed. She could no longer pass through them easily. Nikko began to ask, then demand that they move aside, but Erde could see he was unpracticed at the Glory-thing, and his harsh orders set off bouts of weeping and hysteria among the weakest, and angry mutters among those with more presence of mind. So Nikko shoved harder, and Lealé kept up her steady stream of Glory patter, soothing, seducing a path to open up behind the rough-handed bodyguard. Behind them, the petitioners rose up and followed, murmuring and pushing against Erde and Sedou and N'Doch, until Erde wanted to scream and lash out with arms and fists and anything to keep them away from her. But she didn't, remembering what Earth had told her about fear.

An eternity of seconds later, Lealé was nearly at the door. Beside the towering columns that framed the ceremonial entrance, she turned back toward the crowd, a faceless, dreamlike figure outlined in brilliant white.

"Now, my brave children, my dearest brothers and sisters, you shall rest here in safety, while Glory goes out to put an end to this nonsense! For how can the Word of Light be heard with all that going on?"

Erde heard N'Doch's brief exhalation of disgust. She laid her palm against his back to quiet him.

"Hey, girl," he whispered.

"Hey, bro," she answered, in his own Frankish syllables.

He laughed softly, put his arm around her and hugged her close. "This is where it's gonna get rough. You ready?"

Erde shook her head.

N'Doch wishes he could give the girl comforting words, but he has none. At the door, big Nikko slips the lock and eases the door open just the slightest crack to give himself a view of the situation outside. N'Doch ducks around behind him to peer around his back. Before the door swings shut, he gets a glimpse of the twisted-iron wreckage of the front gate. The pseudo-colonial guardhouse is a pile of rubble. Jack-booted soldiers in camo uniforms are pouring single-file through the gap and fanning out across the front, rifles at ready. N'Doch recalls what Nikko said about the attackers being organized. *Who are these guys?* he wonders. Why spend so much effort on just another cult house? The city's lousy with them. But none of this is a mystery to Nikko.

"Storm troopers, Mr. B. They know we're here."

The phone on Nikko's hip beeps discreetly, like just another business call coming in to enlarge the Big Man's empire. Nikko confers with it briefly.

"Fifteen seconds to the wall," he reports. "Another twelve to the door."

Baraga pats the air, palms down, a silencing gesture. His eyes flick toward Lealé, still soothing the petitioner crowd. Some of them are claiming her personal attention now, and by habit, she is trying to supply them with a calming answer. N'Doch watches the bodyguard balance his maglight on the rim of a tall vase of flowers. He does it without moving the beam, so that the light continues to embrace and magnify the Mahatma Glory even as he moves away from it with Baraga and Jean-Pierre, toward the door. Baraga looks back at N'Doch and jerks his head in a wordless summons. N'Doch feels the chill seep into his gut.

He's gonna leave her behind.

N'Doch tells himself this bothers him because he's soft-hearted where women are concerned. But it's also scary confirmation of the dragon's dead-weight theory of Baraga's escape tactics.

Nikko cracks the door open again, letting in only the slightest wisp of light as he counts down silent seconds to himself. At fifteen, N'Doch hears a grinding, tearing crunch, muffled by the heavy door. Nikko gives Baraga a slow nod.

Look behind you! N'Doch begs Lealé. He's only ten feet away from her. He's got twelve seconds, less now. He could warn her with a whisper, but he can't bring himself to do it. If he does, he could blow his Big Chance. He sees fame and fortune miraculously within his grasp, after a lifetime of dreaming, and the desire for them rages in him as hotly as sex. *Lealé can take care of herself,* he reasons, as the tanks roar up outside the house.

With his pistol held at arm's length, Nikko yanks open the door. Jean-Pierre hugs his boxes and runs for it. Baraga wraps an iron arm around N'Doch's waist and propels him forward.

"Keep your head low, kid."

N'Doch bucks back. He has to at least try. "No! You're leaving her! You can't . . ."

"You want to live and be famous? Two four-man tanks. There's no room."

N'Doch doesn't count heads, he struggles, not even sure why he's doing it, if he feels the way he says he does. The Media King is stronger than he would ever have imagined. The iron arm around his waist is replaced by one around his throat. Baraga drags him through the doorway. N'Doch can't see Sedou, but he guesses the heavy drag on Baraga's other side is his brother hauling on him.

The tanks are firing rounds into the front yard, keeping the assault force down in cover. But bullets are pinging against the tanks' armor and zinging past N'Doch's ear. He's still arguing with himself, telling himself to just relax, let the Media King toss both him and Sedou inside the goddamn tank where they're safe. Nikko can get the girl.

"Nikko!" Baraga shouts. "Get him off me!"

The *girl*!

Off to the side, past Baraga's stranglehold on his neck, N'Doch sees the girl dart out of the door. She's got Lealé in tow, and she's moving fast, using the tanks for cover like she should, except she's not heading toward them, she's . . . *running for the grove*!

He tries to choke out a yell, but Baraga's got him so tight, he can only gag for breath. Now he sees Sedou, grappling with the bodyguard, unable to shake him loose.

"Which one of you is it?" Baraga hisses. "Which one of you's the dragon handler?"

N'Doch takes a wild guess. Maybe Baraga doesn't know. Maybe he thinks *both* the dragons are stashed somewhere else.

"All of us!" he gasps.

"That's not what he told me."

"Then he didn't tell you much!"

The girl's out in the open now, and the rain of gunfire intensifies.

Nikko has Sedou pinned against one of the tanks. Sedou's struggling to fight him off, struggling to hold on to his human-form, failing . . .

—*Sedou! The girl! Stop her!*

The Sedou shape waves, resettles, wavers again. Nikko lets go and backs off from it in horror. He levels his pistol at its head.

"Nikko! No! Don't hurt it! Take the other one!"

If he'd been thinking clearly, N'Doch realizes, he'd have seen the way it was going down. But then Baraga finally makes a mistake. He looses his hold on N'Doch's throat to watch the man they'd called Sedou melt and dissolve before his very eyes and reform into a living creature out of myth. A dragon. N'Doch jerks himself free, off balance, and falls hard on his side. He rolls to his feet just as Nikko levels his pistol at the fleeing women.

"Nikko! Both of them! NOW!"

The bodyguard gets one shot off. Lealé stumbles and drops. A sudden wind has come up. Blinded by dust and outrage, N'Doch throws himself into the line of fire.

The lead ripping into him at close range blows him off his feet. Or maybe it's the wind. He expects the agony of having his chest torn open, but there's only a tingling and a vast roaring. He expects to land hard, in too many pieces.

But he never lands at all.

Chapter Thirty-Seven

He comes to consciousness slowly, surreally aware that he is running, has been for a long time. His lungs ache and his ribs are cramped but his long legs keep pumping away, doing what is needed without his having to think about whether he can keep going or not. He just does.

Being on autopilot lets him check out his surroundings. The air is thick and hot, and the sun's all wrong, too red and not quite round, like it might be at sunset near the horizon, except it's straight overhead. The dusty hills around him are too red, too, and pocked with shell craters. He sees he must have imagined all that blood and tearing and having his chest blown open. By some wonderful mistake the bodyguard missed, even at such close range, and N'Doch's old survival instincts took over: He finally got some sense and ran for it.

But the landscape isn't the familiar flat, dry fields surrounding the City. And N'Doch doubts that even the most organized coup could have leveled all the outlying villages and housing projects as completely as the rubble around him indicates. Plus, it all looks like it's been there a while. Layers of grit have softened the contours of the shattered walls and filled in the crevasses. He searches the hills and horizon for the smoke plumes of fire-bombing, and listens for the clatter of artillery or the wock-wock of the copters in the air.

Nothing. Just hot, dry landscape and a man running. A man who hasn't a clue where he is, or even why he's running. He just knows that he has to, something is after him, but it isn't behind him, it's all around him. . . .

N'Doch wakes abruptly, with a heaving gasp and a

need for air so desperate that it's a long shuddering moment before he can think about anything but breathing. When he gets it under control, he opens his eyes. He still doesn't know where he is.

He's lying in a bed, not just on it but in it, between sheets and under blankets, as far as he can tell. He lets his eyes rove, sees a tall wooden footboard with turned posts at both ends. The blankets are a single thick, airy coverlet. Its soft, coarsely woven fabric makes him think of his mother Fâtime at her loom.

The bed sits in a shaft of light from a small window. The bright cold light leaves the rest of the room in shadow, so while N'Doch gets his breath and waits for his heart to stop trying to break through his ribs, he studies the window in detail, hoping it will help him understand what's happening to him.

The window is square and set well into the wall, so a deep seat is formed by the sill. N'Doch sees a thin, brown cushion and a pile of what might be clothes. He wonders if they are his. The glass in the window is divided into many smaller panes, held together with thin strips of some dull-colored metal. At first N'Doch thinks there's something wrong with his eyes, but then he sees it's the glass. It's all ripply and dotted with minute air bubbles, so that his view of the outside is subtly diffused and diffracted: bare branches, furry-pointed green ones and blue, blue sky. N'Doch has never seen a sky that blue, and he stares at it until he realizes he's been drifting, probably for a long while, because when he becomes aware of himself again, the angle of the light has shifted and the sky is chased with big white and gray clouds. And now there's a woman sitting in the window seat, a white woman, paler than the girl even, dressed in white and with white-blonde hair as fine as spider silk. She's bent over some sort of handwork which she's holding up to the window in order to see. With the bright, white light, her long white dress and her own shell-like pallor, the woman is almost translucent.

N'Doch thinks he's kept still but he must be wrong, 'cause the woman looks up at him with a soft frown of interest and concern, then sets her work aside and comes toward him. Her hands on his cheeks and forehead are cool and professional. He figures he'll lay low and see what she's up to. And then it comes to him like a shock that she's a nurse, maybe a doctor. So he did get blown to bits, and somehow they've managed to stick him back together again. Only he's not sure now of how much of himself he's got left. He's forgotten to check.

The pale woman reaches her arms around him and with the impossible strength of mothers and doctors, bundles him up into a sitting position, supported by pillows and bolsters. N'Doch takes inventory and finds himself complete. Not quite like himself, and as weak as a newborn, but entirely as whole as one, too. It just doesn't make sense. The woman pats his shoulder, then reaches to a low wooden table beside the bed and fills a small clay cup with water from a stoneware jug. The crisp trickle of water inflames a vast thirst he wasn't aware of a moment before, and he drinks without worrying if the water's safe. It's cold and clear and more delicious than he ever imagined water could be. She's holding a third cupful to his lips when his next big revelation hits him, so hard he almost chokes. They did it once, they could do it again. *He's been doctored by dragons.*

Which means it really did happen. The shock of the impact and the ripping and tearing of his vital organs, it's not all a sweat-drenched nightmare. The bullets took him, then the dragons came and took him back, and carried him off somewhere . . . here. . . .

Revelation clicks in once more, and N'Doch understands where he is.

The woman sets the cup down and moves away through the shaft of light toward a shadowy door. She leans out and calls softly down the hall, and N'Doch knows he's figured right. She's speaking the girl's antique Kraut. For cryin' out loud, he's in 913!

He lets that explanation settle for a while to see how its logic suits him. He knows he's not thinking real fast or straight quite yet, but mostly he's just grateful to be thinking at all.

I died, he tells himself. *Or almost. And they fixed me.*

The miracle implied makes him shiver, and the woman comes back to the bed and pulls the covers up around his chest and shoulders. His entirely unmarked, unventilated chest.

"Kalt?" she murmurs. Her eyes look away from him, as if she lets her hands do her talking.

And he is cold, he realizes, not just from shock and revelation. It's cold in the room, and it's probably real cold outside. Now that he's upright, he has a wider view through the window, and he sees why the light streaming in is so hard and white. There's snow on the ground out there.

Snow. Real snow. He's never seen it before, except on the vid. He shivers again, and the woman goes to the corner where a small fire is burning in a narrow stone fireplace. She prods it with a metal poke and throws more wood on. She looks up at the sound of footsteps coming down the hall, light and steady, accompanied by the creak of floorboards. A second white woman comes into the room, shorter and older than the first, and rich with autumnal color in her short, graying hair and layered clothing. She has a brisk, direct presence that makes N'Doch feel obscurely chastised even though as far as he knows he hasn't done anything wrong except die and be resurrected.

"Hello," she says. Her voice is warmly resonant. Immediately N'Doch is thinking how much he'd like to hear her sing. Her French is odd and deeply accented but it's French nonetheless, and he can understand her. "My name is Rose. Welcome to Deep Moor."

Deep Moor. He recalls the name. The girl's back when haven with all the women. But she'd always described it as a paradise of perpetual summer. It doesn't much feel like summer in this room.

He wonders if his own voice will work. "I am N'Doch N'Djai."

Rose smiles. "Yes, I know. I know all about you, so you needn't tire yourself with explanations."

N'Doch is fairly sure now, but he could use some confirmation. "Am I alive?"

"Certainly. But there was doubt there for a while. The dragons worked long and hard. How do you feel?"

"Uh . . . okay." But what he really feels is *different*. If he had to describe this difference, he'd say he feels bigger, not taller or fatter, but bigger *inside*. He's been too distracted so far to search his mind for the dragon presence. Now that he does, he cannot raise them.

"The dragons," he asks Rose. "Where are they?"

"They went back, as soon as they recovered from the great effort of the Healing. They went back to rescue the mage Erde called . . ." She stumbles over the name. ". . . Jarara?"

"Djawara?"

"That's it. Did she say he was your grandfather?"

N'Doch nods, exhales, and lays his head back. He wonders if the old man will come. He's been worried about Djawara ever since going off and leaving him alone out there in the bush, never mind what Lealé says about him being a man of power. . . .

Lealé.

"Excuse me, madame . . ."

"Rose. Just Rose."

"Rose. There was a woman who helped us. Did they say . . ?"

Rose shook her head gently. "The Dreamer was already gone when they got to her. The spark of life had fled." For some reason, her gaze flicked outward, toward the window. "Even dragons cannot make miracles."

N'Doch is not sure she's right. Mostly to keep her talking so he can hear that wonderful voice whose undertones tickle the insides of his lungs, he asks, "There's a war here, too, right? How's that going?"

Again, her gaze drifts to the window. He sees the strain in her then, the worry and exhaustion in her eyes. "The King's forces are in retreat, the barons are fighting among themselves and the mad priest is burning every witch in sight, and a few that aren't. The only good news is that Baron Köthen has gone over to Otto's side. About time, I say. But the war is the least of our problems."

Rose seems to lose herself to the view for a moment. Then she shakes herself out of her reverie. "Still, we're safe for a while yet, and we've food enough in the cellars, so you are to rest and eat and await the dragons' return. You're in good hands." She reaches and draws the younger woman within the circle of her arm. "This is Linden. She is Deep Moor's healer. Unfortunately, she speaks no Frankish, but then, she normally prefers not to speak at all." Rose smiles at Linden as if this was some long-standing joke between them.

"How come you speak French?" Instantly N'Doch regrets his bluntness. He's trying to recall how the girl acts with strangers, so he can do like she would at home, but he sees he just didn't pay close enough attention.

But Rose laughs, a throaty, complex reply to the un-spoken parts of his question. "I've . . . traveled. Now—would you like to get up and move about? Here are garments on the sill. I'd say let's go for a walk outside, but it's frigid with this . . . unseasonable cold. We aren't meant to have weather like this in Deep Moor, and I doubt you're recovered enough for it. But come down-stairs and join us for supper when you're ready."

The women leave him to dress, but at first, even getting up is a problem. N'Doch has a moment of terror where he convinces himself he's paralyzed. But it's more like his body's forgotten how to work, like he needs to apply conscious effort and teach it all over again how to sit up, stand up, and walk.

Different, he keeps thinking. *I feel different. Newly made.* Dragon *made.*

They know. These witchy women know, and they left me alone to deal with it privately. N'Doch appreciates their consideration. He gets the clothes on, pulling them over the longish linen shirt they'd put him to bed in. They're odd clothes, hanging loose and heavy on his slim body, yet meant for a shorter person. When he stands up next to these women, he's gonna tower over them. He has a hard time not thinking of the clothes as a cos-tume, like when he first saw the girl on the beach, when he still thought this whole deal was a vid shoot. It makes him laugh now, but it's a hard laugh, full of unaccus-tomed irony aimed mostly at himself. He wishes he had a mirror.

But the clothes are clean and warm and comfortable, and he knows now that to ask for his own clothes back would be indulging in the macabre. Maybe their re-maining bloodied shreds would make this death and res-urrection thing somehow realer to him. But he didn't die, it seems, not quite. Because Lealé did.

He takes an experimental walk around the room. It's a small square white room with a dark, beamed ceiling just inches above his head, and a wide-boarded floor that complains musically of his every step. There's a wind outside now. He hears it howling in the rough stone chimney. The light at the window has gone gray and flat, and there's actually some of that snow flying in the air. N'Doch watches it for a while but it only makes him feel desolate. His limbs have remembered how to walk in time with each other, and he's chilled and hungry and thinks he'd prefer the company of strange women to the burden of trying to understand what's already happened to him, and what's supposed to happen next. He heads downstairs.

He's halfway down the narrow, steep steps, gripping the railing with both hands, when he feels the dragons' return. *Her* return.

His whole being lifts toward her, and the dragon-shaped emptiness inside him fills with her welcome. But the bright joy that sweeps through him like a searchlight is still freighted with denial, and N'Doch knows he will never fully accept this role that Fate has cast him in without his approval.

But somehow, he tells himself, he'll keep this from her. He owes them now. He owes them Big Time. So for the time being, he'll see this dragon thing out. He'll go off with her, with them, and find this bad dude Fire and see what they can do to settle his hash. N'Doch has a bone or two to pick with the guy himself. Then he'll be free to think about what comes next.

The dream swims up, as vivid as a vid running right there in his mind. He knows where to go now. He doesn't know where it is, or even *when,* but he knows how to get there.

N'Doch pulls his clumsy, new-made body together and goes on downstairs to play along with Destiny.

Tanya Huff

When Henry Fitzroy is plagued by ghosts demanding vengeance, he calls upon newly made vampire Vicki Nelson and her homicide detective lover to help find the murderer. But Vancouver may not be big enough for *two* vampires!